BLUE COYOTE

Motel

Dianne Harman

Blue Coyote Motel

Published by: Dianne Harman

http://www.dianneharman.com

Interior design and typesetting by Amy Eye, The Eyes for Editing

Cover design by MAE I DESIGN

Edited by The Eyes for Editing

ISBN 13: 978-1-480-09435-2

ISBN 10: 1480094358

Blue Coyote Motel

Dedication

To Tom, who raised an eyebrow, put a pencil behind
his ear, and started to edit.

Addiction is hard to understand unless you have experienced it.

PROLOGUE

Jeffrey Brooks believed that, with the use of Freedom, a drug he had secretly developed, there would be no more wars, hatred, or discrimination, which had plagued the world for centuries. They would simply vanish. Religious strife, dictators, and terrorism would all become things of the past. Jesus, Mohammed, Buddha; each had wanted freedom from strife, but each had failed. He, Jeffrey Brooks, would be the only person in the history of mankind to deliver the Holy Grail sought by so many, world peace. Surely he'd be awarded the Nobel Prize and wouldn't those bastards at Moore Labs be sorry they had fired him.

Get a good job. Find a rich man. Get out of the barrio. These were the words of wisdom passed from mother to daughter, repeated over and over, day after day. The very beautiful and sexy Maria Rodriguez had grown up with those words. They became her sacred mantra and Jeffrey became her Savior.

CHAPTER 1

The red engine warning light on the dashboard was blinking without stopping. Doug had noticed it for the last fifty miles, but now it had his full attention. His 1997 Dodge had over 140,000 miles on it and he'd been meaning to get an engine tune-up. He never seemed to have enough money, but it looked like he better find the money and find it fast.

Doug felt like he was on another planet. Nothing existed in this barren part of the world, but endless miles of dirt and tumbleweeds, sweltering and brown from the lack of water. The uninhabitable desert stretched for miles in every direction. The scorched land looked like something from a science fiction photograph. He felt as parched as the barren land before him. There were no signs of life other than an occasional car on the shimmering highway. He idly wondered if what he had always heard was true; that there really were "desert rats" who lived here, people who preferred the solitude of the desert. The thought was incomprehensible to him.

His cell phone rang. He was sure it was Lisa, his ex-wife, making her weekly demand for the past due alimony payments he owed her. Shit, if he couldn't even afford to get an engine tune-up, where in the hell did she expect him to find the money to pay her?

Sweating even more profusely than usual, he answered the phone.

"Doug," his boss Jack said, "how did the sales calls go in Phoenix today?"

Doug pictured Jack in his Armani suit, sitting behind his antique mahogany desk in the high-rise corner office of the Century City Aravalve Western Headquarters. The gold lettering on the door that led to Jack's office read "President." He visualized Jack's sporty red Porsche convertible in the basement of the office building, in the stall numbered "1." In his mind's eye, he also saw Jack's beachfront home in Malibu, the young, tan, blond, arm-candy trophy wife, the requisite two adorable children, and the perfectly groomed yellow Labrador retriever. The annual company Christmas party held every year at Jack's home depressed Doug about as much as anything ever had. The president of Aravalve was cool and successful, everything Doug wasn't. Doug hated him and at the same time, he wanted everything that Jack had.

Doug answered, "Well, not that great. Both customers told me to come back in six months; that they didn't need any valves right now. I gave it the old college try, but it seemed like no matter what I said, they just weren't interested."

"I want you to come to my office first thing Monday morning. You're way below your sales quota. The other salesmen are selling valves. They seem to find a market, but for whatever reason, you're not closing any sales. We need to talk," Jack said.

Swell, Doug thought, *here we go again. Looks like I'm going to be fired Monday morning.* He wondered if he would even be able to get another job. Five jobs in three years was not a great track record and from the way Jack sounded, he doubted that he would be getting a glowing recommendation. In this job market, finding anything new would be hard. He was already dreading Monday morning.

There was a time when everything in Doug's life had been good, really good. He was a lineman on the high school football team, big and burly when it was a good thing to be big and burly. Another 100 pounds later, it wasn't. He had tried everything—the lap band, Weight Watchers, Jenny Craig, and every other diet out there. Nothing had worked and the weight sure didn't help the high blood pressure his doctor kept warning him about.

Both of Doug's parents had died at an early age from heart problems. He was worried he'd meet the same fate, but he just couldn't seem to get a handle on controlling either his weight or his high blood pressure. His doctor had given him pills, but they weren't helping.

It seemed like his whole life had gone downhill after college. Until then, his future had looked bright, particularly when UCLA gave him a full-ride football scholarship. Scouts from the pro teams had been at most of his games during the early part of his senior year. Everyone predicted that he'd be playing pro after graduation and Doug was expecting to be offered a big contract along with a signing bonus. He knew he was really, really good, but during the last regular game of the season, he blew out his knee. It was a career ending injury and his pro football career was over before it had even begun.

Doug had easily been the most sought-after athlete on campus by the coeds. His wavy black hair, sky blue eyes, and large muscular body made every one of them want to take him home and many did. An audible sigh of anguish came from every campus sorority house when word got out that he had married Lisa, the beautiful, blond cheerleader he had known since high school. They married the summer after his junior year in college. A few months after his football career ended, Lisa gave birth to their stillborn son. Nothing between them was ever the same, each silently blaming the other for their son's death.

After he graduated from college, he found there wasn't much of a market for has-been football players. Certain that he would be playing in the pros; he hadn't spent much time preparing for a job in any other field. He began a series of lackluster jobs, enough to financially get Lisa and him through each month. She went to beauty school and got a job as a nail technician. They lived in a small one-bedroom apartment in a seedy, run-down, area of Los Angeles. Money was always tight, but it was all they could afford. The marriage turned into a succession of bitter arguments, just one unpleasant scene after another and five years later, they divorced.

His current life consisted of fielding Lisa's calls for money, trying to hold a job, and worrying about his escalating weight. He knew carrying 325 pounds on a 6'4" frame was not healthy, particularly given his parents' history of heart problems. His doctor always hassled him about smoking and he knew the cigarettes weren't helping his health, but *what the hell*, he thought, he deserved them. His life was shitty enough without giving up one of the few pleasures he had left. His future looked like a black hole of nothingness with no way out. If there was a better way, he hadn't found it.

There was one more thing, something no one knew about. With all the weight he'd gained, women no longer found him attractive. Increasingly, he found himself visiting prostitutes, just to get some sexual relief. The tighter the money got, the sleazier the prostitutes. He hated himself for what he was doing, but he couldn't stop. After all, he reasoned, as bad as his life was, wasn't he entitled to a little relief now and then? Even if it came in the form of a low-life prostitute? Every time he looked in the mirror, he saw what he had become and he felt disgusted with himself.

Forgetting his ongoing problems for a moment,

Doug tried to concentrate on the current situation, the red engine warning light on the dash. *Swell*, he thought, *as if the day hasn't already been bad enough. Now it looks like something is seriously wrong with the car*.

He was smack dab in the middle of the Mojave Desert, otherwise known as the armpit of California. There was nothing to speak of ahead or behind him but miles and miles of empty desert. Blythe was seventy-five miles behind him to the east and the Palm Springs resort cities were another sixty miles or more ahead of him to the west. Interstate 10 was a pretty lonely place when you had car trouble. The outside temperature gauge on his dashboard read 103 degrees, the wind was howling, and tumbleweeds were flying, stopped only by the intermittent fencing on the side of the road. *This is just fucking great*, he thought, *anyone else would have car trouble near Palm Springs, but no, not me. Where do I have car trouble? Seventy-five miles outside of Blythe in the middle of summer*. He took it as yet another omen of how fucked up his life had become.

Just then, he spotted an old, run-down gas station about a mile or so ahead. He pulled in and got out of his car, barely able to breathe in the stifling heat. The dry wind blowing the tumbleweeds sounded like fingernails scraping on a chalkboard. A weathered-looking old man greeted him and introduced himself as Lou. Doug followed him into the small office that was badly in need of a paint job, new linoleum and a floor to ceiling cleaning. He could barely notice any difference from the temperature outside.

"Say," Doug said, "got anyone who knows how to fix an engine problem on that car of mine out there? And how do you stand this heat? Don't you have an air-conditioner?"

"Most air-conditioners don't work well in this heat," Lou said. "They die. Not a brand out there that can stand up to it. Only ones that can are big commercial ones and I sure as hell can't afford one of those. As for your car, sure, I can probably fix it. Let me have a look. I've been doing auto repair for over forty years so there's not much I can't fix. If you need some part, it usually means about a day to get what I need from the auto supply shop in Blythe. Believe it or not, they send new parts out to me by Greyhound bus. I only get delivery once a day, so that's why it takes a day or so to fix any sort of major problem."

He walked out to Doug's car, and took a look under the hood. "Yeah, I can't be sure, but it looks like you need a new water pump," Lou said. "I'll call the auto supply shop and they can send me the part. You're going to have to spend the night, but there's a nice little motel up the way that reopened about two months ago, the Blue Coyote. You can drive my old truck up there. Three miles and you'll see the sign. When I get the part in and the car's fixed, I'll drive up to the Blue Coyote tomorrow and we'll switch cars. You can pay me then."

Doug gave the old man his contact information, got in the truck, and headed up the road. He saw the sign for the Blue Coyote just where Lou said it would be. The endless desert sand blew across the highway in the shimmering heat. Doug hoped the place would be clean and at least have a cold beer. He needed something to eat and also a working air-conditioner that offered some relief. Right now, the cold beer was the main thing on his mind. He could almost taste the beer on his tongue and feel the ice-cold brew sliding down his throat. The heat was ungodly, particularly if you were carrying around 325 pounds of weight. *Shit*, he thought, *I weigh almost one-sixth of a ton. Now there's a happy thought.*

As he started to turn into the Blue Coyote driveway, he became aware of raised high voltage power lines dancing in the distance. When he looked at the power lines a little more closely, he noticed that something was off. It looked like one of the high power lines was going directly into the motel. Although Doug hadn't been a Phi Beta Kappa in college, he remembered something he had read in some magazine about how dependent everyone and everything was on electrical power. He couldn't imagine why the Blue Coyote would need such a large amount of energy feeding into it. Even in this unremitting heat, even if the air-conditioning system ran 24/7, which it probably did, and even if there was a back-up generator, why so much energy? He forgot about the power line after he turned into the driveway, pleasantly surprised by the way the motel looked in this godforsaken out-of-the-way place. Unlike most places in the desert that, almost without exception, looked battered and rundown, the Blue Coyote looked like it had been freshly painted with desert plantings arranged attractively around it.

He parked Lou's old, rusted truck, got out, and entered the reception area. A young brunette with a beautiful smile greeted him. "Hi. I'm Maria. Welcome to the Blue Coyote," she said. "Our rooms are a hundred and twenty-five dollars a night, but they're really comfortable and with the central air-conditioning, you won't even know you're in the desert. There's an honor bar with beer and wine and some other things that can be microwaved. I'll have baked goods for you in the morning."

Doug was speechless. He had never seen a woman as beautiful as the one in front of him. Long, lustrous black hair framed a face that would have inspired poets and artists. And her body! Her body was perfect, from her full, lush breasts to her small waist to her long legs. His mind was numb and his jaw went slack. She rendered him incapable of doing anything but staring. *What in the hell was she doing in this godforsaken place? He wondered if he was hallucinating. This simply couldn't be.* It was impossible to imagine that a woman as beautiful as she was even existed, let alone in this place, but the vision in front of him remained and when he was finally capable of thinking, he realized the most beautiful woman he had ever seen was indeed in front of him.

Doug thought a one hundred and twenty-five dollar room rate in this nowhere place was exorbitant, but there wasn't much to choose from, which was exactly why they probably got that kind of money. He clearly needed somewhere to stay. He wasn't sure if Aravalve would reimburse him, but if he hadn't made the sales calls in Phoenix, he wouldn't be here now. They really owed it to him to pay for his room. Even if Jack fired him Monday morning, Doug was determined to get Aravalve to pay for the room.

He signed the registration card and the young woman gave him his room key. He went to the refreshment area where the drinks and food were located, picked up two ice-cold beers and went to his room. It was a small motel, five rooms in all, but his room was large and clean. The floor was tiled and the bathroom even had spa caliber complimentary shampoo, conditioner, body soap, and body lotion. There was an oak framed painting of a blue coyote on the wall, howling at the moon. Doug had seen the blue coyote motif all over the Southwest, but in this remote place, it seemed particularly appropriate. He wondered if he'd hear coyotes tonight. That could be pretty scary out here. Even so, he looked forward to the coming darkness and welcomed the night.

The air-conditioning felt great. He turned on the shower and stepped in. It felt good to get the desert grime off his skin and the warm water loosened the tension in his neck, shoulders, and lower back.

Endless hours of sitting in a car didn't help his chronic back pain. It seemed the longer he drove, the more it hurt. He was constantly reminding himself to lower his shoulders, to let the tension go.

After his shower, Doug opened one of the beers and lay down nude on top of the bedcovers, letting the air-conditioning cool him off. He watched the news on the room's swing-arm flat screen television and opened the second beer. *Man*, he thought, *someone has put some serious money into this place. Why would anyone invest money in flat screen televisions, spa bathroom items, and designer tiles on a motel in this nowhere place?*

As he began to relax, he decided that maybe things weren't quite as hopeless as he'd thought earlier. Maybe he could convince Jack to give him another chance. He knew he hadn't really tried hard enough to sell the valves. If he could sell more valves, he could get the money he owed Lisa. It wasn't her fault he'd blown out his knee and their life had begun to slide down the rabbit hole. Maybe he could even convince that cute new receptionist at Aravalve to have dinner with him.

Doug felt better than he had in a long time. The hum of the air-conditioner was very relaxing. He wasn't sure, but he thought he could detect a slight scent of sandalwood in the cool air as it flowed across his body. When he was in a college fraternity, he and some of his friends decided to get a massage after a night of drinking and partying. He recognized the sandalwood scent as being the same the masseuse had used.

He got dressed and wandered back to the refreshment area. There were some baked chicken breasts in a food warmer that looked pretty good. He helped himself to two of those along with a fresh-looking salad. He debated about having another beer, but decided against it. *I'm on a health roll here*, he thought, *no sense screwing it up*. He walked back to his room, got into bed and slept the sleep of the newborn and was awakened just before noon by the telephone ringing next to his bed.

"Mr. Ritchie, your car is here. Lou repaired it and he's waiting in the office for you," Maria said.

Doug hurriedly dressed, amazed at how long he had slept. Quickly walking to the motel office, he paid Lou, checked out and drove west, towards the San Fernando Valley area of Los Angeles where he lived. It felt good to be alive. For the first time in a long time, he realized he was smiling. The tension he carried like an albatross around his neck was gone. He decided it was time to join a gym. He even imagined he might have lost a few pounds the last couple of days. Looking back on last night, it was probably the best night's sleep he'd had in months.

He thought about what a refreshing and pleasant place the Blue Coyote had turned out to be. Yesterday he had seen nothing but tumbleweeds and searing blacktop when he drove down the highway, but today he saw the beauty of the desert with its varying shades of brown and the beautiful hills in the distance. Yes, it definitely felt good to be alive.

CHAPTER 2

Monday morning arrived with Doug feeling the best he'd felt in years. The weekend had been great. Without quite understanding why, he had joined a gym down the street from his apartment and worked out the last two days. He had run a mile each day, eaten carefully, and had no desire for beer, cigarettes, or prostitutes. He decided to take a run and hit the gym before his dreaded meeting with Jack.

After he showered and shaved, he stood in front of his closet for some time, picking out a crisp white shirt, muted grey striped suit, matching tie, black belt, shoes, and socks. He knew he had to convince Jack that he could do a much better job and he intended to do just that. He needed Jack to give him one more chance.

Doug lived in the San Fernando Valley, which was part of Los Angeles, but was nearly twenty miles from the downtown area. On his way to the Aravalve headquarters in Century City, the west side freeway traffic was horrible as usual. Doug couldn't understand why anyone would want to live here. *How could you plan anything in your life with a constant traffic jam looking you in the face whenever you wanted to go anywhere?* The side streets weren't much better. Finally, he got to Aravalve's corporate office and said a silent prayer that the upcoming meeting with Jack would go well.

Hurrying into the reception area outside Jack's office, he almost collided with the cute new receptionist. "Sorry, Lacy, I almost ran over you. Guess I'm just in a hurry for my appointment with Jack," Doug said.

"Wow, Doug, you look great! It's good to see you and I'm sure Jack will be happy to see you." Lacy looked at Doug and graced him with a dazzling smile. "Perhaps you need to take me out for a drink after work, considering you almost upended me," Lacy said.

Doug could hardly believe what he was hearing. This was a dream come true. A beautiful woman like Lacy asking him out for a drink, yes, this was shaping up as the best Monday he'd had in a long, long time.

"I definitely need to make it up to you, Lacy. How about 5:00? I'll look forward to that."

Doug smiled at her and it felt like the Doug of years ago, the confident football player whom no one could resist; certainly not Lacy. She didn't remember him being this charismatic. *How could she have missed it?*

The door to the inner office opened and Jack walked forward to shake Doug's hand. "Good to see you. Come on in my office." Jack closed the door after they entered his office, looked at Doug and said,

"What's happened? You look like a different person. Did you go to some spa or something?"

Doug replied, "I know I haven't been working up to my potential. I've been off track for a while, but I'm back now. I'm asking you for another chance. I promise I will be your top salesman within three months or you won't even have to fire me, I'll quit. Please, trust me. Just give me one more chance."

Jack took a long look at him. Something had definitely happened to Doug. His shoulders were squared, he had a confident air about him, and he looked ready to get out and sell. Looking like he did now, Jack sensed it would be hard for anyone to say no to Doug during his next sales call. Even though Doug carried extra weight, somehow it didn't look so bad on him now. He just looked like a powerful, large man.

"I've always liked you," Jack said. "You can have your one more chance. I sense a change. If you can do this job and do it well, I have no doubt that you'll be our top salesman. I'll look forward to hearing about your sales results. Why don't you come to dinner at the house this Sunday? Let's say 7:00. The sunsets are beautiful this time of year at the beach and I know Nancy would love to see you." Jack looked at his watch, indicating that the meeting was over.

Doug stood up, shook Jack's hand firmly and said he would see him Sunday. He walked into the reception area, reminding Lacy he'd be back at 5:00.

It is a good day, Doug thought to himself. *No, it is a very good day*! Doug called on six different businesses and sold large orders of valves to each one. *Jesus*, he thought, *this might be the best day I've ever had*. It was right up there with winning a football game.

As promised, Lacy was waiting. Doug couldn't help but grin when he saw her. She looked like the perfect Southern California beautiful young woman. Lacy was tan and fit with long red hair, big blue eyes, incredibly white teeth, and an "inviting look" that drove men crazy. It certainly did Doug. If the Barbie doll was real and if she had red hair, she'd be a dead-ringer for Lacy. Doug bet she even surfed. As they were walking to a nearby cocktail lounge, he realized he didn't know anything about her and wanted to know everything.

The evening was memorable. From cocktails they progressed to dinner and then to her townhouse. He felt charming; shit, he was charming. It had been a long, long time since any woman had invited him to go home with her. The rest of the night was just as good. She was a joyful lover, giving and warm and very different from the cold-hearted prostitutes he'd been using the last couple of years. Just the thought of them now filled him with disgust. Thank God he had been careful and used protection. He didn't want to ruin this new beginning with Lacy. His luck had changed and he was damn glad it had.

He left Lacy's townhouse just as the sky turned from dark blue to the rosy pink of dawn. It was time for his morning run and workout, then off to make more sales calls. He had only had three glasses of wine during the previous evening, one at the cocktail lounge, one at the restaurant, and one at Lacy's home. That restraint had to be a record in itself. No wonder he felt so great and God knows, he hadn't had much sleep.

Aravalve released the sales results of each of their salesmen every three months and finally, today was the day. Doug knew he had done very well in the last couple of months, but would it be good enough to make him the number one selling salesman? The results were to be announced at 3:00 p.m. that afternoon. The minutes seemed like hours. It was hard to stay focused. The quarterly meeting of the Aravalve sales force was held in the boardroom next to Jack's office. When Doug walked into the room at 3:00 p.m., applause broke out. Looking up at the whiteboard, he knew why. He had outsold the next closest salesman by two to one. Unbelievable. Jack walked over to him and held out his hand. Quietly he said, "I am so happy for you and so glad I decided to give you a second chance. Congratulations!"

The rest of the meeting was lost on Doug. He couldn't believe he had done it. Word of his success spread quickly throughout the building. When he walked to his car, people he didn't even know congratulated him. He noticed several women who had never before spoken to him smiling at him. Yes, life was good.

With his increased sales, his bonus would be substantial enough for him to pay Lisa the back alimony he owed. That would get her off his back and be one less thing for him to worry about. When he got to his car, his cell phone started ringing. He looked at the caller ID. It was Lacy. Doug flipped the phone open and said, "Hi Lacy, I didn't see you at the meeting. I called a few minutes ago to see if you could join me for dinner tonight."

Lacy had been in a meeting with the Human Relations Department concerning her recent promotion to the Marketing Department. She mentioned that he had been the talk of the building and how very proud she was of him. She offered to make dinner for the two of them at her townhouse. Why didn't he come over about 7:00?

What an amazing few months it had been! He'd lost 20 pounds, stopped smoking, really cut down on his drinking, and hadn't even thought about paying for sex. A man would have to be a fool to pay for it when Lacy was so warm and willing. He was working out, running four days a week, and was thinking about running a half-marathon. Doug had been the top salesman, earned enough to pay Lisa off, and was totally involved with Lacy. They were at the point where they were looking for deal-breakers because the relationship seemed almost too good to be true. Life was really, really good.

CHAPTER 3

"*Madre de Dios*, Maria, you have to get this job. You're too choosy. You'll never get out of the barrio," her mother Elena said. Maria thought back to her childhood and she didn't think a day had ever gone by that Elena had not invoked the "Holy Mother" over something. Elena continued, "Maria, you are so beautiful; they will have to hire you. They would be crazy not to offer you a job and if it's a good one, you must take it. Your time is running out."

Maria stood on a stool in front of the small bathroom mirror to get a full-length view of herself. The Rodriguez family couldn't afford to buy a mirror and put it on the back of a door, so the small little mirror over the sink would have to do.

If she was being honest, Maria would probably have to agree that her mother was right when she told Maria she was beautiful. She had jet black hair that hung in soft shiny waves, just touching her shoulders, a stark contrast to her creamy light tan complexion and large brown eyes fringed with double lashes, which an envious classmate had once called "camel lashes." Full breasts led to an incredibly small waist with soft, rounded hips and long, long legs.

Maria read the fashion magazines in the library and knew that many women paid a lot of money for implants trying to get full, lush breasts like hers. She'd also read that some women were willing to pay to have their lower ribs removed so they could have smaller waists. Maria was simply the recipient of a lucky gene pool. Her body and face caused men's eyes to glaze over when they saw her for the first time. When the initial shock wore off, they noticed that she also had a warm smile and full, inviting lips, again a blessing bestowed by nature rather than some scientific injection.

At 5'8", Maria towered over Elena. Years of hard work and bearing eleven children had prematurely aged her mother. There was only a sixteen-year age difference between them, but Elena looked forty years older. Her mottled, lined face was surrounded by nondescript grey-brown hair. Elena's hands were rough from working as a cleaning lady and her body had become thick with constant years of childbearing. Elena carried the weight of her large family on shoulders that were becoming more and more stooped each year.

Today was a big day for Maria, the interview with Moore Scientific Laboratories. The Rodriguez family didn't have a computer, but their priest, Father Ryan, knew how much Maria wanted to find a job outside the barrio. From time to time, he would search the Internet to see if there were any good jobs for her that were within bussing distance. He had called Maria a few days earlier when he discovered that this well-respected company was looking for a receptionist. He knew big businesses like Moore liked to show ethnic diversity and being Hispanic would certainly be in Maria's favor.

When Maria called to make an appointment for the interview, she learned that the head of Human Relations at Moore Labs was a man. Maria was well aware of the effect she had on men. A short black skirt, which showed off her legs, and a creamy silk blouse, which accentuated her high, full breasts, would be perfect to wear to the interview. Actually, it was the only "dress up" outfit she had. She applied a little mascara to emphasize her lashes and lip gloss to set off her smile and lips. The effect was dazzling. She looked incredibly sexy, but very ladylike. It was a difficult look for most women to achieve, but Maria instinctively had "it".

Elena was speaking once again. "Maria, remember, only your beauty will get you out of here. If not, you'll be like every other pretty young woman who stays in the barrio. You'll end up marrying some macho, beer-drinking wife abuser or worse. You've seen what happens to them. They have one baby after another, their children are killed in drive-by shootings by gang members, and drug deals go down on every corner. Remember what happened to Raoul, your younger brother? My heart breaks every time I think about him being mistakenly shot by gang members. *Madre de Dios*. I beg of you, get out while you still have your beauty."

Conversations like this had been going on ever since Maria had been a young girl. She wanted out of the barrio far more than her mother knew. Maria and her father, Fabian, had never told Elena what had happened to her in the alley behind their house on that fateful day several years earlier. The mere thought of what the gang members and the rats had done to her still made her shudder in horror. Most memories fade with time, but that memory was seared forever on Maria's brain.

Her mother had made her deathly afraid of aging, of ending up bent and aged like she was or fat and pregnant like her sister Celia, who had her first child out of wedlock at thirteen and was now pregnant with her fourth child by four different fathers at age nineteen. None of the four fathers had stayed around to help take care of or pay for the children. They all lived in the Rodriguez house; three more mouths to feed with a fourth on the way.

"Mama, if you feel so strongly about it, why didn't you get out? Why did you stay? You always talk about the men of the barrio and yet papa is one. Why is he any different?"

Elena Rodriguez looked at her daughter, "Your father told me if I married him he would never beat me. He told me he loved me. I believed him. He's a good man. He never has raised a hand to me. We don't have enough money to get out and we can barely feed the family. It's too late for us, but it's not too late for you. I know you will be offered a job at Moore Labs. Every morning at Mass, you are in my rosary bead prayers, prayers that you will get a good job, find a rich man, and leave the barrio. When you lose your looks and start aging, it will be too late. You are twenty-three. You can't wait much longer."

CHAPTER 4

Maria's life had not been easy. She always remembered the small rented home in Santa Ana, California. Slum landlords didn't put money into houses in this area and her run-down house was always badly in need of paint, inside and out. The steps leading to the porch were sloped and rotting away. The tired, rusty air-conditioner hung precariously from a bedroom windowsill that threated to come loose any minute. The inside was furnished with just the bare necessities: couch, refrigerator, stove, and an old television her father got from a family who set it out with the rest of their trash. The bedrooms were lined with used bunk beds held together with duct tape. The younger children shared beds while her father slept on the living room couch alongside a folding cot where Elena slept.

Her mother worked long hours as a cleaning lady, spending two or more hours each day commuting on buses to get to and from work. The Rodriguez family didn't own a car. Her father, Fabian, was a gardener's assistant and he, too, worked long hours. The money they earned barely covered the essentials. Fabian and Elena had crossed over the border from Mexico two decades ago, wanting to give their children a better life than what was available for them in Mexico. Maria was the first born and ten more children soon followed, making it even harder for Maria's parents to eke out a meager existence. They were always working, never home. Maria was more of a parent to her brothers and sisters than her parents were. No, it had not been an easy life.

Maria's physical development and beauty occurred early and it had not escaped the attention of the "home boys" in the barrio. "*Grande chichis,*" "big tits," was usually the first thing they yelled when they saw her. When there was no response from her, "*grande chichis*" turned to "*una apretada,*" the frigid one.

Women, particularly young women, weren't regarded very highly in the barrio. The ones who escaped the "home boys'" hoots and yells had ties to the gangs. Those young women were off-limits, under the protection of the gangs, and it was rare for a rival gang member to ever say anything disparaging or sexual to them. If they did, they were usually found dead in a matter of days. Maria's brother had been killed by gang members and she hated them.

The barrio was a frightening place. It was never-ending gang fights, the sound of gunshots late at night, and rats that lived in the alleys behind the houses, eating whatever they could find. Maria would never forget the night when she was twelve years old and had taken the trash out to the alley.

On the night she made a solemn vow to get out of

the barrio, she noticed that the trash had been overflowing in their small kitchen. She knew how tired her mother would be when she finally got home from working all day cleaning houses and then taking a second job, cleaning up from the cocktail party one of the ladies she worked for was having. She thought she would help her mother by emptying the trash.

Maria walked out the back door in the early evening, turned the corner, entered the alley, and immediately sensed there were people nearby. In a matter of seconds, she was surrounded by five young men with prominent gang tattoos. She recognized them as being from the same gang that had been responsible for her brother's death. She turned to run back to her house, but was stopped by one of them who held her arms from behind while another one sprung open his knife and slowly cut each button off her blouse. As her blouse opened, he deftly slashed the front of her bra with his knife, exposing her breasts. The "home boys" were whipping themselves into a sexual frenzy, calling her "*puta*," slut, touching her exposed breasts. Then they pushed her to the ground, tearing at her jeans and pulling them off. Prying her legs apart, one by one they dropped their jeans to the ground, savagely raping her. Violence was common in the "hood" and two of them could only become erect by first beating her; then, and only then, were they capable of raping her.

Maria was a virgin and the brutal assault caused

her to bleed severely from her vagina, as well as bleeding from her split lip where they had punched her. She could feel hot tears on her cheeks as one of them yelled, "*hijo de puta*" to the others, "son of a bitch." The leader of the gang yelled for them to leave, that someone was coming, and in seconds they were gone. As she lay on the ground, battered and bruised, she could hear the rats coming near her, scuttling around with their bright little piercing eyes. She could feel their tails as they brushed against her, licking the blood from her legs. She could feel one crawling up the inside of her leg seeking the source of the vaginal blood as another one inched along her cheek, licking the blood from her face. She was too weak to cry out for help. Mercifully, she passed out from pain and terror.

When her father, Fabian, arrived home from work, Maria's sister told him that Maria had taken the trash out and hadn't come back. Fabian rushed to the alley and with one look at her he instantly knew what had happened. It happened a lot in the "hood". He ran to her, tearing the kerchief off his head and wiping the blood away as he scattered the rats with his boot toe. He gently helped her stand, pulling her jeans on and zipping them. He took off his shirt and put it on her, wiping her cheeks gently as tears fell from his eyes.

"Maria," he said, "Elena must never know. This would break her heart. I will help you into the house. We'll tell the others that you fell when you were dumping the trash and tore your blouse. They don't need to know. No one needs to know. After your mother leaves for work tomorrow, I will go with you to the free clinic to have you examined and treated by a doctor."

He helped her into the house and into the bathroom. She washed herself, getting rid of the rapists' semen. As she looked at herself in the mirror, she felt dirty, ashamed, and violated. For the first time, she vowed to get out of the barrio. It was her mother's mantra, but one that was now shared by her.

In her senior year of high school, she listened enviously to a few of her classmates talk about the colleges they hoped to attend. Very few students graduated from Maria's high school and even fewer had the money or the grades to go to college. When Maria graduated from high school, she knew there was barely enough money to feed her brothers and sisters, much less money for her to go to college. Even if she could qualify for a scholarship, she couldn't go. She was expected to get a job and help the family. College was not an option. Her mother and father had never graduated from high school. Between gangs, drugs, and teenage pregnancies, there was no guarantee her younger brothers and sisters would even make it into high school, much less graduate

After graduation Maria took a job as a receptionist at the "free" neighborhood health clinic just to help the family. She knew it wasn't a career. She decided she would look for a job in a few years that could possibly lead to a career, but for now she needed to make money. Five years quickly went by and she knew her mother was right; time was running out. She needed to find a place to work that was more than a receptionist at a neighborhood health clinic. That would never get her out of the barrio.

She began to have bouts of mild depression. The never-ending work and chores she did for the family coupled with her job as a receptionist at the clinic, made her wonder if there really would be a good life for her, or if her present life was going to be as good as it got. She told one of the doctors at the clinic about the feelings, which she described as "wet wool." The doctor prescribed an anti-anxiety drug for Maria's symptoms and thus began her intermittent reliance on drugs to control the "wet wool."

Being beautiful had its pluses and if the job interviewer was male, she knew she'd probably be offered the job. She decided she would be very careful about choosing what company she would work for. Even if she were to get married and have children, she probably would have to continue working, so she had better choose a company where she could stay a long time. Elena told her that no one hired older women. Elena's words regarding aging were always with her.

Elena constantly told Maria to look for a rich man and that rich men liked beautiful women. Again and again she told her to never have anything to do with the men in the barrio, that with her good looks she could do much better. She told Maria not to waste her looks on someone poor, that men would be willing to pay for her beauty. The words had been repeated so often by Elena that Maria had them committed to memory. Those three thoughts had been her mantra since she could remember. *Get a good job. Find a rich man. Get out of the barrio.*

She'd worked since she'd been twelve, babysitting, cashiering at the local convenience store, and as a receptionist at the clinic. Now she was interviewing for real, grown-up jobs. This was different. She wanted to be sure that she was making the right decision.

She rode the bus ten miles to Irvine where the large high-rise businesses were located, but she wasn't prepared for the company campus of Moore Scientific Laboratories, which was made up of several buildings. Her purse was inspected by the security guard and a wand was passed over her body. Maria had never been through a security line at an airport and all this was quite new to her. After the security guard allowed her to enter the building, she simply stood in awe at what was before her. The lobby was an atrium filled with exotic plants. There was beautiful artwork on the walls and custom tiles on the floor. It was beyond anything she had ever seen.

When she got off the elevator on the floor where

the Human Resources Department was located, once again she simply stood in awe. The furniture, the carpeting, the art on the walls, all of it was like something out of the magazines she read at the library. *So this is what it's like to have money*, she thought. She wondered if the homes of the business executives at Moore Labs were this beautiful. Maria hoped and prayed that she would be offered the job of receptionist. To work here would be a dream come true. She sent a silent prayer of thanks to Father Ryan.

Scott Adams, Human Relations Director, instantly put her at ease. Mr. Adams told her what the duties of the job would be, the benefits, and the salary. At the end of the interview, he told her he was interviewing several other applicants and he would call her within a few days. She thanked him and told him she wanted the position; that she knew she could do a good job for the company.

He went through the motions of interviewing the other applicants, but as soon as he had seen Maria, he was determined to have her come to work for Moore Labs. Scott couldn't keep his mind off of her. Those full breasts in the white silk blouse, the long legs he could see beneath the tight skirt, the small waist, and that incredible smile and those lips. He fantasized about her for two days before calling her and offering her the job. He told her he would pay her more than the ad had indicated; that she had a bright future at Moore Labs, and that he would be happy to help her.

Even though she was very aware that he would like to offer her more than a job, she eagerly accepted and they agreed she would start the following Monday. She couldn't believe her luck. The company was involved in scientific research. Not only would she work in beautiful surroundings, but the work would be interesting. She had gone to the library to research the company and learned that Moore Scientific Laboratories' biggest research project involved developing new drugs and hormones that they referred to as "anti-aging" research. It was hoped that these discoveries would slow down the aging process in the human body. This was a subject in which Maria was vitally interested. Scott had told her that there would be chances for advancement and that many of the scientists who worked at Moore Labs needed personal assistants. The future looked bright.

That evening, after she had received the job offer from Scott, Maria waited at the bus stop for her mother to return home from her long day at work. She couldn't wait to tell Elena the news that she had a real job, a career-type job in a beautiful office, which was going to pay her well, and best of all, perhaps she could pick up some information on how to keep her beautiful looks. Elena was as excited as Maria was. It was just as Elena had prayed for every day at the early Mass she attended before starting her day's work—that Maria could get out of the barrio. "Praise be to God," Elena said, crossing herself.

Maria knew she needed some clothes for her new job. She had no money and no credit cards, but the local Catholic Church had helped her family in many ways over the years and maybe they could help her now. Maria and her family had often gotten clothes, which parishioners had donated, from the church and in fact, the blouse and skirt Maria had worn to the interview at Moore Labs had come from there. The next morning she decided to see if they had anything that she could wear to work at her new job.

Judy Greer, the woman in charge of overseeing donations to the church, greeted her warmly. Judy had been a fixture at the church ever since Maria could remember. She was a mother earth type who still wore Birkenstocks, had probably been at Woodstock in the '60s and hugged everyone she met. Judy only saw the good in people. She was a bit of a saint herself and a perfect person to work at the church.

"Maria, how wonderful to see you! What can I do for you?" asked Judy.

"I was just hired by a fancy business in Irvine to be their receptionist and I start Monday. The problem is, I don't have anything to wear to work. I have one good outfit, the one I got from the church, and what other few clothes I have are too casual or they're worn out. I know that people sometimes donate clothing to the church. Can you help me?" Maria was clearly distraught and Judy was happy to help her.

"I think you're in luck. We have a very wealthy member who brings in sacks of clothes twice a year. Her photo is always on the society page of the local newspapers and she doesn't want to be photographed wearing the same thing twice. She was just here and insisted on showing me every feature on the new Bentley her husband gave her. I haven't even taken the clothes out of the bags. Come, you can help me sort through them. She's just about your size."

An hour later, Maria left the church weighed down by bags of clothes. She had taken almost everything the "rich lady" had donated with the exception of a few fancy evening dresses. The wealthy church member had very good taste and Maria recognized the designer labels from reading fashion magazines at the library. She never thought she would own clothes that had labels like Tory Burch, Celine, St. John, Donna Karan, and Trina Turk. Even the woman's shoes were her size. She looked at the red soles on the Christian Louboutin shoes and wondered how she could have ever been so lucky! There wasn't a single sign of wear or scuff marks on them. Had the rich lady even worn the clothes and shoes she had donated, or had she just bought them because they momentarily had caught her eye? Well, it didn't make any difference. Maria was just grateful the woman had donated them. She said a silent prayer of thanks for the God who must be looking out for her.

She started work on Monday and by Tuesday afternoon word had quickly spread from floor to floor about the beautiful new receptionist. Many a young male employee found an excuse to visit the reception area during Maria's first week on the job. She had a hard time remembering all their names, but they all knew hers. The words "Maria Rodriguez" were very visible on the nameplate on her desk. The one person she did remember was Jeffrey Brooks, because he found some excuse to go in and out of the reception area several times a day. Of average height and build with sandy-colored hair, he wasn't someone who would stand out in a crowd, but what set him apart from the others were his vivid blue eyes, which shone with intensity and curiosity. They were eyes that, once seen, could never be forgotten.

From the office rumor mill she heard that Jeffrey was a brilliant scientist who specialized in research involving anti-aging hormones. The other scientists who worked at Moore Labs felt it was only a matter of time until one of his discoveries would lead to a Nobel Prize. Several weeks went by and then one afternoon, when she was taking her afternoon break in the company cafeteria, reading a library book she had brought with her to work, she heard Jeffrey's voice. She looked up as he sat down across from her.

"Good afternoon, Maria. I'm Jeffrey Brooks. I hope

you don't mind if I join you. I need a cup of coffee to keep my afternoon energy up. So how do you like working at Moore Labs?" he asked.

She put her book down and was a little taken aback at the intensity of his stare. His eyes moved from her face to her bright red sweater, which clearly showed off her full breasts. His eyes lingered there a moment too long for her to feel comfortable, then his gaze shifted to her legs. He had a hungry expression on his face that made her feel slightly nervous.

Maria drew her legs under her chair and answered him. "I like it. It's interesting work and I love meeting people. I would like to know more about the research that's being done here. From what I've heard, the company is world renowned and on the cutting edge of a number of scientific discoveries. I'm particularly interested in the research being done on anti-aging."

"What a coincidence. I'm the lead member on a team that's working in that area and I guess you could say that it's my specialty. I'd be happy to fill you in if you'll have dinner with me tomorrow night," Jeffrey said.

Maria was very good at reading people and there was something about Jeffrey that made her very uncomfortable. He was strange and quite different from the men she'd known before, although he was clearly lusting after her and that was pretty normal for the men who came in contact with her. At times, it was as if he was somewhere else, not fully present. She guessed that was just part of his brilliant mind. If he was as dedicated to his research as everyone said, it probably would be hard to deal with routine day-to-day matters.

Because she was so interested in his research on anti-aging, she thought this would be a good opportunity to find out more. If she could learn anything from him that would help keep her from aging, she was more than willing to go to dinner with him. Once again she was reminded of Elena's words, which had become Maria's mantra. *Get a good job. Find a rich man. Get out of the barrio.* Well, she was one down. Maybe Jeffrey would be the answer to the other two. She promised herself that she would keep her questions light and airy. She didn't want anyone to know how terrified she was of losing her looks.

"Yes, I would like that very much. I get off work at 5:30. Shall I meet you in the reception area? There are lots of restaurants around here; we could just go to one of those," Maria said

Jeffrey smiled. It was a warm and beautiful smile and it caught Maria somewhat off-guard, given her first impression of Jeffrey. Next to lusting for her, it was the first normal thing she had seen him do. "Perfect. I'll make reservations for us. I know a great little Italian place nearby. No notebooks or recording devices, though. A lot of the stuff we do around here is pretty top secret," he laughed.

Maria wasn't sure whether he was kidding or not. He was so different from any man she had ever known. His eyes held an intensity she had never seen before. When he looked at her, he couldn't disguise how much he wanted her and Maria sensed this feeling. She felt threatened by him and yet strangely attracted and drawn to him. He was sexy in a very intellectual way, far different from the macho men she had known. Although she wasn't particularly an egotistical person, she had to admit that the idea of a brilliant scientist being interested in her was very seductive. Certainly, she was no stranger to male relationships, but she'd never met a man like Jeffrey. The men she had known before seemed like children compared to him. She was looking forward to the dinner and learning more about his research.

She glanced at her watch and realized she had gone way over the fifteen minutes allotted for her coffee break. She grabbed her book, told Jeffrey she'd see him tomorrow, and hurried out of the cafeteria. Fortunately, no one was in the reception area when she returned to her desk. She sat down, put her book in her desk drawer, and acted as if she'd been sitting there for quite some time.

The next morning before she went to work, she took everything out of her closet. Nothing seemed right. What do you wear when you're going to have dinner with someone who was probably going to win a Nobel Prize? She didn't have a clue and she also didn't have any money to buy anything new.

She relied on the "rich lady's" clothes and decided on a simple, lavender sweater and matching skirt. It was unseasonably cool for Southern California and she knew the outfit was flattering to her, showing off her hour-glass figure.

As the day went on, she found that she was really looking forward to the dinner. At 11:30 that morning, Jeffrey called her, confirming the time. They talked for a while and she could tell that he, too, was looking forward to the dinner. She wondered if she had misjudged him since he seemed a lot more normal on the phone than he had been in person. Promptly at 5:30, Jeffrey walked into the reception area. "Ready?" he asked.

"Just one minute. I need to shut down my computer," she said. Maria got her purse from the bottom drawer of the desk, secretly pleased that the rich church lady had donated the Kate Spade bag. It looked a lot better than the Wal-Mart special she'd gotten for Christmas several years ago.

The trip to the Italian restaurant was short and when they entered, she could tell Jeffrey had been right. The restaurant looked and smelled wonderful. Maria had spent a lot of time reading cookbooks she had checked out of the library. Her family had never been able to afford to eat out at restaurants and even if they had, they never would have gone to a restaurant as fancy as this one.

As she was looking at the menu, the waiter came and asked if they would like to order from the wine list. Jeffrey asked if he might order for her, that there was one special wine he particularly liked. After the waiter brought them their wine, she sipped it and asked Jeffrey to tell her about it.

"Well, I particularly like this malbec, maybe because it brings back such good memories for me. After I graduated from college, before I began my post-graduate work, my parents gave me a graduation present, a trip to Argentina. For some reason I had always been fascinated with the country and it was an incredible experience. Malbec wine comes mainly from Argentina and every time I drink it, I feel happy, like I did in Argentina.

Maria rarely drank wine other than the sip of wine that she would get at Communion Mass. All of the men she had known in the past preferred beer, but she loved the malbec Jeffrey had suggested. The deep red wine was fabulous and she found that, with Jeffrey's help, she could even detect the hint of plums and berries.

When she ordered, neither the waiter nor Jeffrey suspected that she had never eaten any of the things she ordered. In fact, she didn't even know what they were. Because she was too embarrassed to ask, she just took a chance and ordered. She decided on bucatini with a pork and fennel ragu and a caprese salad. Jeffrey opted for the shellfish risotto with a fresh pea soup. The aromas coming out of the kitchen held the promise that they would soon be enjoying a spectacularly good meal.

"Tell me a little about yourself," Jeffrey began. "Why did a beautiful woman like you decide to come to work for Moore Scientific Laboratories? I'm sure you had a number of other choices."

She gave him an abbreviated version of her interest in what Moore Labs was doing and asked him to tell her more about his research. Clearly, this was his love. Once he started, it was like floodgates had been opened.

Speaking slowly, he began, "I always wanted to be a scientist. Even when I was a little kid, I'd be experimenting with things. The science kits my parents gave me just got bigger and more expensive the older I got. My mother was always worried about aging, so she took all kinds of health food supplements, some okay and some pretty weird. I grew up thinking everyone ate tofu. The other kids in class had peanut butter and jelly on white bread and chips for lunch. I finally convinced Mom to give me peanut butter and jelly, but it was organic, on whole grain bread. I used to console myself by thinking at least the other kids didn't know it was organic and that it wasn't some really weird thing like we often had at home.

"My mom spent hours at the library, trying to discover the secret to the fountain of youth. When she learned about the Internet, it opened up even more possibilities. I guess it was pretty natural that I'd go into this field."

"I'm fascinated by aging as well. I've always wondered if something could be discovered so that people wouldn't have to look older. Wouldn't it be wonderful if we could look like we do now for the rest of our lives? I guess everyone hopes that some drug or product like that will be discovered," Maria said.

"Can you keep a secret?" Jeffrey asked.

"Of course. I really don't know anyone well at Moore Labs and yes, I'm a very good keeper of secrets. With all my brothers and sisters, I had to learn to keep secrets," Maria laughed.

"Well," Jeffrey went on, "I think I'm on the brink of finding the fountain of youth. The research I've done on rats has been incredible. I think that with just a little more tweaking, I can keep us looking exactly like we do now." Jeffrey was oblivious to the shiver that ran through Maria at the mention of rats. Rats brought back the terror of the evening in the alley when she was twelve years old.

He was just starting to go into greater detail when the waiter brought their soup and salad. They resorted to small talk, things like where they had come from, their families, his education, and her lack of education.

As they began to eat their main course, Jeffrey's cell phone rang. "Yes, of course. I'll be right there," he said. He stood up, took several bills out of his wallet, and apologized to Maria. He continued talking as he escorted her out the door. "I have to go back to the lab. My assistant has been overseeing some things that require my immediate attention. Again, I'm sorry. I really enjoyed being with you. Could we try again?" Jeffrey asked.

"Yes, I'd like that very much," she said.

Maria found she had liked being with Jeffrey far more than she had thought she would. He was probably the most interesting man she had ever met, even if he was different. He was completely dedicated to science and to his work. He told her there were a number of things he wanted to work on; experiments that he hoped would lead to important discoveries for all of mankind. He clearly had some grandiose plans for the future and for the good of the human race.

While talking about his future plans, Maria had asked him "What do you have in mind? It seems hard to believe that one person could help the entire word. I mean, I know it's possible, but it seems pretty unlikely."

"Well, I'll keep that for another time, but I do think it can be done. I just need to work out some of the details." Jeffrey replied.

She had never met anyone like Jeffrey. The other men she had known were only interested in beer and sex. Jeffrey had shown her that he could be very normal and she thought what a burden it must be, to be so close to discovering something that everyone would want. How could she not feel flattered that he wanted to see her again? She was smart, but she had never met anyone with a mind as quick as his and it was hard to keep up with his train of thought. *This is a challenge,* she thought, *a very interesting challenge and unlike any I've ever experienced.*

"Well then," Jeffrey said, "could we try for dinner again tomorrow night? Hopefully, I can take care of what I need to do at the lab tonight and tomorrow I'll be available for the entire night. If not, I'll let you know."

"Yes. I'm already looking forward to it," Maria said, smiling, and at the same time mentally wondering what other "rich lady outfit" was in her closet that would compare to what she had worn tonight. She could tell by the way he had looked at her that he had definitely approved of the lavender sweater and skirt.

Maria and Jeffrey spent a lot of time together during the next few weeks. They shared their pasts as well as their hopes for the future. Once, when Jeffrey looked at her and told her how beautiful she was, she shared her fear of losing her looks, a fear she lived with daily. In turn, Jeffrey told her about his childhood and how a lot of people thought he was crazy because he was different. He told her that he was manic-depressive, diagnosed by a psychiatrist while he was in middle school, and that his life had changed for the better when he began taking medication for it.

Jeffrey was thirty-seven years old, but his commitment to science had kept his social life to a minimum. He was enthralled by this young, strikingly beautiful woman, who seemed really interested in his scientific endeavors. He couldn't help but notice that every man who saw Maria paused and stared, unable to believe that anyone could be that beautiful. A beautiful woman was not a bad thing to have as a companion.

CHAPTER 5

Gradually, the friendship turned into something much deeper. They progressed from casual goodnight kisses to passionate lovemaking at Jeffrey's apartment.

Jeffrey was tired from working so hard and his brain felt fried. He thought a short weekend vacation might do him good and give him a much-needed break. He asked Maria to go to Santa Barbara with him for a long weekend, which she readily agreed to, having never been out of Orange County. Jeffrey decided he would splurge and they would stay at the Bacara Resort in Goleta, just north of Santa Barbara.

They each took a day of vacation and left Orange County about 10:00 on a Friday morning, hoping to avoid the moving parking lot, which often made up the 405 Freeway. Fortunately, traffic was light and they easily made it to the Santa Barbara area by noon. Just south of Santa Barbara, in the Montecito area, they turned off Highway 101, leisurely admiring the lush reds and purples of the hillsides covered with bougainvillea vines, the stately mansions, and the beautiful oceanfront homes. When they got to Santa Barbara, they spent several hours exploring downtown, the pier, and State Street. They found a wonderful wine and cheese shop where they bought several different kinds of cheese and some wine to enjoy later in the evening.

The drive to the resort, which was located high on a hill overlooking the Pacific Ocean, was breathtaking. The old world Spanish style architecture of the world-class resort was charming with no detail in luxurious comfort overlooked. As promised, their room faced the ocean and had a small balcony where they enjoyed their wine and cheese before dinner. .

Jeffrey had heard good things about the Miro Restaurant in the hotel so they decided to try it, which proved to be a very good decision. Within minutes of being seated, the waiter brought their menus, water was poured, and warm bread with a red sea salt butter was offered. The wine steward asked what wine they would like to order with dinner and suggested the Cakebread Sauvignon Blanc with their salad and the Switchback Ridge Cabernet Sauvignon with their entree.

The Dungeness crab in Jeffrey's salad had been perfectly steamed and chilled and was one of Jeffrey's favorites. Maria had never had calamari so she decided to expand her taste buds and try it. It, too, was an excellent addition to her salad and she was glad that she'd been experimental when making her selection. The wine steward poured their beautiful red cabernet as the waiter brought their strip steak and loin of lamb. Although they were stuffed from the wine and cheese they'd had in their room and from the large dinner, the waiter insisted they try the restaurant's signature dish, an orange blossom beignet, a fancy New Orleans word for a fritter. They opted to split one order and although they could only manage a couple of bites, the waiter had been right, it was fantastic.

It was a beautiful night as they leisurely left the restaurant to have an after dinner drink on the patio by the fire pit. The roar of the ocean, the warmth of the wine they had ordered, along with the lingering taste of the well prepared food were the finishing touches to a wonderful day. Jeffrey was relaxed for the first time in months. Although he had used being tired as an excuse for the trip, and there was some truth to that, his real purpose had been to propose to Maria in a romantic spot. His instincts had been right; he couldn't have picked a better time and place.

He reached into his pocket and took out a small jewelry box. Maria was looking at the ocean and never noticed his movement. When she returned her gaze to Jeffrey, he said, "Maria, we've spent a lot of time together in the past few months. I want to spend the rest of my life with you. I love you. You make me happier than I ever thought I could be. Will you marry me?"

Her affirmative answer was a foregone conclusion. The thought briefly crossed her mind that her mother would be really, really happy and Maria couldn't wait to tell her she had found a rich man and she was getting out of the barrio. Now she'd never hear that mantra again. She'd never have to see the rats in the alley and the faces of the young gang members who had raped her. Finally, she was getting out. "Jeffrey, let's go to the room. I have to call my mother and tell her. She will be so excited."

As predicted, Elena was ecstatic. Maria hung up the phone and got undressed, walking in the nude to the open balcony doors, knowing that no one on the water could see her. Jeffrey turned the lights off and wrapped his arms around her as they both looked out at the ocean. He gently fondled her high, full breasts, caressing her nipples until they became hard and erect. He let one hand gradually slide down her smooth skin, stroking her luxurious pubic hair. *Thank God she didn't have the money for a Brazilian wax,* he thought, *I could do this the rest of my life and I just may.* As he turned her around to face him, he noticed she had tears rolling down her face.

"My God, Maria, what's wrong? Have I done something? This should be the happiest moment of our lives. Please, tell me what it is! Why are you crying? What have I done?" exclaimed Jeffrey.

"Jeffrey, I'm crying because I love you so much and I don't want to become ugly. I know you love me now, but what's going to happen when I start to age? Will you still love me then or are you going to leave me for some younger, more beautiful woman? I'm so scared of becoming old. Please, just hold me."

"Maria, I will love you forever. You and my work are all I care about. I promise you that I will never leave you. Come, we need some sleep. It's been a long day and we're both tired." He led her to the bed where they did sleep, but not until much later.

A week after they returned from Santa Barbara, Jeffrey took Maria to a fashionable French restaurant. Jeffrey had dined there recently with one of the executives from the company and wanted to share it with her. "Maria, there's something I need to talk to you about."

Maria immediately felt her stomach tighten. Usually those words meant that bad news was going to follow. She waited for the words, "I really like you, but this isn't going to work out."

"Yes, Jeffrey, what is it?" Maria stammered.

Jeffrey began, "I know what I'm going to suggest is unethical, but I believe I have discovered something that will keep people from outwardly aging. The research I've done with the rats in my lab has been extremely positive. All of their outward signs of aging have stopped. Rats normally have a life expectancy of three to five years, at the most. I have one who is nine and jumps around like a youngster. All of their coats are glossy, their eyes are clear, and none of them appears to have aged even one day.

"I know how worried you are about losing your youth and beauty, but I love you for who you are, not your beautiful face or your beautiful body. Yet I understand how important those things are to you. I have been injecting the rats monthly with a hormone I've discovered. I think it will work on humans, and more importantly, I think it will work on you.

"In the United States, the government has made it very difficult for any new drug or hormone to be approved before it can be sold to the public. They want years of data from clinical testing before it can go on the market. It's very unethical to try anything like my newly discovered hormone on a human until it has gone through all of the government approvals. It's also completely against Moore Labs' policies. Hell, I think I even signed something or other when I was hired about that, but I've decided I don't want to wait. I believe I can keep you looking just the way you are now. I do know that it's not a dangerous hormone. There has not been one single adverse effect on the rats. I would never expose you to anything that might harm you. I love you too much for that and I'm willing to do this because I do love you so much.

"There is just one thing I need to ask of you. No one must ever know. If Moore Labs ever found out what I was doing, that I was injecting you with the anti-aging hormone, I would be fired immediately. Worse than that, I would probably go to jail. If you want me to use the injection on you, you have to promise me that you will never tell anyone. What do you think?" Jeffrey asked, looking at her expectantly.

Maria was stunned. She knew that Jeffrey was risking his professional career to help her overcome her fear of aging that she'd had since she was in her early teens. What if someone found out? Would he grow to hate her? Would he later regret making this decision? And yet, for all the questions racing through her mind, the thought of never again having to fear losing her beauty was very compelling and powerful. If she could keep her beauty, she'd never have to go back to the barrio and the terrors that lived there.

Maria began to voice her fears to Jeffrey. "Jeffrey, I love you so much for even suggesting this. You know how terrified I am of losing my looks, but I don't ever want to be the cause of something that could potentially ruin your future. I'm almost sorry that you brought it up. If something were to happen and Moore Labs found out, you probably would be fired and possibly go to jail and it would all be because of me. I would never ask that of you. It's too much. I really don't think we should do it."

"Maria, if I didn't want to do this, I never would have suggested it. I don't see a downside. Neither one of us can ever discuss it with anyone. As long as we don't talk, how will anyone find out? This will work, I promise you."

When people want to believe something, they tend to downplay the negative risks that might be involved. Casting all of her concerns aside, Maria agreed to have Jeffrey administer the monthly injection that she so desperately hoped would keep her looking young and beautiful. It was a decision they both would deeply regret.

Jeffrey told her it would probably be several years before she would even notice anything. About the time others in her age group began to get fine lines around their eyes, thickening of the facial skin, a slight sag in the jawline, and a grey hair or two, Maria would stay exactly as she was at this moment, a stunningly beautiful woman in her prime.

The injections began that night. There was no pain or side effects. Maria looked forward to always being beautiful and Jeffrey looked forward to winning the Nobel Prize.

Their marriage took place at St. Vincent's Church in Santa Ana, the church Maria had attended from the time she was baptized. She took her First Communion there and the family attendance was a Sunday ritual. Her mother was at Mass almost every morning at 6:00 a.m. A strong belief in a rapturous afterlife eased the pain of Elena's present life. From the time Maria had been born, her mother insisted that the Catholic Church be just as important to Maria as it had been to Elena.

Jeffrey believed in science, not in a rapturous afterlife, but he agreed to be married in the church that meant so much to Maria and her family. His family was Episcopal and he had been baptized at an early age, therefore, they would be able to get married in the Catholic Church. Even though his was not a church-going family, Jeffrey knew his parents would understand what it meant to Maria for them to be married in her church. He even agreed to the premarital counseling that the church required.

It was a lovely wedding. Maria looked like a carnal angel when she came floating down the aisle on Fabian's arm. She wore a strapless cream-colored wedding dress with her lustrous jet-black hair pulled up into a bun covered by a short lace veil. Her light tan complexion was in sharp contrast to her dark eyes and hair. Two of her sisters stood with her, dressed in peach-colored, strapless satin dresses. The Rodriguez women were very attractive, but Maria was the beauty of the family. No one in the church could take their eyes off of her. There was an aura of smoldering sexuality and innocent beauty about her that was mesmerizing.

The youngest Rodriguez girl, Magdalena (everyone called her Lena), was the flower girl and the ring bearer was Maria's youngest brother, Miguel. At six and seven, they were adorable. Jeffrey's friend, Dan, from Moore Labs, stood with Jeffrey, as well as one of Maria's brothers. The rest of the brothers were ushers and the guest book was overseen by one of her other sisters. The church was packed with family, friends, and church members who Maria had known since she was a child.

Jeffrey insisted on paying for the wedding, knowing that Maria's family could ill afford to give their beautiful daughter a wedding. The reception took place in the outdoor patio of the church. It was a beautiful spring day, one of those glorious days just before the June skies in Southern California turned grey, as they did every year.

They honeymooned in the Tuscany area of Italy, a gift from Jeffrey's parents. His mother really liked Maria. She had always wanted grandchildren, but with Jeffrey's passion for science, she had long ago decided that a daughter-in-law and grandchildren were not to be. She was thrilled with the size of Maria's family, hoping Jeffrey and Maria would have many children. Maria didn't share with Jeffrey's mother the decision she had made at a very early age to never have children. Taking care of ten children had been enough for her. She told Jeffrey her feelings about not having children when their relationship changed from casual to something more. He understood and really didn't want children either since, in a way, science was his child. Although Maria had no education beyond high school and Jeffrey had his doctorate in Metabolic Medicine, his mother felt that the match was a good one. Maria's lack of higher education was far overshadowed by her nurturing, giving personality.

Tuscany was beautiful. Other than her trip to Santa Barbara, Maria had never traveled. When you lived in the barrio, you rarely got out of the barrio. She eagerly took to the Italian countryside, enchanted with its food, small villages and shops, the art, and the rolling hills studded with grape vines and olive trees. Away from his lab, Jeffrey was able to completely relax and he joined her in attempting to eat and drink as much as they could. For a welcome change, he even seemed somewhat normal.

The Italian men were as captivated with Maria as the American men. Wherever they went, she was the object of slavish male attention. Men passed her in the streets, softly telling her how beautiful she was, sending wine to her at dinner, and blowing kisses to her. If possible, Maria became even more beautiful, glowing in the spotlight of all the male attention. It was an unforgettable two weeks.

Maria and Jeffrey returned to California and settled into married life. They bought a condominium in Irvine near Moore Labs. Maria was soon promoted to what Moore Labs referred to as a "scientific assistant." Her new job consisted of doing secretarial work for a pool of five Moore Lab scientists. She loved the work and felt she was beginning to have a glimmer of what Jeffrey did in his scientific research.

Jeffrey was becoming renowned for his work on anti-aging hormones. Moore Labs had submitted his discovery to the Food and Drug Administration and they were now waiting for the government approvals to be completed. They wanted to be able to get the drug on the market as soon as possible. The FDA had approved their trials on the rats and they were now starting trials on humans. Everyone in the industry knew it would be one of the biggest blockbuster drugs to ever hit the market. The stock price of Moore Scientific Laboratories had risen dramatically in anticipation of FDA approval.

The discovery came at a very good time. The baby boomer generation was reaching their sixties and had a fear of all things which indicated they were aging. This was the generation that wasn't supposed to age. If there was a magic elixir to delay aging, the boomers would be standing in line to buy it. Billions of dollars in new sales were on the line.

Several years, happy years, went by for Maria and Jeffrey. Then one day, disaster struck. It came on a Wednesday afternoon, in Maria's office. She was preparing to leave for the day and decided to go to the ladies' room before she and Jeffrey met in front of the building for dinner at their favorite Italian restaurant. She left her purse on her desk.

Dan, Jeffrey's good friend and fellow scientist who managed the five scientists in the pool for which Maria had been hired, walked out of his nearby office ready to quit work for the day. He definitely looked like his life had been spent in a lab. Pale-faced and overweight with thinning hair, it was apparent to anyone who looked at him that this was a very cerebral man, not a gym rat.

He idly noticed Maria's purse on her desk and wondered if she had forgotten to take it with her. He walked over to it, intending to put it in one of her desk drawers. He noticed that the clasp on the purse was undone and it was open. He couldn't help but see a vial inside which was clearly labeled "Property of Moore Scientific Laboratories." He was very familiar with the vials, as all experimental products must be stored in them. There had to be a designation of what was in the vial so there would never be an inadvertent, dangerous mistake, which could prove costly to Moore Labs. He took the vial out of her purse and saw the designation on it for Jeffrey's experimental anti-aging hormone.

The government was getting close to giving approval for the hormone, but the approval was still months, if not years away. Dan began to have a sick feeling about his discovery. Jeffrey was the only person who knew how to make the hormone or have access to it. Had he allowed the drug to leave the high security lab without company approval? Could he be administering it to Maria? This was a violation of company policy that was both unethical and illegal. Dan heard footsteps in the hall and dropped the vial back into Maria's purse, realizing she had gone to the ladies' room before she had left for the day.

"Maria, I need to talk to you for a moment before you leave," Dan said. "I thought you had forgotten your purse and I walked over to your desk to put it in a drawer for you when I recognized a Moore Laboratories vial in it. Where and how did you get it?"

Maria knew that Jeffrey could be fired if Dan told anyone what he had discovered in Maria's purse. She and Dan had become friends since she had started working as his assistant. A number of different answers to his questions came to mind, but she quickly decided to use their friendship as leverage.

"Dan, can you keep a secret?" Maria asked.

"Yes, but I'm not sure that I should in this case."

"Dan, please, please, please," Maria said. "I'm swearing you to secrecy. Please promise me."

"Okay, Maria. I don't think I'm going to like what you're going to tell me, but yes, you have my promise," Dan said. Dan really liked both Maria and Jeffrey. Everyone knew that the FDA was eventually going to approve the drug, so what if Maria had been using it prematurely? Did he want to be the one responsible for Maria and Jeffrey getting fired or worse?

Maria was clearly very upset. She began by telling him about her fear of aging and how all she had ever heard from her mother when she was growing up was that she had to keep her beauty, that she had to marry while she was still beautiful or her life would be over. Maria told Dan about Jeffrey's decision to give her the drug before it was on the market because when she began the injections, she was at the most beautiful stage of her life. Maria told Dan that Jeffrey had only done this out of his devotion and love for her. She told him that Jeffrey hadn't given it to anyone else, how other drug companies had tried to bribe Jeffrey with promises of huge amounts of money if he would give them the formula, and how he had refused all offers. Maria told him Jeffrey had slipped the vial to her a couple of hours earlier as she was scheduled to get her monthly injection that night. She pleaded with Dan not to tell anyone.

Maria glanced at her watch, realizing she was going to be late meeting Jeffrey. She hurriedly finished by once again asking Dan not to tell anyone and making him repeat his promise to keep the secret. She ran down the hall, rushing to the front of the building where Jeffrey was waiting.

"Are you all right? You look upset. What's wrong?" Jeffrey asked.

Maria knew that Jeffrey would be furious with her if she told him the truth and he'd also be very worried that Dan would end up telling someone. Instead, she made up a story on the spot, telling Jeffrey that she had taken a phone call just as she was leaving and it was some crank call. Some strange person had gotten her extension number and threatened to hurt her if she didn't tell him what type of underwear she was wearing.

It was the only thing Maria could think of on such short notice. It clearly worried Jeffrey, but she told him that she was fine and it was just some anonymous call by a wacko. She reassured Jeffrey that the person never called her by name and probably just dialed randomly and got some sick pleasure from hearing her shocked voice.

He believed her.

CHAPTER 6

Dan felt sick to his stomach when he left Moore Labs after his conversation with Maria. He knew he had promised her that he wouldn't tell anyone about the vial he had discovered in her purse, but the more he thought about what Jeffrey had done, it became clear to him that Jeffrey had made a very bad decision.

Many of the other scientists at Moore Labs had made discoveries which were highly sought after by various other drug companies. Even so, they all abided by the contract they had signed with Moore Labs when they had been hired. Dan himself had made an important scientific discovery resulting in a type of aspirin, which was effective, yet had no adverse side effects, unlike the others on the market. But Dan hadn't given it to any members of his family and it galled him to think that Jeffrey had abused lab ethics and protocol by administering the anti-aging hormone to Maria.

Almost every time one of the scientists at Moore Labs made an important discovery, they would talk about how they wished they could give their discovery to some member of their family who was in pain or suffering from some type of physical or mental ailment, but they never did. It would be a breach of ethics and the legal contracts that each of them had signed when they had been hired by Moore Labs.

Sleep wouldn't come to Dan that night as he weighed the pros and cons of telling the founder and president of the company, Sidney Moore, what Jeffrey had done. Sidney had been Dan's mentor and Dan knew he couldn't face Sidney if somehow he found out that Dan had known what Jeffrey had done, but hadn't told him.

Yet, on the other hand, he had made a solemn promise to Maria. Jeffrey was not only Dan's colleague; he was his friend. They had shared many hours in the lab together as well as often getting together for a drink after work. Dan had also been the best man at Jeffrey and Maria's wedding. He desperately wished that he had never walked over to Maria's desk and seen what was in her purse. This really was a no-win situation.

As dawn broke, Dan came to a decision. He went into his office early and promptly, at 9:00 a.m., when Moore Scientific Laboratories opened for business, he called Sidney's office.

"Sidney Moore's office," answered Monica, Sidney's long-time personal assistant. "May I help you?"

"Monica, this is Dan Weaver. I'd like to schedule an appointment with Sidney. Could he see me this morning?"

"Let me check his schedule. Yes, if you can be here

at 10:00, he has an opening. I know he would be happy to see you. He always speaks so highly of you."

"Thanks. I'll be there at 10:00."

Well, he thought, *there's no going back now*. The next hour passed at a snail's pace for Dan. He dreaded the upcoming meeting with Sidney more than he had ever dreaded anything in his life. There was no way to gloss this over. Later, he wished he had never made the call.

At 9:55, he rode the elevator up to the top floor and walked to Sidney's luxurious office suite. As soon as he entered the reception area, Monica escorted him to the door leading to Sidney's office, knocking on the door, which was quickly opened by Sidney.

"It's good to see you. What brings you to my office so bright and early? A new discovery, I hope!" Sidney said, laughing, with his customary large smile. The enormous success of Moore Scientific Laboratories allowed Sidney to wear custom-made silk suits; have his hair cut and colored by an expensive Newport Beach hair stylist; and have a private trainer come to the gym that had been installed adjacent to Sidney's spacious office three mornings a week. He was proud of his home in Cota de Caza, his Maserati, and his beautiful second wife. Sidney had been a pharmacist before he founded Moore Labs and very much enjoyed the perks of his successful career.

Once again Dan felt sick to his stomach. This had to be about the worst thing that he had ever been involved in, ratting out his best friend. He began, "Thanks for taking the time to see me. I don't think either of us is going to enjoy the next few minutes, but there are some things you need to know, things that I have to tell you."

"Sit down. Tell me what's troubling you." Dan was ashen, his hands were shaking, and he was sweating profusely. One look at Dan and Sidney could tell that he was paying a very high price for whatever it was he was getting ready to tell him. He motioned for Dan to sit on the tan leather couch on the other side of the room, which Dan interpreted as a gesture of trust and friendship. Sidney usually conducted his meetings with people by sitting in a position of power behind his desk.

He told Sidney what had happened from the moment he had seen the vial in Maria's purse to the promise she had extracted from him. He knew that by telling Sidney he had broken his promise to Maria and ended his friendship with Jeffrey. He felt like a traitor and yet he knew he could not have done otherwise.

"Are you sure about this? Are you 100% certain that Jeffrey has been administering the anti-aging hormone to Maria? I need to be very, very certain that what you've told me is true. If you have even a shred of doubt, tell me now. I don't want to be sued for slander," Sidney said.

"Here is what I know and why I'm 100% certain of what I've told you. I personally saw the vial in Maria's purse. I know that it was Jeffrey's. Maria admitted that Jeffrey had been injecting her with his hormone. She even told me that Jeffrey had given the vial to her earlier that day because last night was the night for her monthly injection. Not only did she admit it, but she swore me to secrecy and made me promise I wouldn't tell anyone. I broke that promise and I don't feel good about it, but I felt you needed to know. Yes, I am 100% certain," Dan concluded.

"You know what will happen when this story breaks? There will be a feeding frenzy in the press. This has all of the elements of a really good story with a possible future Nobel Prize winner developing an anti-aging hormone and giving it to his beautiful wife against all company protocol. Yeah, this is a story the press will be all over," Sidney said.

Dan knew that Sidney was worried about the implications of what he had told him. He would have to meet with lawyers and pacify investors. And the hormone itself. Who owned it? Legally, it was the property of Moore Scientific Laboratories. When a scientist was hired by Moore Labs, a contract was signed involving confidentiality and it stated in very clear terms that Moore Scientific Laboratories owned whatever the employee developed. In this case, like in all the other discoveries, although the hormone had been developed through Jeffrey's experiments, Jeffrey did not own the hormone; Moore Scientific

Laboratories did. Dan also knew that if Jeffrey had been supplying the drug to Maria in violation of all company rules and regulations, Jeffrey could just as easily be selling the formula to some competitor, getting rich in the process, against all Moore protocol and contract rights.

Sidney began, "I am very, very sorry that you had to be involved in this. I can't thank you enough for telling me. I know it must have been the most difficult decision you ever had to make and I know that Jeffrey and Maria are good friends of yours. I can only imagine what you must be going through. Again, thank you. I need to talk to our lawyers and get some things in place before I confront Jeffrey. Why don't you take the rest of today, tomorrow, and next week off? Just go somewhere and get some rest. You can come back when this has blown over. I don't think it would be a good idea for you to be here when I confront Jeffrey. Once this becomes public, even though your name will never be mentioned, the press will nose around and probably try to reach you. Naturally, Maria will have to be fired as well."

Dan left the office, sick at heart. He knew he couldn't have lived with himself if he hadn't told Sidney, but that didn't make the sick feeling in his stomach go away. He went home, booked a flight to Cabo San Lucas, Mexico, and left that afternoon. In a few hours, he was sitting on the beach, a much-needed piña colada in hand.

CHAPTER 7

It had not been a good couple of days for Sam Begay. In fact, the last few days had been even worse than usual. He had lost the faith of the Tribal Council; left the sweat lodge before the ceremony had ended; and disappointed Strong Medicine. No, these were not things one wanted to have happen on the reservation. But if he could have known what the next few years of his life would bring, they would seem good by comparison.

Sam, a Native American, left the reservation when he went to college, one of the few from the reservation to do so. He was an extremely bright student and had received a scholarship earmarked for Native Americans. Even so, it didn't fully cover the cost of his education and he still had to take out a number of loans to help pay for his education. He returned during brief vacations from school, but most of his summers were spent in school so he could get more credits and his degree earlier. Just as he was ready to graduate from college, a casino was built on the reservation by his tribe.

The tribe had gone through many changes in recent years. The members had all prospered since a gaming compact had been signed by the Governor, which essentially allowed the tribe to have a casino on the reservation. The casino, financed by Las Vegas casino management firms, had provided wealth beyond any of their expectations. As one of the 241 members of the tribe, Sam received a check every month for $30,000, as did each of the other tribal members.

People drove for miles to come to the casino, which the tribe had made into a destination resort. Like the golf courses in the Palm Springs area, they had put water on the arid desert land which allowed them to build an award-winning golf course. A five star hotel with a fashionable spa rose off the desert floor. The old adage "Build It and They Will Come" had never been truer. Because the casino and spa were on tribal land, it cost far less to stay and play there. It was an easy drive from either Los Angeles or Phoenix. Not only was it competitive with their Palm Springs neighbors, it was also far less expensive than the Las Vegas hotels. Every year the casino and resort saw an increase in revenues. Life for the tribal members was good, except for Sam and his ongoing battle with his anger.

Late in the 19th century, many Native American tribes had been forced onto reservations on lands no one else wanted, lands where nothing would grow and water was scarce. It was in these desolate areas, after tribal gaming had been approved on a statewide ballot, where the casinos had been built by different tribes. They proved to be enormously popular and literally became "money machines" for previously impoverished tribes. The tribal members had gone from eating food out of government-issued cans to buying expensive Kobe beef. Such was the case with Sam's tribe.

Sam knew many people felt that the tribes were making too much money off of the casinos. People who were opposed to Indian gaming argued that because members of the tribes were often prone to alcoholism and abusive relationships, they shouldn't be given an opportunity to receive unlimited amounts of money. They felt that the money would only feed their addictions and be squandered. Sam disagreed. He felt it was payback time. For example, Sam's reservation would soon be home to a new school, a dental clinic, a medical clinic, and a pediatric center. A psychologist had started to work with the tribal members on issues such as alcohol addiction and spousal abuse. None of these things would have been possible without the money from the casino.

Sam lived in two worlds. One foot was strongly rooted in the Anglo's world. He was a medical resident with only a couple of months left until he finished his residency. His specialty was pediatrics. With the new wealth, the tribal elders had voted to pay for the college tuition and graduate school of any child who was a member of the tribe. Sam was the first one in his tribe to go to medical school. His dream in life was to be a doctor and help his tribe, particularly the children.

Even though the money was plentiful, the old ways

died slowly, if at all, for the tribal members. There were so many things that could be done for the children's health. The tribal members didn't trust the Anglo doctors, preferring to get treatment from the traditional tribal medicine man, Strong Medicine. Sam knew that a medicine man's ability to heal was limited, even one as good as Strong Medicine. Sam was of both worlds and he knew once he had completed his medical studies, he could bridge both worlds, helping the members of his tribe by introducing them to modern day medicine coupled with the ancient tribal medicine.

But no matter how much time Sam spent in the Anglo world, his other foot was still rooted in the ancient tribal ways. He had grown up in the old ways and he understood the power they held. Sam needed the tribe to trust him so they could benefit from the excellent medicine which was available from the Anglo's world. Sam's college loans were staggering, but all of his medical school costs were paid for by the tribe. He never could have afforded to go to medical school without the tribe's generous offer. With the heavy workload of medical school, his trips back to the reservation were infrequent. When he finished with his residency, he planned to return to the reservation and work as a pediatrician at the new pediatric center.

In the past, through sheer will power, Sam had trained himself to erase the picture he held in his mind of his mother, Susie, dying in the hospital. But this time he simply could not erase that horrible day from his memory. The picture of her last hours in the hospital filled his mind. He remembered the left side of her face, battered and split from the force of Joe's fist with the big ring he wore, causing a jagged cut. His brutal punches had dislocated her left shoulder and damaged her kidneys and lungs. Neither could be saved, even by the surgery the emergency room doctor had immediately ordered. He had called in an eye specialist who tried to save Susie's right eye, which was hanging out of the socket when Sam found her lying in a pool of blood, whimpering and moaning incoherently.

Sam was afraid to move her, but he didn't have a choice. The paramedics from Blythe were always slow to come to the reservation, if they came at all. Sam knew he couldn't wait for them to take her to the hospital in Blythe. Everything looked broken. A burly neighbor of Susie's helped Sam get her into the backseat of Sam's car. Susie was unconscious and never felt the jolts from the potholes in the reservation road. The main highway was a little better, but it really didn't matter to Susie. She never would know how carefully Sam had driven that day. She died late that night. A deep rage had stayed with Sam after his mother's death, a rage that was difficult for him to contain.

She had been beaten by Joe, the man Sam had known for his entire life as his "father." Just recently, his spiritual tribal father, Strong Medicine, had told him that Joe was not his biological father. His real father was Red Cloud, who had gotten Susie pregnant when they were in high school. Red Cloud had died in a tragic alcohol-related car accident before Sam was born. Not long after Red Cloud's death, Susie had married Joe. Native Americans and alcohol were a bad mix and reservation life was hard and even harder when you were a young woman, pregnant, and unmarried. Joe was the best Susie could do under the circumstances, so reluctantly, she agreed to marry him.

Sam hated Joe. From an early age Sam had learned to leave the house when he could see the telltale signs that Joe's rage was about to surface. When he went back home, Sam could see that once again Joe's temper, fueled with alcohol, had ended with his mother being beaten. The hatred and anger he felt for Joe was always simmering just below the surface.

Sam had always wondered about his physical appearance and why he didn't resemble Joe at all. Where Joe was squat with brown hair, Sam was tall, lean and muscular with sleek black hair. Joe had a swarthy pockmarked complexion, where Sam's was smooth and reddish-brown. Their noses were different. Sam had a strong nose some referred to as a "Roman" nose, although most of the Native American men had the same shaped nose. Joe's nose was flat, probably as a result of some barroom brawl. No, there were few, if any, resemblances between the two men. Certainly nothing that would make one think they were father and son. Sam thought that after he left the reservation and went away to school, when he didn't have to see Joe on a daily basis, his anger and hatred would lessen. It hadn't.

It was no secret on the reservation that Sam had anger issues. He had a history of numerous schoolyard fights, causing him to be expelled several times. The pattern was always the same. Susie would go to the school, cry, and tell the principal that there had been some problems at home that were causing the outbursts at school and the principal would relent, once again allowing Sam back in school. The school didn't have many students as bright as Sam.

As he got older, the fights and anger came out in different ways. Although alcohol was not sold on the reservation, there was a tavern just outside the reservation that had seen Sam in many a barroom brawl. Every time Sam won. When questioned by Susie, he would tell her that the other person had started it, that it was someone else's fault. Sam really believed that he was just a victim; that others were always out to get him. The Tribal Elders wanted Sam to be successful as much as Strong Medicine did, but they were becoming increasingly concerned about his anger issues.

This time, when Sam returned to the reservation from a break in his residency, it was pretty apparent to everyone on the reservation that he better get his anger in check if he was ever going to be an effective doctor. Once again, Sam had gotten into a barroom brawl. Sam still blamed his relationship with Joe as the reason he was angry all the time. He was glad that Strong Medicine had told him the truth about Joe. Sam was relieved to know he wasn't Joe's son and if he wasn't Joe's son, maybe he could begin to control his anger.

One day, during his brief return to the reservation, Strong Medicine asked Sam to meet with him. "Little Bear, it is time for you to join other tribal members in our sacred sweat lodge. You must get rid of the anger you are carrying that's poisoning your mind. Spending time in the sweat lodge with your tribal brothers will cleanse your mind and spirit. It is part of the 'old ways,' but it will help rid your mind of your anger and hatred."

Somewhat reluctantly, Sam agreed to meet Strong Medicine and some of the other tribal members at the sweat lodge before he went back to the hospital where he was completing his pediatric residency.

Sam wished he could change his Native American name, Little Bear. When Joe had married his mother and Sam had been born, Joe had named him. Sam didn't want any connection to the man, but he was stuck with the name. It grated on him every time someone used it.

As requested, he had met Strong Medicine and a few other tribal members at the sweat lodge. It had been a horrible experience and he had disgraced himself and Strong Medicine. The heat was worse than anything he had ever experienced. When the talking stick was passed to him, he spoke too little and too fast. The others spent a long time talking.

Didn't they feel the heat? Sam wanted to scream at them to shut up. He had to escape the heat and the sweat streaming down his body. Maybe this was the purification that Strong Medicine talked about, but he felt like he was going to faint. Maybe he wasn't the man Strong Medicine thought he was but at this point, he didn't care. All he could think about was how he could escape from the overwhelming heat in the sweat lodge. He knew that from time to time people had died at sweat lodges and he didn't want to be the next fatality. Finally, unable to bear the heat any longer, he crawled towards the flap.

Sam could see the disappointment on Strong Medicine's face as he pulled the flap of the hogan open and stumbled into the cool night air. He was ashamed that he had been the only one to leave the all-consuming heat of the sweat lodge. Perhaps the others were stronger and braver than he was. Once again, Sam felt anger wash over him. Maybe he was more like Joe than he thought. Both of them were angry men. He was beginning to wonder if what some people said was true—that one's environment was stronger than one's biology.

Hours later, asleep in the manufactured home that had been his mother's, he felt the hand of Strong Medicine on his shoulder. "My son, it is time to do your vision quest. The tribal fathers have expressed their great disappointment in you. You failed the sweat lodge. The only way to gain their respect is by completing a successful vision quest.

"Most vision quests are done during adolescence, but you were busy with school and then college. The time has come for you to communicate with 'your' spirits. You will fast and pray for two days and one night, seeking relief from the anger you carry. You will also develop clarity for your future. I will help you. My time on this earth is nearing an end and there is much I need to teach you before you will be ready to replace me."

This was the first time that Strong Medicine had expressed a desire to have Sam replace him as the tribe's medicine man. It saddened him to think that the one person he really cared about felt his time here on earth was nearing an end.

Strong Medicine had been more of a father to him than Joe or anyone else in the tribe, even his mother's brothers. He truly seemed to care for the young man who had been so despondent and angry since his mother's death. He had always seen something in Sam that no one else had. It was he who had urged Sam to attend college and later to go to medical school and become a doctor. Sam owed everything to Strong Medicine and he made a vow that, no matter what, he would have a successful vision quest. He would not fail Strong Medicine again.

Strong Medicine had told him to be ready to leave on his vision quest two hours before dawn. Sam would take no food or water with him and would dress only in a loincloth. He was to hike to the top of a nearby sacred mountain, which, for obvious reasons, was called "Rising Sun Mountain".

Giving him last minute instructions, Strong Medicine began, "My son, your vision quest will not be like that of others who embark on a vision quest. Yours will be about proving to the elders that you can be trusted to be a member of the Tribal Council. The tribe needs smart people to help them with the many changes that have occurred since the casino came to our land. If you want to be a doctor and help the tribe, you need to have the respect of the tribe. You can have all the degrees in the world, but without tribal respect, nothing you say or do will matter."

"I will not fail again and disgrace you. I promise you I will complete the vision quest and gain the respect of the Tribal Council. Thank you for believing in me."

Sam started up the trail leading to Rising Sun Mountain before dawn, intent on reaching the summit so he could see the sunrise from the top. He knew the next two days would test him as nothing else ever had. The difficulties he had experienced in being a resident in his last year faded by comparison. When he arrived at the top of the mountain he sat down and waited for dawn to break. The sky began to change from dark blue to turquoise to pink to a fiery red as the sun slowly came into view. It was the most beautiful sight he had ever seen. Just then an eagle flew across the sky, an omen. No matter what happened in the next two days, he knew he would never forget the sunrise on the first day of his vision quest.

He found a spot where he could sit comfortably and spent the rest of the day chanting, as Strong Medicine had instructed him to do. The sun beat down on him and it became intolerably hot. He could feel the sweat droplets on his brow dripping into his eyes. His whole body began to glisten with sweat. Sam became painfully aware of the hard earth under his buttocks. He continued to chant until the sun left the sky.

The temperature dropped and soon it became somewhat bearable. Then he began to hear the night noises: scratchings, the high whistles of animals calling to one another, slithers. This was a long way from the comfortable room in the teaching hospital where he was finishing up his residency. He wondered what his medical mentors would think if they could see him now. Even though the hours he had to put in as a resident were horrific, at least he wasn't worried about snakes and all the other unidentifiable sounds he was sure belonged to things which meant to harm him. Staying awake would not be a problem, but dealing with the unseen terrors of the night would be.

He was hungry and very, very thirsty. Strong Medicine told him he must be vigilant all night and he had given him advice on ways to do this. For Sam, alertness was not the problem. He was terrified of going to sleep and waking up eye to eye with one of those unidentifiable sounds.

As the sun rose, he began his second day. The sun started to shimmer and the horizon seemed to waver. Thoughts flooded his brain in the form of bad daytime nightmares. He wanted to run away, but he wasn't sure he could even stand, much less walk or run. The sun steadily beat down on him and his lips became dry and cracked. His skin felt like it was being flayed. Susie began speaking to him, urging him to forgive Joe, that Sam really hadn't known him; that Joe had been good to her in ways that Sam had never seen.

Strong Medicine came to him in a vision, telling him that soon it would be over, that he must stay and face his demons. His biological father, Red Cloud, likewise appeared, begging Sam's forgiveness for never having had the chance to be a father to him. Other tribal members came and went in his spinning mind. Once again, he felt the all-consuming rage. He wanted to kill Joe for what he had done to Susie. But didn't that make him just like Joe? Joe was not a full blood member of the tribe. His bloodline was only one-sixteenth tribal, not enough to qualify him as a member. However, he preferred tribal life over that of an illegal immigrant, a mestizo. While he and Susie were married, he barely worked, eking out a hand to mouth existence until the casino opened. The night Susie died, the tribe voted Joe off the reservation. No one had heard from him since and you couldn't prosecute someone if you couldn't find them. In the searing heat, Sam swore to kill Joe if he ever returned to the reservation.

The Old Ones say you can feel your spirit during a vision quest. They say that no water, no sleep, and no food strips one of the pleasures of the body. Sam felt the hatred coursing through him. Finally, after many hours, he was spent and exhausted. The rage that had threatened to take over his very life seemed to have finally passed out of his mind and body. Where there had been a tidal wave of hatred and anger, now there was a calm pool and peace of mind.

Strong Medicine told him that the quest would end at sundown on the second day. Dusk came and still he couldn't bring himself to stand up. Finally, he arose. He was completely disoriented. Where was the reservation? There were no landmarks in the dark to guide him. He stumbled down the mountain, unsure of what direction he was going. He walked for many miles in what seemed like a long, long journey.

He could see some lights in the distance. Relieved, he thought they must be lights from the reservation, but as he got closer to the lights, he realized that he must be lost. This was not the way to the reservation. When his eyesight cleared and the movements of his body brought him back to the present, he saw a neon sign that said "Blue Coyote Motel."

Sam became aware that the lights he had seen were coming from the small motel and that there were several cars in the motel parking lot. He desperately needed food, water, and sleep. He had nothing with him. He had no identification or money, but he had memorized his credit card number.

Sam staggered to the front of the motel, opened the door to the office and entered. He was greeted by an incredibly beautiful young woman with jet black hair which reflected the light above the desk. She took in the sight of the nearly naked, filthy Indian standing in front of her with a look of amazement. Forcing herself to remain calm as he seemed to be quite harmless, she said, "Welcome to the Blue Coyote Motel. If you're looking for a room, you're in luck. We have one room left and you're welcome to it."

Sam could only imagine what he looked like. He had not slept for well over forty hours. He was weathered, dirty, and dressed only in a loincloth. He thought the namesake of the motel, the *blue coyote*, must be shaking with laughter. Fortunately, the young woman seemed unfazed by his appearance. She handed him a registration card attached to a clipboard. He filled it out and paid for the room with his memorized credit card. He was relieved when she didn't ask for identification or to see the card.

"Come. Let me show you to your room," Maria said. "We also have a refreshment room with an honor bar which can be added to your room charge. Beer, wine, and food are in there. You look tired. You may want to rest before you eat," she went on. "I think you'll like your room. It's large and the air-conditioning is wonderful. You'll feel refreshed in no time at all."

As he entered the room, he thought he could detect a faint hint of sandalwood in the air. His senses were very acute after his time on the mountain and the air flowing from the air-conditioning vent was cool on his skin. He saw a blue coyote painting on the wall and recognized the artist, one of his tribe.

"I know this is a strange request," Sam said to the young woman, "but do you happen to have any men's clothing here that may have been left behind by one of your guests? I have just finished a vision quest on Rising Sun Mountain and I really would like to have some regular clothing."

"As a matter of fact, I have some clothes that a guest left a few weeks ago. I think they'll fit you. You're welcome to them. I'll be back in a minute." Maria returned shortly with a shirt, pants, underwear, and some sandals. He showered, letting the water wash away the last of the nightmares and the heat of the day. The clothes and sandals fit perfectly. Although it was very late, he used the phone in the room to call Strong Medicine.

"Strong Medicine, I am here in a motel. I finished my vision quest. I got disoriented coming down the mountain and made a wrong turn. I went in the opposite direction of the reservation. I followed the distant lights of a motel, thinking they were the lights of the casino."

"My son, I am so glad to hear your voice. You have been in my thoughts since you left. Do you think your vision quest was successful?" Strong Medicine asked.

"Yes, I feel much better," Sam said. The cool air in the room was in stark contrast to the heat of the day. "I am finished with my hatred of Joe. The anger is gone. I will always miss my mother, but her relationship with Joe was her choice. It was not up to me to change her life. I'm ready to finish my pediatric residency and do whatever I can to benefit the tribe. My plan is to return to the reservation when I complete my residency in two months.

"Can you come to the motel and pick me up tomorrow morning? The motel is called the Blue Coyote and is a few miles west of the reservation on the main highway. You can't miss it. I need some sleep now and this is a very comfortable place."

"I will be there at nine o'clock tomorrow morning. I know of the motel. It's not that far from the reservation. You have probably passed it many times and never paid attention to it. Sleep well. I will tell the Council of your successful vision quest. I am proud of you, my son. We have much work to do to prepare you for your coming responsibilities."

Hanging up the phone, Sam began to feel really, really good. He drank some cool water and walked to the refreshment room. Entering the room, he again noticed the very faint scent of sandalwood. *Strange*, he thought, *why would there be the smell of sandalwood here*?

He heated up a large Reuben sandwich in the

microwave and took a container of potato salad out of the small refrigerator. He decided he would celebrate the end of his vision quest with a piece of chocolate cake he spotted in a small plastic box. He filled out a small form that would result in his purchases being added to his room charge. Ravenous, he sat down at the small table in the refreshment room and devoured the food.

After he finished eating, he headed back to his room, undressed, and got in bed. The soft movement of air coming from the air-conditioning vent felt good to him. Actually, he felt the best he had felt in a long, long time. The sweat lodge event was over and the vision quest had been completed. The anger, which had been so much a part of him for so long, was gone, replaced by a sense of peace and calmness. Sam was really looking forward to completing his residency and having the opportunity to provide much needed medical treatment to the children of his tribe. He soon fell into a deep and dreamless sleep.

At 9:00 a.m. the next morning, Strong Medicine pulled into the motel in his old truck. As he jumped into the truck, Sam waved good-bye to the beautiful young woman standing by the front door of the motel. He was looking forward to working with the tribal children and his work with Strong Medicine. He was feeling really good about the future. In fact, he realized he felt the best he had felt in years. He thought it was because of his successful vision quest. Later, much later, he would learn that it was not just the vision quest that made him feel so good.

CHAPTER 8

The last two months of Sam's residency flew by. Upon completion, he would be a bona fide pediatrician. He couldn't wait to return to the reservation and begin his new life, a life dedicated to helping children. Remembering the terrible childhood he had endured, he had one hope—to make each tribal child's life better than what his own had been.

Strong Medicine had been busy during Sam's last two months of residency. He had overseen the finishing touches of the newly constructed school and adjoining pediatric center. The pediatric center had been constructed to Sam's specifications, with Strong Medicine personally overseeing the project. The reception area was kid-friendly, painted in bright colors with toys and games everywhere. The furniture was small and child-sized, with the exception of a few adult-sized chairs for the parents.

The pediatric center opened six weeks after Sam completed his residency. He was proud of the fact that he was the first, and for that matter, the only doctor on the staff.

One of Sam's very good friends was the same artist who had painted the blue coyote painting Sam had seen at the motel where he stayed after his vision quest. Sam persuaded him to paint murals on the walls of the reception area and in each of the four treatment rooms. The Muppets, Babar, and a host of other cartoon and storybook characters were cheerily painted in rainbow colors on the walls, showing them engaged in all types of fun activities. The children loved them. Even when a child had to have an injection, Sam and the nursing staff were able to divert the child's attention away from the needle and direct it to some sort of activity taking place on the walls. Sam loved his work at the pediatric center. He woke up every morning excited to get to the center so he could care for his young patients.

True to his word, Strong Medicine began meeting with Sam three to four times a week, instructing him in the ancient ways of the tribal medicine man, just as Strong Medicine himself had been taught by his mentor, Laughing Bear. In the evenings, after Sam had finished his work at the center, he would go to Strong Medicine's home, eat a simple meal prepared by Strong Medicine's wife, Little Doe, and continue his studies. Straddling the two worlds was difficult at times for Sam. Having been scientifically trained, many of the things Strong Medicine taught him seemed absurd. The medicine available to doctors was quite different from that dispensed by a tribal medicine man.

Strong Medicine showed Sam which herbs, minerals, and things from nature were effective when treating certain ailments. He taught him when to starve an illness, when to use prayer and when to sing the ancient healing songs. By ancient tradition, passed down over generations, the medicine man secured the help of the spirit world in healing disease and the psyche as well as promoting harmony between humans and nature.

The healing songs were the most difficult for Sam to master. Even though his tribe was not Navajo, it was rooted in the Navajo culture. The language was similar, but the tonal scales taxed his musical ability to the limit. He, as all tribal children, had heard their language being spoken by the elders, but it wasn't allowed in the classrooms because of regulations requiring that only English be spoken in school classrooms. If anything, the children of his era were discouraged from learning to speak their native language. Sam felt like he was starting from scratch and even though the songs were difficult, it left him with a good feeling.

Not only was he expected to learn the music and the language, he was expected to sing them in the presence of a sick patient. He also had to memorize and prepare the natural herbal concoctions that were taught to him by Strong Medicine. At times, it all seemed too much. He had to constantly remind himself that he was doing it for his tribe as well as for the children of the tribe. He didn't want his heritage to be lost or forgotten, and he knew that many of Mother Nature's herbal remedies were probably better for the patients than the synthetic drugs touted by the drug companies.

As if learning all of this wasn't hard enough, Strong Medicine expected him to learn how to forage for the plants that were such an integral part of the herbal medicine prescribed by the medicine man. The barren landscape didn't lend itself to easy foraging and he and Strong Medicine often had to travel far from the reservation to find what they needed. This was not the type of learning one could find in a book. There was no written record about the things that Strong Medicine was teaching him. It was tribal lore and tradition that was expected to be handed down verbally from one medicine man to the next medicine man, generation to generation. Even so, Sam often found himself jotting down notes of various herbal remedies and words of the songs after some of his sessions with Strong Medicine.

The tribal children who came to the center loved Sam and very soon both they and their parents had complete faith in his ability to heal them. As part of gaining the parent's trust, he found that he often had to use the herbal concoctions and sing the healing songs he learned from Strong Medicine. The children were fine with Sam's background in western medicine, the parents not so much. He could insert a little western medicine here and there because the parents could see the positive results that were taking place in their children, but there was still a lot of reluctance and wariness on their part. Sam knew it would take time and resigned himself to learning all that Strong Medicine could teach him, knowing he would use it sooner or later.

Phyllis Chee was a member of the same tribe as Sam. She left the reservation after high school to study at the University of New Mexico. She had taken the name Chee rather than her father's name, Bidzil (the name given to him at birth meaning "he is strong," because of how loudly he cried and how early he crawled and walked). She knew that the name Bidzil would cause endless questions and she wanted to fit into the modern world as best she could. Having to constantly explain the name would make it much harder. She graduated from college with a degree in Medical Management and went to work for a large hospital in Phoenix.

Phyllis returned to the reservation several times a year and was pleased to see that the tribe was building a pediatric center and a school, something she thought was long overdue. She had very bad memories of going to school off the reservation. At the school she attended, which was located nearly twenty miles away, the Indian children had been made fun of for their hand-me-down clothes, their looks, and their different ways. Many of the children simply dropped out of school and returned to the reservation, preferring to give up their education rather than be ridiculed.

In earlier days, even though visiting doctors came to the reservation from time to time, generally a sick child was taken to a hospital in Blythe. The tribe distrusted the white man's medicine. The doctors, all of whom practiced western medicine, just weren't able to connect with the tribal children. When a child had to be hospitalized, it created even more trauma; often enough to thwart the healing that needed to take place. As the children became more fearful, the doctors and nurses became more assertive in trying to heal the child. This often ended up in a lose-lose situation for everyone.

Now that the center was open, the children could be treated by a member of their own tribe and if a child needed to be hospitalized, there were several rooms fitted out for short hospital-like stays at the center. Nothing that could help the healing process had been spared. The equipment was the most modern and sophisticated available, thanks to the ample funds generated by the casino's earnings.

Phyllis had straight, shoulder-length, dark brown hair, which surrounded a heart-shaped face with flawless skin. Soft, liquid brown eyes with long black eyelashes looked out under thick, black winged brows. Long legs and a body built for physical work reflected the genes of the female Native American from olden times. She was a strong, beautiful woman, greatly respected by the tribe. Many of the young men in the tribe had been attracted to her, but none had succeeded in gaining her attention. Her standards were high and she had seen what alcoholism and dysfunction could do to tribal families.

She was well aware that the $30,000 monthly allotment each tribal member received from the casino revenues had killed whatever ambition many of them might have had to work or further their education. Even though the tribe paid for the higher education of its members, very few took advantage of the offer. Phyllis valued her free education and was sorry that others weren't doing the same. She was the first tribal member to leave the reservation to obtain an undergraduate degree fully funded from the casino that opened just as she graduated from high school. She often wondered what would have happened to her if her education hadn't been provided by the tribe. Phyllis knew her parents couldn't afford to send her to college and she knew she probably would have ended up like so many of the other men and women of her age, lots of children and days marked by trips to the store to buy alcohol.

She was also aware that she could pick and choose among the male members of the hospital staff in Phoenix. It was not for lack of invitations that she stayed home and led a rather quiet life; she just didn't find any of the men she met particularly interesting. Her heart was still on the reservation and she was gradually coming to the realization that she was fated to be a spinster and just enjoy her nieces and nephews.

On one of her visits back to the reservation, her

father asked her to come with him, as he wanted her to see the new pediatric center. She treasured her time with her father who was getting up in years. She knew that he wouldn't always be there when she returned home for a visit. Her mother had passed away several years earlier and it still hurt to come back to the small doublewide trailer and not see her mother patting out the fry bread for Phyllis' welcome home dinner.

They slowly made their way up the long walkway that led to the center. Her father had trouble walking after being thrown by his horse many years ago. Without the proper medical care, his broken leg had not healed properly and his limp was very pronounced. Even so, he still kept a couple of horses, as did many of the tribe's members.

The center was just as colorful on the outside as it was on the inside. It had opened a few weeks earlier and most of the kinks typical of a new building had been worked out. Phyllis was thrilled with what she saw. She knew that many future generations of children would benefit from the center. With healthier bodies, she was hopeful that the young people would resist the readily available alcohol and drugs. There was a strong anti-alcohol anti-drug program in the newly built school and if this generation could buck the addictions of the previous generations, there was a strong possibility that these young people could achieve the greatness of their tribal ancestors. The future for the tribe's young people looked particularly hopeful, thanks to the revenues provided by the casino.

As they rounded a corner, preparing to go into the hospital section of the center, they almost collided with Sam and one of his nurses. "Phyllis, is that you?" Sam asked. "How wonderful to see you! It's been what, eight years or so?"

As he spoke, he apprised the young woman in front of him and thought how beautiful she was. She was probably married with several children, although he hadn't seen her on the reservation. Then he remembered someone had told him she lived and worked in Phoenix. Sam thought she'd probably left the reservation long ago, mentally and emotionally.

Phyllis told him she had just arrived for a short visit with her father. He then vaguely recalled hearing that she had gone to school at the University of New Mexico and taken a job at a hospital in Phoenix. He also remembered that she had been the first young person to make use of the tribe's offer of a free education.

She recognized Sam from years earlier. Bedzil had told her that one of the tribal members had become a pediatrician and was coming back to the reservation to practice medicine. He also had told her that Strong Medicine had taken Sam under his wing, preparing him in the ways of the medicine man. She hadn't paid much attention, as Sam was a little older than she was and their paths had rarely crossed.

As Sam gazed at Phyllis, seemingly struck by her beauty, an idea occurred to him. "Didn't you get a degree in Medical Management? What are you doing these days?"

"It's been a long time since we've seen each other. Congratulations on opening this beautiful and much needed pediatric center. And to answer your questions, yes, I did get a degree in Medical Management and I'm working at a hospital in Phoenix."

The nurse accompanying Sam turned to him and said, "Doctor, I'm sorry to interrupt, but we're running way behind schedule. At this rate, we won't finish until late tonight. Please, you're needed right away in Room 2."

"Sorry," Sam said. "I never should have agreed to be both the center's director as well as the only staff physician. I just run from one to the other, never spending enough time at either. It's been good seeing you. How long will you be here?"

Phyllis smiled. "I'll be here for the rest of the week. I'm staying at my father's home, just down the road. The center is wonderful and long overdue. You're to be congratulated."

Sam hurried to Room 2, waving good-bye as he entered the room. Phyllis turned to her father, "Dad, how long has Sam been back? I thought the center was only recently opened."

"He returned a few weeks ago. He's a good man.

He completed his vision quest and will be the tribe's new medicine man when Strong Medicine decides it's time. I like him and the children need someone they can trust. It's so much better for them to be treated here, rather than in Blythe. Before the casino money came to the tribe's rescue, I know of many children whose parents just couldn't afford to make the trip and the children suffered. Come, let's go home. It's time for lunch."

It was late when Sam finished with his last patient. He was scheduled to meet Strong Medicine after work and Sam hurried to his home to continue his studies with the medicine man. "Sam, you are very late. It makes it hard to teach you the ways of the ancient ones when you work such long hours. What happened to cause you to be so late?"

Sam sat down and turned to him. "I don't know how much longer I can do this. I know it's only been a few weeks, but it's getting worse by the day as the practice grows. I can't be both the director of the center and at the same time, the only doctor on the staff. I must have been crazy to have thought I could do both jobs at the same time. However, I have an idea which would solve the problem. Today, Phyllis Chee and her father came to the center to look at it. She's visiting from Phoenix, where she works for a hospital. She graduated with a degree in Medical Management. I don't know much about her, but wouldn't it be great if she could be the director and I would be free to fully devote myself to the children as well as to your teachings?

"I don't know if she would even be interested and the Council would have to approve it. I'm sure she would demand a sizable salary. What do you think?"

Sam hoped that Strong Medicine would agree with him. He found himself hoping even more that the beautiful young woman was unmarried and would be interested in the job. He didn't think he'd seen a wedding ring on her finger.

Strong Medicine looked at Sam. "My son, one of the things that I have taught you is that there are no mistakes. Phyllis came to the center at the moment you were overwhelmed with work. Do you think that was a coincidence? Of course not. The Great Spirit put her there to help you. I will convince the Council that this is necessary and hopefully, she will soon be our new director. All things happen for a reason. Learn from this."

Strong Medicine acted quickly. The next morning, he called an emergency meeting of the Tribal Council and proposed that Phyllis Chee be offered the job as director of the pediatric center, starting immediately. He explained how Sam needed to be able to devote himself to his patients and the teachings he was learning from Strong Medicine. Strong Medicine told the Council that he felt his own time on earth was coming to an end and soon he would be joining their ancestors. He needed to finish his teachings with Sam and he couldn't do it if Sam was working late at the clinic and too tired to continue learning the ancient ways. Strong Medicine was eloquent in his presentation. The Council immediately approved his request to offer the job of director of the pediatric center to Phyllis. As soon as they voted, Strong Medicine called Sam and told him. At lunchtime, the two of them walked over to the see Phyllis and her father.

Phyllis answered the knock on the door. "Please come in. This is a welcome surprise. Strong Medicine, it's good to see you. It's been too long." She walked to the back of the trailer and called out, "Father, we have guests. Dr. Sam and Strong Medicine are here."

They sat down in the small living room. Even though Phyllis' father received over $300,000 annually, he had never bothered to replace the brownish-grey threadbare sofa and chairs or the worn living room rug. Everything was as it had been when his wife was alive. She died shortly after the casino was built. The doublewide had a feeling of a time gone by, a place lost to memories.

When Phyllis returned to the front room with her father, Strong Medicine began to speak. "Phyllis, the reservation is your home even though you have been a part of the western world for many years, first when you were in college and then with your work at the hospital in Phoenix. This morning I called a special meeting of the Tribal Council and they would like to offer you the job of director of the pediatric center. Sam has too much work to do. He can't be a doctor, a director, and a medicine man-in-training.

It's too much. We want you to be the director. You would work with Sam, but running the center would be entirely your responsibility. If you agree, we would like you to start as soon as possible."

Strong Medicine looked closely at Phyllis, who was clearly stunned by the offer. Obviously, she had never even considered the possibility of becoming the director of the pediatric center. She and her father had taken a tour of it simply because her father knew that anything related to medicine interested her. Phyllis wished she could answer immediately, but first she needed to make phone calls.

"Would you give me a couple of days? I need to talk to some people and think about this. I am truly honored you would consider me for the position and I will get back to you no later than day after tomorrow. Will that be all right?" Phyllis asked.

Sam turned to her and spoke softly. "I think we would work well together. It's a chance for both of us to help our tribe, our people. Please think seriously about this. I really hope that you'll accept the position."

She looked at the earnest plea in Sam's eyes and realized not only how dedicated he was to his people and his medicine, but also how very attractive he was, something that she had never previously considered. Her eyes slid down to his wedding ring finger. There was no ring. She knew she would take the position. It was just a matter of arranging a few things.

As Sam and Strong Medicine stood at the front door of the run-down trailer getting ready to leave, Strong Medicine suddenly turned to Phyllis and placed his hands on each side of her face and said, "My child, it's time for you to come home. Your people need you."

The next morning when Sam arrived at the clinic, he was amazed to see Phyllis waiting for him at the locked front door. She turned to him, gracing him with a smile that radiated warmth. "Please show me my new office. I resigned from the hospital yesterday. I offered to give two weeks' notice, but they generously told me if I would give up my two weeks' severance pay, I could start here at the center immediately, so here I am. I do have a few loose ends that I have to tie up in Phoenix. I'll go there this weekend to pack up the things in my apartment. I've also given notice there. The apartment manager was very gracious about it. She said there was a waiting list and she could rent it immediately. It's rather amazing how it all worked out, don't you think?" Phyllis asked.

Sam thought of Strong Medicine and how he had told Sam there were no coincidences. Clearly, he had much to learn from this wise old man. Sam vowed to speed up his teachings with Strong Medicine. They were very important and he was looking forward to it. He was also looking forward to working with this attractive, intelligent young woman. "Where will you live?" Sam asked. "I hope it's fairly close to the center, as emergencies do happen."

Phyllis replied, "When I drove onto the reservation yesterday, I noticed that there were some condos being built just down the road. I was surprised, as I don't remember ever seeing any building of that type on the reservation before. Yesterday, after I talked to you and Strong Medicine, I bought one. It will be finished in a few weeks. My father's trailer is too small for me to live there for very long and quite frankly, I find it sort of depressing. My mother had a way of making everything bright and cheery. My father misses her so much that the trailer has become a shrine to her. I need to be surrounded by things that represent happiness, actually something like what you've done here at the center. Everything just seemed to work out. I still can't believe it. Let's get started."

Phyllis noticed that there were a number of mothers with sick children who were standing a respectful distance apart from Sam and Phyllis. They obviously were waiting to see the doctor and it was very apparent that Sam was idolized by the mothers and children.

Sam unlocked the door, feeling as if the weight of the world had been lifted from his shoulders. He didn't need to worry any more about staffing, payroll, forms, scheduling, etc. He was free to do what he did best, care for and treat sick children.

CHAPTER 9

Sidney, the president of Moore Scientific Laboratories, was in a state of shock upon hearing what Dan had told him about the security breach of his gifted employee, Jeffrey Brooks. As soon as Dan left Sidney's office, he called the in-house counsel for Moore Labs, Peter Lincoln. "Peter, could you come to my office at once? It's important and I need your advice. We may have a major catastrophe on our hands."

Peter Lincoln, a tall, greying, 50ish-looking lawyer, had been with Moore Labs for twelve years. An impeccable dresser, Peter was one of the few men who could get by with always sporting a folded pocket square, which matched his tie, in the breast pocket of his suit coat. He lost no time in getting to Sidney's office. As he stepped out of the elevator on the sixth floor, he thought something must really be important. In the twelve years he had been with Moore Labs, he had never been summoned to Sidney's office. His department dealt mainly with contracts and other legal aspects of the company. His curiosity was aroused as he stepped into the reception area. Monica immediately ushered him into Sidney's office.

"Thanks for getting here so fast, Peter," Sidney began. "An unimaginable breach of trust has taken place that could have far-reaching consequences for Moore Labs. I need to have a very clear understanding about Moore's potential liability in this matter and what we need to do to prepare ourselves."

"What has happened? You've never asked me to come to your office. How can I help?" Peter said.

"I have just been told by a very trusted and reliable employee that Jeffrey Brooks, the brilliant young man who discovered the anti-aging hormone, which we have submitted for approval to the FDA, has been injecting the hormone into his wife for some time. I can't believe a man of his talent and intellect, someone who many of us expect will garner the Nobel Prize for his efforts, would be so stupid."

"Wait a sec," Peter said. "That's clearly a violation of our standards and to my knowledge; none of our other scientists has ever done anything like this. Are you sure?"

"Yes, Jeffrey's wife admitted to my source that Jeffrey was doing this after my source happened to see a Moore Labs vial in her purse. I don't need to tell you that this is not only illegal, but just as important; it is completely against our company policy. I am going to have to fire both of them, but first there are some things I need to know."

Sidney continued, "I need to be sure of our legal position and I need to know his legal position. It is my understanding that the hormone he discovered is the legal property of Moore Labs. Office rumors say that he has been courted by several other drug companies, but I believe that we own the formula because of the contract he signed when he started with us. My concern is that he will go to one of those drug companies or a drug company in some foreign country and sell the formula to them. Other countries don't have the long approval waiting periods we have here in the United States and the drug could be sold in another country within the year, completely undercutting Moore Labs. I don't need to tell you what a nightmare that would be for our company and its stockholders who have been waiting for FDA approval for some time. Obviously, I need some advice and I need it fast."

"That is my understanding as well, but I'll need to see the contracts he signed when he became an employee of Moore Labs. Do you have them?" Peter asked.

"I had Monica go to HR and get Jeffrey's personnel file. All the documents that he signed when he was hired by Moore Labs are in it. Take a look and tell me what you think. Here's the file."

Peter opened the large manila file folder Sidney handed him and began reading, trying to ignore Sidney, who was nervously pacing back and forth in the large office. Thirty minutes later, Peter closed the file.

"Well, it's just as you thought. Jeffrey did sign a

confidentiality agreement, a non-competition contract, and a contract regarding experiments. The last one, regarding experiments, is the one that provides that all discoveries are the legal property of Moore Labs. However, the problem is trying to enforce these contracts. If it's true that he has violated the contracts, and you seem certain that he has, you could sue him," Peter said.

"If we sue him, can you imagine the adverse publicity we would get? I don't think that our stockholders and investors would be very happy about that. I also wonder if the questions that would surround the hormone would slow down FDA approval. That would make the stockholders and investors even angrier," Sidney responded.

Peter continued, "It would be very hard to extradite him from another country if he leaves the United States and then sells the formula in that country. Plus, litigation over ownership of his discovery would probably tie the hormone up in the courts for a long time, which would not sit well with Moore Labs' investors."

"Well," Sidney said, "If you were me, what would you do? After all, this is what I pay you for."

"You're probably not going to like my advice. I'm looking at this from a practical standpoint as well as a legal standpoint. Legally, you win. Practically, you lose. Why don't you offer him a large sum of money and get him to leave Moore Labs? It's going to cost him the Nobel Prize either way. If what he has done is ever released to the public, the Nobel Committee will never award him the prize because he violated the terms and conditions of his employment. The Nobel Committee will never allow itself to become involved in a scandal. Unfortunately, because a company cannot receive the prize, only an individual can and no more than three at that, Moore Labs will not receive the publicity you were hoping to get if Jeffrey won."

Peter went on. "If he leaves Moore, the company still owns the anti-aging hormone and he won't be eligible for the award because he doesn't own the hormone. Is my proposed solution perfect? No, but under the circumstances, it may be the best one for everyone. Don't you have access to some kind of slush fund so no one would know what has happened? One that wouldn't involve other people? Moore would simply release a statement that, due to health reasons, Jeffrey decided to take an early retirement. It happens all the time. Is it the end of his career? Probably, but he's the one who made the choice."

Sidney didn't like to be put in a box, particularly one drawn by an employee. However, the more he thought about it, Peter's recommendation of an out-of-court settlement did provide a solution to a potentially devastating situation. This way, no one would ever know what really happened. After the initial statement and story, the press would no longer be interested and Moore would retain all its rights to the hormone.

Sidney wondered how much money he'd need to pay Jeffrey to silence him. As the president of the company, he knew there was a large fund for just such a contingency. Not surprisingly, he was the only one who had access to it. The more he thought about the plan, the more convinced he became that it might just work.

"Thanks for your counsel. Naturally, I don't want any of this conversation repeated. It's probably just as well that I don't tell you what I have decided to do. Under the circumstances, I think the less even you know; the better. This is a very delicate situation and I need to act fast. I'm worried about collateral damage and all that. Monica will see you out."

Sidney spent the next few hours developing his strategy and at four o'clock that afternoon, he asked Monica to call Jeffrey's secretary and have Jeffrey come to his office at five.

CHAPTER 10

It was just getting dark when Jeffrey rode the elevator up to the sixth floor. He entered the luxurious reception area, noting the Granville Redmond painting on the wall directly across from the window, which provided a panoramic view of Saddleback Mountain to the east and the blue Pacific to the west. Monica asked him to be seated, said Sidney would be with him shortly, and went into his office to let him know that Jeffrey had arrived.

Monica had been with Sidney for twenty years. As his first employee, she had seen the spectacular growth of the company. Sidney had changed from a bespectacled pharmacist to a powerful captain of industry. Although Monica was extremely well-compensated, to look at her one would never know it. Her clothes had not been in style for many years, her hair was a mousy brown-grey, and she wore no make-up other than lipstick. The overall effect made her look as if she still belonged on the Midwest farm she left when she was eighteen years old. Monica had never married and was devoted to Sidney and the company. He was her life. She knew as much as Sidney did about the company he had founded.

Sidney said, "Monica, I want you to sit in on this meeting. I am going to have to fire Jeffrey Brooks. The reasons will become clear during the meeting. I know I don't need to ask you not to divulge to anyone what takes place in the meeting, but I feel better for having said it. This is probably not going to be pleasant, but it needs to be done and it needs to be done now. When we're finished, I want you to draw up a statement that our communications office can send to the press, but run it by me first. Now, please show Jeffrey in."

Jeffrey was surprised to be summoned to Sidney's office. This was a first for him. He couldn't think of any reason why Sidney Moore would want to see him. Things were on hold with his anti-aging hormone while they waited for approval by the FDA. He had many other experiments and tests underway, but nothing that would merit a summons to Sidney's office. He called Maria and told her he'd meet her in her office after meeting with Sidney. She, too, thought it was strange that Sidney had asked Jeffrey to meet with him, but decided it was probably something as simple as finding out how his experiments were coming along. She had heard that Sidney regarded Jeffrey as "the number one scientist" in a company where there were many fine scientists.

Monica opened the door to Sidney's office and asked Jeffrey to come in. He sat down in one of the chairs across the desk from Sidney and was surprised when Monica did the same. Sidney began, "Jeffrey, it has come to my attention that you have violated your contract with Moore Scientific Laboratories. I won't go into the particulars or how I found out, but I know that you have been administering the anti-aging hormone to your wife. As you well know, this is in violation of all that Moore Labs stands for, ethically and legally."

Sidney heard Monica gasp. He knew that this secret would be as safe with her as it was with him. He trusted her completely.

Jeffrey was in shock. His mind raced, trying to figure out how Sidney had found out. The only person who knew was Maria and she had everything to lose if Moore Labs ever found out what he was doing. He also knew she really did love him and she would never disclose "their little secret" to anyone. He was caught off guard and no plausible lie came to him.

"Jeffrey, as of this moment your employment with Moore Labs is terminated. You, as all the employees at Moore Labs, are an 'at will' employee, so I have the right to summarily terminate you at any time. I know you have been courted by pharmaceutical companies and even foreign countries regarding the anti-aging hormone. I want to emphatically state that our legal counsel has made it very clear to me that Moore Labs owns the rights to the hormone even though you discovered it. If you were to go to any of those third parties and sell them the formula, we would have no choice but to sue you. It would be difficult for both of us and your reputation would be destroyed.

"I have a proposition for you. Two million dollars will be transferred to your bank account tomorrow and another two million dollars will be transferred to your account in one year. Moore Labs will immediately issue a statement that you have taken an early retirement for reasons of health. If we hear of the drug being produced by any other drug company or in any other country, the second installment will not be transferred to you. We will then issue a statement declaring the true reason for your leaving Moore Labs. There is no point in signing contracts or agreements, as you clearly feel that they mean nothing to you. It goes without saying that Maria must leave Moore Labs as well. The necessary paperwork for both of your terminations is being prepared by HR as we speak."

Jeffrey couldn't believe what he was hearing. Where would he go? What would he do? He had so many new scientific ideas that he wanted to test. And yet, could he subject Maria, her family, and his family to a scandal? The scientific world was a very tightly knit world and bad news traveled fast. He knew he had better take the money and figure out later what he was going to do after he left Moore Labs. In spite of the money being offered, Jeffrey recognized that his future looked grim.

He felt like someone had punched him in the stomach. Never in a million years could he have anticipated leaving Moore Labs under these humiliating circumstances. His mouth felt dry and for a moment, he felt like he was going to faint. He hadn't cried since he had been a child, but right now all he wanted to do was curl up in the fetal position and sob like a baby. All of his hopes and dreams had been destroyed in a matter of moments. And how would he explain this to Maria, who thought he was the most brilliant scientist in the United States? He struggled with these feelings as he spoke to Sidney.

"I'm sorry. This is not how I wanted my relationship with Moore Labs to end. I wanted to win the Nobel Prize and Moore Labs was a big reason why I felt I could. What I did was really not that wrong. The only person I administered the hormone to was my wife and there are personal reasons for my having done that. I guess I have no choice but to leave as I can see that your mind is made up. Transfer the money to my bank account and we have a deal. My paycheck from Moore is deposited electronically into my bank account by the payroll department, so they have all the information they need to access my bank account."

Jeffrey was not a bad person. He loved Maria and knew that he alone held the power to keep her deepest fears from coming true. He had made a clear distinction between Maria and Moore Labs in his mind. Since his experiments were responsible for the development of the anti-aging hormone, he felt he should be able to administer it to his wife. Moore Labs didn't see it that way and he had violated their rules. Jeffrey understood Sidney's concerns. If he had violated some of their rules, what other ones would he be likely to violate in the future? It was too risky for Moore Labs and he reluctantly understood why he had to go.

Jeffrey shakily stood to leave. "I've enjoyed working here, Sidney. I'm really sorry it's ending like this." He turned and almost stumbled as he left the room.

Monica turned and looked at Sidney. "I wonder what will happen to him. What a shame. He's a brilliant man. Look what has happened to him. He lost his job, ruined his career, and threw away a chance to be awarded the Nobel Prize. I hope his wife is worth it."

For the first time since Dan had come to his office that morning, Sidney began to feel better about the situation. He had taken fast and decisive action. Jeffrey seemed to realize that Sidney had no choice but to do what he did. The stockholders, fellow employees, and the press would never know. Thank God it was over. He walked over to the credenza, which housed a full bar, asked Monica if she would join him, and poured two stiff Maker's Mark bourbons on the rocks.

He raised his full glass and clinked it with Monica's. He noticed that her skirt had slid up her leg dramatically. He made a mental note not to fumble with the clasp on her bra like he had last time. Monica smiled sweetly at him with adoring eyes as he stood up and moved closer to her, sliding down the zipper on his pants. Yes, everything was going to be just fine for the president of Moore Labs.

CHAPTER 11

Jill knew she couldn't keep on running. Once again, she was driving across country trying to outrun the past. It had been six months since Rick had died. Six months of unremitting pain, tears, depression, and agony. It was a sensation that gnawed unceasingly at her very soul.

The trust fund that Rick had established made it very clear that Jill was to get everything, including the large house in Newport Beach, California, the second home on the golf course in the California desert community of La Quinta near Palm Springs, the Mercedes and the BMW (which she had sold), a large bank account, the stocks, and mutual funds. She was worth over twenty million dollars, but her wealth did not take away the feeling of complete emptiness she had experienced ever since Rick's death. She had visited Las Vegas, Miami, Denver, New York, and San Francisco and was currently returning to California from Dallas, trying to run faster than the past but it always seemed to be gaining on her.

She was utterly and totally depressed. She no longer wanted to live. Living was too painful. The only way out seemed to be suicide. Jill found herself thinking more and more about dying. Actually, she had gone beyond thinking about it and now found herself contemplating when she would do it. She knew she couldn't do it with guns or knives. She remembered a phrase she had read somewhere about "wanting to go gently into the night." That's how she would like to go. No more pain, just going to sleep for a long, long time. At her request, her doctor had given her a prescription for sleeping pills when she told him all she did at night was cry while lying awake and staring at the ceiling. She hadn't told him the real reason she wanted the pills, knowing that he would immediately refer her to a psychiatrist. Her hand drifted to the pocket in her purse where she kept the medication.

It wasn't that she was afraid of dying; it was that she was more afraid of living like this. She was looking for the right place to die. None of the places she'd been felt right. Jill really didn't want to be a burden to anyone so when she did do it; she wanted to be in some out-of-the-way place where she didn't know anyone. Her conscience wouldn't allow her do it when she was staying in some friend or family's home, leaving them to deal with all that went with the aftermath of a suicide.

Glancing down at the speedometer, she realized she was going 95. *Not a good idea in this early evening light,* she thought. She had no idea that she'd been going that fast, once again lost in past memories. Jill had been on the road for over 14 hours. Although she was an excellent driver, her reflexes were shot, she was exhausted, and she knew she shouldn't be driving. Her car showed an outside temperature of 99 degrees, even though it was past 8:00 p.m. If she had a flat tire or some other type of car problem, she wasn't sure she could survive for very long in this god-awful heat.

She noticed some lights in the distance and a roadside sign that said "Blue Coyote Motel." She desperately needed sleep. Maybe she could keep the waking nightmares at bay for a few hours with some decent rest, or maybe this would be the place she would end it. Months later, she would wish that she had gone the extra 65 miles to her home in La Quinta and never stopped at the Blue Coyote Motel.

Pulling into the motel, she was pleasantly surprised at how well the motel was kept up. Recently painted, the cream-colored Southwest style motel with its red tile roof reflecting the last rays of the setting sun was a pleasant backdrop for the desert plantings someone had very carefully placed around the premises. The brightly colored species of cacti and succulents were well cared for. Entering the office, she walked to the small reception desk.

Tears were starting to well up in her eyes. Obviously, she was more exhausted than she realized. "I need a place to stay tonight. Do you have any rooms?" she asked the lovely dark-haired young woman behind the desk.

The woman stepped around the reception desk and gave Jill a big hug. "I'm sorry, but with those tears in your eyes, I just thought a hug might help.

And to answer your question, yes, I have one room left. It's nice and the air-conditioning feels so good after this brutal desert heat. We also have an honor bar and a few things to eat in our refreshment room. Just fill out the registration form and I'll show you to your room. I promise you, you'll feel much better in a little while."

Jill quickly signed her name, Jill Loren, on the paperwork and followed the young woman to the refreshment area where she helped herself to a glass of wine, carrying it to her room. Just as the woman had said, the room was quite pleasant and the air-conditioning felt wonderful. She noticed the painting of a blue coyote on the wall and thought, *how very fitting in this godforsaken place. The only animals that would want to be here are the coyotes.* She briefly wondered why the beautiful young woman was working here, in the middle of nowhere. With her looks, she certainly could get a better job in the city.

Jill took off the clothes she'd been traveling in all day and felt the cool tile on her bare feet. Lying down in her underwear on the bed, the air-conditioning began to refresh her. At a height of 5'7", with straight ash-blond hair, an enviable body, and a million dollar smile, Jill was a very attractive woman. When Rick was alive, people were always telling him how beautiful she was and how lucky he was to have her as his wife. Rick was a doctor and she knew that doctors were fair game for lonely patients and aggressive nurses who wanted to "marry up." She and Rick laughed a lot about that since they both knew a number of doctors who had succumbed to this form of professional liability.

The commitment that she and Rick had made to one another was so strong she never worried about the other women who constantly surrounded her husband. The extra attention Rick received at the charity events, the hospital donor dinners, and the political events they attended had been nothing more than a source of amusement to both of them. She honestly felt she had never had a jealous moment, even when some of the women had made their intentions crystal clear with a dramatic display of cleavage when they leaned toward Rick to whisper something privately.

She knew what people said about her life and they were right; she had been lucky. She had plenty of money, good looks, and a beautiful home on the Gold Coast. Just living in the Newport Beach area of Orange County gave her an elite status. Their home was located on a hillside overlooking the Pacific Ocean. Every home in the area would sell for several million dollars. It was such a prestigious enclave that the residents used "Newport Coast," rather than "Newport Beach" on their checks and in mailing addresses.

Jill's life with Rick had been fabulous. She was adored by and married to a well-respected cardiologist. Designer clothing and Judith Lieber bags were a staple in her closet. People expected the doctor's wife to look good and she didn't disappoint. Her husband enjoyed having a woman who looked like a trophy wife on his arm, even if she was a valued "first wife."

The only thing she would have changed about their life was that she was unable to have children. She had been through numerous in vitro fertilization procedures and none had worked. Both she and Rick had been tested and doctors couldn't find any reason why Jill had been unable to conceive. Her gynecologist had suggested they look into adoption, but it really didn't appeal to either of them. If they had been honest, they would probably admit they just wanted their very own little Rick or Jill. Finally, they had decided that parenthood wasn't going to happen for them. Wrapped up in a world of their own, maybe it had been for the best. If Jill could have seen into the future, she would definitely have known that their decision was the right one.

Rick had a private practice in Newport Beach and was on the Board of Directors at Newport Hospital, a silk stocking hospital catering to the wealthy. The hospital was built on high ground overlooking the Pacific Ocean with a spectacular view of the city and the yachts at anchor in front of multimillion-dollar waterfront homes. People dreamed of a life like hers, but what they didn't dream about was how fast it had become a nightmare.

A screenwriter would never have been able to sell the script that had become her life story; an esteemed cardiologist having a major heart attack in his office, then dying a few hours later at age 42 in the Emergency Room at the hospital where he practiced. If there was a God, this had to be the cruelest joke he or she had ever played. Jill would never forget the phone call. Rick's partner was in tears. She had driven frantically to the hospital. The shrill sound of the EKG machine attached to Rick had flat-lined, indicating that there was no heartbeat. It was etched forever in her mind. There had been a steady stream of nurses and doctors at the hospital going in and out of the Emergency Room, hoping against hope that the rumors were wrong, that Dr. Loren was still alive, that it was all some macabre misunderstanding. He was loved and respected by his colleagues and now, suddenly, he was gone.

Jill let the cool air blowing gently from the air-conditioning vent wrap itself around her. She started to feel a little better, somewhat like the Jill she had been before Rick's death. She let her thoughts roam. Perhaps it was time to stop running. But if so, what would she do with the rest of her life? How could she get up each morning without Rick beside her? Money certainly wasn't a problem. The problem was that she felt useless. She had always known exactly what to do and everything had seemed pretty simple. She just supported Rick, whenever and however she could. Now that he was gone, she felt like a balloon, randomly floating here and there.

Her friends had been telling her to get on with

life, that the chapter with Rick was closed. She knew people were starting to avoid her, even longtime friends. She had become uncharacteristically quick-tempered, given to crying jags and temper tantrums. Recently, she had yelled at her favorite private shopper in Nordstrom's when she couldn't find Jill's size in the striking St. John knit suit she wanted to try on. At night she cried herself to sleep, often thinking about the bottle of pills in her purse.

Jill had passed beyond the unwritten time society allotted for grieving. Whatever new tragedy was occurring in her friends' worlds was now the thing vying for their attention. Rick's death had become yesterday's news. The crying shoulders that had been so plentiful in the beginning had moved on. She was alone with her thoughts and memories of Rick.

She sincerely liked people and people genuinely liked her. She had been a top fundraiser for whatever charitable organization she had agreed to help. A master at getting donations for silent auctions or getting companies to underwrite events, Jill was highly sought after as a board member by local charities. If she didn't take the sleeping pills, she'd need to think about what to do with her life. Maybe she could get a job with one of the nonprofit organizations to which she had donated so much time. She'd need a resume, but what could it say? Experience: nurturing my husband. She doubted if there were jobs where that was a requirement. She and Rick had never discussed her working because there had never been a need.

Another potential option involved her friend, Barbie, who was a staple at the local Buddhist temple and had been urging Jill to go to Nepal with her. There was a festival in November, the Mani Rimdu festival, where all the sherpas came from throughout the Himalayas to reconnect, party, and worship at the Thyangboche monastery. Barbie said they would fly to Bangkok, Thailand, and then go on to Kathmandu, Nepal. She kept telling Jill the change of scenery would be good for her and would take her mind off the past. God, it sounded exotic and beautiful. She had never been to that part of the world and maybe it would be good for her. There would be no past memories of Rick, only new memories on which she could build.

As she lay on the bed at the Blue Coyote, promising herself that she would look into both of these options after she got home, she drifted off to sleep, waking up two hours later feeling refreshed for the first time in months. She got dressed and decided to have another glass of wine and something to eat. She wouldn't need the pills tonight. She was beginning to think she might never need them.

Jill walked to the refreshment room where there were a number of sandwiches and other foods that could be warmed in the microwave. She chose a plate with meatloaf and mashed potatoes, warmed it up, and thoroughly enjoyed her meal along with a second glass of wine.

She knew her friends were probably right; it was time to move on. Finishing her wine and food, she returned to her room. As she unlocked the door, she once again realized how very tired she was and how inviting the room and the cool air were. For the first time in months, sleep came easily and she slept like a baby; even her dreams were kind to her.

Jill awoke to the sun streaming in her window at 11:00 a.m. the next morning. She couldn't believe it. She hadn't slept this long since Rick had died. She felt great and, for the first time since Rick had died, she felt hopeful. The depression seemed to have lifted and she didn't feel like crying or cursing. She practically leapt out of bed, ready to get on with her life. She packed quickly, grabbed a couple of slices of the freshly baked banana bread from the refreshment area and gave her room key to the young woman at the desk.

"Thank you so much," Jill said. "You were absolutely right. I slept like a baby and I feel wonderful. I don't know what magic you have here, but it works." She smiled and waved as she drove away.

Yes, the woman thought, *that's what they all say when they leave. They're refreshed and ready to get on with their lives.*

Jill turned westward onto Interstate 10. She reached into her purse, found the pill bottle, opened her window, and tossed out pill after pill, letting the wind take each one. Soon, the harsh desert elements would absorb the pills into the barren land.

CHAPTER 12

It had been almost a year and a half since Rick's death and Jill's life had changed dramatically. She had gone from a woman who had it all when Rick was alive, to the depths of despair. She had been a walking suicide time bomb looking for the right place to end it all. But now, six months later, she had snapped out of it and was back in the world of the living.

The first thing she had done when she got home from her drive back from Dallas was to call her friend Barbie and ask if the invitation to accompany her on the trip to the Mani Rimdu Festival in Nepal was still open. Barbie assured her she would love to have Jill join her. After the conversation with Barbie, Jill called another friend, Marge, who was in charge of the annual fundraiser for Newport Hospital. It was a huge affair and it usually raised over a million dollars, which went toward various charitable programs supported by the hospital, particularly the Women's Treatment Center, for which the hospital had a world famous reputation.

"Marge, I've decided that it's time for me to get back into community volunteering. I hear that you're the chairperson of the annual Newport Hospital fundraiser this year and I wonder if I could help. I'm pretty good at getting people to donate items. I've done it for several charities in the past and I thought if you could use some help, I'd love to work on the silent auction."

"Oh, Jill, this is wonderful," said Marge. "Yes, yes,

yes. I really could use some help. The woman who's in charge of the silent auction hasn't even started to get any items donated and I'm starting to get concerned. The silent auction is a major part of the money we raise. Let's get together for lunch. How about tomorrow at Il Fornaio? Could you join me then? I'd like to get started as soon as possible. I'm so glad you called! They made plans to meet for lunch at noon the following day.

Jill felt genuinely enthused for the first time in a long time. Once again her life had some purpose. She wasn't aimlessly drifting. She was glad she had thrown the sleeping pills out the window in the desert and never looked back.

She knew she was excellent at getting people to donate to charities and she began to make a list of the various people and businesses she could contact. Soon her list filled five single-spaced sheets of paper. *Well*, Jill thought, *that's a good start. Now for Nepal.*

She called Barbie again to get more information on exactly when they would be going, what reservations needed to be made, and to get some idea of what was involved in the trip. She found information about the Mani Rimdu festival on the Internet and spent the next couple of hours researching her upcoming trip.

She'd heard the word "trek," but she didn't know exactly what it meant so she looked that up too. *Swell*, Jill thought, *the dictionary says it's a journey involving difficulty or hardship.* She decided she'd better start working out and strengthening her legs in anticipation of the mountains she'd soon be climbing on the trek Barbie had planned for the two of them.

Jill had heard of Nepal, but wasn't exactly sure where it was located, only that it was in Asia. She learned it was a landlocked nation in Asia just north of India. One source even said it was where the "ice cold Himalayas meet the steamy heat of India," which might make selecting the clothes to take a challenge. Heat or cold? She decided to buy clothes that could be layered.

Next she wondered about the word "Himalaya." What did it mean? Once again she consulted the Internet and found that "Himalaya" meant "abode of snow." She idly wondered if she would be able to see Mt. Everest. If she could, that would make some great cocktail party talk. Even if someone hadn't heard of Nepal, they'd probably heard of Mt. Everest. Feeling like she was beginning to get a handle on the upcoming trip, she made her reservations through Snow Lion, a company Barbie had recommended. Jill was very excited about her upcoming adventure. Seeing a festival held in one of the most remote areas on the planet would be something that no one in her circle of friends had ever done.

Jill remembered asking Barbie how she had become interested in this trip and what made her want to go to Nepal. Barbie told her about a 50th surprise birthday party she had attended for a friend. Most of the people didn't know one another, so they were asked to wear a name badge, but instead of their name, they were told to put a vacation or trip destination on it, a place they'd like to go. Barbie had studied Buddhism for years, so she put Nepal on hers, thinking of the Mani Rimdu Festival held there every year. After a few minutes she realized no one was going to come up to her and inquire about Nepal. The places she saw on the nametags of the other guests were Las Vegas, Paris, New York, and for God's sake, Laughlin, Nevada. No, these were not people who would be interested in Nepal. Then and there she made the decision to go to Nepal.

Wow, Jill thought, *I've done more in the last few hours than I've done in the last few months.* She decided to start the wheels in motion for the charity fundraiser before she left for Nepal so she would still have two months to finalize everything after she returned. February was a good month for fundraisers. Christmas was over, bills were paid in January, and tax day, April 15th, was still a ways off. The charity checks always began to flow again in February.

The next few weeks were filled with contacting potential donors, buying cold weather gear, and working out. She had read that the trek to the Thyangboche Monastery where the festival was held would be a killer. True to her promise to herself, she spent as much time as she could hiking in the hills above Crystal Cove, working on strengthening her legs for the trek. She knew she would be in extremely high altitudes, but she wasn't too worried about getting altitude sickness. She had practiced yoga for years and with the breathing exercises involved in that discipline, she didn't think that would be a problem for her, but you never knew.

Finally, it was time to depart on their adventure. The flight left Los Angeles at 2:30 p.m. and with the difference in time and the 14 1/2 hour flight, it would arrive at 7:00 p.m., Bangkok time. They were going to spend the night at a hotel located in the airport, and fly on to Kathmandu the following day, giving them two days to explore Kathmandu before taking a helicopter to Lukla, where they would begin their trek.

Barbie had been insistent that they fly Business Class from Los Angeles to Bangkok. It was a long flight and flying in coach would make it seem even longer. After a couple of hours, Jill had two glasses of wine and slept through most of the flight. She awoke refreshed in time for dinner. Customs and Immigration inched along slowly, but it helped to know that their hotel was just a short walk away. Jill was glad they had decided to spend the night in a hotel located on the airport premises rather than taking a taxi to a hotel in the city. From just flying over it, she saw that Bangkok was like every other big city in the world, full of noise, bright lights, and people.

The next morning dawned clear and beautiful. They boarded their plane for Kathmandu, the second leg of their journey. Everything about this trip was so different, so foreign, and so exotic. In spite of the fact that Jill and Rick had traveled extensively during their marriage, this part of the world was completely new. The views from the plane were incredible. As they flew over the Himalayas, the pink-capped mountains and cloudless blue skies seemed to go on forever. *So this is the top of the world,* Jill thought, as they approached their destination, *how utterly gorgeous.*

She shuddered as the thought occurred to her that if she had taken the overdose of sleeping pills, she never would have experienced this incredible scene before her. Thinking back to the woman she had been, depressed, despondent and utterly hopeless, she simply couldn't recognize that woman. There was no longer any frame of reference between that woman and who she was now. She made a silent vow that she would never allow anything to put her in that place again.

It was warm when they landed. Although Kathmandu's temperature was in the 60's and 70's this time of year, similar to the weather they had left in Los Angeles, they would soon be trekking up to an elevation of over 12,500 feet. At that altitude, it would be cold, bitterly cold.

Kathmandu was a city in motion. Everything was foreign and fascinating. Their cabby took them to their hotel, which was an oasis in the middle of the city. The hotel gardens were gorgeous. Jill thought wood must be cheap and abundant in this part of the world because in every direction she saw exquisite wooden carvings. Their room overlooked a Buddhist temple where huge prayer wheels were being turned by passing local residents. Brightly colored prayer flags were everywhere and exotic scents filled the air. It was truly a feast for the senses.

As planned, Jill and Barbie spent the next two days exploring the city. Barbie insisted on visiting several of the beautiful Buddhist temples located in the city. In one of the temples, both of them were given long white ceremonial khata scarves as welcome gifts by a lama. While there were a few tie-dyed hippies from Western countries who had stayed too long looking for enlightenment, the majority of the tourists in Kathmandu were simply travelers anxious to explore this remote area of the world. The food was different from anything Jill had ever tasted. Yak tea? Who knew there was such a thing?

Kathmandu was the starting point of many treks in the Himalayas and many shops catered to the trekkers. While Jill and Barbie were buying some last minute things their guide had suggested, they met several mountain climbing teams from around the world who were hoping to scale Mt. Everest. Although the teams would be taking the same route as Jill and Barbie, the teams would continue on to Base Camp One, near the foot of Mt. Everest, while Jill and Barbie would end their trek at Thyangboche Monastery, about 15 miles from Mt. Everest.

After weeks of planning, the day finally arrived for them to begin their trek. If everything went as planned, they would land in Lukla and immediately start trekking, getting to the first stop where the sherpas, who had been hired to assist them with their heavy bags, would set up camp in the late afternoon.

There was only one helicopter flight daily from Kathmandu to Lukla. Their trip information brochure contained a warning that flights were often delayed because of bad weather in the Himalayas. Now that she was involved in this adventure, Jill sincerely hoped they would be able to take off and land in good weather. Bad weather and unstable air currents in the Himalayas were not things Jill wanted to experience.

By prearrangement, they met four other people who

would trek with them and their guide. There was a couple from New York, obviously fit and the type who would probably race each other up the mountain. There was a teacher from Chicago looking for adventure. The last person in their group was a single man from San Francisco, a very attractive doctor who was studying Buddhism. It didn't take Barbie long to make his acquaintance. *Well,* Jill thought, *this whole trip was Barbie's idea. It would be the icing on the cake for Barbie if she found her soul mate while she was trekking in Nepal. She'd already looked for a soul mate in every Buddhist temple in Southern California and how ironic it would be if she found him here.*

They had to wait at the Kathmandu airport for several hours until there was a window of clear weather. Suddenly, their guide called to them, "Hurry, we must go now." Jill looked out the window and saw a rusty old Russian helicopter. There was a "no smoking" sign on it, which the pilot was ignoring. She felt the protective safety net that had always been such a large part of her life, begin to slip away. There was no turning back. She raced for the helicopter with great anticipation. Once again, the colors of the mountains, the snow on the mountain caps, and the skies were incredible. No artist could do them justice.

Because there was no airport or landing strip at Lukla, they landed on a soccer field and within minutes, they began their trek. Jill had a backpack that contained water, some snacks, and extra clothing that she could put on in layers as the temperature dropped. The rest of her daytime trekking gear was carried by her sherpa, Minga.

The days of the trek passed quickly. A new experience took place each moment of each day. There were fields of rhododendrons, temples clinging to cliffs, yaks with bell collars announcing their presence, swaying suspension bridges over rushing rivers, brightly painted houses, and children greeting them at the side of the road. As they walked past them, the children would say "Namaste" and hold their hands over their hearts in the traditional prayer position. Jill had no frame of reference for what she was experiencing. She took each thing as it occurred and enjoyed it for what it was, with no comparisons available or necessary.

When they arrived at Tyangboche Monastery, Jill could only stare in amazement at all of the brilliant colors and the beauty of the nearby mountains. They were breathtaking and in the distance, she could see Mt. Everest, the tallest mountain in the world. She was in awe. There were simply no words to describe this beautiful, majestic area of the world and she felt humbled by the sheer massiveness of her surroundings. Very few people in the world ever had an opportunity to observe what she was seeing and she knew it was something she would never forget.

Sherpas and their families came from all over the Himalayas for the Mani Rimdu festival, reconnecting with old friends and family members. It was a time of celebration and revelry. Dancing, drinking, and beautiful ceremonies in the Monastery were all part of the two day festival. For this short time they forgot about how hard life was in this rugged, beautiful high country and simply enjoyed themselves. The revelry went far into the night.

Everywhere Jill looked, she saw happy people. Although they possessed few material possessions, she sensed that they had something inside that she lacked and she resolved to find whatever it was. Maybe it was Buddhism or perhaps they had discovered something that didn't exist in her Western world. Where she came from, people would be protesting or rioting if they had as little as these people did.

When she observed the children, Jill realized she had never seen a child have a temper tantrum or even cry. The children were cherished by their parents and their extended families. Infants were carried by their mothers or strapped into slings on the mother's back so that the babies wouldn't touch the ground during the entire first year of life. There was an old wives' tale that this was done to separate them from the animals. It was a charming tale and maybe it worked. The young children certainly seemed to be happy.

The trek back to Lukla was just as breathtaking. They stopped at several teahouses and Jill found she had developed a taste for the local yak tea and yak butter. When they got back to Lukla, the helicopter was waiting for them. Jill realized that soon she would be back in her Newport Beach home, her body the same, but her spirit very, very different. With growing confidence, she looked forward to the next chapter of her life.

CHAPTER 13

Jeffrey couldn't believe what had just taken place in Sidney's office. He was the star of the company, the anointed one; literally, the future financial success of Moore Labs rested on his shoulders. All of his dreams of being awarded the Nobel Prize had just gone up in flames. Where would he go? What would he do?

He went to Maria's office in a fog. "Darling, what's wrong? You look like you've just seen a ghost," Maria said.

"Maria, get whatever you have in the desk that belongs to you. We've both just been fired from Moore Labs. Pack up and please, make it fast. I want to get out of here before I see anyone." Ten minutes later they walked out the front door of Moore Labs for the last time. Maria kept looking at Jeffrey, wondering what was going on.

"Let's go down the street to Kelly's. I need a drink. I'll explain everything to you there. But first, I need to know one thing. Have you told anyone that I have been giving you the anti-aging hormone?" Jeffrey stopped walking, turned to her, put his hands on her shoulders, and looked intently into her eyes to see her reaction.

Maria realized that whatever had taken place in

Sidney's office had something to do with her and she made an instant decision to never let Jeffrey know about her conversation yesterday with Dan. Now she knew why Dan had taken the day off. "Of course not! We decided long ago that no one should know about it. You know I would never do anything that could hurt you. Plus, I would have everything to lose if I told anyone. It makes absolutely no sense to think I might have told anyone."

A few minutes later, they arrived at Kelly's and went directly to the bar area. The restaurant had that intimate, clubby feel of restaurants that had been popular in the 60's. Jeffrey quickly walked to a leather booth in the rear of the room. He didn't want to see anyone from Moore Labs. The bar filled up fast with workers needing a drink before they headed out for their long commute home on the freeways. Kelly's had a reputation for fast service, something the workers needed. Maria and Jeffrey placed their order and were quickly served their drinks.

"Maria, everything's changed. Somehow Sidney found out that I've been giving you the anti-aging hormone. It's the end of the Nobel Prize for me and it's the end of my work as a scientist at a prestigious company like Moore Labs. I don't know what we're going to do. Moore is going to issue a statement that I left for medical reasons. We both know that's the kiss of death in this industry. Everyone will assume that I have terminal cancer or that I've entered some rehabilitation program."

"How can they do that? You're the most important scientist they have. Without you, the anti-aging hormone will never win the prize for them, much less bring in billions of dollars in new revenue for the company," Maria said.

"They were never going to win the prize. It can only be awarded to a person or in some cases, up to three people. They were just going to ride on my coattails, get the publicity for being the lab where the hormone was discovered, and then market it. It would translate into big dollars for them.

"The deal is, I signed several contracts when I went to work for them," Jeffrey said. "Every scientist they hire is required to sign a bunch of stuff. I violated their contract when I gave you the hormone. Sidney caught me off guard and I didn't lie to him when he asked me if I had given it to you. Also, they probably would have called you in and I didn't want you to be hurt any more by this than you're going to be. Sidney felt that he couldn't trust me any longer and told me that if I'd violated that part of the contract, there was a good chance that I would violate other parts."

"Maria interrupted him, "But you're the one who discovered the hormone. Doesn't it belong to you? Since you're the one who discovered it, wouldn't every laboratory around still want you to work for them?"

"I wish," Jeffrey said, "but the contract spells out

that any discoveries made by scientists in the employ of Moore Labs belong to Moore Labs. I'm irrelevant now that I've been fired. My contract was 'at will' so they had the right to fire me without notice. I'm pretty sure that no other company will hire me now. I suppose the bright side is that we won't have to worry about money. They gave me four million dollars, half now and the other half in one year if I don't sell the formula to some other company. I don't know where to go or what to do. Science has been my life. They could sue me, but evidently they have decided an out-of-court settlement is better for them. At least that's a bright spot in my day. It's kind of sad when the brightest spot in your day is that someone has decided not to sue you."

Jeffrey put his head in his hands. "I'm not sure if any of the other employees in the lab know what has happened. The only one I met with was Sidney. Oh yeah, he had his secretary there as well. He probably wanted some backup in case I did or said something crazy."

Maria looked at Jeffrey and said, "Let's leave town for a while. We need to make some plans and that's going to be hard to do here. Everyone from your fellow scientists at Moore to all your other friends are going to be calling and asking you what happened. Finish your drink. We'll go home, pack a few things, get in the car, head east, and see where it takes us."

She stood up, put on her coat, and headed for the door, looking neither right nor left. There was no trace of her usual warm smile. Her lips were grimly drawn together. She appeared pale and terribly worried. It suddenly occurred to Maria that Jeffrey might not be able to acquire the materials and chemicals he needed to make the anti-aging hormone. She began to panic just thinking about the future. All of her old fears came crashing back. It had been a few years since she had even considered the possibility of aging and it was not a pleasant thought. She walked by a table of Moore employees and looked straight ahead without acknowledging them. When they called out her name, she didn't answer, pretending she hadn't heard. Jeffrey took a few bills out of his wallet, threw them on the table, and quickly followed her out the door.

They drove to the condominium they bought shortly after they were married, parked the car, and took the elevator up to their third floor unit, closing the door behind them. For the first time in the last few hours, Jeffrey felt safe. As the enormity of what had just happened began to sink in, his shock turned into an ice-cold anger. Maria started to cry. The reality of the situation was becoming very clear to her. She told Jeffrey how scared she was that she wouldn't be able to get the injections anymore; that she'd be cut off from the hormone and would become old and ugly. Even in his pain and anger, Jeffrey couldn't stand to see Maria in tears. He promised her that no matter what happened, he would find a way to continue the injections. He told her they'd talk more about it later, but right now he wanted to get out of town before anyone came to the door or the phone started ringing.

Maria didn't know how long they'd be gone so she watered the plants, transferred a few things from the refrigerator to the freezer, and packed a small travel suitcase. She made sandwiches and put some sodas in a cooler.

Jeffrey checked to see that he had his credit cards and threw some clothes into a tote bag. He changed the message on the answering machine, asking the caller to call his or Maria's cell phone, allowing them to monitor whoever was trying to get in touch with them. Both of them were anxious to get out of Irvine.

They took a freeway route that headed towards the Inland Empire area in Riverside County. Jeffrey just wanted to be in the open spaces and let the desert clear his head. He didn't want to see anyone or talk to anyone. From Riverside he took the freeway route that traveled through some of the most barren and desolate areas of California. Before entering the desert, they made a quick stop at a gas station and then Jeffrey turned the car towards Phoenix.

By now it was 9:30 p.m. and the wintry, desert air had turned cold. The car handled easily on the nearly empty highway. Between the high speeds and the cool wind, Jeffrey began to feel a little better. He knew he could never return to Irvine and that he had to find work somewhere else. The four million dollars promised to him by Sidney would not last forever. He needed some sort of long-range plan, hopefully one that would allow him to continue working on the development of his hormone discovery

Sidney wouldn't be giving him a glowing recommendation; that he knew for sure. He was also certain that Sidney wouldn't go into the details of the dismissal with any companies that might have an interest in him. Sidney would describe the incident in such a way that no company would ever hire him, no matter how brilliant he was. He was screwed and he knew it. He looked over at Maria, still enchanted at how stunningly beautiful she was, and he knew if he had to, he'd do it all over again.

They'd been driving for two and a half hours and he was tired, physically and emotionally. He was on the verge of exhaustion when he saw a roadside sign advertising a motel at the next off ramp. "Maria, I'm tired and I don't think I can go on. Is it OK with you If we stop at this motel up ahead and spend the night? Things will look different in the morning. We don't have to be anywhere and I'm pretty sure there's not much between here and Phoenix. I just don't think I can safely drive for a couple more hours."

"I'm tired too," she said. "Yes, let's stop here. It's late and we've only stopped once since we left Irvine. It's been one hell of a day, one I would like to see end, even if it's in the middle of nowhere."

As he turned into the broken down service road that

led from the freeway off ramp, he noticed a number of high voltage wires, more than he would have expected in this out-of-the-way place. He pulled into the empty motel parking lot. A cold wind was blowing and tumbleweeds scuttled across the lot. It was an unforgiving land, yet for some reason he was drawn to it. The desert was a lonely place, but in his present situation, the loneliness appealed to him. Other than Maria, he really didn't want to ever be around people again. He just wanted his experiments, his science.

A naked light bulb hung from a frayed cord above a sign that said "Recepion." If the owner couldn't even spell "Reception," Jeffrey could just imagine how great the room was going to be. Maintenance at the motel had been badly neglected. Jeffrey thought some desert rat probably owned it. He figured that the owner either didn't have any money to put into repairs or so few people stopped at the motel the owner simply didn't feel there was any reason to spend money fixing it up. Old, decaying buildings like this were not that unusual in remote desert areas. Time had passed them by and Mother Nature was slowly taking the upper hand. Theirs was the only car in the parking lot.

Maria and Jeffrey got out of the car and walked up to the door with the word "Office" printed on it in faded blue letters. Entering the unlocked door, they rang the bell on the reception desk, waiting for someone to acknowledge them. After a few minutes, a grizzled old man with a cigarette dangling from the corner of his mouth shuffled into the room from the back and asked if he could help them. His shirt was stained with food and his huge belly hung over the big turquoise belt that struggled to hold up his pants.

"My wife and I need a room for tonight. Do you have anything?" Jeffrey asked.

"Sure. It ain't the best motel room in the world, but if yer tired, it'll be a good place to sleep. It's cheap, only $50.00 and it's clean," the old man said.

Maria knew how tired Jeffrey was and decided they would spend the night there no matter how bad the room was. It was that or risk an accident. She hadn't said anything to him, but she was sure he had nodded off a couple of times during the last half hour he'd been driving. Jeffrey filled out the guest registration form the old man gave them and paid for the room with his credit card. The old man handed them a key and told them to follow the walkway to room number 2.

The walkway cement had huge cracks and parts of it were just holes where once there had been cement. An old children's saying played in Maria's mind as they walked to their room, "Step on a crack, break your mother's back." She didn't know where that was coming from. Maybe it was the sense that she was a child again, not knowing what the future held.

While the room wasn't great, it was just as the old

man had described, clean and cheap. Faded wallpaper peeled away from the wall under a heating vent over the bathroom door. The bathroom had no amenities other than a plunger standing guard next to the toilet. Maria hadn't had much experience with motel rooms, but even she knew that having a plunger on "standby" was not a good sign. She was glad that she had brought her own soap and shampoo. The blankets were thin and the towels were worn, but the room would do for the night. They ate the sandwiches she'd fixed earlier. Exhausted, they got in bed and immediately fell asleep.

When they awoke the next morning, the desert air was crisp and clean and the sky was a spectacular shade of blue. There was not a bit of city smog and you could easily see for twenty miles. It was as if they could reach out and touch the nearby Eagle and Coxcomo Mountains. Having no desire to stay at the motel any longer than necessary, they returned the room key to the old man. As they were walking away, he said, "By the way, if you know anyone who wants to buy this joint, I'd sell it real cheap. I'm getting too old to run it and my health has taken a turn for the worse thanks to those damn cancer sticks I'm always suckin' on," he said. They told him they'd keep it in mind, got in their car, and headed back towards the highway.

Maria and Jeffrey arrived in the Phoenix area just before noon. "Let's get some lunch. We haven't eaten anything since last night and it's too early to find a room." Maria said. "There's a restaurant in Phoenix I've read about that's supposed to have the best Mexican food in the world. I entered the name of it on my iPhone. I'll call them."

Several minutes later they were on their way to the restaurant after realizing they were just a short distance from its location. They pulled into the packed parking lot. Obviously, they weren't the only ones who had heard about it. The small building was painted in the colors of the Mexican flag, red, green, and white. A large handwritten menu was taped over a window where a man was taking orders. To his left was the kitchen where an old woman was hand forming and frying one tortilla after another on a hot griddle. The take-out style food that the small kitchen was turning out was mouthwatering. The only seating available was at small tables located under a large, white canvas awning. Maria and Jeffrey took their iced teas, found an empty wooden table, and waited for their number to be called.

They looked around. The tented room was filled with every type of desert cactus that could be grown in the Phoenix area, their spikey cactus blooms jutting out of the various shades of green in a myriad of colors. The review Maria had read in the magazine said the restaurant catered to a cross section of the Phoenix population. The review had been right. There were well-dressed men in suits sitting next to ranchers in cowboy hats. Students, medical personnel in their scrubs, and women who spared no expense in personal upkeep were all there. The food was the best Mexican food they'd ever had and Maria was pretty critical when it came to Mexican food. They shared chili rellenos, baked cheese, fresh tortillas with salsa, and an incredible pork stew. Stuffed, they walked out of the restaurant, feeling good for the first time in 24 hours.

"Well," Jeffrey said, "now what? Where do we go and what do we do? I'm absolutely lost."

"I've been thinking," Maria said. "You know how that old man back at the motel said it was for sale? Well, what if we bought it? Don't say no until you hear me out. It couldn't be too much money. I mean, how many buyers do you think he's going to have? It looked like there was a small house in the back where we could live and you've always talked about what you would like to have in a lab if you could build your own. Well, this is your chance. You could build your own lab just the way you want it and then conduct your experiments right on the premises where we live. You will have the best of both worlds. The place is remote and no one will be watching over your shoulder. You could sell any new discoveries you make to drug companies and since they'd be new discoveries, your past work with Moore Labs wouldn't be a problem. We have enough money. We could fix up the motel and make it inviting with a better welcoming sign along the highway."

Jeffrey interrupted her. "Wait a minute. What are

you talking about?"

Maria continued, "I bet we're not the only travelers who got tired on that long drive and there's nothing else for miles. We could get some better electricity and install Wi-Fi. Most importantly, we'd be together. If we buy that motel we can accomplish the two things that are most important to us, being together and continuing your research. I'd be fine being alone with you in the desert. We decided before we were married that we wouldn't have any children, so being far away from schools and city life really wouldn't be a problem for me. I love to cook and I could make things for travelers to eat, not a full service restaurant, but things they could heat up in a microwave. I could prepare casseroles at night and coffeecakes for in the morning. You wouldn't have to do anything concerning the day-to-day operation of the motel. I'll do it all. While I take care of the motel, you could continue your research full time. What do you think?"

Jeffrey was at a loss for words. He had promptly forgotten the conversation with the old man. *Just idle talk*, he thought. Clearly though, Maria had given it a lot of thought on the drive to Phoenix. At first, it seemed like the craziest thing he had ever heard, but as he thought more about it, he realized her idea had some merit. There were a number of new experiments he wanted to try. Some were only quasi-legal and he knew no bona fide scientific laboratory would allow him to do them. There were ideas he had that might work, but only if no one was around to monitor him while he conducted his research. If he lived at the motel, he would be totally alone with no one snooping around or asking dumb questions.

He liked the idea of complete privacy that the motel's location provided. If one of his projects didn't work out, no one would know and he could just go on to the next one. He knew where he could get the supplies and materials that he would need. Maria was probably right about the motel not being expensive. He couldn't imagine there would be a bidding war going on for a run-down motel in the middle of nowhere.

During the last year or so, another thought had come to him from time to time. Maria was taking the anti-aging hormone and clearly, she was not aging. If anything, she was more beautiful than ever. Jeffrey knew that some of the best scientific discoveries in history had been made by older scientists who were getting up in years. When he started work on his anti-aging hormone, he had decided he wouldn't take it. That was before he met Maria. He had started to worry that as he aged, she would begin to look around for a more attractive man, one who was younger. There was a fourteen-year age difference between the two of them and while it didn't seem to matter now, later on it might.

Certainly every person who saw her was struck by her incomparable beauty. He was still completely mesmerized by her shimmering black hair, her high cheekbones, the large welcoming smile, the incredibly white teeth, and a female figure that could serve as a poster for every plastic surgeon in Beverly Hills. What people didn't know was that everything about Maria was natural with the exception of the anti-aging hormone, which kept her looking young. If they lived at the motel, he could keep her to himself. He knew she needed him for the hormone and he also knew she really loved him. The chances of her leaving him for a younger man might be dramatically reduced if he agreed to her proposal. Buying the motel might just be the answer to everything.

Jeffrey weighed the consequences of Maria's suggested course of action. He didn't want to ever see anyone from Moore Scientific Labs again. He didn't want to answer questions and he didn't want to discuss what had taken place in Sidney's office. He and Maria both loved to read and they enjoyed a quiet type of life, but could they live the rest of their lives alone in the desert with just an occasional traveler to talk to besides each other? He didn't know. But he was also pretty sure that he was looking at a menu of very limited choices.

"Jeffrey, let's go back to the motel. Let's take our time and really look at it. We need to think about what we could do to improve it. And just as importantly, we need to find out how much he wants for it. I know it sounds crazy, but it might work. We can't spend the rest of our lives running from place to place. The cost of improving it will probably be far more than what we'll pay for it. We could sell our condominium and the beauty of the motel's location is that we'd still only be a few hours from our families. By the way, we need to think of something to tell them. If we bought the motel, we could just say you're suffering from burnout and we decided to do something totally different. It would work. I feel it."

A lot of what Maria said was true. He agreed to go back and look at the motel. *Good God, this is nuts*, Jeffrey thought. *I'm going to look at a motel in the middle of nowhere with the idea of buying it, fixing it up, and living there. This is a long way from being interviewed for winning the Nobel Prize, but what the hell; it might just work.*

CHAPTER 14

Maria and Jeffrey were both quiet on the drive back to the motel, each lost in their own thoughts. Maria felt that the motel had "good bones" and they could begin with that. She knew it was going to take a lot of work, but the small desert town of Blythe wasn't far from the motel. There had to be some contractors in Blythe who probably needed work. She imagined there wasn't much work available, particularly in these tough economic times.

What she couldn't get in Blythe, she was sure she could get in Phoenix. She already knew that she would need new furniture, paint, and light fixtures, which was probably just the tip of the iceberg. When the motel was open, she could make one trip a week into Blythe for groceries and miscellaneous items. They had passed a UPS truck a while ago so she knew that she could order things from the Internet and have them delivered to the motel. She'd have to discuss the matter of Wi-Fi and electricity with the contractor, as she wasn't quite sure how all of that would work. She became lost in a world of colors and decorating ideas, making for a very short trip.

While Maria was absorbed in thoughts about decorating the motel, Jeffrey was thinking about the lab he would build. He knew he'd need a lot of electricity for some of his experiments and he would prefer not to draw attention to the motel by using such a large amount of electricity. What if he installed a number of solar panels to generate electricity? Jeffrey had been thinking for a long time about how to harness and store solar energy. He knew there was no present technology available for storing solar energy, but he wondered if he could build a big battery that would store the energy and then it could be used when there was no sunlight. Until he could get the solar power technology worked out, he knew he could always get electricity by using a gypsy line which would divert the energy that was coming through the high voltage wires he had seen last night near the highway that led to the motel. He began to make a mental list of what he would need.

Now that he was no longer employed by Moore Labs, he would have to get the ingredients for the hormone he was injecting into Maria from some new source. He knew where Moore Labs had purchased the materials and he was pretty sure he could do the same. It might cost a little more because they would have to be bought in smaller quantities, but he didn't have any choice. The basic ingredients came from extracts of plants that grew in the Amazon. It was illegal to bring them into the United States, but a laboratory in Mexico had been processing and selling the distilled products in the United States through a special trade agreement. He would have to make a trip to Mexico and find a way to get the raw materials he needed. They were an essential part of the monthly injection he was giving to Maria.

For many years, Maria had suffered from occasional bouts of depression. Jeffrey thought he could probably compound a drug that would help her, but he hadn't been able to do it while he was working at Moore Labs. He could always tell when one of her periods of despair was coming on. It began with her talking about feeling like she had "wet wool" in her brain. She would take a few days off from work, stay in the condo with the lights off, wear an old robe and slippers, and close the blinds. She had taken various drugs such as Xanax and Prozac, which helped her for a while, but then a few weeks or months later, the depression would always recur. Jeffrey was certain it was tied to her fear of aging, but he couldn't quite figure out what he could do to treat her. He decided when he went to Mexico to get the extracts for the anti-aging hormone; he would also get other supplies he felt could become part of a "feel-good" drug he was certain he could make.

His mind raced with ideas for other drugs. There would have to be space for the laboratory rats that he planned to use in his tests. Moore Labs had followed all of the governmental rules regarding animals and testing to the letter of the law. In this new environment, Jeffrey knew the only rules he would have to follow would be his own. Without any government oversight or inspection, he could easily speed up the time it took to test his experiments.

He smiled to himself with a sense of satisfaction that he would no longer be under the thumb of government rules and regulations. He could be a real "cowboy" in the industry, free to do whatever he wanted with no one supervising him. The more he thought about it, the more he was beginning to like the idea of moving to such a remote, desolate area. It definitely would make testing his experiments easier.

Maria and Jeffrey arrived at the motel; both intent on taking time to really look at it. They got out of their car, took a deep breath, and entered the office area. Once again, no one was there to greet them. They rang the bell and the old man shuffled in, ever-present cigarette dangling from his mouth, dressed in the same clothes he had worn the night before and earlier that morning.

"Back already? I ain't even made up the room. You gotta give me a few minutes," he said.

"Actually," Jeffrey said, "we're here to look at the motel. You said it was for sale and we'd like to see what you have here. We're kind of tired of the city rat race. Would you show us around?"

Are you kidding, the old man thought, *you're the first people to even want to look at it. Maybe, just maybe, I can get the hell out of here.* "Sure. Follow me. You got questions, just ask."

The motel was located on a large piece of fenced

property, although a lot of the fencing was damaged and needed repair. There were two buildings behind the motel, one that looked like a house and the other that seemed to be a storage building. People who lived this far from civilization always kept "stuff" because someday they might need it, whether it was an auto part or the plug for a bathtub. No landscaping had been planted to break the harshness of the desert. The doors to the rooms looked tired and most were sagging from their hinges at odd angles. The motel sign in the middle of the parking lot was mounted on a pole that was broken and tilted. It looked like someone had backed into the pole with their car.

The drab motel was in the style of the auto court motels, which had been popular in the 50's. The "L" style motel plan had an office on the left with a door leading to a kitchen, which was in serious need of some updating and tender loving care. Coagulated grease, old appliances, food-specked walls along with dirty and dented pots and pans all cried out for attention. The covered outdoor porch dog-legged to the right, connecting six rooms which were exactly alike, separated by "faux" pillars. Maria thought she would make the last room into a "refreshment room" where the guests could get drinks and food. A couch, refrigerator, microwave, table, and chairs would fit into the room. The parking lot was dirt and gravel with a space in front of each room for a car. Naked light bulbs hung over doors with paint peeling from them. The windows looking out from the rooms were caked with dust and didn't look as if they'd ever been washed.

Threadbare carpeting covered the floors of the rooms, which were badly in need of new furniture, paint, lighting, and bedding. The bathrooms were old and uninviting with linoleum floors stained from years of leaking basins and toilets. New tile floors, showers, basin fixtures, and linens, in addition to the painting and light fixtures, were added to the list Maria was making.

The one-bedroom owner's house, connected to the motel by a breezeway, had a large living/dining room and a kitchen. The bedroom was also surprisingly large. There were windows across the entire back with nothing to see but the vast desert. The bathroom and kitchen were adequate. Everything was in need of repair and updating, but structurally, the motel was in a fairly sound condition. Whoever had originally built it had done a good job. It needed a lot of cosmetic work, but just as Maria had thought on the drive back from Phoenix, the basic bones of the motel were good. Putting time and money into updating the structure would make it a place where people would want to stay.

The list of items to be bought and things to be fixed went on and on. Everywhere they looked, something cried out for attention. The money needed for improvements was definitely going to be far more than the asking price of the motel.

"Oh," the old man said, "there's one more thing.

It's the basement. The person who built this place was scared as hell of a nuclear bomb, so he built a bomb shelter. He was sure that the Feds was testing bombs out here in the desert. I just call it the basement, but you probably oughtta take a look at it."

At the far end of the motel the old man opened a door marked "Basement" and led them down steps to a door which opened up to a room that ran the length of the motel. Jeffrey could barely contain his excitement as he entered the room. He had assumed he would have to build a separate, free-standing laboratory for his experiments, but this basement location would be the perfect place. He could partition it into several rooms. One room would be the actual lab where the experiments would take place; a smaller one would be a storeroom for the supplies needed for his experiments; a third would be for the test rats; and he'd also need a very small office. There was even a bathroom, although it, too, was filthy and badly in need of repair.

After completing the inspection tour of the motel premises, Jeffrey asked the old man, "What are you asking for this place? It needs a lot of repairs to make it into a motel where people would want to stay or even revisit. There's a lot of traffic on the highway, but in the two times we've been here, I haven't seen anyone else. Are you open year round?"

The old man remained silent for what seemed like a long time. He debated what number to put out as his asking price. He didn't want to scare them off with a high asking price. They were the first people to ever even ask about the place and he really wanted out. He and his wife had bought the motel when he retired, but cancer took her the second year they were here. He blamed himself for her death because she hadn't wanted to buy the motel in the first place. It had been his idea and now that she was gone he was lonesome. The young couple was right, very few people stopped or stayed at the motel. His son, Josh, kept asking the old man to join him at his place in Montana. Josh had a small ranchette with a trailer where the old man could live. He knew his expenses would be minimal.

"Tell you what. I want to get outta here so I'd be happy with $120,000, cash. You'd get everything but the car. I need that to go to Montana," the old man said. "If you're interested, I'll leave tomorrow and you can get started on them things you need to fix."

"I need to talk to my wife. We'll meet you in the office in a little while," Jeffrey said.

Jeffrey and Maria followed the old man back up the stairs and walked out to their car in the parking lot. Maria took a couple of soft drinks out of the cooler they had brought, handing one to Jeffrey. "Well," Jeffrey said, "what do you think?"

"Yes," Maria said. "Let's do it. The basement is perfect for your lab and I can fix up the motel rooms. The only things we'd need a contractor for would be your lab, the bathrooms, and maybe the kitchens. We can get started as soon as we go back to Irvine, list our condo, get a U-Haul, and bring our belongings out here. Jeffrey, this is a new start. Financially, we'll be fine with the money from Moore Labs, the proceeds from the sale of the condo, and with whatever you can make selling the new drugs you invent. It will be more than enough and who knows? We might even make a little money on this motel. You'll have all the peace and quiet you need for your experiments. I would be happy just doing things around here like cooking and reading. Neither of us would miss the city life. Please!"

Maria's large brown eyes were shining with excitement. When she looked at Jeffrey with those pleading eyes, it was a done deal. Actually, he, too, was excited about this strange turn of events and ready to get on with a new life, knowing there was going to be no turning back. Their earlier lives were over. The future lay in this run-down old motel in a god-forsaken part of the California desert that wasn't even on his radar twenty-four hours ago. *Strange where life takes you,* he thought. *I've always heard there are no coincidences. If I wasn't a believer before, I am now.*

He walked over to Maria, putting his arms around her. "Are you very, very sure about this?" he asked.

"Yes, this is the answer. I just know it." She started to cry with joy and excitement. It was an emotional moment for both of them as they each realized that this really was a turning point in their lives. They were exchanging the known for the unknown, preparing to start a new life in the barren California desert. Even as they embarked on their new adventure, blowing tumbleweeds surrounded them as the desert wind picked up. They were in unchartered territory. It was terrifying, yet at the same time, exhilarating.

They walked back into the office and as they rang the bell, the old man walked in. "Well," he said, "made a decision?"

"Yes," Jeffrey said. "We'd like to buy it. Since there's no real estate agent involved, we'll both save on that. I need to have some title documents drawn up and recorded. I'll give you a down payment today and the balance when we close escrow. I'd like to get started in a few days. We'll go back to our home in Irvine and take care of some things there. You probably need to do the same here. We'll be back in three days. Will that work for you?"

The old man felt like saying, "*You kidding me? I never thought I'd unload this dump*," but he kept his mouth shut, trying to hide the smile that threatened to take over his face and just nodded. "Why don't you give me that check and I'll write you up a receipt. I got a lawyer friend in Blythe who can draw up the papers. I'll have 'em for you in three days."

Jeffrey wrote out a check for $25,000 and handed it to the old man. He and Maria spent some time walking the property they had just bought, got back in their car, and headed for Irvine to end one life and begin a new one.

Little did they know their new life would become a living hell.

CHAPTER 15

It was a crisp fall day and Sean had been driving for hours on his way to El Monte, California, from Santa Fe, New Mexico. Currently, he was driving through the desolate desert area west of Blythe. He was unsure what the future held and only knew that the part of his life he treasured, the part of his life he had devoted to God, was no longer to be.

Sean couldn't remember a time when he hadn't wanted to become a priest. He came from a large Irish Catholic family where it had been a tradition for the oldest son to join the priesthood. The Moriarty family brought the old Irish tradition with them when they emigrated from Ireland. As the oldest of the seven Moriarty sons, it had always been assumed that Sean would follow in the tradition. Even if there hadn't been a tradition to follow, Sean would have become a priest.

Whenever Sean entered a Catholic church, he felt like he was coming home. It was a feeling he had experienced since he had been a little boy. For the past twenty-three years, his home had been the church. His vocation was that of a priest. To Sean, it wasn't a profession; it was simply who he was. He loved the devotions, the liturgy, the rites, and he knew he had helped many people during his career as a priest.

The one person Sean couldn't help was himself. And now what? How could he face a future in which he could no longer be a priest? The Bishop had called Sean in early that morning and told him that he was being relieved immediately of all of his priestly duties. From that moment on, he could not take part in any ministry, wear any cleric's clothing and could no longer call himself a priest. The visibly angry Bishop told him that serious allegations of child molestation had been made against him. He revealed that an investigation indicated that the allegations were true. Fortunately for both Sean and the Church, the victims, who were now adults, had agreed not to press charges or go public with the allegations because of a confidential cash settlement the Church's lawyers had worked out with the victims. Under a Church Charter adopted in 2002, the Bishop had no choice but to officially defrock Sean.

There had only been a few unfortunate incidents. Sean had been able stop himself from approaching young boys for a long time. It was only when his dependency on alcohol began to spin out of control that Sean couldn't seem to help himself. He was grateful that his alcoholism seemed to have escaped the Bishop's attention. It was either that or the Bishop didn't feel he needed to raise the issue since child molestation itself was cause for mandatory defrocking. Child molestation trumped alcoholism. Even though the public would forgive an alcoholic they drew the line at child molestation. Sean was glad his alcoholism hadn't been discussed. The memory of being drunk and officiating at a Baptism last week was a memory he'd rather not revisit.

When had he started to depend on beginning the day with the sacred rite of Communion? When had the words "The blood of Christ" started to mean far more to him than the words of the Mass? When had he started to fill the chalice to the brim, knowing that part of the rite consisted of the priest drinking whatever was left in the chalice?

He could still remember when he was seven and how the sip of wine had made him feel when he made his First Communion. His body glowed with the warmth of the wine. A year later, he became a young acolyte, turning the pages of the Bible for the priest. Later, he became a senior acolyte and was always available to help with the ceremonial duties of Mass whenever he was asked. What always made it worthwhile was the sip of wine and, as he got older, more than just a sip.

It was easy enough to lie to himself. He told himself how much he loved being a part of the service, doing God's work. In seminary school, there was Mass every morning. He could justify wine in the morning because it was part of the religious rite. The evening wine shared with friends was what most college men did, right? Even those in the seminary. As a young priest, he began to officiate at daily Mass. At some point, a little wine with lunch became a routine thing to have. After all, the Italians did it and wasn't the Vatican in Italy? Then a glass or two with dinner. Then a glass or two before dinner. Then a glass or two after dinner. Over time, wine had become a very important part of his life.

Sean couldn't remember exactly when the wine had changed to vodka. He read somewhere that people couldn't detect the smell of vodka on a person's breath. Maybe that was when it started. He did know that he felt a lot more comfortable when he had the vodka bottle in his pocket under his vestments.

He wondered what defrocked priests were expected to do. Was there a twelve-step program for them? How would he introduce himself? "Hi, I'm Sean. I used to be a priest, but I was defrocked for buggering little boys." Yeah, that would be a great line at a party. The party days were probably over anyway. When the word got out, he rather doubted he would be a welcome guest anywhere. He'd miss the parties. Sean was charming and had been widely sought after as a guest at all kinds of social events. People loved to have a priest at their party because it gave the party legitimacy. It also made it a lot easier for everyone else to relax when their own priest was clearly enjoying himself.

Sean liked everything about Santa Fe. The adobe buildings and the pueblos always interested him whenever he spent time away from the parish. Santa Fe was a very social town with a high percentage of the wealthy being Catholic and Sean knew them all. He enjoyed the social scene and rarely turned down an invitation to attend opening night at the world-renowned Santa Fe opera or the art gallery shows on Canyon Road. He particularly looked forward to Indian Market, which was held every August with over 1,000 local artisans displaying their wares in the central plaza. It had become a tradition for him to join several of the parishioners for dinner after the Market at Pasquale's restaurant on Don Gaspar, just off the central plaza.

His car was heading for Southern California after his morning meeting with the Bishop. Sean was traveling towards the old family home in El Monte where one of his younger brothers still lived. Since he had left to join the priesthood, the area had changed. Now it was a haven for gangs and the Irish families he had grown up with were long gone. Maybe this was a blessing because right now he couldn't bear the thought of facing his childhood friends.

He knew his family would have no choice but to take him in, but he didn't know if he could stand to see the disappointment in their eyes. Thank God his mother was gone, since the pride and joy of her life had been her son, the priest. Sean often thought she felt his being a priest elevated her to a place just below the Virgin Mary. His brothers had also been proud of him. "My brother is a priest," they always said. Well, not anymore. They never even suspected that he had a penchant for young boys or alcohol. Irish families enjoyed their drinks and being a celibate priest in the Catholic Church meant women were simply not an option for him.

Sean remembered the first boy. Although it had happened a few years ago, the memory was seared forever on his brain. It had been right after a morning Mass. Jake was thirteen, just coming into puberty. There was innocence and a latent sexuality about Jake that morning that made it hard for Sean to keep his attention on Mass.

After Mass, Jake and Sean went into a small room located behind the altar to change clothes, Sean to his day robes and Jake to his jeans and a T-shirt. Sean undressed and felt Jake's eyes on him, hungry eyes. Before Sean could stop himself, he had Jake in his arms, kissing him, feeling searing heat in his rising penis. Sean pulled Jake's underwear down and fondled his small, immature private parts. Jake moaned with pleasure. Sean reached for the bottle of holy oil, gave it to Jake, and told him to rub it on Sean's penis. His brain had ceased all thought processes between the warmth of the oil and the small hand on his fully erect penis. Sean turned Jake around, leaned him up against a wall, entered him from behind, and exploded in a violent orgasm that caused Sean to sag to his knees. He held on to the boy's hips, raising himself to his feet, and whispered in Jake's ear, "God loves you, Jake. God loves you for letting me do this. Remember it always!" Afterwards, he felt sick with shame and revulsion.

He had turned Jake around, ready to apologize,

when he realized Jake was smiling. Jake had enjoyed it. He wondered if this was Jake's first time. He couldn't bring himself to ask. Sean really didn't want to know. He only knew he could never, never do this again. And to think he had done this in God's own house. What he had done was beyond blasphemy. Sean also knew he could never confess his sins to one of the other priests, but he made a silent vow to do penance and atone for his sin.

Sean soon learned that while the mind may be willing, the body was weak, very weak. He prayed for strength, but the second boy was just too beautiful. When Sean was in the small room behind the altar after Mass with young Gene, all the strong resolutions he had made left and once again he found himself having sex with a young boy. When he turned Gene around, he saw the terror in the young boy's eyes. Sean profusely apologized, told Gene he had never done anything like that before, and pleaded with him never to tell anyone. Having a priest ask anything of you is hard to resist, particularly one as well loved as Sean. To Sean's knowledge, Gene never told another soul.

There were several other incidents like those with Jake and Gene. How many, Sean couldn't remember, maybe six or eight. He really didn't know and didn't want to remember. All of them left Sean loathing himself and the only thing that seemed to give him relief was the vodka. It had become necessary to numb himself so the feelings of self-loathing and revulsion wouldn't overtake him. He idly wondered which of the boys had told on him. It didn't really matter now, but he was curious.

When Sean was in college, in addition to his Master of Divinity degree, he had also gotten a Master's Degree in Psychology, but he'd never practiced it. He probably had used it over the years when he counseled his parishioners, but who knew whether it was the psychology or the religion that seemed to help people? As long as the counseling worked, it never had mattered and even if someone had asked him if it was religion or psychology that he had used, he really couldn't separate the two.

Maybe he could help other priests who needed counseling. He was sure there was a code of ethics against allowing a priest defrocked for child molestation to be anywhere near children. And anyway, who would want to be counseled by a priest who had been defrocked for child molestation? He probably wouldn't even be welcome at school events for his nieces and nephews.

He thought there was some law about sex offenders and his "crime" fit that category. It involved keeping a certain distance from schools. That brought up another thought about being a "registered sex offender." He vaguely remembered according to the Church's charter adopted in 2002, that if a priest was defrocked for child molestation the Bishop was required to report him to the authorities. But since the church had settled out-of-court, he wondered if any of that would apply to him? *Swell*, he thought, *one more thing to put on the list of "things I need to do when I get to Southern California"—find out if I need to register as a sex offender and wait for the authorities to come knocking on my door.*

But first, he had to get his life in order. The silver flask on the passenger seat called to him once again. He needed another swig of vodka. He wanted some wine; no, he needed some wine, and a lot of it; right now. For the hundredth time since his meeting with the Bishop this morning, he swore to himself that after today, he would quit drinking. The one thing he didn't know was how he was going to shut up the insistent inner voice that demanded a drink, the voice that caused him to unscrew the cap on the flask and take another swig.

He knew if he hadn't been addicted to alcohol, he would have heeded the voice of reason in his mind. No matter how strongly he felt the urge to touch and be touched by young boys, he had always been able to listen to that voice of reason in his mind. It was only in the last couple of years that he began to ignore the voice, seducing the boys in the small room behind the altar, swearing them to secrecy. What he had done was criminal and immoral. How could he forgive himself or for that matter, how could anyone else ever forgive him? He never would have been a child molester if alcohol hadn't affected his judgment. He had never been in denial about his alcoholism; he just hadn't wanted to quit.

Sean was a large bear of a man with a roadmap of red veins covering his nose and cheeks. He was pale from spending most of his life indoors and his steely grey hair was cut short. He was dressed in a pair of old khakis and an out-of-date sport shirt. He rarely dressed in anything other than his daytime clerical clothing or the robes he wore when he officiated at Mass. It felt very strange not to be wearing his stiff priest's collar.

He was still wearing the huge silver cross that almost covered his chest. It had been given to him when he became a priest. He knew he should take it off, but not yet. Never again would he hear the words, "Father, I have sinned. Forgive me." Once again, the enormity of what had happened that morning swept over him. As he reached for his flask, he veered off the road and almost sideswiped a bridge abutment. He realized he'd had too much to drink and was under too much emotional strain. A strong voice inside him cautioned him to pull off the road and get some sleep. He wondered if God was talking to him. Now that he was no longer a priest, maybe God felt it was time to help him.

Ahead of him, just to the right of the shimmering blacktop, he noticed a sign for the Blue Coyote Motel. He couldn't go any farther. Sean was seriously drunk and he knew it. He turned off the highway and entered the driveway of the motel. Perhaps this was a place where he could try and deal with his devils, staying at this motel in the middle of nowhere. Later, he would recall that his decision to stop at the motel had been as bad a choice as the young boys and alcohol had been.

He staggered and caught his balance as he got out of his old car. There hadn't been much need for a car for the last twenty-three years, as most of his time was spent in the parish. Looking at the car with new eyes, he realized that he had better make getting a new car a top priority. If he kept it any longer, it would probably have value only to an antique collector. One more thing to put on the "things I need to do when I get to Southern California" list. Fortunately, he had been able to save most of his salary, as his basic living needs were met by the parish. Room, board, and clothing were furnished to him. The only expense had been his alcohol and that wasn't much because after Mass he was often able to secretly take the leftover wine back to his room.

He stepped into the motel office area. "Do you have a room for tonight?" he asked the beautiful young Latina woman standing behind the desk.

"Of course, Father, we would be happy to have you stay here," The woman said, smelling the alcohol on his breath and noticing the broken red veins on his nose and cheeks. *He really needs to be here*, she thought. *We can help him.*

He didn't bother to correct her. He looked like a priest and how many people wore a cross as large as his? She'd probably noticed the "St. Michael's

Church" bumper sticker on his car, which the church had sold as a fundraiser. Probably not too many people with that bumper sticker and a large cross checked into this motel. He signed the registration book as Father Sean Moriarty, knowing he no longer was a priest, but unwilling to admit it.

He wondered where she lived. There wasn't a city for miles. He had noticed what looked like a house attached to the rear of the motel. Maybe she stayed there, but even in his befuddled state, he wondered why a beautiful young woman would work at a motel in the middle of a nowhere desert.

"Let me show you to your room," she said. "We'll stop by the refreshment area on the way. Beer and wine are always available on an honor system and we have some food and a microwave. The weather is so hot here in the desert that we have provided a commercial grade air-conditioner in each room. I think you'll find it very comfortable."

"Thanks," Sean said. As she showed him the refreshment area, he thought how he could take a couple of glasses of wine to his room and finish off the vodka. *Might as well* he thought, After all, this was the last day he would ever drink again.

His room was larger and more comfortable than he would have thought. The namesake of the motel, the blue coyote, figured prominently in the decor of the room. A framed painting of it was on the white adobe wall.

The room was beginning to spin. He must have had more to drink than he thought. Sean remembered going back to his room at the rectory and drinking some wine while he quickly packed. He'd also stopped at a rest area and refilled his flask from the vodka he kept in the trunk. He decided to lie down. Stripping off his clothes, he flopped down on the bed and quickly fell asleep.

Sean awoke an hour and a half later and realized he was very hungry. He got dressed, ready to go to the refreshment area. As he walked out of his room, he turned left and inadvertently passed the door to the refreshment area. He heard the steady nearby thrum of some type of machine, possibly a generator. Sean thought they must need some type of backup electrical system in this desert heat. Whatever it was, it was getting louder. At the end of the sidewalk he saw a door with a sign on it that said "Basement." *Strange*, he thought, *I didn't think there were basements in the Western United States and especially not here in the desert.*

Curious, Sean started down the darkly lit steps and saw two other signs that read "Danger" and "Keep Out," which were posted on a door at the bottom of the stairs. There was a lock on the door and the thrumming sound coming from behind the door was quite noticeable. He tried the doorknob, but the door was securely locked. He decided it was some heavy-duty equipment that powered the motel's air-conditioning system. *It must take a lot of energy to keep an air-conditioning unit running in this heat*, he thought. He walked back up the stairs, turned to his right and immediately saw the light from the refreshment room.

Sean chose a chicken salad sandwich and some potato chips. The usually insistent voice that cried out for wine whenever he ate food was strangely quiet. The soft drinks in the cooler looked inviting. Sean took the food and a soft drink back to his room, once again enjoying the coolness the air-conditioning afforded. He reached into his suitcase for the latest novel he was reading, thinking that at least the library would miss him. *When I'm finished I better send these books back by FedEx*, he thought, *One more thing to put on my "things to do when I get to Southern California" list.* Sean spent the next two hours comfortably resting, feeling the stress of the day begin to leave him. He looked at the flask. It was one of the few material things that was important to him. His name and a cross had been etched on it, "Father Sean Moriarty." He might as well throw it in the trash. He was no longer a Father and he had sworn that as of tomorrow he wouldn't need the flask. Now it was just a bad reminder of the last twenty-three years of his life. He soon fell asleep, cooled by the air-conditioner and soothed by the slight scent of sandalwood in the air.

As long as he had been in the priesthood, he had awakened before daylight, spending the next few hours in prayer or service. He didn't need an alarm clock or a phone call. It just happened automatically. It was like God calling to him, saying, "Sean, it's time for you to wake up and start my work."

The next morning when he woke up at the Blue Coyote, he saw the sun shining in his window. His first thought was that he would be late for Mass. When he became oriented, he realized the sun looked like it had been up for hours. He checked the bedside clock, which read 10:00 a.m. He couldn't believe it. He hadn't slept that long in years and he felt very rested. The yearning in his groin that always preceded his desire for a new young boy was gone as was his craving for the morning wine at Mass. This was his first morning without Mass; his first morning as an ex-priest; his first morning without alcohol.

He hoped that this might be a new beginning. Maybe without the constant cravings he could find peace of mind, which had eluded him ever since he could remember. Maybe he was being given a chance at redemption. Maybe the God he had prayed to for so many years was indeed answering his prayers.

He took a shower, shaved, and quickly repacked the few things he had taken out of his suitcase. A little over 24 hours; was that all it had been? From the depths of despair to this wonderful feeling of hope? Well, he knew God worked in mysterious ways and this sure seemed to be one. Whatever was going on, he welcomed it with open arms and stepped out of the motel room, leaving behind the cool, refreshing air-conditioning of the room.

He put his battered suitcase in the trunk of his car and checked out. "Have a good day, Father," the beautiful young woman said. "Drive carefully." *Yes*, Sean thought as he turned onto the highway, *I think it's going to be a good day.*

CHAPTER 16

A few months later, standing in front of the mirror as he went through the daily ritual of shaving, Sean thought back to how different his life was now from what it had been. The reflection in the mirror showed a man with smooth skin and clear eyes. The broken veins in his cheeks had disappeared and his former pallid complexion was rosy. He looked like a very healthy middle-aged man.

His abstinence from alcohol had caused many changes to take place in his life, surprising him more than anyone else. The first couple of weeks had been rough, no denying it. But strangely, as he stood here this morning, he had absolutely no desire for alcohol or the companionship of young boys. It was adjusting to a life that was not centered around the Church that he found so difficult. After a few days back at the family home in El Monte, he knew Thomas Wolfe had been right with his novel *You Can't Go Home Again*. As he had expected, the family's first born had not been warmly welcomed when he returned to the homestead. He needed to find a place where he could make a fresh start. The past was still alive in El Monte and he was no longer a part of that past.

Sean had remained friends with a couple of priests he'd met in seminary school who had been assigned to the Denver diocese. He had visited them several times over the years and discovered that he liked Denver. There was no denying the city's beauty. While he'd never considered himself much of a physical person, he had enjoyed skiing the couple of times his friends had talked him into joining them on a short ski trip to the nearby Rocky Mountains. Denver was a city that revolved around skiing.

When he made the decision to leave El Monte for good, he called his old friends in Denver, mentioning that he had left the church for personal reasons and that he was thinking of moving to Denver. If they knew what had happened to him, they never mentioned it. They immediately asked him to come to Denver and help them with a charitable project. They explained to him that a large donor in their church had a family member who had been greatly helped by the treatment he had received at a counseling center. The donor wanted to set up a non-profit outpatient counseling clinic, but he didn't want it to be church-oriented. Since his friends were both Catholic priests, they could hardly open up a clinic and not have it be a part of the church, but Sean could. Very soon, he was on his way to Denver.

He couldn't believe his luck. Almost immediately upon his arrival in Denver, Sean found himself employed as the lead psychologist and director of the non-profit clinic his friends had told him about. Although it was not yet open to the public, it was nearing completion. Sean immediately became immersed in the numerous details involved in getting it ready to open its doors.

Just as the donor wished, it was to be non-religious in nature. There would be three other psychologists, one who would deal with young people, one who would deal with the large local homeless population, and one who would deal with individuals and families facing the challenges of Alzheimer's. Sean was to oversee the three psychologists and also be available for private consultations. It was similar to the counseling he had done as a priest, but the money was a lot better.

He bought a condominium with a view of the Rocky Mountains. It felt strange to have so many "things" after leading such a spartan lifestyle for so long. He needed furniture, kitchen items, and linens. For the first time in his life, he had to make decorating decisions regarding colors and motifs. He found he really liked to cook and spent many nights unwinding from the day in front of his stove, carefully following the directions of a food expert he had seen on TV.

But the strangest thing of all, the thing he still had trouble even admitting to himself, was that he was attracted to one of the female psychologists he had hired. Jeanne was her name and she had spent her whole life in Denver. She'd attended local schools and ultimately obtained a Master's Degree in Psychology at Denver University. She put herself through school teaching skiing during the winter months and working as a fly fishing guide during the summer. She was in her early 40s, had never been married, was athletic, fit, and had the smoldering sex appeal of the classic American outdoor woman.

Sean first met Jeanne when he interviewed her. During the initial interview Sean mentioned that he had enjoyed skiing the few times he had been. He thought little of it until a few months later when Jeanne asked if he'd like to come skiing with her after New Year's. Jeanne said that was the best time to ski, right after the local schools had started back up after the holidays and the crowds on the slopes had disappeared. Sean told her he'd like to try it, but to remember that he was a beginner and she was an expert.

The day Sean spent with Jeanne on the slopes was one of the most enjoyable days he could ever remember. Jeanne's parents had been alcoholics and she refused to drink. Although Sean had no desire now for alcohol, it just made his developing friendship with Jeanne that much easier. Under her guidance, he discovered he was a passable skier. It was an enchanting day, a day that Sean would never forget. Several more days together followed, each just as enjoyable as the first.

As if to counterpoint how wonderful his new life was, occasionally Sean would wake up in the middle of the night, drenched in sweat as he slowly came out of a nightmare from his past. Young boys and vodka – the remembrances terrified him. Whenever the nightmares occurred, he swore to himself that no matter what, he would never go back to that way of life. He would rather die.

Long ago Sean had come to terms with the fact that he was a homosexual. Now he was beginning to question it. Could it be that since he had been forbidden by the Church to marry or have sexual relations with women, he had simply found another outlet, one not suitable in mainstream society, but one that was often quietly condoned by the Church? Was that what had caused this compelling interest in young boys?

A couple of months after they had first gone skiing, Sean admitted to himself that he'd fallen in love with Jeanne and he knew he had to tell her about his past. To go any further in their relationship without telling her would not only be unfair to her, it went completely against the honesty that was integral to the counseling programs they sponsored each week. To take ownership of whatever your problems and shortcomings were was a very important element in healing and moving on. With that thought in mind, Sean invited Jeanne to have dinner with him at his home.

After a wonderful meal of braised short ribs, homemade bread, spinach salad, and a dessert of lemon meringue pie, Sean said, "Jeanne, there's something I need to tell you. Actually there are several things I need to tell you. The first one is that I love you. You've come to mean everything to me. I never thought something like this would happen to me, but it has. However, this may be the only time you'll ever hear me say that because the other things I need to tell you may destroy any feelings you might have for me." He wrung his hands as he spoke to her, clearly nervous and agitated.

"Sean, wait," Jeanne said. "If you're going to tell me how you were defrocked for seducing young boys and about your alcoholism, I know all about it. I had you checked out completely before I ever agreed to work at the clinic for you. I will also tell you that the man who did those things is not the man I've come to know and love. We all would like to change things in our past. You're not alone, but I love a man who cares about people, who gets up each day wondering how he can make the world a better place, a man who loves the beauty of nature and takes great pleasure in cooking. Sean, I love you for who you are now, not what you've been."

"You knew all about my past and you still agreed to work for me?" Sean asked incredulously.

"Yes," Jeanne said, "and I've been waiting for you to tell me you love me for quite a while. Come, you can begin to show me as well." Jeanne stood up, took his hand, and led him to the bedroom.

Sean's mind was spinning. She knew and now she wanted him to make love to her. He had never been with a woman. What if he made a fool of himself? Even if his past hadn't ruined the relationship, the next hour very well might.

Jeanne was no stranger to the carnal world and deftly guided Sean in the beginning. Sean's male instincts gradually kicked in and as the heat of the moment grew, with a willing and warm woman under him, he climaxed with guttural, animal sounds. Afterwards, Jeanne gently guided his hand, helping her to climax as well. Both were perspiring heavily as they lay in the warm aftermath of their lovemaking.

"Jeanne, I know it's sudden and unexpected, but I want to marry you. I'm not getting any younger; I know what I want and what I want is you. Please say you'll be my wife."

"Yes, yes, yes," Jeanne screamed. To his utter surprise, she jumped on top of him and rhythmically stroked him to a stage of excitement he had never experienced before, feeling the uncontrollable heat for the second time that night. When they made love again, Sean knew to hold back, letting Jeanne climax before he did. He thought he could become quite good at this. As they lay locked in each other's arms, Jeanne whispered to him, "When can we get married?"

"As soon as possible. Why wait? Let's go to that little church we passed on our ski trip. Let's do it right away." Sean pulled her close and vowed he would do everything he could to deserve her faith and love. "Jeanne, spend the night and move in with me tomorrow. I want to be with you every moment. At our age, there's no reason to wait."

Jeanne and Sean never spent a night apart from that moment on. His days were filled helping people, something he passionately loved. He loved Jeanne just as passionately and proved it to her every night, sometimes several times a night. It was the best of times for Sean.

CHAPTER 17

Maria spent most of the four hour ride back to Irvine making lists. Fortunately, their condominium was small, so their furniture would easily fit into a U-Haul truck. The old man at the motel had very little furniture in the house behind the motel and from what Maria had seen, there was nothing there she would want. She needed to pack the kitchen items, bedding, and their clothes. She made a note to drop off her work clothes at the church, thinking it rather fitting that the "rich lady" clothes she still had would be going back to the church. Jeans and tees would be her new wardrobe staple.

Moore Labs had a dress code which required that all of the scientists who worked there wear ties. They didn't have to wear suits because of their extensive work in the labs, but Sidney Moore wanted them to look professional, so even under their lab coats they wore ties. Maria made a note to donate most of Jeffrey's ties to the church as well.

Late in the day they were back in Irvine. Jeffrey called the real estate broker who had originally sold them the condominium and made an appointment to meet with him the following day to put their unit on the market. Next, he called a U-Haul center and made arrangements to rent a truck in two days with a proviso that he would drop it off in Blythe after they unpacked at the motel. In the meantime, Maria drove around the neighborhood getting cardboard boxes from several stores and began to pack up the household goods.

That night, the enormity of what they were about to do kept Maria from sleeping. The old aging fears returned, looming larger than ever. What if Jeffrey couldn't get the extracts he needed to make the hormone? Would the desert air cause her to age? What about exposure to the sun and wind? Would the physical work that she would be doing cause her to age? The days of being inside a building protected from the elements would be gone. Would her skin become leathery and lined because she would be living in a place where the furnace ran full time in the winter and the air-conditioner ran constantly in the summer? Maria and Jeffrey rarely used their furnace or air-conditioner in Irvine. She worried what such a sudden change would have on her physical appearance. Finally, she fell asleep, letting her future rest in God's hands, just as her mother and the church had taught her to do so long ago.

They were up early on Sunday, preparing for what they knew was going to be a very busy day. Jeffrey was to meet with the realtor and then go see his parents, telling them what he and Maria had decided to do. Meanwhile, Maria cleaned out the refrigerator and the pantry. She decided to take a few refrigerator items in a cooler with them, knowing she and Jeffrey wouldn't have time to stock up in Blythe the day they arrived at the motel. The rest of the food she packed up to take to her parents. When Maria had called and told them of their plans, they were not happy. They were very close to one another and Maria and Jeffrey spent a couple of nights each week at their home. This was going to be very hard on Elena and Fabian.

Next on her "to-do" list was the church. When she knocked on the "Outreach" door at the church, it was quickly opened by Judy Greer. "Maria, I haven't seen you for years. You don't look a day older than the last time I saw you! What's your secret? I've often thought about you, wondering how you were doing. Since your wedding, I've lost track of you. I guess we must be going to different church services. From the looks of you, your life must be going well."

"My life is going very well, thank you." Maria said. "Actually, my life is changing. That's why I'm here. Jeffrey and I bought a motel just off the 10 Freeway, out in the desert on the road between LA and Phoenix. He's got a bit of scientific burnout and we decided to do something entirely new. I'm really excited. I've got some boxes of clothes I'd like to donate to the church. Maybe they will help some young woman the way the 'rich lady's' clothes helped me. I don't think I'll need them in the desert."

"I wish you well, Maria. You're one of the few young women who ever made it out of the barrio. I'm happy we could help. The "rich lady" who donated the clothes the day you got your job was another one who made it out of the barrio. That's one reason she always donated so much. I always thought that maybe she bought clothes without ever wearing them just so she could give them to us. She wanted to help someone and it looks like she did. Her husband was transferred to San Francisco a few years ago and I haven't seen her since.

Guess there's kind of a lineage in these clothes. We'll see who gets them next."

Judy gave Maria a big hug and said, "I'll help you get the boxes from the car and when you get ready to open the motel, let me know the name and some information about it. If I hear of anyone who is going that way, I'll tell them to stop in and say hello. I really wish you all the best of luck. It sounds exciting!"

Maria drove back to the condo, arriving just in time to let in the professional cleaning crew that the realtor had been able to arrange on short notice. Actually, Maria was very glad he had. She was running out of time and if she had to do a deep clean on the condo, plus the packing, she'd be up all night. That was no way to start a new life!

Monday morning they looked around the condo for the last time, feeling a bit sad to be leaving it. Maria remembered how excited she had been when they bought it. It represented everything good about getting out of the barrio. There were no rats or gangs in Irvine. She remembered how happy and proud her mother had been of her. She and Jeffrey had carefully picked out each piece of furniture, each piece of linen, the kitchen items, and everything else that made a house a home. It had been their home for several years, a happy home. Now they were leaving for a new and uncertain life.

She looked back one last time with tears in her eyes. Out of the corner of her eye, she saw Jeffrey wipe something out of his eye. While the new was exciting, the old had been very, very comfortable.

CHAPTER 18

The drive from Irvine to the motel was uneventful. Jeffrey drove the U-Haul truck, while Maria followed in their van. Just as he had said he would, the old man was waiting for them, ready to leave, with his car packed.

"Here's them papers you wanted drawn up. Had my lawyer friend do it. This sheet of paper has the address and telephone number where I'll be if you need me. My lawyer friend will take care of the rest of the sale. You'll have to pay the balance of the sale price to him through an escrow account he's set up. I'm gettin' outta here. Hope this place makes you happier than it did me," the old man said.

He got into his rusted old Lincoln, lit a cigarette, and waved good-bye out of the broken window on the driver's side. He was sure that whatever waited for him in Montana was better than what had happened to him here. He left in a cloud of dust, glad to be rid of the place where his wife had died.

Maria and Jeffrey unpacked for the next couple of hours, moving the little furniture that was left in their new house outside. After they unloaded the U-Haul, they packed up the old man's furniture to take to the Goodwill in Blythe the next day on their way to return the U-Haul.

Exhausted, they ate what Maria had brought in the cooler and got into the bed they'd made. They could hear the desert wind howling outside their window. The stars in the sky provided the only light and they shone brilliantly. It was cold and desolate in the desert winter. Even though the howling wind was a foreign, eerie sound, it was strangely comforting. Nothing mattered but that they were alone in the desert and they were together. They snuggled, eager for the warmth of the other, and soon both fell into a deep sleep.

At 2:15 a.m., Maria was awakened by the sound of the roaring wind which had intensified. *Oh well*, she thought, *as long as I'm awake I might as well go to the bathroom*. She didn't want to wake Jeffrey so when her eyes had adjusted to the darkness, she made her way into the bathroom. The full moon shone through the small window, bathing the bathroom in a soft light. Walking the few steps to the toilet, she passed by the medicine cabinet mirror and stopped. It was cracked in the center in a jagged line and as she looked in the mirror, it was as if she was looking at two people.

By some strange play of the moonlight, the face she saw on the right side of the crack was exactly as she looked now, but gasping involuntarily, she stared at the left side of the crack and saw herself as she would look twenty years from now. She stood stone still, rooted to the spot. Several minutes went by while she simply stared, looking first to the right side of the crack, then to the left. She realized what she was seeing was her future if Jeffrey failed to get the extracts he needed for the hormone. She continued to stare into the broken mirror, becoming more and more terrified. In a few minutes, the light changed and both sides of the cracked glass merged, reflecting her as she was now, young and beautiful. She breathed a sigh of relief.

As she got back in bed, she could feel her heart racing and in that moment she knew she would do whatever was necessary to make sure that Jeffrey kept her looking young. She didn't want to look old. She refused to accept aging and swore it would never happen. A cold tingle of fear ran down her back. The mere thought of getting old terrified her. *No, I'm not going to let that happen*, she thought as she finally drifted off to sleep.

CHAPTER 19

This was not fun. This was not how it was supposed to be. Weddings were supposed to be joyous occasions. Just before Jorge and Luisa Ortega boarded the flight from Rio to Los Angeles, they discovered that all of the Southern California airports were shut down due to an air controller's strike. They were finally able to get a flight to Phoenix with a two hour layover in Miami where they cleared Immigration and Customs. From Phoenix, they were to drive a rental car to Laguna Beach, located on the coast, south of Los Angeles.

Luisa's sister, Selena, was getting married in Laguna Beach in three days. Jorge and Luisa had planned on leaving with the rest of the family a week ago, but, as usual, Jorge had gotten tied up with his business in the Amazon. Luisa could have predicted something would happen. It always did. With Jorge, business came first. Jorge and his father, Tomas, owned a huge gold mining operation located in one of the most remote areas of the Amazon. It was a wild and lawless area. With gold prices on the world market approaching $1,800 per ounce, their efforts were well compensated. The Ortega mining operations were estimated to hold thirty percent of the known gold reserves in the world.

Presently, they were working at a furious pace

trying to get it out of the earth and out of the Amazon as fast as possible in order to take advantage of the spike in world gold prices. The mining, refining, and transporting of gold was a long, difficult process. The mines operated by Jorge and his father were massive open pits, hundreds of feet deep. The bottom of the pit, where the gold was located, was often flooded with four to six feet of polluted and sometimes toxic water. At any one time, hundreds of miners would be working in the pit, operating heavy equipment as well as hand tools.

It was very dangerous work and accidents and even deaths were common occurrences. A lot of the gold from the mines was stolen by the miners. There were tales of the Brazilian natives, who made up the major part of the work force at the mines, trying to escape with the gold by swimming across the river. The river was home to both crocodiles and swarms of piranhas, fierce flesh-eating fish that could reduce a full-sized man to nothing but bones in a matter of minutes. The rivers of the Amazon carried many dangers.

The local and national newspapers, constantly writing exposes about the poor working conditions at Ortega Mines, had not been kind to Jorge and his father. There also were stories about how the Ortegas were damaging the environment with reckless and harmful mining practices. These "attack pieces" in the press seemed to be never-ending. It had gotten to the point where Luisa just told people Jorge traveled a lot with his job. She never told them about the nature and extent of his business operations. She was tired of always having to defend his business. When Jorge returned to their home in Rio, after spending some time at the mines in the Amazon, he was drained and emotionally spent with the constant strain of dealing with the natives, the government, and the environmentalists, not to mention his father who could be a hard taskmaster. Traveling to California for a wedding was the last thing he wanted to do.

After two long flights and no sleep, Jorge was exhausted. His mind kept churning. How was he going to be able to get the gold they needed for their investors out of the Amazon? He continued to think of the investors and his father and they were not happy thoughts. And now this, the long drive in the rental car. The drive to Laguna Beach would be nearly six hours and Jorge had not driven in a long, long time. He and Luisa had a driver in Rio and Luisa had never learned to drive.

They took the shuttle bus to the rental car agency at Sky Harbor airport in Phoenix where Jorge showed them his international driver's license. The SUV seemed huge after the Ferrari his driver drove when he was in Rio. He took the wheel and began the long drive. The evening rush hour traffic only added to his exhaustion and stress.

On the drive across the desert, Jorge continued to worry about the business. He was tense and filled with stress as he thought about how their house of cards could collapse. Even though the gold business was very lucrative, at the moment the financial affairs of the business were stretched pretty thin. Banks had begun to press Ortega & Ortega for payment and he was constantly worried that there would be some disaster in the mines or that the world financial markets would change and gold prices would collapse. The Ortegas had borrowed heavily in order to get the gold out of the mines. As he drove west towards California and the miles melted away behind him, Jorge thought he couldn't go on like this much longer. He knew he needed to find a way to distance himself from the problems associated with the mines. He made a vow that, somehow, he would find a way to deal with the tension he was constantly under.

Like Jorge, Luisa was also dealing with stress in her life. But her kind of stress was much different. Hers was self-inflicted. Luisa's way of dealing with stress had developed into a nasty little habit. Between the bad press, dealing with the mining operations and Jorge's stress, it seemed the only thing she had any control over these days was deciding what she would put in her mouth. Huge amounts of food soothed her. She started to gain weight, something she had fought all her life.

When she had been younger and in college, a friend had told her that if you threw up what you ate, you could eat anything. She had dismissed the whole idea as nauseating, but recently, she had been so frustrated about her weight, she decided to try it. She soon discovered that her friend had been right. She could eat anything she wanted as long as she put her finger down her throat afterwards, causing her to throw up. An added bonus was that for the first time since she could remember, she didn't have to worry about her weight. Luisa knew what she was doing probably wasn't good for her body. She'd read enough about bulimia to know that it could have some adverse effects on the body and teeth if it was done for a long time, but she didn't plan on doing it that long.

While Jorge worried about the gold mines, Luisa worried about how she could throw up on this trip without anyone finding out. She knew Jorge would not condone what she was doing, and she didn't think anyone else would either. It was her little secret. She liked being able to eat anything she wanted. Binging and purging had become a constant way of life for her.

As they drove west in the darkening night, Luisa thoughts turned to her sister and the upcoming wedding. Selena had traveled to the United States to attend college on the East Coast. While she was there, she met and fell in love with Jim Henderson. They both planned to attend law school at the University of Southern California.

Selena visited Jim's family in Los Angeles and promptly fell in love with Southern California. The proximity to the ocean and the high energy and action-packed lifestyles of the Los Angeles residents reminded her of Rio. They finished law school together, passed the bar, and began making their wedding plans. Jim was to be the fourth generation to work at the family-owned law firm of Henderson and Henderson, which was opening a branch office in Orange County. He and Selena were going to work at the new branch. They decided to settle in Laguna Beach and rented a condominium on a bluff overlooking the ocean.

An hour and a half after Jorge and Luisa left Sky Harbor airport, Jorge barely missed a car he was passing. He was beginning to take dangerous chances and Luisa was becoming concerned. She knew there was no way he was going to be able to make it all the way to Laguna Beach in his present sleep-deprived state. They needed to find a place to stop and spend the night.

"Jorge, pull into that motel up there, the Blue Coyote. I just saw a sign. We're in the middle of nowhere and you can't make it to Laguna Beach. There may be nothing else for miles and miles. You can get some sleep and we'll drive to Laguna Beach tomorrow. We're fine on time, so stopping here won't delay our plans for the wedding festivities."

Looking back, she wondered what their life would have been like if she hadn't uttered those fateful words. She didn't know that just sixty miles ahead of them, the sprawling resort cities of the Palm Springs area beckoned with every type of accommodation possible. Selena had planned the wedding with her careful thoroughness, but no one had anticipated the air controller's strike. Luisa had traveled with her mother to Southern California several times in the last year, helping Selena with the wedding details. She knew if they got in tomorrow, rather than tonight, it didn't matter. The rehearsal dinner was the day after tomorrow.

"You're right. I am exhausted. A few hours of sleep will really help me."

Jorge was always tired. He worked too hard and was under too much stress, none of which was helping their marriage or her chances of getting pregnant. It had been a long time since Jorge had even touched her. She loved him, but secretly she had begun to wonder if marrying him had been a mistake. They turned into the motel driveway, parked the car and entered the office.

"We need a room for the night. Do you have anything?" Jorge asked the lovely young brunette behind the desk.

"I have one room left. You look like you could use some sleep. It's so quiet here, you'll be asleep in no time," the woman said. "Just fill out this registration form. I'll show you to your room and our refreshment area where you can get something to eat before you retire for the night."

"This will be fine," Jorge said. "It's warm and the air-conditioner feels wonderful. Thank you. I think we'll get something to eat and then some much needed sleep."

Luisa didn't know what to do. Usually after she ate, she immediately went into the bathroom and threw up. For some strange reason, tonight, she didn't feel the need. *Well, that's for the best,* she thought. *It would really be tricky in the bathroom with Jorge nearby.*

An hour later, they turned off the bedside lamp, surprisingly relaxed, and fell asleep instantly. The quiet humming and the coolness of the air-conditioner lulled them both into a deep, dreamless sleep.

Later in the night, Luisa stirred, realizing that Jorge was drawing her to him. She felt the long-forgotten bulge against her buttocks. Eagerly, she turned to him. Their lovemaking began softly and slowly. It had been so long that she had forgotten how he felt against her and in her. Rio, the Amazon, the gold, bulimia, all of the problems fell away as they began the timeless dance of love, reaching a crashing crescendo together. Afterwards, they held each other, once again falling into a deep and dreamless sleep, the coolness of the air-conditioner blowing softly over their heated bodies.

In the morning when Luisa awoke, she kept her eyes closed. She wanted this closeness, this feeling, to never end. As tired as they both had been, it had been a magical night. She knew that Jorge must feel the same way. She realized that the marriage had not been a mistake, that she really did love him. It was as simple as that. She vowed to be a better wife, to be more understanding about his business, to be more supportive and not add to his concerns.

Jorge slowly woke up to the sun streaming into the room. He rolled over, pulling Luisa once more to him. He wondered why it had been so long since they had made love. He wanted her again, just as much as he had earlier. Her warmth filled him with joy. Afterwards, he promised himself he would be a better husband; he would put her above the demands of his business.

"Luisa," he began, "I'm so sorry for what I've put you through this last year. You're far more important to me than my business. I have to travel, yes; it is part of the business, but I have been taking everything out on you. I'm sorry and I promise you it won't happen again. This morning, I feel like a changed man. I love you more than anything."

They dressed, eager to continue their trip to Southern California and the wedding. They both felt better than they had in a long time. It was unspoken, but both knew that there had been some form of magic in their room. They were grateful to have had the night together.

As they left their room, Luisa thought she could detect the faint smell of sandalwood. She was familiar with the scent from her years of yoga practice. Her teacher had often burned incense during the classes and sandalwood was her favorite scent. It brought back fond memories.

CHAPTER 20

Selena's wedding in Laguna Beach had been beautiful. Luisa and Jorge made the drive to Laguna Beach in plenty of time to help with the rehearsal dinner the following night. People kept telling them that they looked like the newlyweds and candidly, they felt that way.

Although Luisa had visited the coastal region of Southern California on her past trips, it was Jorge's first visit. He immediately knew he wanted to live there and started thinking about how he could do it. He knew he needed a little space away from his father. The business of mining and exporting gold from Brazil was difficult at best. The demand for gold from their mines far exceeded the supply and there was constant pressure put on him by his father and the company's customers to produce more and more gold. The environmental agencies made it all the more difficult because of their incessant demands and lawsuits to stop all mining operations in the Amazon. Jorge's father expected him to be at the mines outwitting the environmental agencies, the natives, and the Brazilian government. It was no wonder he had been so tired when he left Brazil, but he didn't feel tired now. In fact, he felt the best he had felt in years.

Making a spur of the moment and somewhat

impulsive decision, Jorge decided he would adopt a work schedule that would allow him to be in Brazil for two weeks a month and then in California the following two weeks. It seemed to be a workable solution and it still gave Jorge some breathing room. He insisted that they buy a house right away. Although Luisa was surprised at Jorge's sudden and seemingly impulsive decision to leave Rio and move to California, she readily agreed with his decision. Jorge's business, for all of its problems, had made him an unbelievably wealthy man; plus, he had inherited a great deal of money from his grandfather, an early discoverer of gold in Brazil. But if Jorge couldn't find the time to enjoy any of it, what was the point of being wealthy? Luisa and Jorge knew they could easily afford to make the move to California.

He and Luisa began looking for a home on the coast. They looked from Long Beach to Dana Point. Jorge wanted to live on the water and have a boat. The house had to be large enough to accommodate the many visitors they knew would be visiting from Brazil. Jorge and Luisa were from large families and there would be a never-ending stream of houseguests. They would be living near Disneyland and everyone wanted to see where Mickey Mouse lived.

They found the perfect house on the water in the Huntington Harbor area of Huntington Beach. There was a separate guest wing with two bedrooms and two bathrooms, a large "great room," and a full size kitchen. The main part of the house had four bedrooms and six bathrooms. The sixty-foot boat dock sealed the deal. The bedrooms were upstairs with harbor views as well as views of their swimming pool. The kitchen was a chef's dream with two ovens, two refrigerators, a center island with a range and sink, and a walk-in pantry for storage. It was everything that Luisa or their cook would ever want.

By a lucky turn of fate, the present owners were moving to Northern California and preparing to lay off their maid and cook. Jorge and Luisa hired them and were quite pleased with the house, boat slip, and the built-in services of a maid and cook.

The house had been on the market for a long time. The owners were anxious to sell and readily agreed to a thirty-day escrow. Jorge and Luisa made arrangements to fly back to Rio to put their affairs in order and decide what personal items needed to be shipped to California. Jorge opted to keep the Rio condominium, as he needed somewhere to stay when he was there. They couldn't wait to get settled in their new home. They both had learned English in school, but an English tutor was going to be pretty high on the priority list when they got settled.

A couple of weeks after she returned to Rio to put their affairs in order and get ready for the move to Southern California, Luisa woke up one morning with an upset stomach. Luz, her maid, brought Luisa her usual breakfast of fresh fruit, lightly buttered toast and coffee. Luisa took one look at it and promptly went in the bathroom and threw up. She wracked her brain trying to remember what she had eaten for dinner the previous night. She recalled that she'd eaten grilled flank steak, salad, and steamed vegetables. *Nothing strange there*, she thought. *It's pretty much what I always have when I'm at home.*

Some would call Luisa voluptuous, but she simply thought of herself as being round, like her father, Diego, with a tendency to gain weight. Luisa was terrified of ever returning to her bulimia and purging days. She had easily given them up after her stay at the Blue Coyote Motel, but she never wanted to binge and purge again. Overall, her life was almost idyllic and she had no desire to go back to her former bulimic habit. She was almost neurotic when it came to eating and watching her weight. Very little food ever passed her lips unless it had some redeeming quality. No, it couldn't be last night's dinner. *Maybe I'm getting the flu*, she thought as she got back in bed. She told Luz to wake her in a couple of hours, glad that Jorge was deep in the Amazon so she couldn't expose him to whatever it was she was getting. He was exposed to enough dangers in the Amazon and he didn't need her adding to his problems.

Luisa slept fitfully for a couple of hours, waking up when her maid quietly entered her room. Suddenly she was ravenous. She said, "Luz, please,

I'm starving. Make me some torresmo from the beef last night; bring me a big glass of milk and hurry!"

She spent the rest of the day tying up loose ends in preparation for the move. Late in the afternoon, she suddenly remembered that she had promised her parents she would join them at their home for dinner that night and she knew she'd better hurry if she was going to make it on time.

"Welcome, darling," her mother, Juanita, said, "Come in. I have some exciting news for you. At least I hope it's exciting for you!" Juanita was beautiful in a mature way. Tall and slender with silver hair pulled up into a bun, she was the picture of moneyed elegance. Diamond earrings and a diamond and gold necklace highlighted her bronze complexion.

Luisa's father, Diego, was as round as his wife was slender. His skin was ruddy and his hair was still as black as it had been when he was a small boy. They were an odd pair. Luisa's mother was often featured on the society and fashion pages of Brazilian magazines and newspapers, while her father looked like he should be working on the docks. Not only were they total opposites in their looks, their backgrounds had been just as opposite.

Juanita's family had been among the early settlers in Rio with a great deal of wealth and social status. Diego came from a family of dockworkers, just scraping by to put food on the table. He had made it out of the slums of Rio, going to the local university and then to law school. He began representing the unions and their injured workers, particularly those who had been hurt while working on the docks. The law firm he had founded had done extremely well, now employing well over seventy-five lawyers. As it grew, it expanded far beyond the docks to white-collar crimes and divorces, which had become rampant in Brazil. Diego worshipped Juanita. He still couldn't believe she was his wife, even after all these years. It may have been a marriage of opposites, but it worked very well for them.

He handed Luisa a glass of wine as he kissed her on each check. She normally loved a glass or two of wine, but looking at it, she could feel her stomach turn. "Thanks, Papa, but it doesn't sound good right now. Maybe later," she said. Turning to her mother, she asked, "What's the news? You're positively beaming."

"I am so excited. Your father and I have decided to move to California to be near you; first Selena and now you. We contacted the real estate agent you bought your house from and she told us about a house for sale that's only a block from yours. It's not on the water, but we've never been particularly interested in owning a boat. The house is smaller than yours, but it will be fine for us and Selena's home isn't far away. We talked to a real estate agent here and we're listing our house tomorrow. What do you think?"

Luisa could hardly believe it. She was very close to

her parents and the only reservation she had about her pending move was leaving her parents.

"This is the best news I think I've ever heard. I didn't want to tell either one of you, but I've spent so many hours crying because of leaving you. And now you'll be near me. I am so happy!" She hugged each of them and couldn't wait to tell Jorge the wonderful news. His relationship with his father, Tomas, had become increasingly difficult after the death of Jorge's mother. Tomas had never really recovered from her death from breast cancer at the young age of fifty-two. Luisa's parents had loved Jorge like a son from the moment they had met him. The rest of the evening was spent talking about the move. It was new beginnings and a very exciting time for all of them.

The next morning Luz brought in Luisa's usual breakfast. Once again, Luisa took one look at it and quickly made her way into the bathroom. She slept the rest of the morning and woke up very hungry. *What is going on?* Luisa wondered. *It's almost like I am having morning sickness. Surely I couldn't be pregnant. Jorge has been so busy, but there was that magical night at that motel outside of Phoenix. What if?*

She quickly dressed, called her driver, and asked him to take her to the nearest drugstore. She bought a home pregnancy testing kit. As soon as she was back in her bathroom, she peed on the stick. The result window on the home pregnancy test clearly showed a plus, indicating she was pregnant. For a long time she stood looking at it in disbelief. From the time she and Jorge had gotten married eight years ago, she had wanted a baby and now the test showed she was pregnant. When she could trust herself to speak, she dialed her gynecologist and made an appointment for the following day. She wanted to be sure before she told Jorge and he was due to return from the Amazon in three days.

The next morning was a repetition of the past two days. Fortunately, by early afternoon she felt better and rode to her doctor's appointment in high spirits. The waiting room was filled with expectant mothers-to-be. In the past when she had waited for the nurse to call her name for her annual female exam, she resented every pregnant woman in the room. Why were all these women pregnant when she couldn't conceive? It just didn't seem fair. Every year she was more disappointed than the year before.

This time, however, she felt like an insider. She knew at a very deep level that at long last, she was pregnant. The exam and the test that followed confirmed it. Her doctor gave her a long list of things to do and not do. Her only question was about traveling. Could she fly in a couple of weeks? The doctor assured Luisa that as long as she rested before and after, she would be fine.

She left the doctor's office resolved to do everything she could to make her body the best vehicle any baby could ever have. She instructed her driver to take her to the Galleria, where the most exclusive shops in Rio were located. She knew there was a very elegant maternity shop there and several thousand dollars later, she returned to her car, arms loaded down with bags.

Luisa could hardly wait to tell Jorge and her parents. She decided to ask them to have dinner with Jorge and her the night he returned from the Amazon. She would tell all of them at the same time. When she returned home, she asked her cook, Manny, to come to her room. She wanted to give him instructions about preparing a special dinner for her parents and Jorge when he returned home in two days.

Luisa was familiar now with the routine of her morning sickness. The thing that got her through the first couple of hours was knowing that she would be fine by noon. She was sure she was beginning to gain weight from the huge amounts of food she was putting away at lunch and dinner. Manny and Luz took notice and privately had many conversations about Luisa. They were pretty sure she was pregnant and they wondered if she knew, but they knew better than to ask her. Luisa had a fiery temper and was a very private person. She would tell them when she was ready.

Two days later, promptly at 6:00 p.m., Jorge arrived home, driven by his chauffeur in the red Ferrari. He walked into the large entry hall, dropped his suitcase, and wrapped his arms around Luisa.

"I'm so glad to be home. I missed you so much. How are you?" he asked.

She didn't tell him just how great she was. That would come later. "I'm fine, just glad you're home. Luz is fixing you a drink. Go upstairs, wash up, and change into some comfortable clothes. Mom and Dad are joining us for dinner and Manny has prepared all of your favorites: stuffed sirloin steak, scalloped potatoes, Caesar salad, green beans with slivered almonds, fresh baked bread, and for dessert, a chocolate mousse."

Jorge pulled back and looked at her, "What's the occasion? You know we've always reserved that meal for special occasions. Are you keeping something from me?"

"Of course not. I just want you to be glad you're home. And it is a special occasion; you're home." Luisa playfully pushed him up the stairs and went into the kitchen to see how Manny was doing with the preparations.

"Manny, what am I going to do without you?" Luisa said. "I depend on you. Are you sure you won't reconsider and come with us to California?"

"I'll miss you for sure, Miss Luisa, but my family is here. Everything I know is here. I have to stay, but it sure won't be the same without you and Senhor Ortega." Manny looked like he would cry and with Luisa's raised hormone levels, she knew she would for sure. She quickly walked out of the kitchen into the dining room and busied herself lighting candles and rearranging the table flowers.

She heard her parents drive up. Even though her father was now "of counsel" at the law firm he had founded, a fancy name law firms used when a wealthy partner semi-retired, he had kept his driver and much of their household staff. Like Manny and Luz, they, too, would not be accompanying her parents to California. Luisa knew that the move meant lots of changes, but the loss of their trusted household staffs might be the hardest.

She greeted her parents as Luz handed each of them a glass of wine. Jorge came down the stairs and warmly embraced them. They talked of Jorge's most recent adventures in the Amazon, the move to California, and news of friends and family until it was time to sit down for dinner. Luisa had refrigerated some champagne, and just as they were being seated, she asked Manny to put it in an ice bucket, letting him in on her secret.

He was thrilled for her and it made his decision to stay in Rio even harder. As Luz served the salad to the four of them, he carried in the champagne bucket and placed it next to Luisa.

"Manny, would you please pour some champagne into each of our glasses?" Luisa said.

Jorge turned and looked at her. "What's going on? Not only is this a special occasion dinner, but now, champagne? Luisa, is there something we need to know?"

Luisa lifted up her glass. "Please, all of you lift your glasses. Let's toast the future father, Jorge, and the new grandparents, Diego and Juanita. I'm pregnant!" Luisa touched the rim of the glass to her lips, but following her vow to make her body the best environment she could for her baby, she traded the champagne for Perrier.

Juanita and Jorge both started to cry and Diego was just about to when Luisa stopped them all. "Please, no tears, even if they're tears of joy. I want smiles and laughter."

It was by far the happiest day of Luisa and Jorge's life.

CHAPTER 21

Maria and Jeffrey located a contractor in Blythe who gave them what they felt was a fair estimate for the work they couldn't personally do: tiling the floors, redoing the bathrooms, kitchen electrical work, lighting, upgrading the air-conditioning and heating, fixing the fence, installing solar panels, and partitioning and building out the basement. The price went up as they discovered other things that needed doing, but that was to be expected and the contractor, whose name was Jim Sullivan, seemed to be honest. He and his crew began working on the motel a few days after Maria and Jeffrey hired him.

Maria made a couple of trips to Phoenix for paint, bedding, towels, furniture, window coverings, and kitchen and serving items. On one of her trips to Phoenix, she took a break and wandered into a Native American art gallery. Her attention was immediately drawn to a 5' x 7' painting of a blue coyote on the far side of the gallery. She and Jeffrey had spent many hours throwing motel names back and forth and they were still undecided as to what to call their newly acquired motel. When she saw the painting, she knew. They would name it the "Blue Coyote Motel." The painting would be perfect for the office.

"Excuse me," Maria said to the handsome young Native American man sitting at the desk. "I'm interested in that painting. Can you tell me something about it?" Jet black hair hung to his shoulders and his complexion was the color of mahogany. Sparkling white teeth shone when he smiled. He was dressed in a crisp white shirt, blue jeans, and the most beautiful turquoise and silver belt Maria had ever seen.

"Oh, that's the Blue Coyote," the young man said. "In my tribe it translates to 'turning in the darkness.' It's part of the creation myth and we consider it sacred. It was painted by a tribal member whose reservation is not too far from here."

How perfect for a motel, Maria thought, "*turning in the darkness*" *and isn't that just what travelers will be doing when they stop to stay at the motel*? She could hardly contain her excitement. "How much do you want for it and do you have any other paintings of the Blue Coyote?" Maria asked.

"It's listed at $500.00, but I think the artist would take $450.00. And yes, I have several other paintings of the Blue Coyote by the same artist in our storage area," the young man said, realizing that this might be a very good day for the gallery.

"I'll take it and I'd like to see the others. I need eight paintings in all, if you have them."

"Give me a few minutes to find the others. May I get you some water or coffee?" the young man asked.

"No, thanks. I'm fine. I'll wait here and look around. You have so many wonderful things," Maria said, walking slowly through the gallery.

She found a number of Native American art pieces which spoke to her. On an oval wooden pedestal, there was a marble carving of a woman with her hair pulled back in the traditional Navajo style. She found brightly colored geometric rugs that would be beautiful on the tiled floors of the motel, Navajo wedding baskets, squash blossom necklaces, and other pieces she thought were incredibly beautiful. Maria wanted to buy a number of them, particularly the rugs. She promised herself that she would return when she had more time and a better idea of what she could use at the motel. For now, the Blue Coyote paintings would be perfect. She knew Jeffrey would be pleased, although he had left most of the decorating to her, preferring to supervise the work in his soon-to-be lab.

"I can't believe this. We have seven others, but they're a little smaller, 3' x 4'. Each one is somewhat different from the others, but they're all of Blue Coyote and all by the same artist. The price is $375.00 per painting, but since you're buying so many, I can do better on the price. The total for all eight would be $3,125, but I'll take $2,750 for all of them," the young man said.

Maria took out her debit card and paid for them. "I really like some of the other pieces that you have on display, but I need to think about what I can use.

I'll be back in a few weeks. You've been so helpful, thank you."

"If you call before you come and tell me what you're interested in, I'd be happy to have some pieces ready for you. I hope you enjoy the Blue Coyote paintings. May I ask what you'll be doing with so many?" the young man asked.

"Yes. My husband and I bought a motel just off Interstate 10 about an hour and a half from here. We're remodeling it. It doesn't seem like there are any others along that particular route. It's remote, but we think vacationers, traveling salesmen, and people who are tired after a long day of driving will stop and spend the night with us. We want to provide them with a really nice place to rest. Yes, I will call you the next time I come to Phoenix. Again, thanks, you've been most helpful!" Maria exclaimed.

The young man wrapped the paintings in bubble wrap and helped her load the Blue Coyote paintings in her van. She could hardly wait to get back to the motel and share with Jeffrey what she'd bought.

CHAPTER 22

The design, construction, and remodel of the laboratory space claimed every waking minute of Jeffrey's time. He told the contractor, Jim, what he wanted in his lab. He showed him how the basement needed to be divided into three main rooms with a small office. Jeffrey showed him where he wanted to place the back-up generator, running water, and sink. It was essential to Jeffrey that there was a built-in desk with a large television screen over it and a counter next to it for his microscope and other scientific equipment. The image on the microscope needed to be projected onto the television screen. He told Jim he had an idea for purifying air in the lab, then feeding it into the motel rooms, so he needed a large commercial grade air-conditioner to be put in the basement with vents leading to all the motel rooms, plus the main house, the office, the lab, and the refreshment area.

Jeffrey picked out the type of sink, the paint for the walls, the canisters he would need in the storage areas, and the cages for the laboratory test animals. He let Jim think that he would be involved in breeding dogs and any experiments done on the dogs would be done to improve the breed. No need to tell him what he would be doing to the rats he used in his tests and experiments.

Ideas for new drugs and new experiments were flooding Jeffrey's brain. He was constantly making notes and had even resorted to keeping a pen and pad next to his side of the bed, waking up several times in the night to jot down fresh ideas.

As the lab was nearing completion, Jeffrey sat down and began to make a timeline, deciding which experiments he wanted to start first. For several years, he had played around with an idea he had for a narcotic substance which could be pumped into the air people breathe, calming them and allowing them to feel happy and stress free. He had thought about it initially because of Maria's bouts with depression.

Jeffrey chose to call the drug he was making for Maria "Freedom" because it would free Maria from her bouts with depression. He decided to wait to tell her about it until he perfected it, but he was pretty sure he could do it. The more he thought about it, he determined it would be an airborne type of Xanax. If it worked as he envisioned, it could be administered to every person on the planet. It might even be responsible for bringing about world peace. *Imagine,* he thought, *there would be no more wars, hatred, discrimination, strife, terrorism, or dictators, because everyone on the planet would be exposed to Freedom.*

This new and exciting drug would allow people to be at their best at all times. They would be productive, happy, and free from anxiety, stress, and depression. He was quite familiar with Xanax, Prozac, and the other anti-anxiety drugs on the market, but they were nothing like the one he was planning. All of the products presently on the market had to be prescribed by a doctor and were intentionally taken by the patient. Freedom would be airborne and disbursed into the environment. People wouldn't know that they were taking a drug because it would be in the air. However, they would quickly begin to feel better once it was administered. He knew that technically it was a narcotic and narcotics of that type could only be prescribed by a licensed physician; all the better reason for no one to know what he was planning to develop in his lab. If he was successful, he knew he could sell Freedom for huge amounts of money.

He had read where sandalwood had been used in drugs in China and Tibet over 4,000 years ago. It was also frequently used in Native American ceremonies. Sandalwood incense was quite common and could be bought anywhere incense was sold. The scent of sandalwood would mask the odor of the other elements in Freedom and would be an integral part of his mixture. The odor of sandalwood was common in the Southwest, so no one would notice if he used it in Freedom.

The rest of the narcotic compound Jeffrey had in mind consisted of ingredients not available on the open market. Their sales in the United States were strictly regulated and controlled. The extracts he needed to make Freedom would be difficult for an individual to obtain. He also had to get the ingredients for the anti-aging hormone. He decided it was time for him to take a trip to Mexico. He remembered the name of a distributor who imported plants from the Amazon, distilled the plants, and shipped the processed end product to various distributors in the United States. It was the same distributor Moore Labs had used. Jeffrey didn't have the needed government permits to purchase the drugs in the United States as Moore Labs had been able to do; however, for the right price, anything was possible in Mexico.

CHAPTER 23

A few days later as he was driving to Sky Harbor airport in Phoenix, Jeffrey thought back to the last couple of months. He and Maria were getting close to opening the motel, his laboratory was almost finished and he was off to Mexico to get the products he'd need for the anti-aging hormone and procure the basic ingredients for his new Freedom drug. He felt good. He had been a little worried that the 24/7 motel arrangement with Maria might soon get old. But if anything, it had strengthened their relationship. Now he was about to begin working on an exciting experiment that was every bit as important as the anti-aging hormone.

Jeffrey was pleased that he'd thought to install a false bottom in his carry-on luggage so he could conceal the cash he'd need in Mexico. He knew he could get through the metal scanner at security with a large amount of cash, but Customs could pose a problem. Jeffrey had been to Mexico enough times to know that the searches they conducted upon arriving in Mexico were nothing like the ones conducted in the U.S. *But even so*, he thought, *I better be prepared in case I am searched*. He smiled, thinking of everything he had accomplished.

He parked his car at Sky Harbor airport and after clearing security, boarded the Aeromexico Airlines plane for Guadalajara. Jeffrey had read that the airline was having financial troubles, but you'd never know it from the completely full flight. In addition to the Mexicans returning to their homeland, there were a number of American women. Many of them looked like they might be candidates for cosmetic surgery at the American hospital in Guadalajara. Cosmetic surgery was a lot cheaper in Mexico than it was in the United States. One could get a nurse, a margarita, and luxurious accommodations while recuperating from cosmetic surgery, all at a quarter of the U.S. costs. Many American women had their "work" done in Mexico.

It was a smooth flight and Jeffrey was glad that over the years he had kept up his fluency in Spanish. He easily conversed with his seatmates and the flight attendant. Being able to speak Spanish, rather than having to use an interpreter, was going to make it a lot easier to deal directly with the supplier with whom he would soon be doing business.

As he stood in the Customs line, he felt himself beginning to perspire. He could feel the moisture under his arms and on his face. He hoped it didn't show. Even though it had seemed like such a good idea back in his lab, now that the line was moving, he was increasingly nervous about the false bottom in his carry-on. Then he realized he was going to be lucky. The Customs official was only searching every fourth person and so far, he, Jeffrey, wouldn't be that person. The searches being made were just as he remembered from earlier trips to Mexico—they were poorly done, lazy searches. The BIENVENIDOS sign on the wall caught his attention, reminding him he was in Mexico. The Customs official waved him through as the red light turned to green.

Jeffrey casually strolled out of the airport and made his way to the taxi stand. In smooth Spanish, he told the driver to take him to the Hilton Hotel in the city, about a thirty minute drive. He checked in and took the elevator to his room, which overlooked the hotel's pool and the brilliantly colored tropical plants in the garden. The pool was empty. It was still late winter in Guadalajara.

Jeffrey recalled the name of the drug distributor he would need and placed a call to Hernandez Compania. It wasn't a large company and he was able to make an appointment with the general manager for the next day.

Next, he called Maria and told her he had arrived, had been able to make an appointment with the man he needed to see, and expected to return home the next night. He unpacked his carry-on bag, hanging up the shirt he planned to wear in the morning. Mexican men did not dress casually when they conducted business. Jeffrey had worn a sport coat on the plane, which he would wear over the dress shirt with one of the few ties Maria had not donated to the church. He was ready for his meeting and was hopeful it would be productive.

Traveling was tiring. There was no way around it. Hurry up and wait. Hurry up and wait. The luxury of arriving at the last minute for a flight was no longer an option. A long line in security could easily result in a missed flight. He went to the Vinifera lounge in the hotel, sat down at the bar, and ordered a margarita, some chips, and a couple of tacos. By now it was 8:00 p.m. and he knew tomorrow was going to be a long day. Even though Guadalajara was two hours ahead in time and his body didn't feel that tired, he decided to go back to the room. After a good night's sleep he would be fresh for tomorrow's meeting.

The next morning, he showered, shaved, and as he got ready to put on his shirt, he discovered that one side of it was badly wrinkled. He needed to conduct this meeting from a position of power and a wrinkled shirt was not an option. Jeffrey quickly pressed the shirt, finished dressing, and rode the elevator down to the hotel dining room. After a breakfast of huevo chorizo scramble and jalapeno corn cakes, he walked a few blocks to the offices of the Hernandez Compania. Nothing had changed since the last time he had been in Mexico. There were unfinished buildings with exposed steel rebar, the constant sound of blaring horns, and streets filthy with litter, excrement, and mud. Young children were still on every corner begging for money and selling Chiclets.

Hernandez Compania was located on Rincon de Las Praderas. When he entered the low-lying industrial building, he told the receptionist that he had an appointment with Señor Jose Perez. A few minutes later, a door leading from the reception area opened and a handsome older man walked over to Jeffrey, introduced himself, and shook his hand. Sr. Perez was an elegant looking man with a mane of white hair surrounding his dark brown face. To Jeffrey, he looked to be part Mexican, part Indian. Although he wasn't very tall, he had the powerful build of someone who had spent a lot of time working out.

Sr. Perez asked Jeffrey to follow him. They walked down several long, narrow halls, finally entering a large office tastefully decorated with plush carpeting, Mexican artifacts, and the usual picture of a wife and children displayed prominently on the desk.

He told Sr. Perez that he was a scientist who was starting a company and would like to purchase some items from his company. He explained that he had applied to the US government for the necessary permits, but that it often took a long time to receive them and he was anxious to get started right away. He told Sr. Perez he could give him a large cash retainer today to apply as a draw against future purchases. Jeffrey said after he had spent the initial amount, he would again travel to Mexico and give Sr. Perez another cash payment to cover any future purchases.

Jeffrey knew that he couldn't ship or carry the items he needed into the United States. It would be illegal for them to be in his possession. Sr. Perez assured him that the items could be sent to his company's distribution center in California and then shipped to him. The drug companies were a powerful lobby in Washington D.C. and the agreement between Mexico and the United States, which had been made several years earlier, allowed the drugs to be shipped from Mexico to the various distribution points without any questions or inspections.

He took out a typed list of what he wanted. He had gone over it several times to make sure that everything he needed for the anti-aging hormone and other experiments would be included as well as several substitutes in case the experiments didn't go exactly as planned. Sr. Perez looked at the list and assured Jeffrey that the items would be delivered to him within a week to ten days.

Sr. Perez said the cost of the items on the list would be $45,000. Jeffrey opened his briefcase which contained bundles of bills. Each bundle contained $5,000. He carefully counted out nine bundles, $45,000. He deliberately let Sr. Perez glance inside the briefcase bottom to see that there was plenty of cash left after he extracted the $45,000. He wanted Sr. Perez to think he was a rich American with plenty of cash and would be back. Jeffrey told him no receipt would be necessary. He doubted the money would ever see the bookkeeping office of Hernandez Compania, but as long as he got what he wanted, he didn't care.

Before closing his briefcase, Jeffrey took out another $10,000 and handed it to Sr. Perez, saying, "When the shipment is delivered to me in the United States, I don't want any record made of the materials on the list or that they were delivered to me."

Sr. Perez smiled ever so slightly and said, "No problem, Sr. Brooks. We do this all the time." Just as Jeffrey thought, *corruption was still alive and well in Mexico. That's how things got done here. I didn't make the rules but I sure can play by them.* He knew the carrot insuring delivery would be the next $45,000 he would bring when he made his next trip to Mexico to get a resupply of the ingredients he needed for his experiments.

When he got back to his hotel, Jeffrey asked the concierge to make a reservation for him on the first flight back to Phoenix. He went up to his room and packed. The concierge had been able to book a direct flight from Guadalajara to Phoenix, which was leaving in three hours. He had time to get to the airport, check in, and get something to eat. He missed Maria and couldn't wait to get back to her and his lab. His meeting with Sr. Perez had gone well, even better than he had hoped. He had a secure source for the ingredients he would need and felt confident that he would succeed with his dream of producing an earth changing drug. Freedom was going to be made. He knew it would work. He couldn't wait until his shipment of requested materials arrived and he could get started.

CHAPTER 24

Jeffrey returned from Mexico eager to begin his experiments. However, there was no doubt in Maria's mind that being fired from Moore Labs had taken a toll on him. He had always struggled with feelings of being different from other people and some people thought he was slightly crazy, but those feelings seemed to have intensified in the last couple of months. He was having spurts of extremely long hours of work followed by overly long hours of sleep. He had always been meticulous in his grooming, but now it no longer seemed to be important to him. When they would talk, she noticed that his speech and thought processes seemed to be jumbled, and at times, incomprehensible.

Jeffrey had been taking medication for his manic-depressive condition for many years and he began to wonder if it was losing its potency. He was aware that he was alternating long hours of work with long hours of sleep. He was also aware that his personal grooming was becoming less important than his work in the lab.

"What's going on?" Maria asked one day. "Something is wrong. I know how difficult the Moore situation was for you, but you seem to have changed. I'm also worried about your sleeping. It seems like every time I wake up in the middle of the night, you're not there. I didn't know you before you started your medication, but I've read that people in manic states often don't sleep for days. I've also noticed that when you do sleep, it's sometimes for hours and hours."

"Maria, I was called 'Crazy Boy' when I was growing up. For some reason, all those god-awful childhood memories have been coming back to me. Maybe it's just a delayed reaction to the stress of being fired by Moore Labs," Jeffrey said. "As for not sleeping, I've had so much on my mind with building the lab, going to Mexico, and getting ready to conduct the experiments, sometimes I just can't seem to make myself sleep. When I do sleep, I want to get as much as I can so I'll be clearheaded when I conduct the experiments. Don't worry, I'll be fine once I get started on all the things I'm planning to do. Actually, I'm very excited. This is a transitional time for me." Secretly, he hoped that Freedom would help him as well.

Maria didn't have a good feeling after their conversation. She felt Jeffrey was beginning to spin out of control. Yet, maybe what he had told her was true. It couldn't have been easy to have everyone think you were crazy when you were a kid. And certainly there had been a lot of work and planning to do in the last couple of months. Maybe it was just a reaction to the stress he had been under. She decided to let it go for now and accept that this was just a temporary situation.

The complete shipment of drugs and supplies from the distribution center in California arrived as promised. Sidney had been true to his word. Two million dollars had been placed in Jeffrey's bank account the day after Jeffrey was fired. That money had become essential in view of the costs of remodeling the motel, building the lab, and buying the supplies he needed.

The laboratory was complete and was a dream which had come true. Jeffrey would often stand in the middle of the laboratory and marvel at what had been done. Shining metal counters gleamed under recessed overhead lights that could be dimmed or brightly lit by a touch of the switch. The walls had been soundproofed. Security doors and new stairs had been installed. One set led to the front of the motel, the other leading to the rear of the motel. He didn't want to encounter motel guests each time he went in and out of the lab. He looked around at the results of his elaborate planning and design, thinking of the cost overruns, but he just didn't care what it had cost. It was a state-of-the-art laboratory and he couldn't help but smile with satisfaction at what he had created and accomplished.

While Jeffrey was busy finishing up the lab, Maria was putting the final touches on the motel. The plumbing had been replaced, furniture delivered, and fresh white linens were on each neatly made bed with colorful Southwest style bedspreads. The bathrooms had been tiled and new fixtures installed. The small kitchen adjacent to the office and the one in their house had new appliances, cookware, ceramics, and glassware. The motel had been freshly painted, inside and out. A landscape nursery in Blythe had delivered and planted the succulents and cacti, which surrounded the motel, softening the harsh, desolate landscape. The motel was as attractive as any motel could be in that remote area.

Now that they were close to opening the motel, Jeffrey was anxious to experiment with the new drug, Freedom, before it opened. "Maria," Jeffrey said one night at dinner after he had received the shipment from the California distribution center, "I really think the Navajo rugs you told me about would look great in the guest rooms. They'd be perfect on the tile floors. Why don't you go back to that gallery in Phoenix that you liked so much and get them? Spend the night and see if you find anything else we need. You've been working so hard. You could use a day of shopping, which I know you enjoy."

"Thank you. I know you're going to love the rugs. They are so beautiful and really would finish off the rooms. I also need to get a couple of other things while I'm there. I'll go day after tomorrow. Is that OK with you?"

"I could use a few things as well. Let me make a list. I'll stay here at the motel and finish up what needs to be done before we open. We should be able to turn the highway sign on next week."

Jeffrey got his pen and paper and began making a list. Secretly, he was looking forward to Maria being gone so he could perform his first test of Freedom. He was pretty sure the test he was planning would work. He had been over and over it in his mind, tweaking the ingredients and adding and deleting various materials. He had an uncanny ability to mentally put different compounds together and envision the finished experiment in his mind before it had ever been tested. It was one of his strong suits as a scientist. He felt confident that the experiment he was contemplating would work, but you never knew until it was tested.

Two days later, Jeffrey kissed Maria good-bye and told her to drive safely. As the dust kicked up by

Maria's van faded into the distance, he quickly went down to the lab, assembled the materials he'd need, and began his work. It took many long hours to get the right combination of different ingredients. Jeffrey worked late into the day, but finally, the time had come to test Freedom. Would it work?

He slowly opened the valve on the compressed gas container and heard the low, familiar hiss of gas being released from the container. The container looked like a green oxygen tank, similar to the type commonly seen in hospitals and used to dispense oxygen to a patient. It was four feet high and constructed of round, heavy gauge steel. The regulator mechanism to release the gas at the selected rate was located on the top.

When he was building the laboratory, Jeffrey had purchased fifty of the tanks from a Los Angeles medical recycling company and had them shipped to his laboratory. The gas being released from the container was his own invention and design. He had attached a small hose to the regulator located on top of the compressed gas cylinder. The hose was connected to the air-conditioning duct that led to all the motel rooms, the office, and their home. The Freedom gas itself was colorless and odorless; however, Jeffery had added a slight amount of sandalwood scent to give the gas a distinctive, yet pleasant, aroma.

A powerful fan pushed the gas through the air-conditioning ducts. The jerry-rigged system of hoses, vents, and fans looked as if it was working perfectly. He was pleased that his invention seemed to be performing just as he had anticipated. His months of careful planning were taking shape. The Freedom drug was on its way to its first test site. Now it was up to him to see if it would work on a human being as he had planned.

He ran up the steps from the basement and made his way to the Blue Coyote office. There was a slight scent of sandalwood in the room. He stood quietly for a few minutes, breathing in the scented air that was coming out of a vent high on the wall behind the reception desk. Jeffrey didn't notice any side effects. He didn't feel dizzy or sick to his stomach. Actually, he felt pretty good.

Jeffrey left the motel office and walked into the courtyard outside the office. He let himself into the empty motel room located across from the office. He didn't detect any sandalwood, which meant there was no seepage from one room to another. The air-conditioning system had been designed by Jeffery so that the flow of Freedom's air could be manipulated from room to room by the controls he had installed in the lab.

He went back to his lab and turned the control valve so the Freedom mixture would enter the motel room he had just been in, but not the others. After he walked back up the stairs, he entered the room and now detected the scent. He walked into the room next to it, detecting no odor. The pipes and vents were working perfectly.

Next, he needed to see if the dosage level of the mixture would produce the "good feeling" he was hoping for. He poured himself a cup of coffee, got his latest copy of Scientific American, and sat down on the leather couch in the office. An hour later he felt better than he had ever felt in his life.

Jeffrey dialed Maria's cell phone. She answered on the first ring. "Maria, is there any way you could come back this evening instead of tomorrow? Nothing is wrong, but my experiment, the one I briefly told you about, the "feel-good" one, seems to be working out better than I had expected. I can't wait to see what you think and how it makes you feel."

"That's great." Maria said. "The timing is absolutely perfect. The 'wet wool' feeling I always get just before a bout of depression has started. I'm on my way to the gallery to pick up the Navajo rugs. It's my last stop. I have an appointment at the gallery in a few minutes, so I can be home in about three hours. I love you and thank you for doing this for me."

Maria couldn't wait to get home to Jeffrey and the experiment. She bought eight of the Navajo rugs; one for the office, the refreshment area, their home and the rest for the guest rooms. They were truly works of art. She knew she was spending a lot of money on the motel, but she had convinced herself it was a wise investment. She hoped it would appeal to people and perhaps they would stay at the Blue Coyote whenever they were in the area. She hoped it would be a "word of mouth" success.

Jeffrey was really pleased. The months of mulling everything over in his mind had paid off. He knew he had discovered something that drug companies would be very interested in purchasing. As he waited for Maria, he thought about how he should market the mixture. He was pretty sure he could easily sell it for a huge sum of money. If he tried to sell it here in the United States, issues would be raised about clinical trial tests and there would be a long waiting period. The FDA would no doubt put a ban on using it while they did testing. Other countries didn't have the strict regulations that stifled the development of new drugs in the United States. When new drugs were developed outside of the United States, they could be sold at a much lower cost because the years of research and development needed in the United States were pretty much side-stepped at overseas locations. Jeffrey thought the pendulum had swung a little too far here in the good old U.S. of A.

He had determined that the solution to avoiding the FDA's strict rules, regulations, and unacceptable delays, would be to use the motel guests as his clinical trial. He was sure there would not be any damaging physical, mental, or emotional effects from taking the drug, but he planned to monitor the dosages very carefully.

Jeffrey also decided that from time to time the mixture would be piped into the house which was attached to the motel by a breezeway. When the commercial air-conditioning unit had been installed, Jeffrey made sure that the air-conditioning vents for the motel were also connected to the house at the rear of the premises. He felt certain that both he and Maria would benefit from occasional doses of Freedom. Jeffrey knew there would be no problems with Freedom, and decided to self-administer the drug to both of them.

Jeffrey had never been so wrong.

CHAPTER 25

Maria turned onto westbound Interstate 10 in Phoenix, happy to be heading home. She couldn't wait to share her purchases with Jeffrey and she was ready to try the "feel-good" drug. Her bouts of depression always started with a dark cloud that seemed to fall over her mind. She thought of it as "wet wool," although where that thought came from, she had no idea. As the bleakness deepened, the cloud turned to near total darkness.

She had been to numerous doctors who had prescribed different kinds of anti-depressants, beginning with the one she had first consulted at the "free clinic." The drugs eased her despondence, but didn't entirely take it away. Usually, these bouts just had to run their course. Before going to the gallery to buy the rugs, she had taken the most recent anti-depressant prescribed by her doctor and felt a little better. She hoped and prayed that Jeffrey had discovered something that would make her bouts disappear completely. She knew the signs of depression well and it would be wonderful to never have to experience them again.

The drive from Phoenix was uneventful. As she was getting ready to pull off the highway onto the road leading to the motel, she saw where Jim had installed the pole for the neon sign advertising the Blue Coyote.

He'd done a good job placing the sign and she hoped it would bring business to the motel.

She was pleased with what she and Jeffrey had been able to accomplish in such a short time. They were almost ready to open the doors to the public and could hardly wait for the first guests to arrive.

The motel looked like a jewel in the setting sun, a creamy adobe color with a red tile roof, very Southwestern. The landscape plantings she had so carefully chosen were perfect for the look they wanted. Various forms of cacti and succulents reflected the desert setting and required almost no water.

The large solar panels that Jeffrey had installed were on the back side of the motel and out of sight. He wanted to use the solar panels as the primary source of energy and knew a high electricity usage in his laboratory would trigger a visit from the local electrical company. He wanted his work to be free from scrutiny and the extra energy he hoped to produce with the solar panels would insure that no one would be coming to the motel to check on him. If the solar panels malfunctioned, he still had the gypsy electric power line he could rely on.

Jeffrey had turned on the outside lights and the whole motel area where they had worked so hard glowed with a warm and inviting look. Maria was certain that anyone who turned in the driveway and saw the motel would want to stay. She drove to the rear of the motel where their house was located. It was lit up as well, a welcoming beacon in the lonely, harsh desert.

"I'm home. Come help me unload the car. I can't wait for you to see the rugs I bought," Maria yelled out. She opened the trunk and carried some of them into the house.

"It will have to wait for a few minutes. Please, come with me. You have to experience what I've been doing; then I want to see how you feel. And just how are you feeling now?" Jeffrey asked. Maria looked tired and Jeffrey sensed that one of her periodic bouts with depression was beginning to drain her.

He gently led her to the big leather chair in their living room and poured her a glass of wine. Jeffrey told her to stay there and that he'd be back in a minute; that he wanted to try out his experiment on her. He ran down to the lab and connected the vent feeding their house with Freedom. As he turned the switch, the green light on the control console lit up, indicating that the mixture was being fed into their house.

He knew from his experiment earlier that afternoon that it would take about fifteen minutes for the drug to begin to work. Excitedly, he hurried back to the house and poured himself a glass of wine as he and Maria talked about their day. She began to tell him about the beautiful things she had seen at the Native American gallery. After a few minutes had gone by, he noticed that Maria was smiling. Maria never smiled when she was having one of her bouts. *This is encouraging*, he thought, and as they continued to talk, he noticed a sparkle in her eyes that hadn't been there when she had returned from Phoenix. He watched her closely and after about fifteen minutes had passed, he asked her how she was feeling.

"I feel better than I have all day. I smell something, which I think is sandalwood and it's very pleasant. I think I'll just sit here awhile and enjoy it. Judging from how I feel, I think your experiment is a huge success," Maria said happily.

"Okay. I'll unload the car while you relax." Jeffrey was thrilled. His experiment was indeed a huge success. He knew that Maria couldn't pretend to feel good when she was down. It had worked. He had been able to get rid of Maria's depression.

He was back in a few minutes, arms loaded with the Navajo rugs. "These are beautiful! They probably cost a fortune, but I'm glad you bought them. They'll finish off the whole Southwest theme we've developed here at the Blue Coyote. Is one of them for our house?"

"Oh, Jeffrey, I just knew you'd love them as much as I do. The third one down is for the house. We have a lot of leather in here and I thought the browns and deep reds would go well with the leather. I also bought one for the office and one for the refreshment area. The rest are for the guest rooms. I'll decide which ones go where tomorrow, but for now, I just want to sit here and enjoy feeling good. Your experiment is an absolute success because I feel one hundred percent better. You know that dark cloud I've told you about, that 'wet wool' feeling I get? Well, it's gone and it has to be because of the success of your experiment. I hope and pray this will work from now on. I feel like I've just received a miracle. Thank you so much! Now, explain how it works."

Maria had come to dread the "wet wool" and was

thrilled to think it might be a thing of the past. Jeffrey seemed much happier as well. *Maybe*, she thought, *this wonder drug he has created will be a very good thing for both of us as well as for our marriage.*

Jeffrey told her what he had done, how the vents could feed the mixture into any location on the premises. He told Maria how he had named the drug "Freedom" because hopefully, it would free her from her bouts with depression. For now, he said, he would only infuse the mixture from time to time into their house, the office and his lab. He said he was going to use Freedom on some motel guests as a sort of clinical trial so that he could get a sense of how it was doing, although he didn't anticipate any problems. Maria would choose which of the guests she felt would benefit most as she would be the one checking them in at the front desk. Jeffrey knew she had a sixth sense about people and he trusted her judgment.

He thought there could be legal issues, possible lawsuits, and potentially, even criminal prosecution if anyone ever discovered that he was infusing a controlled substance into a guest's room. After all, he was administering a drug to people who had no knowledge they were receiving it. There was a total lack of personal consent. On top of that, the drug had not been sanctioned or approved by the United States government. Jeffrey knew he should file for a patent to protect his discovery, but that would probably start an investigation into what he was doing. His motto had become "The fewer people who know what I am doing, the better."

"Do you think there could be any side effects? I feel great, but if we use this for a long period of time, and we probably will because it makes us feel so good, could we be at risk for some type of adverse reaction, perhaps even becoming addicted?" Maria asked.

Jeffrey replied, "I honestly don't think so. None of the ingredients by themselves would be a problem. I suppose it's a case of one plus one doesn't necessarily mean we get two. I think it's worth taking the risk. As for our guests, one night of this stuff shouldn't hurt them. If anything, it will help them and the effects will last for quite a while. I think of it as a type of therapy. Feeling better will help them get better, both physically and mentally. We'll try it for a few months and see if we notice anything different in our day-to-day lives. Is that okay with you?"

"Absolutely," Maria replied. "I just wouldn't want to unknowingly hurt our guests. I imagine we could be liable if anything happens to them." Maria knew nothing of FDA standards, relying on Jeffrey's knowledge of the world of science.

"Don't worry," he said. "The only thing they will notice is the slight smell of sandalwood. They'll think we're burning incense somewhere and that's a pretty common smell in this part of the country. It's been a long day for both of us. Let's get something to eat and go to bed. We only have a few more things to do before we open the motel to the public. I found a guy in Blythe who's a computer website guru. He's coming out tomorrow to help me design our website. We really are coming down to the finish line!"

CHAPTER 26

It was April in the desert, the most beautiful time of all. Brightly colored wildflowers carpeted the desert floor and climbed up the hills. The earth looked like it had erupted in a riot of color. The air was crisp early in the morning and turned balmy as the day became warmer. It was a welcome passage between the bitter cold of winter and the searing heat of summer.

Tomorrow was the big day when the motel would finally be ready to open. Just a few more things remained to be done. Maria and Jeffrey were meeting with Jim, the contractor, in the early afternoon for a final walkthrough. Their dream had become a reality, a charming reality.

While Maria was cleaning up after breakfast, Jeffrey told her he wanted to get a few more things ready for the experiments he would soon be starting and left for the lab. As she put the last dish away, the beautiful spring day beckoned and she walked outside. This would be a perfect day to take a walk in the desert with Jeffrey. She knew that it might be their last carefree day for a long time. Between motel guests and Jeffrey's work, they wouldn't be able to leave the property together for a while.

Maria entered the door marked "Basement" and took

the steps down to the lab. Today was the last day Maria would feel comfortable about going down to the lab. The test rats for Jeffrey's experiments were being delivered tomorrow and rats reminded her of her awful days in the barrio and the horrible experience of the gang rape. Maria was deathly afraid of rats. She decided she wouldn't think about them today.

"Jeffrey, this is by far the prettiest day we've had since we moved here. Let's take a long walk before we meet Jim. This might be the last time we can take a leisurely walk for a while," Maria said.

"Okay. Let me turn off a couple of the machines. I'm at a place where I can take a break and I couldn't agree more; let's enjoy today. We deserve it!" Jeffrey turned off the machines, flicked the switch on the laboratory lights, and together they walked up the stairs.

By now, it was 9:30 a.m. They went to the main house, put on light jackets, and began walking. Behind their property was an arroyo, a dry desert ravine teeming with lupine, desert ironwood and canyon bursage. They walked beside it for about an hour. Desert animals skittered and the brilliant blue sky covered Maria and Jeffrey. It truly was the most beautiful time of the year in the desert.

Maria's eyes welled up. "I've never been happier. I love this place and now that we have Freedom, I feel wonderful all the time. Really, this is the best time of my life. Thank you, thank you, thank you. I'm so sorry about Moore Labs, but I think we've come out just fine. And you, are you okay with what we're doing?"

Jeffrey took her hand in his, stopped walking, and answered her. "I couldn't agree more. I am so excited about my experiments. What you've done to the motel is incredible. It looks as good as any motel in the Palm Springs area and I love my laboratory. I love the quiet and peace of the desert and most of all, I love you. Yes, I'm not only okay with what we've done, I am very, very happy." They turned around and began the long walk back to their new life, looking forward to the results of Jeffrey's experiments and the opening of the motel.

Jim arrived promptly at 2:00 p.m. for the final walkthrough. The three of them went into each room, testing the lights, the water, the air-conditioning, and the furnace. They made sure that each room was finished properly. They checked to see that the computer was working in the office, as well as the lights and kitchen appliances. They turned the lights on outside each unit. In the refreshment room they checked the microwave, coffee maker, and refrigerator.

One of the things they wanted after buying the property was a swimming pool. They situated it so pool users would have an unobstructed view of the nearby Eagle and Coxcomo Mountains. It was a brilliant decision. The pool was full and sparkled in the sun. They admired the brightly colored umbrellas and chaise lounges surrounding the pool. After Jim assured himself that everything was working properly in the rooms and at the pool, they went to the main house to see if there was anything Maria and Jeffrey had overlooked there. They'd been living in the house and hadn't noticed any problems, but Jim was a perfectionist, insisting they do a thorough walkthrough.

Hiring Jim had been a stroke of luck. He turned out to be far better than they could have asked for, giving them great advice and showing them numerous ways they could save money on the remodeling project. Probably the best part was that because he was such a perfectionist, nothing had been done in a haphazard manner. He had been a class act from start to finish. Who would have thought they would have found a contractor like him in Blythe?

After they finished the walkthrough, they went back to the office where Maria happily wrote a check to Jim for the remainder of the work he had done. He had been worth every cent.

One last thing remained to be done. Jim finished the final wiring needed on the highway sign and tested the neon lights. It was perfect. The words "Blue Coyote Motel" glowed brightly, a beacon for weary travelers. With the lights on, the motel was officially open. Maria and Jeffrey high-fived each other and went into the office where the phone and computer were now up and running. There was nothing to do but wait for their first guests.

CHAPTER 27

The past few months had gone by quickly for Doug. They had been very good months. Even though the recent past had been ideal in many ways, he still occasionally would have a flashback of the person he used to be; a loser, broke, fat, smoking, drinking too much and visiting prostitutes. When the flashbacks ended, he would be bathed in sweat, his heart racing and vowing once again to do whatever it took to never become that person again.

He consistently was the top sales producer at Aravalve. Jack couldn't have been happier with his sales performance and had given him a much larger territory, the Western United States including Hawaii. He particularly liked the frequent trips to the San Francisco Bay Area and Hawaii. He had a generous expense account, which allowed him to eat at great restaurants, stay in hotels with beautiful surroundings, and take Lacy with him when she could get away. After his disastrous start with Aravalve, he never would have foreseen this new development in his life.

Doug had never been to Hawaii and he quickly fell under its spell. His sales calls took him mainly to the islands of Oahu, Maui, and Hawaii. While most of the tourists gravitated towards Maui and Oahu, he enjoyed the peacefulness of the island of Hawaii, or as it was called by the locals, the "Big Island." It was a little sleepier, no nightlife to speak of and fewer tricked-out expensive resorts. He found the port town of Hilo to be especially charming. The farmer's market with its colorfully extravagant displays of Hawaiian flowers like plumeria, anthurium, and orchids delighted him. Doug loved the nearly empty beaches, lava formations, waterfalls, and the warmth of the Hawaiian people. He'd even gotten to like Spam, a favorite dish of the local island residents.

Doug became reliant on his daily workouts and runs to keep his energy up. His busy travel schedule and being "on" all the time for his customers was not easy, so staying in top physical shape was important to him. Everyone is motivated by something different. Doug was a goal-oriented person. Whether it was achieving a certain weight or a certain sales quota, he did much better when he knew the expectation. He decided that he needed to take on the challenge of a half-marathon and he began training in earnest for such an event.

He and Lacy had started living together in a townhouse on the south side of the 101 Freeway in Woodland Hills, located northwest of Los Angeles in the San Fernando Valley. Since moving in with Lacy, he had changed his eating habits and was feeling much better with this change in diet. A Southern California girl, Lacy had embraced vegetarianism at a young age and had eaten a meat-free diet ever since. She was an excellent cook, but if Doug wanted meat, he had to prepare it himself. Since she was such a good cook, he rarely felt the need. If he had a craving, he could always order it when he was on the road. He had been a fast food junkie all his life, but his body was responding very positively to his new eating habits. Weight kept coming off and he didn't feel the least bit deprived. It was amazing what Lacy could do with different grains, fruits, and vegetables.

They had fallen in love with the townhouse because of the view of the hills which separated the San Fernando Valley from the Pacific Ocean. To achieve his goal of running a half-marathon, Doug charted out a running schedule. The hills were filled with paths. He started with a walk-run combination and went on to a full run, usually five to seven miles, four mornings a week. After that, he would shower, eat some fruit and grains, and spend the rest of the day making sales calls.

He had run sporadically over the years, but nothing like he found himself doing now. Even when he was on the road, he stuck to his schedule. When Doug was in Hawaii, he always ran on the beach, just because he could. He loved how it made him feel. There was something about the sand on his feet, the light spray and sound of the surf, and the salty, clean smell of the ocean that made him feel fully alive, every sensory nerve in his body awakened.

Southern California weather made it the perfect place for marathons and half-marathons. Doug pulled up the half-marathon schedule for races in

Southern California on his computer. He decided to start with one that was three months away. He had been running for several weeks and with three more months to train, he felt he'd be prepared. He spent the months training intensely for his race. As the date for the half-marathon neared, he knew he had done everything he could to prepare himself. He just hoped it was enough.

The half-marathon race day dawned bright and clear. It was early spring in Southern California and as usual, it was beautiful weather. He had chosen Santa Monica as his half-marathon site, a short drive from their home. He planned on leaving about 5:00 a.m., knowing at that time of day, on a Saturday, there would be very little traffic on the freeway, always a consideration. He arose at 4:00 a.m. and heated up some oatmeal then topped it with fruit. He wanted to get protein in his stomach before the 6:30 a.m. starting time and the natural sugar in the fruit would give him some energy as well.

Doug and Lacy pulled into the parking lot in Santa Monica where many of the runners were already doing stretches and sprints in preparation for the race. He made his way to the registration desk, filled out the information form, paid his entrance fee, and picked up a free T-shirt being handed out by the sponsors of the race. He did some stretches, drank some water, and got in place for the half-marathon.

Officially, a half-marathon is a little over thirteen miles, but to Doug it felt like ten times that amount.

Although he had faithfully stuck to his training regime, he had never run that great a distance. He gritted it out. Three hours later, he crossed the finish line to the sound of Lacy screaming and yelling her support. She was jumping up and down with joy and pride. Relief flooded over him. He had done it; he had completed his first half-marathon. He was hungry, thirsty, and just plain exhausted. Then it began to dawn on him—he really had completed his first half-marathon. While it had seemed grueling while he was doing it, now he was already thinking about running a full marathon. He wondered if running a marathon was like childbirth; after it's over you tend to forget the pain.

During the next few months, he entered more races and stuck to his training regime. He was in great shape. When he thought about it, he realized this had to be the best time of his life. The money was flowing in, he and Lacy were crazy in love, and he looked and felt great. Life seemed almost perfect.

Then a couple of flies landed in the ointment. One morning, he noticed a few grey hairs around his temples when he was shaving. It seemed a little premature. He was only 34.

The second fly in the ointment regarded his relationship with Lacy. He loved her very much, but could sense she was beginning to get frustrated with him. Sometimes he just didn't feel like making love. She was hurt and couldn't understand why. Recently, Lacy had told him she thought he should see a doctor because he looked tired. She asked if he was worried about anything or if something was troubling him.

Doug didn't say anything, but lately he'd noticed that his sales had really slowed down. He'd started to miss his cigarettes. He seemed to have lost his enthusiasm for the early morning runs. He was bothered by chills, sweats, and occasional bouts of nausea although he didn't feel sick. Some mornings it was just easier to push the snooze button on the alarm clock, pull the covers over his head, and try for more sleep.

He knew he needed to call on some of his customers in Las Vegas, but whenever he went there, the constant noise of the casinos, the smoke-filled rooms, and the frenetic nature of the city exhausted him. He was feeling tired almost every day and the thought of going to Vegas did not really appeal to him. Even so, he decided he'd go a couple of days before the Memorial Day weekend, which would allow him to get back home and rest up over the three day holiday.

The Wednesday before Memorial Day, he flew into McCarran airport in Las Vegas. As soon as he landed and got off the plane, he could hear the incessant sound of the slot machines in the terminal and figured he'd better get used to it for the next couple of days. He went to the car rental kiosk the Aravalve sales personnel used and got a mid-size car. He was staying at the Venetian and it was just a short drive to the hotel.

Doug checked in and went to his room to make appointments for later that afternoon and Thursday. The Venetian was a "suite" hotel, which Doug preferred. He liked having some space in his room, as he often spent a lot of time doing paperwork. The room was great. It had a TV in the bedroom and in the bathroom. He'd be able to watch baseball in both of the rooms. Doug eyed the fully stocked refreshment center, craving a cold beer. It was a little too early and he had calls to make, but he decided he owed it to himself to have a couple of beers later on. Maybe that would make him feel better.

He set up his calls and went down to the hotel valet parking, got his car, and set out. The old spark just wasn't there. He couldn't seem to set the hook. No one wanted valves right now. *How had it been so easy only a few months ago?* he wondered. He drove back to the Venetian in the late afternoon, gave his car key to the valet attendant, and stopped at the first hotel bar he saw. The cold beer went down easy and the second was even better. *Well, what the hell,* he thought, *it's been a lousy day. I just hope tomorrow is better.* He quickly lost $20 to the electronic poker machine in front of him on the bar counter, ordered another beer and fed another $20 into the machine. After the third quick beer and down $40 he went up to his room, showered, and changed clothes.

The beer made him feel better. He decided to go to

the sports lounge and bet on a couple of the baseball games that would soon be underway. The smoke was thick in the bar, making him want a cigarette even more. *Well,* he thought, *why not? I don't know anyone here and I'll quit tomorrow.* He walked out of the sports bar and found the hotel convenience shop, which had all the necessities anyone in Las Vegas needed —condoms, beer, wine, cigarettes, and magazines in every language.

Doug lit up. The first pull on the cigarette almost made him sick. The next one was better. It was kind of like riding a bike. You never forgot how. It had been awhile since a pack of cigarettes had been in his shirt pocket. Actually, it felt pretty natural. He promised himself the beers and cigarettes were just for tonight. He knew he should call Lacy, but he decided to go back to the sports bar instead. He'd call her later.

He drank several more beers and, seeing some people next to him with an order of chicken wings and onion rings, decided to have those as well. The more beer he had, the better the cute little cocktail waitress looked. "Hey darlin'," he said, "When you get a minute, I'd like to order some food and another beer. What's your name? I always like to know the name of the person bringin' me my beer."

"My name's Britney. I'll be right back with your beer." She gave Doug a big smile. Britney was dressed in a tight black corset, which pushed her ample breasts over the top. She wore black fishnet hose, high heels, and a very short skirt. She looked like she was farm-fed, fresh from Kansas, just one of the legions of young women who came to Vegas hoping to find a rich man, but instead, found themselves selling their bodies to make a living. The casinos and bars in Vegas swarmed with beautiful young girls like Britney. Sex sold well in Vegas.

When Britney brought his beer, she leaned over Doug, placing it on a napkin. He could smell her. All he wanted to do was run his hand over her breasts and touch her almost visible nipples with his fingers. God, he wanted her. *This is insane,* he thought to himself. *What in the hell am I doing? What about my commitment to Lacy?*

"Britney," he said in a ragged voice, "what time do you get off work? I'd like to buy you a drink."

She gave him another one of her big smiles. She leaned over him once again, cleaning the ashtray on his table. He could feel her in his hands, feel her under him. Whatever the consequences, he had to have her.

"I'm off in an hour. Why don't we meet in your room? Management doesn't like us to have drinks with the customers in the lounge. What's your room number?" Britney asked.

"1461," Doug said. "I'll meet you there in an hour."

He ate his chicken wings and onion rings, ordered another beer, and decided to place one last bet. His baseball bets had been a disaster. He had dropped $500 in just a couple of hours. Doug decided to bet on a horse race instead in an attempt to recoup his losses. There was a long shot in the race, Commando II, that looked pretty good. It was the last race, so Doug bet $500. The horses were out of the gate and the announcer was screaming that Commando II was in the lead. Doug jumped out of his chair, his attention fully focused on the big screen showing the long shot ahead by several lengths. Doug knew his luck was turning. Commando II was going to make a bundle for him and he'd go back to California a big winner. As he watched the screen, he heard the announcer saying, "What's this? What's happened to Commando II? He's barely moving. This is unbelievable." Doug watched in horror as the rest of the horses ran past Commando II on their way to the finish line. The jockey finally got Commando II to slowly move to the finish line. He came in last.

Doug stumbled out of the bar and made his way to the elevator. The door next to his room was ajar and he could see a bunch of young men inside the room that couldn't be over nineteen or twenty. It was obvious they had been partying all day and intended to keep going. *Swell*, he thought, *just what I need; a bunch of post-teenyboppers partying all night.* He thought about Lacy and knew he should call her, but knew he wouldn't be able to disguise his drunkenness. Anyway, Britney would be coming for a drink in a few minutes and he needed to get the room presentable.

He hung up the clothes he'd taken out of his travel bag and put away the clothes and towels he'd thrown on the floor. He opened the drapes and stood in amazement at what water and gambling had done to the desert. In every direction buildings were ablaze with neon lights. He looked down at the cars, one long line of headlights, moving to the next casino, the next drink, the next sexual encounter. Whatever you wanted, Las Vegas had it.

Doug promised himself he'd just have a drink with Britney, nothing more. Even though she made him so damn horny he thought he would explode, he'd just have a drink with her. He was committed to Lacy. However, the alcohol was dulling his resolve.

Well, maybe I'll have a little drink before she comes, just to be ready, he thought. He opened the door of the refreshment center and found a small bottle of bourbon and a club soda. They were chilled and went down smoothly. Doug tried to set the alarm clock on the bedside table, but his brain wasn't fully functioning by this time. Instead, he left a wake-up call with the front desk; then he heard a knock on the door.

Doug opened it for Britney. She had changed out of her serving costume into a tight, white sweater and jeans. It was obvious she wasn't wearing a bra, her erect nipples showing beneath the sweater. One look at her and every promise he had made to himself went down the drain. He wondered if she was wearing any underwear at all. "You are the sexiest woman I have ever seen," he said.

She walked over to him, ran her hands up his chest and then behind his neck, kissing him deeply. "I wanted you from the moment you walked into the lounge," she said. She pressed up against him, her breasts warm and large against his chest. He just wanted to rip off all her clothes and it was all he could do to restrain himself. She began to unbutton his shirt with one hand, her fingers lightly grazing his nipples. Her other hand drifted down to Doug's crotch and she deftly massaged the huge bulge in his pants with strong, urgent strokes. *Oh my God,* thought Doug, *I've died and gone to heaven.* He kissed her again, backing up to the bed, drawing her on top of him. She pulled her sweater over her head and unzipped her jeans, pulling them off easily. She reached down and unzipped his pants, releasing his large, fully erect penis.

"Roll over," he said, panting. "Let me in you." He mounted her as she lay on her back with her legs spread invitingly open. He made one giant deep thrust into her wetness and came instantly. His eyes seemed to roll into the back of his head and he collapsed on top of her, releasing a deep primordial moan. It had happened too quickly, but Britney was a pro and lied, telling him how wonderful it had been for her. As drunk as he was, he believed her. He closed his eyes, intending to fall asleep, but hearing rustling noises, he opened them in time to see Britney taking money out of his wallet.

"Honey," she said, "I usually get $300, but I like you, so I'm just going to take $200. Thanks. We can have that drink next time."

All Doug wanted now was sleep. He knew if he stayed awake and sobered up, he was going to hate himself for giving in to all of it, the alcohol, cigarettes, and a prostitute. He slept until the sound of the wake-up call the following morning shattered his sleep. His head hurt, his body ached, and his mouth felt like it was filled with cotton. *Oh God,* he thought, *I don't think I've ever felt this bad.* He staggered to the bathroom, pouring himself a full glass of water. *Aspirin,* he thought, *maybe that will help. Where in the hell did I put them?* He found them in the side pocket of his carry-on luggage, quickly gulping four, when he remembered that he hadn't used a condom. It was pretty clear to him what Britney's main source of income was and it wasn't working as a barmaid. He felt panicky as he realized that last night he had unprotected sex with a hooker. Even in his bad days, he'd never forgotten to wear a condom. What if he'd picked something up? How could he ever explain it to Lacy?

Just then, the phone rang for a second time. It was Lacy. "Why didn't you call me last night?" she asked. "I waited until I fell asleep. Where were you?"

"Lacy, I'm really sorry, but I went to dinner with some customers. We ended up seeing the Blue Man Group and when I got back to my room, it was too late to call. I didn't want to wake you. I was just about to call you this morning before I left for a breakfast meeting, but you beat me to it. How is everything?" Doug lied.

They talked for a few minutes. The aspirin began to work. When he hung up, he started the shower. *I hope this helps*, he thought. The shower felt good, a purging rite, something he desperately needed. Doug realized he had to get some food in his stomach, that there was no way he could make it to his first appointment feeling as he did now. He ordered eggs, bacon, toast, and a pot of coffee from room service.

As he got ready for his first appointment, he began to feel blessed that at least he was alive. He called on three companies, but only made one sale, a small one at that. At lunch he thought maybe he could fit a nap in before his scheduled afternoon appointments.

He went back to his room, saw the cleaning lady in the room next to his, and knew she'd be in his room in a matter of minutes. *So much for the nap*, he thought. He sat down at the desk, opened his laptop, and checked his email. Just then, there was a knock on the door. "Housekeeping," the voice said.

"Come in," Doug responded. A middle-aged African-American woman wheeled her cart in.

"I'll come back later if that would be easier," she said.

"No, go ahead and make up the room. I'll just sit here and do some work on my laptop. I'll stay out of your way," Doug said.

He looked carefully at the woman, noticing a slight bulge in the hemline of one leg of her pants. She followed his gaze. He didn't want to ask what the bulge was, but thought it was really odd. Doug idly wondered if she had some deformity. He turned back to his screen and began to answer his email.

Looking up, he noticed that she was looking around the room, seemingly surprised. "What is it?" he asked.

"Well, this room's pretty neat. Don't look like you spent much time here. Looks like you had a shower, slept, had a drink, room service, and that's it. You wouldn't believe what some of these rooms look like," the housekeeper said.

"You must see some pretty unbelievable things," Doug responded. "I've always heard that Vegas had everything," he said, inwardly cringing as he remembered the night before.

The woman appeared anxious to talk and began to tell him of the things she had seen while working in Vegas hotels. She told him of a fire which started in a room caused by people making meth, the $30,000 of gambling chips stolen from a blackjack table while people were playing, and even the recent murder of one of her fellow housekeeping workers. She told Doug that something bad happened just about every week, but you never read about it in the newspapers. The Visitor and Convention Bureau made sure those kinds of stories stayed out of the papers. They wanted everyone to think Vegas was clean and wholesome. The housekeeper told him about the underground rumor mill. Every worker in Vegas knew what was really going on.

"I saw you looking at the hemline of my pants a few minutes ago," the housekeeper said. "I got a knife I keep there just in case I got a problem customer. Don't wanna be the next dead housekeeper." She pulled up her pants and there in a scabbard was the knife. She took it out. It was a scary thing with a big, wide blade. She idly tossed it from hand to hand then put it back. "No sir, anyone thinks about hurtin' me, they're gonna get this shiv shoved in their gut first."

Doug began to feel even worse than he had. This really was a sick place. If you scratched the underbelly of Vegas, the maggots came out. All he wanted was to get out of there and go home.

"Well, I think that's it," the housekeeper said. "You seem like a nice man; might be good for you to go home. This ain't no place for a good man to be."

Doug finished his emails, checked his appointment book, and left for his afternoon calls. Four hours later, he headed back to the Venetian. Despite his best efforts, he had only made one sale. *This may have been the longest day of my life*, he thought, *the company won't break even on this trip*.

He went downstairs to have dinner. He didn't feel like gambling, drinking, or smoking. He still felt sick to his stomach. He admitted to himself he hadn't felt this bad since he'd stayed at the motel in the desert on the way back from Phoenix and going toward his dreaded meeting with Jack. *What was the name of that place? Oh yeah, the Blue Coyote.* He had felt great when he left there and he'd kept that feeling, but lately he could feel himself losing it. He was beginning to slip back into patterns of the old Doug, the Doug he had grown to hate. He had really thought that Doug was gone. The flashbacks were becoming a reality. Maybe there was something about that motel? Maybe he should go back. His mojo was gone and he needed to get it back.

The more he thought about it, the more it seemed like a good idea. Memorial Day weekend was coming up. He decided he'd call the rental car company and return it when he got back to California on Sunday.

He'd leave tomorrow morning, drive south on Highway 95 to Blythe and then west to the hotel. It was a long drive and out of the way, but he didn't care. Visiting the motel again was the only thing he could think to do and perhaps regain the good feelings he had when he left there.

He went back to his room to call the Blue Coyote to see if they had any rooms left for the Memorial Day weekend. Before he made the call, he decided a couple more aspirin couldn't hurt. He walked into the bathroom to get some water. He looked at the mirror and was shocked by what he saw. No wonder Lacy had commented on how tired he looked. He seemed a lot more than tired; he looked old! What in the hell was happening? Where was the charismatic guy from a few months ago? What was going on? He'd aged over five years. He tried smiling at the mirror. That helped to erase the lines. He guessed he'd have to go around smiling all day. He knew he owed Lacy some sort of explanation, but for the life of him he couldn't come up with anything plausible.

I probably do need to get away, he thought. *I've been working harder than ever. Maybe it's beginning to take its toll.* He placed a call to the Blue Coyote Motel. The phone was answered by the beautiful Latina woman he remembered. He made a reservation for the coming Memorial Day weekend, telling her he would check in the next day and would be leaving Sunday morning. The young woman told him she looked forward to seeing him and asked how he was doing.

"You wouldn't believe how great my life has been since the last time I was at the Blue Coyote," Doug said. He began telling the young woman about the last few months. He related just how great he'd felt when he left the motel, how his life had turned around, but unfortunately, now he was feeling like he was losing it and going back to his old ways. He wondered if maybe his motel stay had something to do with it, he said, so he had decided to go back for a second visit. He told her he'd see her tomorrow. When he hung up, he was embarrassed that he'd divulged so much about his personal life. It was very unlike him. *Well, at least she'll know why I'm there—to get my life back together.*

Doug called Lacy and got the answering machine. "Lacy, you know how I've been tired lately. Things haven't been great at work or at home. I know it's me, not you. I've decided to drive to that motel I told you about, the Blue Coyote. It's the one located in the desert out in the middle of nowhere. I'm going to spend the weekend there and drive home Sunday. Perhaps I'll feel better after I've been there. I love you and I'll see you in three days." He hung up, feeling optimistic for the first time in weeks.

After Maria hung up from talking to Doug, she turned to Jeffrey. "Doug Ritchie just made a reservation for the Memorial Day weekend. He'll be checking in tomorrow and he's not doing well. It probably wouldn't hurt to pipe Freedom into his room a few hours in advance. He was a nice guy. I'm sure he'll feel better after he gets here."

CHAPTER 28

Luisa and Jorge's move from Rio had gone smoothly. Soon, they were settled in their new home in California, eagerly awaiting the birth of their much wished for baby. Jorge was ecstatic when the sonogram showed that the baby would be a boy. They decided on the name "Carlos" to honor Luisa's maternal grandfather. She had been very close to her grandparents, spending many summers on their ranch located not far from Rio. She was an accomplished horsewoman and she dreamed of the day she could have her own horse and ranch. Luisa decided to wait until Carlos was out of his infancy, but she definitely wanted him to enjoy the experience of being on a ranch as much as she had.

Luisa was adjusting to the new maid and the cook she had inherited from the former owners. They were good, but she still missed the easy relationship she had with Manny and Luz. They knew exactly what she wanted and how she wanted it. She knew it would take time to adjust to the new help. Although she liked the food that Joey, the cook, prepared, she was having a hard time getting used to California cuisine. She was well aware that all the fruits, vegetables, and grains were good for her, but she longed for the free range beef and chicken she was used to eating in Rio.

Now that Luisa was pregnant, she was even happier that binging and purging were behind her and nothing more than an unpleasant memory. She had vowed to make her body the perfect vehicle for her baby-to-be and being bulimic was no longer an option. Looking back, she realized the living hell she had been in and swore to herself that she would never do it again.

She had interviewed a number of nannies to care for the new baby, but so far, none of them seemed to be right. Her mother, Juanita, offered to come over daily to help her, but Luisa was still intent on finding the perfect nanny. Juanita had enough to do adjusting to her new life in California without the added pressure of having to help with the daily care of a baby, even though it was her first grandchild. Luisa would just have to keep looking. When she found a nanny, she knew her mother would still find plenty of excuses to be with her grandson.

Jorge was getting used to his biweekly trips from California to Brazil and back again. While he loved California and his new life, he suffered from an ongoing sense of guilt. When he was in Brazil, he felt guilty for being away from Luisa. When he was in California, he felt guilty for being away from the family business. He decided he needed an outlet and the time had come to indulge in his hidden passion. Jorge had always wanted to own a boat. Their new home had a dock right outside the back door and there was really nothing to hold him back.

On a beautiful sunny day, he and Luisa drove down Pacific Coast Highway to Newport Beach to look at boats. It didn't take very long until Jorge found the perfect one he had to have. It was a gorgeous brand new 58' powerboat. The galley and main cabin were outfitted with the latest in boating interiors, as was everything else on the boat. Warm woods, polished to a burnished sheen, made the airy cabin and staterooms inviting. There was even a bathtub, which was unheard of on pleasure boats of this size. The smaller stateroom would be perfect for baby Carlos. Luisa and Jorge felt they could do without their household help on boating weekends. The sunroof, ample headroom, and freeboard all contributed to the roomy feeling. It even came with a 13' Boston Whaler, perfect for when they were anchored and needed to get to shore.

Although Jorge had been on many boats, he had never owned one. His father, Tomas, was an accomplished sailor. Jorge had always preferred powerboats, but his father loved the quiet movement of the sailboats with the challenge of setting the sails just right in order to catch the wind. Jorge was impatient and wanted to get where he wanted to go faster than a sailboat would allow.

Arrangements were made to have the boat brought up the coast to the dock in back of their house the following week. Jorge could hardly wait. When the boat pulled up to the dock, their next-door neighbors, John and Becky Richards, came over to admire it. John had introduced himself to Luisa and Jorge the day they had moved into their home. Over the past few months, they had talked a number of times and John was the one who had recommended the boat dealer where Jorge bought the boat. As soon as the boat was tied up, John asked if he could come aboard. An accomplished yachtsman, he knew just about everything there was to know about boats.

As he stepped aboard, John said, "Jorge, you've done well. She's a beauty. I'd love to go out with you when you're ready. You'll need a few shakedown cruises before you take her too far. I'd be happy to help." John couldn't hide his joy at being the first guest on Jorge's beautiful new boat. They made plans to go out the following day.

The boat handled beautifully and Jorge felt comfortable as soon as he stood at the wheel. It was equipped with the latest in electronic gadgetry and he and John spent much of their time figuring out what was important to learn right away and what could be postponed until later. Once they got beyond the artificial breakwater that protected the harbor and entered the open ocean, they discovered just how easily the boat handled as she skimmed over the waves. Farther out in the ocean, they were able to easily run her up to eighteen knots. She rode steady and smooth. Jorge felt like he'd been behind the wheel of the boat all of his life. He loved the feeling.

"Jorge, what are you going to name her?" John asked.

"I don't know. The people at the boat dealership wondered the same thing. I told them I'd wait a day or two to register and name her. They cautioned me against waiting too long. I guess there's some kind of fine assessed if you wait too long," Jorge replied. "I think I'll name her *Luisa* in honor of my wife. If it wasn't for her sister's wedding I'd never be here today and I would never have had the opportunity to own this boat. Yes, that's what I'm going to do; *Luisa* it is."

They took *Luisa* back and Jorge carefully guided her up to the dock located adjacent to the rear of their house. It seemed like the most natural thing in the world to him. "John, let's christen her now. I'll get Luisa, some champagne for us, and Perrier for her. You get Becky. I'll meet you back here at the dock in five minutes."

Luisa greeted Becky and John. Turning to Jorge, she said, "Why are we all down at the dock? I've been on the boat and I'm glad you're enjoying it, but I really don't want to be out on the water until after the baby is born. I'm finished with morning sickness and I don't want to get seasick."

Jorge took a bottle of champagne and neatly cracked it across the bow. "I christen you *Luisa* in honor of the love of my life, my wife, Luisa," he said quite formally. Luisa had no idea Jorge was even thinking of naming his prized possession after her. She was speechless and started to cry. Not many women had a beautiful yacht named after them.

"And now we drink this second bottle of champagne to *Luisa*!'"

John turned to Jorge and said, "Jorge, I belong to a yacht club over on Catalina Island. It's called the Fourth of July Yacht club. It's named after a small protected cove. Let's take *Luisa* over there one of these days. I think you'll like it."

He was really looking forward to taking Jorge to Catalina Island on his new boat. He couldn't wait to introduce Jorge to the island. It was one of his favorite places. During the summer months, John's wife and children had spent many weeks staying in the small rustic cabins located at the yacht club while he commuted to his commercial real estate business via his boat.

They made plans to go the following Saturday morning. The day broke clear and sunny; a perfect day for a boat trip to Catalina. A glassy sea made the two and a half hour trip go fast. With John's help, Jorge felt more and more in control of the boat. As they approached the island, they contacted the Harbor Master by radio and were told that there was a mooring available in the Fourth of July Cove. As soon as the boat was secured, Jorge and John lowered themselves into the Boston Whaler and made their way to the yacht club's dinghy dock, a small dock reserved for members who could tie up their small boats while going ashore.

The clubhouse had a beautiful view that overlooked

the protected cove. Jorge thought it would be a very safe place for children. Steep hills rose from the ocean's edge; isolating the cove. The only way in or out was either by boat or by a small dirt path that ran along the top of the hills which surrounded the yacht club. Anyone walking along the path was completely visible to the members of the yacht club. In the forty years the club had been in existence, there had never been a problem with theft or vandalism. The worst problem seemed to be an occasional member drinking too much and having trouble maneuvering his way back to his boat.

Membership in the club included priority mooring in the Fourth of July Cove and unlimited use of all of the club's many amenities, such as private outdoor showers and the large commercial kitchen in the clubhouse, which the boaters could use to prepare meals. The highlight of being a member of the yacht club was the weekly Saturday night party. Each Saturday night, during the summertime, several members co-hosted a theme party and prepared hors d'oeuvres. It was a bring-your-own-bottle and main course type of party. Games, snacks, and movies for the children were a big part it. Jorge couldn't wait to tell Luisa about the club. Everyone was very friendly and helpful. He asked John how difficult it would be to become a member. It seemed like a very exclusive club and Jorge thought it would probably take several years to qualify for membership.

"John, I think Luisa would love it over here. I would

like to apply for membership. How should I go about it?" Jorge asked.

"I think you're in luck, Jorge. Usually it takes several years to become a member, but since I'm the head of the Membership Committee, I rather imagine I can get you approved as soon as you apply. When we get back home to the mainland, I'll bring you an application."

Jorge couldn't believe his luck. He had no idea that John was such an important member of the club. While they were ashore and having dinner in the clubhouse, John introduced him to a number of members. Back on the *Luisa*, they had a nightcap on the deck, watching the lights of the other boats swaying in the gentle swells of the protected cove. It looked like a magical fairyland. Jorge couldn't wait to bring Luisa and their soon-to-be-born baby to the cove.

They returned home the following day. Everything on the boat had worked perfectly during the previous night they had spent on board the *Luisa*. Even with heavier seas during the return trip to the mainland, the boat was a joy to handle. When they got home, they washed the boat down with fresh water and took care of a few maintenance items that were part of owning a boat. The boat wouldn't be used again until Jorge returned home in two weeks. At dinner that Sunday night, Jorge eagerly told Luisa about his trip to Catalina and the magical little yacht club. He told her he was going to apply for membership when he returned from his trip to Brazil. Luisa couldn't wait to see the club.

Although Jorge was gone for two weeks every month, it was a wonderful time in Luisa's life. Now that morning sickness had ended, she felt terrific. Her one indulgent concession to pregnancy was a welcomed afternoon nap. She saw her parents almost daily. Since her sister Selena and her husband Jim only lived about fifteen miles away, most weekends Luisa and her parents went down the coast to Laguna Beach to see them.

After returning home from Catalina with the boat, Jorge left the next day for Brazil. He was the happiest he'd ever been. He was married to a beautiful woman with a baby on the way. Living the dream, some would say. If one believed in karma, one would say his karma was good. He also had a lovely home on a protected inland waterway in Huntington Harbor, about an hour south of Los Angeles. Houses in the area were protected by a seawall with floating docks located in the rear of each house. Access to the dock was via a gangway leading from the resident's backyard.

There were several thousand homes in the upscale community with selling prices starting at well over a million dollars. Jorge had an outstanding boat tied up to his dock and enough money to do whatever he wanted. His life was very good and he knew it. Although he and Luisa tithed to the local Catholic Church, Jorge decided it was time to make an extra donation in honor of all the blessings bestowed upon him.

His driver picked him up at the Galeao International airport in Rio when he landed and took him to his home. It seemed empty to him now that Luisa and the help were gone. Luz still came every other week to clean for him, but it wasn't the same as having Luz and Manny there all the time. Jorge had been thinking about getting a small condominium, but that would require finding the time to look for one. When he was in Brazil, there were not enough hours in the day to do what needed to be done.

The next morning, he went to the Ortega & Ortega headquarters. His father, Tomas, had decided long ago that trips to the Amazon were not for him. He always became ill—from the lack of good drinking water, the humidity, the heat, the malaria-carrying mosquitos, and little sleep. Fortunately, Jorge could weather the trips and he became the face of the company at its locations in the depths of the Amazon.

In the 1980s, parts of the Brazilian Amazon Great Basin had become a gold rush area very similar to the 19th century "American Wild West." Mining activities had leveled off in the '90s, but in 2008, it once again became a prime destination for get-rich-quick entrepreneurs and schemers. However, it was difficult to get to the Brazilian interior where the gold was located. Dangerous trips on small river tributaries on less than safe boats were just the beginning. Drugs, prostitution, crime, malaria, and undrinkable water added to the mix.

The men who worked the gold mine pits were a fearless breed and corruption and violence were commonplace. Even when they could be kept under control, the indigenous tribal people were every bit as much a threat. They hated the gold miners because the pollution and erosion created by them led to toxic water conditions that caused a decline in the plants and animals of the area. For centuries, these indigenous people had depended on the river for their food and for their very existence. They were committed to doing everything they could to stop the mining, which was rapidly ruining all of the rivers in the "Gold Rush" area.

Guards and guns were everywhere to protect the mines from the indigenous tribes and the lawless gangs of renegade miners intent on stealing any gold they could. Additionally, the deforestation caused by clear cutting and burning the trees on the land resulted in enormous environmental damage, including the extinction of numerous plants found only in this unique area of the world. The indigenous people had been dependent on these plants and their healing properties for centuries. The local environmentalists only added to the problems of the mine owners. The "enviros" didn't like any part of the mining and did everything they legally could to stop it, including numerous lawsuits in the Brazilian courts.

Not only did a gold mine owner have to guard the mines, but guarding the gold itself as it was being taken out of the Amazon basin required even more guards and guns. With gold selling for record high prices, marauding bands of outlaws were not uncommon. Jorge had never told Luisa about the dangers he was exposed to when he went to the Amazon. Even though he was constantly surrounded by armed guards, he knew that if he was killed, a lot of people would be happy to see his head on a spear. Sleep did not come easily in the Amazon. A hammock hung between trees, disturbing night sounds coming from the nearby jungle, and knowing the high stakes involved in the game made for very fitful sleeping. Jorge always counted the days until he could return to the golden land, as he had come to think of California.

As dangerous and difficult as the job of owning a gold mining company was, the rewards were astronomical. The potential for wealth was unimaginable. The owners of companies such as Ortega & Ortega were the ones who reaped the benefits, much to the exclusion of the thousands of miners who worked the mines. The conditions in the mines were simply terrible. Like so many other businesses, the farther down the employment ladder, the more difficult it was for those at the bottom to make a living. At the bottom of the ladder were the garampieros, the lowly workers who could only get back to civilization to see their families every four or five months because of the overpriced passages to the coast, whether it was by way of a river boat or small plane. They worked in the mines because it was the only work available and yet, because of the mines, they could no longer live off of the land. It had become a no-win situation for them

It was a hard life for everyone, a life fueled by the promise of riches. As dangerous as it was, Jorge couldn't deny there was a part of him that was exhilarated by the risks. He felt fully alive in the Amazon, adrenalin running at full tilt. After completing each trip, there was that moment of "Ah, I made it." He couldn't explain it; it was how he always felt when he returned to Rio from the interior. As much as he disliked his time in the Amazon, a part of him thrived on the experience. His personal safety required very careful planning and Jorge was a very careful man. Every one of his senses was heightened when he was in the Amazon. He knew he had been one of the lucky ones and now, with a baby on the way and his new life in California, he vowed to be even more careful.

The months went by and Jorge arranged his schedule to be in California the week before and the week after Luisa's due date. Now they were simply waiting for Carlos. Her doctor assured both Luisa and Jorge that he would induce Luisa if she went a couple of days beyond her delivery date. The baby was big and any more growth after that date could threaten her health, as she was not a large woman.

Jorge had made it very clear to the doctor that he wanted to be with Luisa when the baby was born.

The day Carlos was born dawned bright and clear. Jorge was trying to keep himself occupied and decided to do some minor maintenance work on his boat. Luisa was one of those women who was a natural for childbirth. When her water broke, she calmly called Jorge and told him it was time. He ran up the gangway and excitedly dashed into the house. Luisa called her parents, who immediately drove to her home. Her travel bag had been packed for weeks and the four of them quickly made their way down Coast Highway to the hospital in Newport Beach. Two hours later, Luisa gave birth to a healthy 9 lb. 6 oz. baby boy. Their beautiful new son, Carlos, had joined the world. Jorge had insisted that she get a suite for her stay in the hospital so that he, her parents, and Selena could be with her and Carlos while they were in the hospital.

During her first night in the hospital, after all of the family members had left, Luisa rested in her bed. It was getting late and the big hospital was quiet. Carlos was asleep in his bassinet at the foot of her bed. She looked out the window at the nearby ocean. It was dark, but there were a few lights from passing boats and she could see the line of headlights from the cars on Pacific Coast Highway, just below the hospital. She thought to herself that her life was perfect. She wouldn't change a thing. Jorge and she had never been closer, she loved her new home and everything about California, her beloved parents and sister were nearby, and now this miracle of a baby named Carlos had joined them. She felt truly blessed. She made a mental note to give a large contribution to the church she had been attending since she had moved to California. The parish priest had paid a visit to her earlier that day to make plans for baptizing Carlos. She knew that life was not always perfect, but right now, this was perfection.

Luisa and the newest member of the Ortega family, Carlos, arrived at their Huntington Beach home two days after he was born. A week later, after making sure that Carlos and Luisa were comfortable, Jorge left for Brazil. Luisa's parents, Diego and Juanita, had promised Jorge that they would check in on Carlos and Luisa a couple of times a day. The nanny Luisa hired was staying downstairs in the maid's room. Luisa and Carlos would be well taken care of in Jorge's absence.

Motherhood came easily for Luisa. Her breasts were engorged with milk, but Carlos was a willing feeder. She had heard that a lot of women had problems breastfeeding, but to Luisa, it was the most natural thing in the world. She felt like she was born to be a mother.

The next few months assumed a rhythmic pattern. Jorge was at home for two weeks, followed by two weeks in the Amazon. Carlos was an easy baby, increasing in weight and becoming more and more aware of the world around him.

One weekend, Jorge and Luisa left Carlos with her parents and took their boat to Catalina Island. Jorge had submitted his membership application to the Fourth of July Yacht Club and true to his word, John made sure that the Ortega family was admitted.

Luisa had no experience on boats, but she loved the freedom of being on the ocean and took to it naturally. She even went below to make sandwiches in the galley, something even the seasoned seamen preferred not to do because of possible seasickness. Louisa never had a queasy moment during the two and a half hour trip to the island.

Jorge guided the boat into the mooring at the Fourth of July Cove, easily attaching the bowline to the floating buoy that was anchored to the sea floor. He took Luisa ashore to show her the clubhouse and walked her around the premises. He had visited the Fourth of July Yacht Club a few times during her pregnancy and he introduced her to some of the people he had met. Luisa loved the ambience of the club and couldn't wait until Carlos was old enough to join them. She envisioned sitting on the sandy shore, watching him play in the water. She agreed with Jorge, of how safe this place would be for Carlos. Even so, she made a mental note to enroll Carlos in swimming lessons as soon as he was old enough. Between the pool and ocean water at their home in Huntington Beach as well as the yacht club, he needed to be "water safe."

On the trip back to the mainland, she noticed that

Jorge seemed tense and withdrawn. "Jorge, what's wrong with you? Are you coming down with something? You're not your usual happy self," Luisa said.

"I'm fine," he replied. "I just wish I didn't have to leave you and Carlos all the time. The older he gets, the harder it is for me to leave and fly to Brazil. Even if he was old enough and could come with me, I would never want him to witness what happens in the Amazon. We'll go to Rio when he's older, as I think it's important for him to know his heritage, but never to the Amazon."

Luisa was surprised at the vehemence in Jorge's voice. He had never spoken like that before. She hoped his enthusiasm for life would return soon because this was quite unlike him.

Jorge left for Brazil two days after they returned from their boating trip to Catalina Island. While Jorge was in Brazil, Carlos developed colic and began to lose a little weight. It seemed to Luisa that he was awake around the clock and so was she. She could feel herself getting really tired as the days came and went. She had been to Carlos' pediatrician several times, but he assured Luisa that Carlos would outgrow the colic. He asked if anything was bothering Luisa, for often if the mother was tense or upset, it was passed on through nursing and then the baby became colicky. When Luisa thought about it, she realized that lately she had been somewhat tense and irritable. She had snapped at Carlos' nanny, argued with her parents, and even gotten mad at John for going aboard the *Luisa* without asking her permission. She couldn't come up with any reason why she felt so anxious and nervous. On the surface, life was perfect. Maybe it was Jorge's schedule that was causing her to feel this way. She couldn't think of anything else that was bothering her. She vowed to be more accepting of Jorge's schedule.

It had been a rough couple of weeks for Jorge. Just before he left California for his trip to Brazil, he received word that three of his most trusted guards had been murdered during a botched hold-up attempt. Whenever he left the mines, he had concerns about those he had left behind. The loss of these three employees seemed to reconfirm to Jorge the dangers that lurked in the Amazon. The area where the mines were located was getting more and more lawless each time he went there. The only thing he could think to do was put more guns and guards in place. Two of the mines were barely producing any gold and he felt the time had come to close them down. However, that still left five others, each with its own set of operational problems.

He felt depressed just thinking about what lay ahead. The newspapers and enviros were having a field day with claims of pollution and environmental destruction. In addition to these claims, the murders only confirmed everything that could go wrong in the mines. A recent malaria outbreak hadn't helped and the enviros had traced it to one of the Ortega mines. It was a land-dredged mine causing water runoff, which had become a breeding ground for the mosquito-borne malaria disease. Many of the garimpieros who worked the open pit mines had come down with the illness. All of this recent publicity had definitely not been good for the Ortega & Ortega Company.

When Jorge returned to Rio from the mines where he had spent the better part of two weeks, he was tired and out of sorts. He hoped he'd feel better when he returned home to Luisa and Carlos. He slept fitfully the first night he was back in Rio and was awake long before his driver was due to take him to the airport. As if he didn't feel bad enough, the long plane ride home was filled with violent turbulence caused by a hurricane forming in the Gulf of Mexico. The captain made the flight attendants take their seats for most of the flight. Jorge just wanted to be in his bed in California and sleep for as long as it took him to regain his usual easy-going nature.

Arriving home, he turned his key in the front door lock and heard Carlos crying. The cries the baby was making were like none Jorge had ever heard him make before. He kissed Luisa and asked what was wrong with Carlos. She told him about the colic and how Carlos cried nonstop. Luisa and the nanny were taking turns staying up with him. Jorge picked Carlos up from his cradle and tried rocking him to sleep, but it didn't do any good; Carlos just continued to cry.

Putting Carlos back in his cradle, Jorge said, "Luisa,

I'm sorry to do this to you, but I need some sleep. The flight was horrible and the last two weeks have not been the best. I'm exhausted. I'll help you with Carlos tomorrow."

Jorge tossed and turned in bed throughout the night and got little sleep. It seemed that whenever Jorge would finally get to sleep, Carlos would start crying again. Clearly, Luisa was just as exhausted. She didn't want to tell Jorge, but she had begun to blame herself for Carlos' incessant crying.

Early the next morning, Jorge, bleary-eyed and exhausted, walked into the kitchen to make some coffee. He was surprised to see Luisa at the kitchen table, already dressed and on her second cup of coffee. Luisa said, "Jorge, we have to do something. I feel depressed and it seems like you do too. I've been thinking. We were both so happy at the time of Selena's wedding. We were exhausted and out of sorts when we landed in Phoenix and then, after we stayed at that motel along the highway, we felt so much better. Remember?"

She didn't tell him that she had been fighting a losing battle with bulimia before they stayed at that motel. Now, the more depressed and tired she became, the more she just wanted to eat everything she could in hopes it would make her feel better. She couldn't tell Jorge, but she was terrified it was only a matter of time until she would begin to binge and purge. Her commitment to the health of her baby was the only thing that was stopping her.

"Yes, "Jorge said, "Funny you'd mention it. I've been thinking about that little motel too. Maybe we need to get away, just the two of us. It's not a world-class destination, but we both have good memories about it, so why not go there? We'll go over the Memorial Day weekend. I'll be in California that week. We could ask Diego and Juanita to take care of Carlos and hopefully, we'll both come back refreshed. You'd feel better about Carlos and I'd feel better about business. What do you think?"

"Yes," she sighed, "That's a good idea. I'll do about anything at this point. Hopefully, we can both last a few more weeks. It's only one more business trip for you and I can do anything for that short time. I'll make the reservations. Thank you." Luisa was excited for the first time in weeks. She really hoped that the upcoming visit to the motel would sprinkle a bit of its magic on them, like it had when they had been there before.

Luisa was an obsessive list maker. She made a record of every place they had ever stayed, every restaurant they had ever eaten in, and anything else she felt should be committed to paper. She went upstairs to her office, opened the desk drawer, and quickly found the notebook in which she had written down the name and phone number of the Blue Coyote Motel. She placed a call to the motel. On the second ring a familiar voice answered. "Blue Coyote Motel, may I help you?" Maria asked.

"Yes," replied Luisa. "My husband and I stayed with you over a year ago and I was wondering if you would have a room for the Memorial Day weekend. We'd like it for two nights, Friday and Saturday. The last time we stayed at your motel we lived in Brazil, but since then we have moved and now live in Southern California."

"Yes," replied Maria. "I remember you. You're Mrs. Ortega, aren't you? As I recall, you and your husband had just flown in from Rio and were hurrying to get to your sister's wedding in Laguna Beach."

"What a great memory you have," Luisa said. "How did you remember us and know it was me?"

"Well, you speak English beautifully, but you do have a slight accent. Not many people come here with a foreign accent. I have you down for a room for two nights on Memorial Day weekend, Friday and Saturday. I'll look forward to seeing you then. Have a safe trip driving over."

After speaking with Luisa on the telephone, Maria buzzed Jeffrey on the motel intercom. "Jeffrey, would you believe it? We already have two rooms booked for the Memorial Day weekend and they're return customers. You'll need to make a fresh batch of Freedom. I'm sure that's why they're returning. They just don't know it. We can really help them."

Back in Huntington Beach and two hundred miles from the Blue Coyote Motel, Luisa hung up the phone looking forward to the upcoming trip. For the first time in weeks, she felt hopeful about the future.

CHAPTER 29

Sean and Jeanne's marriage was performed by a priest Sean knew at a little chapel in the Rocky Mountains, outside of Vail. It was late winter and there was still plenty of snow. It was a very small wedding and neither Jeanne nor Sean had invited their families. Sean knew his family would be disappointed by the wedding. They still expected him to act like the priest they had known him to be. Jeanne's family was so dysfunctional that she had little to do with them. A few of their friends came as well as some employees from the clinic. After the ceremony, Sean and Jeanne hosted a dinner for their guests at a local bed and breakfast.

He had never been happier. He discovered he was a natural counselor. Sean had hired other good psychologists and the clinic was thriving. The media was beginning to give it attention, both in print and through television and radio. Sean thought the reason the clinic had become so successful so fast was that it filled a need which had not been addressed other than by bits and pieces, here and there. It offered numerous workshops and groups dealing with Alzheimer's, homelessness and problems associated with simply growing up. The old term "hardening of the arteries" had been replaced by the term "Alzheimer's" and almost every family had someone who suffered from dementia. This condition affected the whole family and the clinic not only dealt with it, both in counseling and education, but it also offered classes and counseling for the caregivers, who had often been overlooked.

Denver was a compassionate city and its local officials were very interested in working with the homeless to get them off of the streets. The mayor and the city council made it a top priority. Sean's clinic offered workshops, classes and counseling for the homeless. The founder of the clinic had been instrumental in setting up workshops and programs designed to help the homeless get jobs and with their new income, they no longer had to resort to living on the streets. The successful results were tangible.

The city was a mecca for young people who lived to ski, but after the season ended, many found themselves with no resources and often resorted to selling and taking drugs, as well as prostitution. Under Jeanne's wise tutelage, programs dealing with those problems were also implemented and they, too, had the backing of the mayor and the city council.

It may have been as simple as being in the right place at the right time, but for whatever reason, the clinic was a huge success and greatly appreciated by the citizens of Denver, many of whom made it a top priority when they wrote their checks to non-profit organizations.

The more attention given to the clinic by the media,

the more people wanted to be associated with it. A number of retired psychologists donated their time as did a few doctors and nurses. The clinic was expanding rapidly and with the growing case load, they were soon going to need more space.

Many of those who came to the clinic were insured, so the cash flow was substantial. Patients could go elsewhere, but they had heard impressive stories about the clinic and they chose it instead. Not only was Sean using all his counseling skills, he was also taking classes on management, a subject completely foreign to him.

Sean had always been a people person. His genuine warmth and caring nature effortlessly drew people to him. He found that many people wanted to work for him and he was able hire his employees from a large pool of well-qualified applicants.

Jeanne was thriving as well, both in the marriage and in her work at the clinic. She was very skilled at connecting with young people because of her troubled background. She could identify with and speak to the problems her clients brought to her when they sought her guidance.

Sean was surprised to find that he really enjoyed skiing. Jeanne was a world class skier and a very good teacher. Under her guidance he was becoming quite accomplished. They spent every weekend in the mountains. Everything about his life had changed, with the exception of the counseling. He found he enjoyed being outdoors, which he thought was strange after all of the years he had spent in church praying and conducting services. He didn't drink, he had a wonderful wife, and the thoughts of young boys no longer haunted him. That was all in the past. If someone had told him that he would be leading this type of life a few years ago, he would have thought they were crazy. It was a life he couldn't have imagined in his wildest dreams.

As a priest, he had never been interested in the rapidly growing world of technology. Smart phones, tablets, and computers held no fascination for him, but as director of the clinic, he was forced to become technologically literate. A thriving business depended on websites, billing programs, scheduling, and calendars. Soon Sean found that he was able to master and enjoy this new world. He realized that, like so many others, he had even become dependent on his smart phone and his portable tablet.

Relaxing while having lunch one day and surfing on his iPad, he discovered an app on birding. He had no idea that it was one of the most popular outdoor recreational activities in America. Sean became fascinated with the activity and talked Jeanne into traveling to the mountains after the ski season to go birding. They took their first birding trip early in the spring, just as the last of the winter snow was melting. Jeanne had always loved any outdoor activity and enjoyed taking photos of the many species of birds native to the Rocky Mountains.

Between their winter ski trips and the birding, they were spending almost every weekend in the Rocky Mountains. They talked of buying a small cabin in the mountains since they were spending so much time driving back and forth on the weekends. They contacted a real estate agent and began looking at properties. Sean didn't think life could get any better.

Then things began to change. For several weeks, Sean had begun to notice that something wasn't quite right with him. Sometimes he felt like he had a fever, then that would go away only to be replaced by a feeling of nausea. At other times he felt chilled and noticed he was sweating more than usual. He began to snap at Jeanne and found he was becoming impatient with almost everyone and everything. His wonderful new life came crashing down one morning when he woke up and realized that he had dreamed of seducing young boys while drinking vodka with them. He got out of bed, drenched with sweat. *Dear God, please no,* he silently prayed. *Not again. No doubt about it,* he thought, *the dream had been highly erotic.* Even though emotionally he was disgusted with himself, his fully erect penis indicated some baser part of him had responded to the dream. As if the dream hadn't been enough of a wake-up call that something was happening to him, when he made his way to the bathroom to shower and shave, he noticed that the stubble on his face was white, rather than gray.

He started thinking about some of the other physical changes he'd noticed lately, but hadn't really paid much attention to, like the veins on the back of his hands, which stood out prominently, and the trouble he was having sleeping. He'd recently admitted to himself he felt really tired, but he couldn't seem to get a good night's sleep. He tended to blame it on his hectic schedule, but now he wondered why he seemed to be aging prematurely.

Sean walked into the bedroom where Jeanne was getting ready for her busy day and asked, "Have you noticed anything different about me?"

"Well, I didn't want to alarm you, but yes, I've noticed that you don't seem as energetic as you were a couple of months ago. I thought maybe with working so hard during the week and playing so much on the weekends, it was beginning to take its toll on you," Jeanne answered. "I'm sure it's nothing. Perhaps we should stay home the next couple of weekends. The last few months have really been hectic. We could both use a little rest."

The day seemed like it would never end. For some reason, Sean's mind kept focusing on the past and all of the problems associated with it. He was unusually sharp with his employees, finding fault with everything, and being less than empathetic with his own patients.

Finally, as the day wore on, Sean was forced to admit to himself that the siren song of alcohol was beginning to sing to him. From his background in psychology, he knew he couldn't stop the seductive thoughts of alcohol, but it was how he reacted to those thoughts that could be a problem. The mere thought of taking a drink scared the hell out of him. *And then what?* he thought. *Would the fantasy of young boys become more than a dream? Would it rear its ugly head as well? Would Jeanne leave him? Would he be forced out of the clinic?* He felt he was going down a steep and slippery slope, that everything he had worked so hard to overcome was about to come crashing down, destroying his new life. He was becoming increasingly anxious and nervous. Sean tried to think of something he could do that would reverse these bad thoughts that were coming to him.

For some reason he began to think back to when his life had turned around. He remembered the little motel in the desert where he had stopped when he'd realized that he was too drunk to drive. He felt overcome by a strong urge to return to that little desert motel. Who knew, maybe there was some healing magic there?

Coming home from the clinic, he pulled his car into the garage and walked into the kitchen, where Jeanne was beginning to fix dinner. "I've been thinking," he said. "I know I've told you about this little motel in the California desert where I stopped last year and it may seem crazy, but I wonder if there's some healing process going on there. I keep remembering how optimistic I was and how good my future looked when I left there, even though I was at the lowest point of my life. There was supposed to be a number of holistic healing places in that area of California and Arizona. You know, hot springs, mineral springs, things like that. Maybe there's something like that going on at that motel.

"Anyway, if you don't mind, I think I'll go there over the Memorial Day weekend, spend a couple of nights, and see if I feel any better. I don't want to alarm you, but not only have I been having some strange physical things going on, I've also been quick-tempered and impatient, which I'm sure you've noticed. But the thing that really got my attention was a dream I had last night. It was about young men and vodka. Quite frankly, it scared the hell out of me on one level, but was tantalizing on another. I'll make the trip by myself. You stay here and enjoy some quiet time without me to bother you. I'll be back before you know it, hopefully back to my normal cheery self. I love you and I will do whatever it takes to keep you and preserve and protect this wonderful new life we've built together. I refuse to go back to who I was. I can't. It's not an option. I'd rather die than go back to that hellish double life."

"Oh Sean, I've been so worried about you. Yes, of course, if you think it will help; then go. Set yourself free once and for all. You've told me a number of times how desperate you were and that suddenly, when you woke up at that motel, you felt optimistic, that there might be a future for you after all. Whether or not there is any healing going on there doesn't matter. What does matter is that you need to feel good again. That's all that is important. We both know enough to understand that these things often have no scientific factual basis, but they work. Call and make your reservation while I finish dinner."

Sean couldn't remember the name of the motel. He racked his brain, but nothing came to him. He recalled that he had used his credit card and perhaps the name of the motel would be in his credit card file. He went upstairs to his office, pulled open the desk drawer, and quickly found the file he was looking for. He leafed back through the pages, and there, in the charge column, was the name "Blue Coyote Motel." Now he remembered the neon coyote sign on the side of the road. He opened his iPad, pulled up the browser, and typed in "Blue Coyote Motel." The motel website immediately popped up with the phone number. He still marveled at technology and how you could find anything you wanted on the Internet. It was amazing.

He took out his cell phone and tapped the phone number onto the keypad. The phone was answered immediately by the lovely young woman who had called him "Father." He recognized her voice and remembered her well. A beautiful Latina, although at the time, he hadn't been particularly interested.

"This is Sean Moriarty. I stayed at the Blue Coyote Motel almost a year ago and I'd like to stay there

Friday and Saturday of Memorial Day weekend, if you have room."

"Of course, Father, I remember you. We would love to see you again. See you in a couple of weeks," Maria said, her voice warm and comforting.

Swell, thought Sean, *how in the devil do I tell her I'm no longer a priest and that I'm married? Being Latina, she's probably a devout Catholic who could never understand how a priest could become defrocked. Oh well, I'll cross that bridge when I come to it. Just a couple more weeks and I'll be there.*

Feeling optimistic for the first time in several weeks, the aroma of the chicken roasting in the oven brought him back to the present and he hurried down the stairs to Jeanne.

CHAPTER 30

Barbie called Jill one Sunday afternoon a few weeks after they had returned from Nepal. "How about coming to a Zen meditation session with me later today? You seemed to enjoy the Tibetan aspect of Buddhism when we were in Nepal. I'd like to introduce you to a type of meditation called sitting meditation. It's associated with Japanese Zen Buddhism."

Barbie picked her up later that afternoon and drove her to a nearby Zen Center. On the way, Barbie filled her in on what she could expect, cautioning her about keeping silent and trying to limit her physical movements. She told her how to sit on a pillow called a zafu and where to place her hands.

They parked the car and entered a vibrant, flower-filled courtyard. A few minutes before 5:00 p.m., they walked up the steps to the meditation room along with a number of other people. The room was oblong and everyone sat on a zafu facing a wall. Candlelight filled the room and there was the smell of incense, a sandalwood scent that Jill was familiar with from her bi-monthly facials. She knew she'd also smelled it somewhere else, but she couldn't quite remember where.

There were two sitting meditation sessions of twenty minutes each and a walking meditation in between. The hardest part for Jill was trying not to swat the fly that kept landing on her face. Barbie had been very clear about keeping her movements to a minimum. Evidently, part of the Buddhist philosophy was a non-attachment to anything whatsoever; that all things would pass. The fly that kept landing on her cheek gave a new meaning to this concept for Jill. She kept waiting for it to pass.

After the meditation, they turned around, faced one another, and listened to the Zen priest give a talk. Following the service, tea and snacks were served in the courtyard where candles were brightly glowing. It was enchanting. Jill started thinking about how she could get this effect on the patio at her home.

She felt a tap on her shoulder. "Excuse me, but weren't you recently on a trek in Nepal?" an attractive man asked her. Looking closely, she recognized the doctor from San Francisco, the sixth member of their trek. Jill remembered him, but she had forgotten just how attractive he was. He was about 6'2", dark hair with graying temples, green eyes, and a great body.

"Yes, I was. How are you?" Jill replied. "I thought you lived in San Francisco. What brings you to Orange County?"

"I had a medical conference in Los Angeles this week and my parents live in Newport Beach. I've heard good things about this Zen Center so I decided to stay over the weekend and try it. And you? Are you a member of the center?"

Jill replied that her friend Barbie had attended services at the center for a long time. After their trip to Nepal, Jill had mentioned to Barbie that she would be interested in attending a service at the center. She told him that this was her first time.

Aaron Nichols was the doctor's name. Jill was surprised when he asked if he could take her to dinner that night. He explained that he was flying back to San Francisco the next day and friends had recommended that he try a new restaurant owned by a celebrity chef who had just opened his restaurant in Newport Beach. Jill was even more surprised when she found herself accepting his invitation.

The people at the center were extremely friendly and very well educated. It seemed that every other one was a doctor, a lawyer, or a psychiatrist. Jill had read somewhere that Zen appealed to the intellect rather than the emotions. This group certainly seemed to underline that.

Jill found Barbie and told her she wouldn't need to take her home. She said the doctor they had met in Nepal was there and that he had asked her to dinner.

"Well, you certainly are doing better than I did," Barbie said. "I tried to get his attention the whole time we were on the trek. Guess I'm not his type! I'm glad you're going out with him. It's time and Rick would want you to make new friends, particularly a handsome doctor from San Francisco."

The dinner with Aaron was thoroughly enjoyable. He was attractive, smart, and entertaining. Jill enjoyed being with him and having been a doctor's wife; she could easily understand and talk about his world. The evening went by quickly and when he took her home, Aaron asked if he could see her again. He explained that he would be in the area during the holidays and asked if she would have dinner with him then. Jill said she'd love to. He pulled out his Blackberry, consulting his calendar. "How about the 23rd of December? As I mentioned earlier, I have family in the area and I usually spend every other year down here for a few days during the holidays."

He walked her to her door, again telling her how much he had enjoyed being with her. Aaron mentioned that he had been attracted to her on the trek, but she had a "Do Not Disturb" air about her. He had made some inquiries and found she was a recent widow and not open to any male overtures. She liked the fact that he had sense enough not to intrude at that time and found she was looking forward to the 23rd.

While she didn't feel "enlightened" after she returned from the Zen Center, she felt pretty good. She didn't know if the good feelings were from the Zen Center or from Aaron. She decided to try and sit in meditation for twenty minutes a day to see how it felt. Aaron said he had been doing Zen meditation for years and credited it with being able to deal with the world from a place of calmness. Jill went to the Internet and found a Zen supplier who carried zafus and ordered one. *I might as well be comfortable if I'm going to do this*, she thought as she placed the order.

Jill was dreading Christmas without Rick and she decided to accept every invitation that came, hoping it might help to ease the pain and loneliness she knew she was going to feel. Maybe if she kept busy, she wouldn't feel quite so lonely.

The 23rd of December came and with it, dinner with Aaron. She again enjoyed herself, perhaps even more this time than the first time. He asked if she was up to being his date at a family dinner the next evening, Christmas Eve. He told her it was a very casual thing. Family and friends traditionally came to his parents' home on Christmas Eve for drinks and food. It wasn't a sit-down formal affair, just lots of extended family and a table loaded with fabulous food.

It took her a moment to reply. Her first instinct was that she should mourn Rick on Christmas Eve and Christmas Day, but in the next moment, she knew that Rick would be the first to insist that she find happiness wherever she could. Theirs had been a wonderful love affair, but that was in the past. It was time to move on. "I can't think of anything I would rather do. May I bring something?" she asked.

"A hungry tummy and a hollow leg," Aaron replied. "There's a lot to eat and drink. I think you'll like my family. We're a bit of a Heinz 57; Jewish,

Catholic, Muslim, and now me, a Buddhist. We're a true American melting pot. My mother is Irish Catholic—I get my green eyes from her—and my father is Jewish. My sister married a Muslim. It can be a bit chaotic, but we get to celebrate a lot of different things, and always with food!" Aaron was clearly delighted she would be joining him and his family.

True to his word, the table groaned with every wonderful food imaginable and waiters were quick to fill an empty glass. Aaron's parents lived on Lido Isle, located on the water in the heart of Newport Beach. The entire neighborhood was alive with Christmas lights. Aaron's father was a doctor at Newport Hospital and had known Rick. There were several other doctors and their wives at the party, many of whom Jill knew. Aaron's parents were delightful. They had been married for over forty-five years and were clearly still in love. They were a joy to be around.

What a combination, Jill thought when she met them. Aaron's father was balding, tall, and thin with large horn-rimmed glasses. His mother was short and squat with a fair but freckled complexion, green eyes, and beautiful shoulder-length red hair. It was only fitting that her name was Maureen. *I would have bet anything that would be her name*, Jill thought, grateful for the warmth they extended to her. It was a wonderful evening and Aaron had been charming and attentive. She was not blind to the numerous kisses and hugs other women felt compelled to bestow on Aaron. She even sensed a bit of jealousy in a few of the women as she was introduced to them by him.

February came and true to her word, Jill had been an integral part of the most successful fundraising event in the history of Newport Hospital. Her silent auction was a huge success. The final amount raised was well over three million dollars. The five-star hotel where the fundraiser was held had done an incredible job of catering to the wealthy with a fabulous meal and tables that gleamed with silver, crystal, and Spode china. Massive floral bouquets had been placed throughout the dining and silent auction rooms. Each dining table floral centerpiece was a smaller version of the large bouquets. The jewels the women wore blazed in the candlelit room.

Bidding was fierce for the donated items. The Rolls Royce topped the list, followed by a one-month stay at an oceanfront compound in Maui and a chalet near Mont Blanc in the Alps. It brought in more money than any past auction. Jill enjoyed soliciting the donations. It was fun and it made her feel she was needed. When she was recognized by Marge and asked to rise to a standing ovation, she felt great. It was good to be acknowledged for something. It was a feeling Jill hadn't experienced in a long time.

Jill and Aaron spent a lot of time together whenever he visited Newport Beach. In mid-May, she made plans for a trip to San Francisco to see her friend Samantha. She mentioned to Aaron that she would be visiting. Of course he wanted to see her and she had to admit that she wanted to see him just as much. After she got off the telephone with him and was getting ready for bed, she looked in the mirror and noticed some grey roots in her hair. She made a mental note to herself to call her hairdresser and make an appointment for a touch up.

That's odd, she thought. *I could swear I was in the hair salon just a couple of weeks ago.* She went to her computer and pulled up her calendar. *Yes, just as I thought, I had my roots done three weeks ago. I've never had to do them that often. I wonder why?*

She turned the computer off and went back into the bathroom. Several people had asked her lately if she was feeling okay. She took a long look at herself in the mirror and could see why. She looked tired. There were lines where there never had been lines before. *I need to get a facial*, she thought. But hadn't she had a facial just a few weeks ago? She went back to the study, turned the computer back on, and once again, pulled up her calendar. It showed that it had only been two weeks since her last facial. She began to seriously wonder what was going on with her physical appearance. She stripped down and stood nude in front of the full-length mirror attached to the back of the bathroom door, taking a long look at herself. There was no mistaking the fact that her skin was beginning to sag and that her breasts, which had always been what people called "pert," had begun to droop. Her stomach, which had always been flat, looked saggy. Jill's skin and particularly her lips felt unusually dry. Something was happening to her body. She decided to see her doctor when she returned from San Francisco.

The next morning it was all she could do to get out of bed. She had an early board meeting with one of her charities, but it didn't interest her. All she wanted to do was sleep. After the meeting, she was scheduled to fly to San Francisco to see Samantha and Aaron. Even that didn't excite her. She got through the next few hours in a fog.

Samantha met her at the San Francisco airport. "Are you feeling alright?" She asked after giving Jill a hug. "You look like you could use some rest."

"I don't know what's wrong with me," Jill said. "I'm just bone tired."

Samantha took a long look at Jill. "I think you need to have some tests done. You don't look well. Promise me when you get back home you'll go see your doctor."

"I've already scheduled an appointment for Monday morning, but first let's just have a great time this weekend. Aaron's picking me up tonight for dinner, so you'll get a chance to meet him. I'd like your opinion," "Jill said.

Aaron arrived at Samantha's home promptly at 6:00 p.m. to pick up Jill. Samantha lived in a home the San Franciscans called a "painted lady," homes that were unique to that city. Several streets on steep hills were lined with these narrow, three-story Victorian houses which were painted in a variety of pastel colors. After Samantha's divorce, she had decided to completely redo her home and it was a beautiful combination of old and new. She loved to show it off and willingly gave Aaron a tour.

When Jill and Aaron got in his car to go to the restaurant, he took a long look at her. "Are you all right? You know I'm a doctor. You look like you may have picked up a bug. Have you been to your doctor? I'm worried about you."

She told him that she had made an appointment for the day after she returned. Aaron asked if she'd noticed feeling any differently recently. She told him she didn't have any energy and felt like she was aging a lot faster than she should be. She said she didn't hurt anywhere; that she had just done her monthly self-breast exam and everything seemed to be completely normal, but still she felt like something was "off."

He made her promise to call him after she saw her doctor. The rest of the evening was just as wonderful as every other time she had been with Aaron. She realized she was falling in love with him; something she never thought would happen after Rick, especially this soon. After dinner, it felt natural for them to go to Aaron's home overlooking the San Francisco Bay. She had never thought she would want another man, but she wanted Aaron and knew he felt the same way. He suggested she call Samantha and tell her she would see her tomorrow. Jill hung up the phone as Aaron was turning the lights off. The drapes were open to a spectacular view of the city skyline with the lights on the boats in the bay gently bobbing and swaying below them.

Their bodies fit together as if in a mold, and the lovemaking was easy, yet passionate. For a fleeting moment, Jill wondered what Aaron was thinking of her body, particularly if she was aging prematurely as she suspected, but as passion filled both of them, the analytical part of her brain shut down.

They spent most of the weekend in bed, hungrily exploring each other. Both were passionate, inventive lovers and Samantha's carefully constructed plans for the weekend never materialized. Aaron and Jill wanted nothing more than to be with each other. Sunday night came far too soon. Aaron took Jill by Samantha's home to pick up her suitcase on the way to the airport, kissing her passionately at the curb as they said good-bye to each other. Once again, Aaron made her promise that she would call him after she had seen her doctor.

Jill got on the plane and took a window seat. She loved to look at the ocean as the plane pulled away from San Francisco. She took the airline magazine out of the seatback in front of her and noticed that her hands were trembling. *I know I didn't have much sleep, but this is ridiculous*, she thought. She didn't want her seatmate to notice the trembling and put her hands underneath the open magazine. *Where is this coming from?* She wondered. She willed the trembling to stop. It didn't.

The next day, Jill dressed carefully for her doctor's appointment. It was always a challenge to figure out what type of clothing could be removed easily in the doctor's office without completely ruining hair and makeup when changing into the unflattering gown that was required. She settled on a simple beige skirt and matching silk blouse. They were clothes that were easy to get in and out of.

Dr. Mathis stepped into the exam room. "Jill, what brings you here? I haven't seen you in a long time, but that's good news in this business." He reminded Jill of Santa Claus with his white hair, ruddy face, round belly, and booming laugh. She adored him.

"Dr. M, I don't know what's wrong," Jill said. "I don't have any energy. My skin is really dry and has lost its elasticity. The roots of my hair are greying way too fast and I feel like I'm aging every time I look in the mirror. And my breasts have begun to sag. I know I came to you after Rick died because I was tired, but this is completely different. Plus, I have found a man I think I'm in love with, so if I could just get rid of these physical things, my life would be just about perfect."

"Hmm," Dr. Mathis said, "let's have a look." He gave her a thorough examination. "Jill, I don't find anything that causes me concern. I'm writing a prescription for a number of tests, which may tell us more. My nurse will call and make an appointment for you at the lab in the building next door as soon as I finish. I'll have the lab expedite the results and I'll call you this afternoon."

"Thanks, Dr. M. I really appreciate it. I don't feel that anything is seriously wrong. I'm just off. I've felt really good these last few months. In fact, I started feeling good after a trip last summer. I pulled off the road and stayed at a little motel in the middle of nowhere. When I got up the next morning, I felt terrific. Maybe it was the desert air, although I have a place in La Quinta so you wouldn't think it would be all that different. Maybe I should go back there."

"Well, let's see what we're dealing with. I'll call you this afternoon. June, who works at the front desk, will have your lab prescription ready for you as soon as I type it into my computer. Don't worry. It's probably just a delayed reaction to all of the stress you've been under after Rick's death. Stress can do strange things to the body. It was really good seeing you and I'm happy that you have a new friend."

After Dr. Mathis left the exam room, Jill dressed quickly. She hadn't told Dr. M about her hands shaking. She had heard that people who were withdrawing from drugs had shaky hands. She loved a couple of glasses of wine, but she wasn't an alcoholic. Still, she thought that was something better kept to herself. Jill picked up her prescription and headed for the lab. After a series of tests, she went home and waited for the call from Dr. Mathis. She wondered if she should have told him how suicidal she had been before she stopped at that little desert motel, but once again, she was afraid he would insist that she see a psychiatrist. Jill filled the time with busy work while waiting for him to call. Plants needed watering, phone calls needed returning, and it was time to start making a list of possible donors for next year's auction.

The phone rang late that afternoon. "Jill, it's Dr. Mathis. I have the results from the lab tests and I'm pleased to tell you that everything appears to be completely normal. Oh, your cholesterol is a bit high, but after spending a weekend in San Francisco, I'm not surprised. Maybe you should just go back to that desert motel. A little rest away from the hustle and bustle of your busy lifestyle might be good for you. Well, anyway, you're just fine now. If you notice anything else, call me, but I don't see anything that would be a cause for alarm. I'm giving you a clean bill of health and again, I'm really happy for you!"

Jill called Aaron and told him the good news. He was clearly relieved to hear the results of the exam and tests. "Jill, maybe you should go back to the motel in the desert you told me about. I'd be happy to go with you, but it would have to be at least a month from now. My scheduler books my appointments a month in advance."

One of the things Jill loved about Aaron was his lack of ego. He was one of the leading oncologists in the United States. People traveled from all over the world to see him and she knew that his schedule was probably booked a lot longer into the future than a month.

"Thanks, but I'm perfectly capable of driving there myself. Actually, I think I'll go over the Memorial Day weekend. I can drive down to my home in La Quinta. I haven't been there in a while and I should see if everything is   okay. Don't worry, I'll be fine." They hung up after making plans for Aaron to fly to Orange County on the coming weekend. Jill would pick him up at John Wayne Airport. They decided not to tell his parents that he would be in town. They didn't want to share each other with anyone.

Jill spent the next few hours looking for the name of the motel. She couldn't find it anywhere. She tried both the Internet as well as telephone information, but since she didn't know the name of the closest town, if there even was one, both of those usually reliable sources of information were of absolutely no help to her. She had paid cash so there was no credit card receipt. She remembered it was something about a color and an animal.

She began to get panicky, hoping against hope that the thoughts of suicide wouldn't come up again. She started a list in her mind of all the things she had to live for. Aaron headed the list. And what was going on with this intermittent shaking of her hands? It had been happening on and off ever since her flight from San Francisco. That was really strange.

Her hands seemed like they were developing a life of their own.

That night she awoke suddenly at 3:00 a.m. The words "Blue Coyote" were running through her mind. She sat straight up in bed and thought to herself, *That's it. That's the name of the motel. I was right. It's a color and an animal. I'll call in the morning.* She wrote the name down so she wouldn't lose it like she often did with dreams that were so clear in the middle of the night, but slipped away like wispy clouds, disappearing in the morning.

"Hello, Blue Coyote Motel. May I help you?" Maria said into the phone.

"Yes. My name is Jill Loren," Jill said. "I stayed at the motel last September. I felt so good when I left, I decided I need to come back to rest and refresh myself. Would you have a room available over the Memorial Day weekend? I'd like to reserve a room for Friday and Saturday nights."

"Yes, I can accommodate you," Maria said. "I have you down and I'll look forward to seeing you a week from Friday. It should be beautiful that weekend. The desert days are quite warm, but the nights are magical." She vaguely remembered Jill as being a rather troubled woman and thought to herself that she probably needed a little Freedom "tune-up."

CHAPTER 31

When Sam was a young man witnessing the abuse of his mother at the hands of the man to whom she was married, living on the edge of poverty, watching his fellow tribe members struggle with addiction and social illnesses, he would have never been able to predict his present life.

After observing the poor choice his mother had made, he was taking his budding relationship with Phyllis Chee very slowly and carefully. They thoroughly enjoyed each other's company and looked forward to the time they spent together. Their burgeoning romance had not escaped the watchful eyes of the nattering old women of the tribe and a lot of idle gossip centered around the two of them and their future. For their part, they were happy to just let everything gradually unfold.

Sam knew he was making an important contribution to his tribe. The overall health of the tribal children was flourishing under his medical care and supervision. Likewise, the new school built on the reservation was a vast improvement for their educational opportunities. A committee had been set up for oversight of the school, a committee on which he willingly served. Although the tribe was a sovereign nation, the school fell under state mandates.

The committee had the option to standardize the teaching to the state requirements or opt to set higher standards for the students and their teachers. They chose the higher standards and the results proved that they had made the right decision. The children were testing far higher than their peers in other parts of the state. It had been a controversial, difficult choice, but it was paying off, not only for the respect the school was garnering throughout the state, but in the children's education. For the first time that Sam could ever remember, the children's eyes shined with hope for the future. Many of them spoke of getting college educations. Parents were attending back-to-school nights and meetings with the teachers. In the past, such meetings had been poorly attended, if at all.

The pediatric center was thriving too. The children's parents were becoming increasingly interested in a better lifestyle for themselves and their children. Sam added a dietician to the staff to educate them about the benefits of eating healthy and avoiding junk food. He made use of two nurse practitioners, a male and a female, who had returned to the reservation after their schooling was completed. They knew the tribal families and their needs, both modern and traditional. He found he had a little more free time for himself because of the nurse practitioners. On the weekends, they were the ones on call at the center. As nurse practitioners working under him, they could dispense medicine and make limited medical decisions. This extra time on the weekends allowed Sam to finally be able to spend some time on his other passion, horses.

Almost every family on the reservation had at least one horse. They were like pets and many a young man had proven his manhood by breaking a wild horse. Most of the tribal members knew about, but few spoke of Strong Medicine's gift of being able to sing to wild horses. Only a very few privileged people had accompanied him into the hills where he sang the ancient songs, calling the wild horses to him. Strong Medicine had more horses than anyone on the reservation.

Sam remembered one particular evening when he was in his early teens and Strong Medicine asked Sam to follow him into the hills. They waited until the stars filled the sky and somewhere around midnight, Strong Medicine began to chant in a singsong voice. Soon they could hear the horses coming out of the hills to join them where Sam and Strong Medicine were seated on the ground. Wild appaloosas and pintos, who moments before had been snorting or wildly pawing the ground, became calm and stood quietly in front of Strong Medicine.

He continued singing, deftly passing three noosed ropes to Sam, pointing to the three horses he wanted Sam to harness. Soon Strong Medicine stopped chanting, stood, and told Sam to lead one of the horses back to the reservation. He led the other two. Sam was amazed that the horses were quiet, calm, and gentle. They provided no resistance to the ropes looped around their graceful necks. Sam and Strong Medicine had never spoken of that night, but its memory had stayed with Sam over the years.

When Sam was in medical school, one of his fellow students asked if he wanted to join a few of them who were going to a nearby race track that afternoon. Tired of studying and having been brought up with horses, he eagerly accepted the invitation.

There had always been races on the reservation, but this was different. Sam went to the paddock area before the first race and carefully looked at each of the horses. He knew horses and he had a pretty good idea which ones were ready to run. He bet $2.00 to win on Gypsy Wind, a long shot. When the race was finished, Sam discovered he had won $122.00. Eight races later, his winnings totaled more than $800.00. It did not escape the notice of his friends. For the rest of his time in medical school, during his internship, as well as his residency, he spent time at the track whenever he could. Sam understood horses. It was almost as if the horses spoke to him and said, "Sam, bet on me. I'm going to win." Even though Susie was getting a monthly check from the casino earnings, he still gave her all of his winnings. He never asked what she did with the money he gave her. He didn't care.

Strong Medicine was a very wise tribal leader. After the citizens of California approved gambling on tribal lands, he kept in close contact with elders from the other tribes. He knew that his tribe must always be aware of what was going on in the world of gaming if the casino was to do well. He had been contacted by a non-profit organization called NCLGS, the National Council of Legislators from Gaming States, which presented seminars throughout the country on issues relating to the gaming industry. They were neither pro-gaming nor anti-gaming.

He felt it was important for the tribe to be represented at the meetings and it provided an opportunity to meet with legislators, not only from California, but from the other states as well. Some of the other tribal leaders had attended the conferences and felt they had benefited from the information shared on gaming issues. Strong Medicine decided to attend one of the conferences being held in the Florida Keys.

Strong Medicine asked Sam to go with him and he readily agreed. They flew to Miami, rented a car, and made their way down Highway 1. The terrain was completely different from what they were used to in Southern California. In many parts of the Florida Keys, the highway was built on an elevated causeway with water on both sides and mangroves spilling almost onto the highway. The abundance of fish and fishermen was new to Strong Medicine and Sam.

At the conference there were a number of tribes represented from throughout the United States.

Strong Medicine and Sam learned about the common problems other tribes from around the country had encountered as they became involved in gaming. The information proved very beneficial as their casino continued to flourish.

What Strong Medicine and Sam had not been prepared for was the large turnout at the conference by representatives of the horse racing industry, which was huge in other areas of the country. They listened to the problems that the industry was having: declining attendance at the tracks, problems with trainers and employees who doped horses, horse farms that were neglecting the health of the horses, and what to do with the horses once their racing careers were over.

Several of the California horse owners who attended the conference shared their concerns about the industry. They cited racetracks being closed, diminishing purses, unreliable horse farms, and lack of places for boarding and training their horses. Strong Medicine sensed that the California horse and track owners felt that the Indian casinos had really hurt their industry. On the East Coast, racinos, which were a combination of a racetrack and a casino, had helped the racetracks stay in business, but racinos were not allowed in California because of the terms of the compacts between the tribes and the State of California.

As Sam and Strong Medicine prepared to return home to the reservation, they had a different outlook on where tribal gaming and the horse racing industry, in particular, were headed. Both of them had an interest in doing something with horses. They talked of nothing else on the long plane ride home. Somewhere over Texas they came up with the idea of building a world-class horse ranch slightly away from the reservation, up in the hills, catering to the East Coast breeders and the horse owners in California.

They knew that this would be a tough sell to the Tribal Council. While all of the Council members had horses, very few of them revered horses the way Strong Medicine and Sam did. They began to draw up a plan. Strong Medicine and Sam attended more NCLGS conferences, where they met members from other tribes and particularly, members of the horse racing industry. Due to his medical commitments, Sam often couldn't travel with Strong Medicine, but they were constantly in touch. Strong Medicine began subscribing to magazines and journals that catered to the horse industry. He researched horse farms and ranches and how they operated. With his own money, he hired an architect to draw up plans for a horse ranch that could accommodate five hundred horses. He began to look for land.

One day, Sam's cell phone rang as he was returning to his apartment. When he picked up the phone, Strong Medicine said, "My son, I have found the land for our ranch. It is perfect. You must see it. Could you be ready in an hour? I'll pick you up." Strong Medicine was usually a man of few words and very reserved. Sam had never heard this much excitement in his voice.

"Of course. I'll see you then." Sam was just as excited and could barely keep his voice from showing it. He jumped into the passenger seat when Strong Medicine drove up in his old truck. "Tell me about it. Why do you like it so much?" Sam asked.

"Well, it's about 2,500 feet higher than the floor of the desert where the reservation is located," Strong Medicine said. "The temperature is much cooler and will be better for the horses. There's a little valley between the hills that would be perfect for the horses, the barns, paddocks, a six-furlong track, a main house, a guest house, and the other outbuildings that we'll need. You haven't seen the plans I've been working on, but we're going to need a lot of land. The property is one hundred fifty acres and perfect for what we need. I think the price is fair and I don't think too many people are going to want to buy a piece of property that big that far away from any town. No developer is going to sit on it and hope the population increases enough to justify building on it."

Strong Medicine continued, "The problem is the money. I don't think I can get the Tribal Council to buy it now. Later, when we're successful, I think they'll be interested. I don't know what kind of money you have. I know the tribe didn't pay for your undergraduate education, but they paid for your medical education and you've been getting over $300,000 a year for several years now from the casino's revenue, so you must have something. I have saved my casino payments and I think you and I should buy the property. The plans have already been drawn up. It will take a couple of years to build it, which is fine with me. It should be ready when you finish your residency and return to the reservation. This will give us time to get the word out to the breeders and to the other horse people so when we're ready, they'll be ready.

"We'll need a manager and a lot of people to work the ranch, but that's the beauty of it. Our young people, those who don't want to go to college, could work on it. One of the buildings would be a ranch house for them where they could live. What do you think?"

That was the longest speech Sam had ever heard from Strong Medicine.

"You know how much I love horses. I think it's a wonderful idea. The horses would be well cared for, it would give our tribe a sense of pride, and I particularly like the idea of having our young people work at the ranch. I have saved some money and yes, count me in."

The rest of the day went by in a haze. They met the real estate agent for a tour of the land, offered a price much lower than the asking price, and two hours later found that they were the owners of a soon-to-be-built horse ranch.

Over the next two years, Strong Medicine was involved in every phase of the construction of the ranch. The more Strong Medicine read, the more things he added to the original plans. The finished ranch was beautiful. Strong Medicine asked Sam if it would be all right if they named it "Legacy Ranch" in honor of their forefathers. It would be a legacy to them. When it was finally completed, it was perfect in every detail. Word quickly spread and soon, the ranch began to develop a loyal clientele.

When Sam returned to the reservation to work at the center, he found he was spending every minute of his free time at the newly completed horse ranch. Even after several months of visiting the ranch, every time Sam drove up to it, his heart soared. The horse breeders were bringing their stud horses and mares to the ranch and word soon spread in the industry that it was the Cadillac of horse ranches. Water misters cooled the horses on hot days. There were special rooms for breeding, foaling, and grooming and a small grandstand had been erected. The young tribal men and women were naturals when it came to training the horses. Four of them did nothing but break the young horses that had never been ridden and had been brought to the ranch.

The heart of the massive operation took place in the ranch's office. A special computer program had been designed to keep track of each horse, what stall it was in, what it was to be fed, and any other information necessary for the horses' welfare. Very soon, the horse ranch, from a financial standpoint, was a successful operation.

The Tribal Council became interested in acquiring the horse ranch as one of the tribe's many business investments. They knew a key component for their tribe to be successful with the management of their newfound wealth was to diversify their investments. They offered to buy the horse ranch from Sam and Strong Medicine, who agreed to sell it to them. It really was the best of times. The ranch manager and his family lived in the main house and Sam spent so much of his off-time there that he decided to move into the guest house on the weekends. Although the ranch manager, Rick, was in charge, it was clear that not many decisions were made without Sam's input.

As passionate and excited as Sam was about both the horse ranch and the center, once again he was beginning to feel overwhelmed, but now it was in a different way. Whenever he went to the ranch, the manager would greet him with a litany of the latest problems. Each morning when he went to the center, the nurses and Phyllis would greet him with their litany of the latest problems. Where previously he had found it invigorating to solve these problems at both places, lately he had begun to dread them.

He felt angry that everyone was so dependent on him. His temper became short and he noticed that people were beginning to look at him differently. Rather than smile and look him in the eye, they would avoid having eye contact with him. He began to lose weight. He had always been slender, but now he was downright skinny. When he looked in the mirror, he was certain that he looked older. The intermittent bouts of nausea and vomiting he'd been having the last couple of weeks weren't helping. And he'd never felt this tired. He began to wonder if there was something seriously wrong with him.

Sam realized he loved Phyllis, but he was getting tired of her morning briefings. He knew he was overreacting, but he felt that she was constantly complaining and it made him angry. A good director must keep the primary doctor aware of everything that was going on in the center, but the way she communicated with him about the problems at the center didn't feel good to him. What had happened to the excitement he had for the beginning of each day and when had he started to look and feel older than he was? He wondered where his feelings of rage were coming from. What was going on?

He was a doctor and should know the answers to these questions, but he was at a loss to understand his symptoms. He was getting very concerned about his mental and physical health.

Strong Medicine asked to meet with him. He began, "Son, people are talking. They say you have changed in the last couple of months. Rick said you took a whip to a horse last week and that you put your boot to Rebel, the dog you've called your best friend. There are rumors that you stopped at a bar off of the reservation to have a beer and ended up in a barroom brawl that resulted in a man being badly beaten. The rumors also say that no one has seen the other man in the fight since that day and that you paid him well to leave the area so you would not be reported to the authorities. What is going on? This is not the man I've known for many years."

Sam replied, "I don't know what's going on. I feel angry, like after my mother died, before my vision quest. I'm having bouts of nausea and vomiting. I feel like too many people are asking too much of me. I don't have any energy. I can't sleep and I'm tired all the time. I'm angry at everything. It seems like the slightest little thing can send me into a blind rage."

He continued, "Yes, the rumors are true about the man in the bar. Believe me, I'm not proud of that moment. I saw red and I went to an emotional place where no one could reach me. There were others in the bar who tried to get me to stop hitting him. I didn't. I couldn't. Now I lay awake at night, terrified it might happen again. Next time, I might kill someone. I know when I'm in a rage I'm capable of it. Can you give me something from the old traditional ways that might help me?"

Strong Medicine looked closely at him. "I remember when you came back from the vision quest, when I picked you up at that small desert motel. You were full of enthusiasm and hope for the future. You need to recapture that feeling. Another vision quest is out of the question. A man only gets one in his lifetime. I think you should go back to that motel and spend a couple of days there. Relax. Take some time for yourself; maybe that will help. Between the center, the ranch, Phyllis, and my teachings, you have had very little time to yourself. Try it. See if that works."

Sam went back to his apartment, which was attached to the pediatric center. He easily remembered the name of the motel, the Blue Coyote. His friend was the artist who had painted the blue coyote series of paintings that hung on the walls throughout the motel.

He got the number from the motel's website. He dialed, trying to remember the name of the woman who had given him the clothes, the beautiful Hispanic woman, but to no avail. The phone was answered on the third ring. "Blue Coyote Motel, may I help you?" said Maria.

The voice was that of the young woman he had met last year. "Perhaps you might remember me," Sam said. "I'm Sam Begay, the one who had just come down the mountain from a vision quest. You were kind enough to give me some clothing."

Maria laughingly answered, "Of course I remember you. I hope you're calling because you're coming back and that this time you will be wearing clothes. How can I help you?"

"Actually, I would like to stay Friday and Saturday of the Memorial Day weekend. I hope you still have a room available. I felt really good when I left your place. I don't know what you have there, but I need some of it now," Sam said.

"I'm glad you're coming back and yes, we have one vacancy. I can almost guarantee you that you'll feel better after your stay with us. We'll see you that Friday. I have you down for two nights, Friday and Saturday." Maria said.

She smiled as she hung up the phone. Memorial Day weekend was going to be a full house, all return customers, all of whom needed Freedom. She made a note to tell Jeffrey he definitely would need to mix up a little extra "medicine" for that weekend.

CHAPTER 32

The Friday before Memorial Day was one of those rare beautiful desert days that seem to happen only once in a while, with a soft blue sky and warm temperatures. The desert's searing summer heat was still a few days away and the bitter cold of winter had gone. It was a perfect time to be in the desert.

Maria went to each of the five rooms in the motel that morning, making sure that everything was perfect for the returning guests who were scheduled to arrive later in the day. She remembered them all. She liked them and was happy that once again she could take part in making them feel good about themselves.

After she carefully inspected the rooms, she made sure that the refreshment area was well stocked with food and drinks. She had precooked a number of meals, which just needed reheating in the microwave, so there was plenty of food for the guests. The motel was literally in the middle of nowhere with the nearest town and restaurant miles away, so any food or drink that the guests wanted had to be made available on the premises.

She walked down the steps leading to the lab, carefully holding on to the handrail. The lighting had never been very good and she was always afraid she would miss a step. She hated to go down there because of the rats in all the cages. She could hear them squeaking and every time she went there; it reminded her of the gang rape and the rats' tails brushing up against her when they licked her blood. She shivered at the thought. Anxious to get back upstairs, she quickly asked, "Jeffrey, the guests will be here later today. Is everything ready for them? Maybe you should start piping Freedom into their rooms."

Jeffrey was beginning to look exactly like one would expect a mad scientist to look. He spent every waking hour in his lab. His hair had turned to a dirty brown-grey, hanging to his shoulders. He was so engrossed in his research and tests that he often forgot to bathe or shave. He'd lost so much weight his dirty clothes hung on him like a scarecrow. He'd lost interest in pleasures such as eating and Maria couldn't even remember the last time they had made love. She wondered whether she even still loved him.

The man she had known was gone and the man who had taken his place frightened her. She tried to talk to him about the day-to-day problems that occurred in running the motel business, but her words fell on deaf ears. When he did talk to her, he often talked so fast she couldn't follow him. When she was able to catch a word or two, it seemed that he thought he could save the world with his experiments. If he made everyone "feel good" there would be no more wars. He would be a Messiah. He was obsessed with one thing and one thing only, his experiments. He was slipping away from her and his hold on reality was becoming tenuous at best. At least he still knew how to make Freedom and the anti-aging compound. She pushed away the thought that he might be slipping into insanity and how that might affect his ability to make the compounds in the future.

What Jeffrey hadn't told her was that he had decided to stop taking the bipolar prescription medicine he had been taking for years. She knew that he'd had a rough childhood, that people often thought he was crazy. A lot of his behavior must have seemed abnormal to other children. He was always the odd man out, the one picked last. She knew he hadn't had any friends when he was growing up. He had told her that his life became much better when a doctor finally diagnosed him as being bipolar and the medicine had become part of his daily routine.

Maria had never known him when he was manic or depressed, but his behavior now was pretty classic bipolar. Not sleeping or sleeping for days, loss of appetite, grandiose rantings, and inattention to personal grooming were just some of the signs he was exhibiting. Ever since Maria had known him, he took his daily medicine that prevented the extreme highs and lows. He was proud of his achievements, but not boastful and he had never thought he was the most brilliant scientist in the world. She feared he did now.

For some time, she had noticed that Jeffrey had begun to have a wild, crazy look in his eyes. He was beginning to stutter and stammer when he talked to her. It was like his brain had become short-circuited. Maria felt uncomfortable around him because she didn't know what he might do or say. It was an unsettling feeling.

Maria didn't know that in addition to stopping his

psychiatrist's prescription medication, Jeffrey had been self-medicating for several months. He devised a formula, which he believed was a clone of the medicine his psychiatrist prescribed. As he became more delusional, he reasoned that he shouldn't have to see the psychiatrist for a prescription refill when he knew he was capable of making it himself. He didn't tell Maria, instinctively knowing that she would insist he continue with the annual check-ups with his doctor. He was oblivious to the signs that his own medicine wasn't working; worse yet, that it contained levels of ingredients that could prove to be fatal. He was sure that the medicine he had concocted for his condition was just as good as the one prescribed by his psychiatrist. His refusal to admit the obvious and deal with it was one of the telltale signs of his deteriorating mental condition.

Jeffrey had never written down the formulas for the ultimate products that he produced as a result of his experiments. He had pages of notes of the tests and research he had done, but the finished products were committed to memory. Maria began to worry not only about Jeffrey's memory, but his mental and physical wellbeing as well. *What would I do if something happened to Jeffrey?* She pushed the thought aside. She'd deal with it after this weekend. There was still a lot to do to get ready for the weekend ahead.

In response to Maria's question about an adequate supply of drugs for the guests scheduled to arrive later in the day, Jeffrey told her, "Yes, I've already started piping it into their rooms. Don't worry. I have prepared an ample supply of Freedom, enough to make each of them happy and feeling the best they have in a long time. In fact, they will no doubt feel the best they have since the last time they stayed at Blue Coyote. I've also been successful in converting Freedom into pills. I'm thinking of selling the pills to them; then they wouldn't have to come back to the Blue Coyote when the effect of Freedom gradually wears off. It would probably make them feel a lot better knowing that they can keep their good feelings by simply taking a pill.

"From the research I've done with the rats, it seems that one pill lasts about a month; then the aggression and depression reappears. I think it will work the same way on humans. Maybe I'll have a meeting with them and tell them what I did to them the last time they visited the motel. At first, they'll probably be angry at how they were used as clinical test rats, but they'll want to keep the good feelings that only I can provide to them. When I work out how I can put Freedom in its gaseous form into shopping centers and other public places all around the world, they'll probably feel honored that they were the first ones to participate in my plan to heal all the people of the world from the anger, hostility, and depression that haunts mankind. It should go fine," Jeffrey concluded.

Within a few hours, each of the guests had checked in. The warm spring air had given way to the early heat summer promised and each of the guests was happy to spend the late afternoon and early evening in their air-conditioned rooms, unwinding, knowing they had made the right decision by coming back to the Blue Coyote.

They trickled into the refreshment area when they were thirsty or hungry. Introductions were made and then forgotten as they went back to their respective rooms, feeling better with each additional hour they spent at the motel.

Saturday dawned bright and clear. The pool, which lay idle during the winter months, beckoned and soon, all of the guests were relaxing poolside in the warm sunshine. The talk was effortless, sharing stories and simply enjoying the lazy day. All of the guests were feeling much better than they had when they had arrived at the motel the day before.

Luisa overheard Sam talking to Jill about his horse ranch. "Excuse me," she said, "I couldn't help but overhear you talking about your horse ranch. I spent many summers riding on my grandparents' ranch in Brazil. I didn't know that a horse ranch such as you have described existed in the United States. If you don't mind, I'd love to know more about it." Luisa and Sam spent several hours talking horse talk. She hadn't realized how much she had missed being around horses and was thrilled when Sam invited her to visit the ranch in a couple of months. She couldn't wait.

Sean was completely relaxed for the first time in a long time. No therapy, no clients, just a good feeling and the warm sun beating down on his body. *This weather sure beats the erratic weather in Denver*, he thought. Once again he wondered about this place. *Why do I feel so good here*? He glanced over at the young man lying on the chaise next to him. Doug had his eyes closed, letting the warm sun wash over him. He sensed someone was looking at him and opened his eyes.

"Hi. I don't think we met last night. I saw you in the refreshment area, but I didn't get a chance to introduce myself. My name is Sean and you are…?"

"My name's Doug. I'm from Los Angeles. I don't know what it is about this place that made me want to return and I know it sounds silly, but I just feel really good when I'm here." Doug laughingly went on, "I don't even need a beer. I'm a salesman. I was in Las Vegas on some sales calls and decided to drive the extra 200 miles to stay here on the return trip. And you, what brings you here?"

"I'm a therapist. I'm here to get away from my clients, have a little down time, and reboot myself." The psychologist in Sean took over and he couldn't help himself when he said, "Tell me about yourself. I'm always interested in hearing what has led someone to this place or that place."

"I had some car trouble," Doug began, "and had to spend the night at the Blue Coyote. My life was going downhill fast. I couldn't seem to sell anything, my ex-wife was harassing me about the back alimony I owed. I was really overweight and drinking and smoking too much. After I spent the night here, I felt great."

"It's funny," Doug went on, "When I got back to Los Angeles, my life turned around. I asked my boss for another chance and have been the top salesmen ever since, I've lost weight, run half-marathons, paid my ex-wife everything I owed her, quit smoking and really cut down on my drinking, but best of all I have fallen in love with a wonderful lady. My life has been great, but recently I've felt like things are beginning to unravel. I thought that if I came back here I might be able to get those good feelings back."

As Doug spoke, Sean began to experience a sense of déjà vu. The details related to him by Doug were slightly different, but the pattern was generally the same. He wondered if the other guests were there for the same reason as he and Doug were. Sean decided to talk to each one. He could always use the excuse that he was a therapist and very interested in people and their lives.

He overheard the continuing conversation between Sam and Luisa. "It's interesting," Luisa began, "When Jorge and I arrived at the Blue Coyote, we were exhausted. We had been on two long plane rides and had driven over from Phoenix. Jorge has a driver in Rio and hadn't driven a car in a long time. He had been dealing with the usual problems of gold mining in the Amazon and couldn't sleep on either flight. He was exhausted and I wasn't much better. Once we'd been here for a little while, we both began to feel better and let go of the stress that we were under.

"Actually," she continued, "Our son Carlos was conceived here, so of course I have wonderful feelings about our stay here. But it was more than that. Our lives seemed much happier after we came here. We moved to California and things have been wonderful until recently. Jorge spends two weeks in California with us and then travels to the Amazon to take care of his gold mining business for two weeks. The stress he's under is incredible. He has to deal with keeping gold production at as high a level as he can, the environmentalists, the natives, and his father. For over a year, he's handled it well, but lately, we've had petty arguments, we've been depressed and both of us have felt off." She went on, "Tell me what brought you here and why you've come back."

"I was disoriented when I came down the mountain after I completed my vision quest and thought the lights of the motel were those of the reservation. It was too late to do anything but stay here. For as long as I can remember, I've had problems with anger and rage. I'm pretty sure I know where it comes from, but I couldn't seem to get rid of it. The tribe and my spiritual father, Strong Medicine, felt I had to get these feelings of rage under control if I was going to be able to effectively practice pediatrics at the reservation. Strong Medicine told me he wanted me to be the next tribal medicine man; that his time on earth was coming to a close."

Sam took a long drink from his iced tea and continued, "After I left here, my life was as perfect as one can be. My feelings of rage and anger were gone. A lovely young tribal woman by the name of Phyllis took over as director of the clinic, which allowed me to devote myself to the children's health. She and I have been seeing each other ever since and I've fallen very much in love with her. The horse ranch has succeeded beyond our expectations and I spend every spare minute there. But like you, lately things have begun to unravel. The feelings of rage have begun to return and

I'm really concerned I'm going to lose everything including Phyllis, my pediatric practice, my medicine man training, all of it. I thought maybe if I came back here I could regain those good feelings that I experienced after my first visit."

Sean was beginning to get a bad feeling. Something more was going on here than random guests stopping by for a weekend. He knew why he, Sam, Luisa, Jorge, and Doug were here. He needed to find out if Jill was here for the same reason.

He got up and saw her sitting under an umbrella on the other side of the pool. Even though it was spring, the sun was strong and she had wisely taken refuge, not wanting to get sunburned. Sean walked over and asked if he might join her, telling her that he had met everyone else gathered around the pool except her and he wanted to introduce himself.

"Jill smiled her dazzling smile and invited him to take a seat. He told her she looked relaxed and asked her where she lived. She replied, "I have a home in Newport Beach and also one in the Palm Springs area. I could just as easily have gone to my desert home to soak up the sun, but something about this place makes me feel so good."

I know what you mean," Sean said. "There seems to be a bit of magic here. I think everyone feels it."

Jill continued, "I happened to come here a few months after my husband's death. I had no plans to stop and spend the night. It just happened because I was too tired to drive anymore and I was afraid I might fall asleep at the wheel. I wasn't coping with life very well and I really didn't feel there was any reason to live. In fact, I was seriously contemplating suicide. I couldn't imagine that I would ever feel good again, but after spending the night here, I felt wonderful. Everything changed. My life had meaning again and I fell in love with a wonderful man that I subsequently met. Then, starting a few weeks ago, my old sense of nothingness returned and I seemed to be aging much faster than normal. My doctor gave me a complete physical and can't find anything wrong with me. On a whim, I decided to return to the place where I had felt so good, right here at the Blue Coyote Motel. I feel much better. I think it's working for me again."

"I'm sure you'll find whatever you need," Sean said. "There must be a little magic here for everyone to feel so good. I feel it myself. Well, I think I'll go in and take a nap. Any more sun and my skin will be fried. I enjoyed talking to you, Jill. I'll see you later."

Sean couldn't wait to be alone. He needed to think about everything he had learned. Something very strange was happening here. He had spent a lot of time in therapy sessions and facilitating groups of recovering drug addicts. What he had heard this afternoon was not unlike what he often heard from his patients. There definitely seemed to be some nexus between the motel and the good feelings people got when they stayed here. All of the guests had been having problems before they came. Then, all of a sudden, for some time they all felt better after coming to the motel, but for reasons that were unclear, they all reverted back to the feelings they had before they had come to the Blue Coyote the first time. All of them decided to return and all of them for the same reason; they wanted to get back the "feeling good" sensation they had after the first time they visited.

What was happening here didn't seem to be much different from the garden variety of the drug abuse cases that Sean had seen on many previous occasions. The usual cycle of events with a drug-dependent person started with unhappy feelings alleviated by taking a drug. When the drug stopped working, the drug-dependent person looked for a stronger drug to get back the good feelings. The cycle continued to repeat itself, oftentimes in a downward spiral.

In theory, his thinking worked. In reality, it didn't. No drug had been given to him. There had been no magic pill, nothing. He had simply come to the motel, stayed, and felt better. *What am I missing?* He asked himself.

As he had been getting ready to go back to his room, Sean had overheard Luisa talking to Sam, telling him about Jorge and a little about the Amazon. Sean wondered if Jorge knew anything about drugs, if something could have been given to them without them knowing. He promised himself he would talk to Jorge and see what his thoughts were as to why they were all feeling so good.

All of this heavy thinking made Sean sleepy and he quickly fell into a deep and dreamless sleep. He awakened feeling refreshed and ready to get back to Denver and Jeanne. *What is making me feel so good*? He again asked himself. *Do the others feel it*? He dressed and headed for the refreshment area, hoping that Jorge would be there. He felt a pressing need to talk to him.

The refreshment area was empty and Sean spent some time looking over the dinner choices. Meat loaf, lasagna, chicken, and a beautifully composed salad were arrayed before him, along with some vegetables and fruits. For dessert, there was chocolate mousse in the refrigerator. He had just picked up the lasagna when the door opened. As if answering Sean's unspoken call, Jorge walked in.

Sean turned to him, held out his hand, and said, "I'm Sean Moriarty. We haven't met, but I talked to your charming wife earlier today. I understand you spend a lot of time in the Amazon. It's always been an area of the world that fascinates me. I was wondering if you could spare some time to chat with me later this evening."

"Of course. I couldn't join everyone out by the pool as I had to take care of some business, but my wife told me of your wonderful work at your clinic in Denver. It would be an honor to talk to you. Let me get something for Luisa and me to eat and I'll come to your room in about an hour. Will that be all right?" Jorge asked.

"Certainly. Take your time. I'm in room 3 and I look forward to talking with you."

Sean went back to his room and thought about what he was going to say. He hoped Jorge would understand and agree with him, that something strange was definitely going on at the Blue Coyote.

An hour later there was a soft knock on Sean's

door and he opened it to see Jorge standing there smoking a cigarette. "I hope you don't mind, but Luisa has become a true Californian. Now she won't let me smoke around her or in the house and an after dinner cigarette is a must for those of us who enjoy them. When I travel, there is always the cigarette dance between California and Brazil. In Brazil no one cares if you smoke, while here in California, you feel like an outcast or worse. This is the one thing I have had a hard time adjusting to since we moved."

"I understand," Sean said. "It was not too long ago that I, too, had to have that wonderful after dinner cigarette. Enjoy! If that's the worst habit you have, you're still better off than most of the people I know."

Sean invited Jorge into his room and closed the door. They sat opposite each other at a small writing table in the room. "What I'm going to say to you may sound strange, but please, just take a moment to listen to me. I wanted to talk to you because of your knowledge of the Amazon and I would like to hear your perspective based on what I have read about the Amazon and the addictive, mind-altering drugs, which I understand are readily available in that area of the world.

"I really think something is going on here at the Blue Coyote. All of the guests have returned to the motel because, when they came here before, they were troubled with one thing or another. All of them felt wonderful when they left. The good feelings continued for a substantial period of time and then suddenly, all of the negative feelings returned. I have done work with drug addiction and the situations are very similar."

Jorge sat in his chair, very still and very quiet. Sean could tell he was giving the matter a great deal of thought. Finally, he spoke. "I noticed a strange smell the first time I visited here. It smelled like sandalwood. That is used throughout the world in incense and often, to mask a chemical odor. I think you may be right. Something must be going on here. We all had problems before we came here. After we left the Blue Coyote, all of us felt better, much, much better. Now our problems are reoccurring. We've all come back and all of us seem to be feeling great once again. That cannot be coincidence. But if that is so, how are we getting this drug?" Jorge was clearly giving Sean his full attention.

He went on, "We are not knowingly ingesting drugs. That leaves the drinking water, the food, or the very air we are breathing. I would have to rule out the water because Luisa and I only drink bottled water. It's a habit we got into because of my travels in the Amazon. That leaves either the food or the air we are breathing. We have our choice of whatever food we want and it would be very hard to standardize the amounts of a foreign substance planted secretly in the food. Weights vary, appetites vary, and some people are even on special diets and bring their own food. If what I've just said is true, then the only thing left would be the air. I suppose drugs could be piped into the rooms somehow. I can't think of any other rational explanation," Jorge concluded.

Sean spoke again. "I have been doing a little research. I googled the motel and found that it's owned by Jeffrey and Maria Brooks. Maria is the woman at the front desk. You were still in Brazil when the news story about her husband broke. It was quite a story, particularly here in California. Jeffrey was rumored to be in line to win the Nobel Prize for his research on an anti-aging hormone and had actually formulated a compound for it. When he left the company he worked for, Moore Scientific Laboratories, they released a statement saying he was leaving for health reasons.

"The underground press wrote that he had given the drug to his wife, Maria Brooks, while he was an employee of the lab, in violation of his contract with them and that he was actually fired by Moore Labs. Supposedly, they gave him a large financial settlement. Apparently, Maria and Jeffrey bought this motel and retired out here. A couple of things interest me.

"First of all, have you really looked at Maria? She's gorgeous and I don't think she's aged a day since I saw her the first time. Based on the Internet search, she would have to be well into her thirties by now and she doesn't look a day older than twenty-two or twenty-three. Secondly, with Jeffrey's intellect and his knowledge of drugs, it's entirely possible he could invent something that would make people feel good; some sort of a feel-good drug. I suppose, like all drugs, it would have an expiration date, after which it would no longer be an effective remedy. From what I read, no one has seen or heard of him in well over a year. If we're going to get to the bottom of this, maybe we should start right here with Jeffrey. Why not try to set up a meeting with him? Everything points to him."

Sean didn't know where all this was going, but he had a hunch he was on the right track. But even if he found out that Jeffrey had been administering some kind of "feel good" drug to all of them, so what? All of the guests had come back to the Blue Coyote so they could once again feel good. They probably didn't know or realize it, but it might be they needed the drug. Their desire to regain their good feelings was really a craving for an addictive drug. Perhaps even if they knew they had been drugged, would they care, as long as it made them feel good?

Jorge sat back in his chair, digesting what Sean had told him. "Sean, I think we should tell the rest of the people what we're thinking and then maybe have a joint meeting with Jeffrey."

"You're absolutely right." Sean said, "Let's get the others and meet back in my room. We're all leaving tomorrow, so tonight is the best time to do it."

They agreed that Sean would go find Jill and Doug,

while Jorge would bring Luisa and Sam back with him. Within a few minutes they were all assembled in Sean's room. They sat on the bed and the floor, wherever they could fit. The rooms at the Blue Coyote were large, but seating was limited.

Sean began, "Jorge and I have been talking about a certain situation here at the Blue Coyote Motel and we'd like to share some of our thoughts with you. You may disagree with us, but we feel that we need to bring some unusual things to your attention."

He went on to tell them about Jeffrey, what he had found out from his search on the Internet, and his suspicions about why they all felt so good when they were at the motel. At first, their faces registered disbelief. This was the United States. It was against the law to administer a drug without a person's consent. They seemed shocked to realize that maybe the drug was an illegal drug as well. They couldn't believe that the owner of a motel in the middle of nowhere would have the wherewithal to do something like that. Clear and simple, it was a violation of their rights and definitely illegal. The more they listened to Sean and then to Jorge, who had come to agree with Sean, the more they were forced to consider that what they were hearing just might be true. Sean told them he thought they all needed to meet with Jeffrey to find out if his suspicions were true. They agreed.

Sean and Jorge walked over to the reception area where Maria was closing up for the night. "Maria, the other guests and I would like to talk to your husband. None of us has met him. We have some questions we'd like to ask. Would it be possible for us to meet with him tonight?" Sean asked.

Maria had noticed the other guests going to Sean's room and could only guess what was going on. There really was nothing she could do. If she didn't call Jeffrey and request the meeting, there was a chance that they would go to the county sheriff. After growing up in the barrio, Maria had a deep-seated fear of anything related to law enforcement. The last thing she wanted was the police nosing around the motel. She had heard horror stories of how they could close down a motel for small things, such as the mirrors in the rooms not being low enough for a disabled person in a wheelchair.

After quickly weighing the options, she decided it would be best for her to call him on the intercom connected to the basement lab. "Jeffrey, the guests would like to meet with you. Evidently they have some questions. Is it okay if I send them down to the lab in a few minutes?"

Jeffrey was surprised at the call, but not concerned. In fact, he had no concerns about anything, as he believed he was on the road to greatness. There was nothing that could stand in his way. He had thought about meeting with the guests and had even mentioned it to Maria. He was proud of his invention, Freedom, the new drug he had developed, if that's what they wanted to talk about.

Unfortunately, the longer he took the drug he had created to control his bipolar condition, the less he was able to filter the real world from his delusional reality. In his present state, he was sure that the people would recognize his genius. This was the manic side of being bipolar.

"Of course, send them down. I'd like to meet with them. I'd like to share my discoveries with them. I'm convinced that the things I've accomplished here in the lab will change the world as we know it today. Why not share the medical breakthrough with the very people who were the first to receive Freedom and experience the miracle of 'feeling good' all the time," Jeffrey said.

Maria had a bad feeling about the meeting. In Jeffrey's present state of mind, he was not capable of realizing that what he was doing was illegal and that potentially, he could be arrested for it. She had no choice but to lead the assembled guests to the stairway that led to the secret basement laboratory. She hoped they would want the drug enough to keep quiet about it.

CHAPTER 33

Maria opened the door leading to the basement lab, cautioning her six guests to watch their step as the stairway was not well lighted. It was just as Sean had remembered it. The "Emergency" and "Keep Out" signs were still on the door. There was a collective gasp as they opened the door to the laboratory. In front of them was a state-of-the-art scientific laboratory that stretched the length of the motel. A huge computer screen, which doubled as a microscope screen, was over a desk in the center of the room. Beakers, tubes, and bottles filled with different substances were spread everywhere.

Through a doorway, they could see cages housing the hundreds of rats Jeffrey used in his experiments. Sophisticated electronic apparatus was   mounted on custom-made tables and stands made especially for their use. A huge glass-front, walk-in refrigerator dominated one of the short walls, housing plants and herbs of all types. Track lighting dimmed by switches on the walls covered the ceiling. A large electric range and a microwave took up one corner of the room. Racks fitted with various microscope slides were laid out on a counter. Clear plastic pneumatic tubes were arranged on a wall in order of their size. A small glass front second refrigerator was filled with food items.

As they tried to absorb the spectacle in front of them, a side door from the small office opened and Jeffrey stepped into the main lab. His hair was unkempt, a dirty shirt was half tucked into his pants, and his beard was shaggy, but his eyes told the full story. They were the eyes of a madman, red-rimmed and gleaming with an unnatural light. It was hard to look into those eyes and not think that you were looking at a person who had gone over the edge.

Sean took over. He had experienced madness before and he knew he was looking at it now. The first rule when confronting a person displaying symptoms of madness is to act as if nothing is wrong, even if the person is obviously mad.

He extended his hand to shake hands with Jeffrey and said, "Hi, you must be Jeffrey. I'm Sean. Let me introduce you to the other guests." They took their cue from Sean and acted as if meeting a madman in a state-of-the-art laboratory in the basement of a motel in a godforsaken place in the middle of nowhere was the most natural thing in the world.

Jeffrey gave them a tour, explaining the purpose of each piece of equipment and even showed them some of his most recent experiments. As mentally unbalanced as he was, they soon realized they were in the presence of a genius. His experiments were light-years ahead of anything any of them had ever heard of or read about. The two who were the most knowledgeable about science, Sean and Sam, were clearly in awe of the man's mind and his accomplishments. If there were any lingering doubts as to whether or not Jeffrey was capable of introducing some unknown substance into the air supply in their rooms to make them happy, those doubts quickly disappeared. That thought alone was terrifying. If he could do that, what else could he be capable of doing or had already done that they didn't know about?

After he finished the lab tour, Jeffrey spoke to them. "I understand you wanted to meet with me. Actually, I had thought about asking you to meet with me, so this works out perfectly. Tell me, how have you been feeling?"

Sean began, "Jeffrey, I think I can speak for all of us. When each of us came here the first time, we were dealing with various different life issues, and not handling them well. After spending the night here, we all awoke feeling great. The feelings continued and all of our lives changed for the better. Then, for reasons that are still unclear to us, our lives have begun to unravel. All of us have returned to the Blue Coyote hoping to regain those good feelings."

"Let me explain and show you something," Jeffrey said. He asked them to step to the side wall where there was a large cabinet door. He opened it, revealing nine pipes. Below each of them was a large, clear glass beaker and adjacent to the beakers, a series of switches.

"I developed a gaseous drug, which causes people to

feel good, and I don't mean just sort of good, I mean really good. The beakers are filled with a compound, which becomes a gas and flows into the pipes. I've mixed the compound with the scent of sandalwood to mask any odor. Using the switches next to the beakers, I can select which of the rooms in the motel I want to introduce the drug into. It causes no side effects. It simply makes people feel better.

"I pipe it into the motel rooms, the reception area, the refreshment area, my home, and the lab. Maria decides which guests she thinks will benefit from the gas and then I pipe it into their room. I call this new wonderful drug that I have invented Freedom. You have been my clinical trial 'test rats.' Different dosages were given to each of you, which resulted in some of you receiving the benefits of the drug for a longer period of time than others."

Sean could feel the eyes of others directed at him. His instincts had been right. They had been drugged without their knowing about it. The guests looked shocked and dismayed. A ragged edge of fear was starting to show on each one of their faces.

Jeffrey continued, "After I started making the drug and after I administered it to you the first time you came to the Blue Coyote, I suspected you might want to continue with the drug. I also thought it would probably be difficult for you to come back to this remote desert location for a 'pick-me-up' whenever the drug wore off. For the past few months I've been working on converting the drug to a pill form, which can be taken monthly. Just recently, I successfully tested the new pill and my tests indicate it performs as well as the gas form of the drug.

"The raw materials for my drug come from some unique and relatively unknown plant substances that are shipped to me by a dealer in Mexico. Although I can combine the products and make the drug, I can't grow the plants here so I'm forced to pay an exorbitantly high price to get the raw materials I need to make the drug. I know that what I'm doing would not be considered legal by the authorities, but here is the offer that I have for you. The price for a year's supply of the drug is $25,000. If you're interested, you can send me an annual check and I'll send a supply of pills to you."

Jill was the first to speak. "How do we know that the pills are safe to take? Have you ever tested them on humans? And what about the aging process? I know when the drug began to wear off, I experienced depression, lack of energy, uncontrollable shaking in my hands and premature aging. It was horrible."

The others vehemently nodded in agreement. Not only had they experienced symptoms ranging from chills to vomiting, each of them had experienced the aging problems as well.

Jeffrey began, "Yes, it's true that one of the side effects of even a slight withdrawal from Freedom is premature aging. However, many years ago I developed an anti-aging hormone, which Maria has been taking. If you look at her, she looks exactly as she did when I met her when she was twenty-three. I have put a small amount of that drug into the new pill form of Freedom. I think that will take care of the aging problems and also keep you looking younger.

"As to the side effects on humans, no, the pill has not been tested on humans. I can tell you that I have been giving these pills to the rats in the cages and they are fine for a month or so and then they begin to show signs of depression and aggression. But as soon as the pills are re-administered, they become happy once again. I made this pill to act as fast as the drug that was piped into your rooms. Within a short time of taking the pill, you will start to feel good again. The good feeling created by the airborne variety lasts for several months, depending on the dosage, while the pill variety lasts about a month. As to aging problems, as long as the rats take the pills, they show no signs of aging. Is it experimental? Probably. Will it work? I have every reason to believe it will and I have never had a failure. I refuse to accept failure.

"Let me tell you something else. I'm going to share this drug with the rest of the world. After that happens, there will be no more wars, terrorism, or inhumane actions, because everyone will feel good. Soon, every place where people gather will have Freedom. I alone can and will change the world."

Jeffrey was becoming more and more agitated. His voice had been rising as he talked to the guests and now he was literally shouting at them. His facial muscles had developed a nervous twitch and spittle was starting to come out of the corner of his mouth. His eyes began rolling around in their sockets. Sam and Sean were certain he was in the throes of a complete mental breakdown.

Sean became concerned for the safety of the group. It was time to get away from this madman. He acted as the spokesman for the group once again and said, "Thank you, Jeffrey. The tour was fascinating and I think I speak for each one of us when I say that it was one of the most interesting things I've ever seen. As far as your drug proposal, we need some time to think about it. It's getting late and I would suggest we meet here at 8:30 tomorrow morning. That will give us at least an hour before some of us have to leave. Would that be all right with you?"

Jeffrey had no doubt that each of them would want the drug, but he agreed to meet them in the lab at 8:30 the next morning. He told them that the pills were ready for them, neatly counted out in batches of twelve. He had already put them into small white vials.

The assembled group of guests closed the lab door behind them and made their way up the dark staircase. When they shut the door to the basement, Sean turned to them and said, "I suggest we meet in my room at 7:30 tomorrow morning. Each of us has a lot of thinking to do and I'm sure that the longer we think about it, the stronger some of our feelings will be. As a therapist, I think it might be a good idea to share our feelings, thoughts, emotions, and yes, probably our anger."

They agreed to meet in his room the next morning and with hardly a word to each other, the guests hurried to their rooms, wanting to be alone and to digest what they had just seen and heard.

At 7:30 the next morning, they met once again in Sean's room. From the looks of them, they had slept little, if at all, during the ten long hours since they had left one another.

Sean was the first to speak. "I don't know how any of you feel, but the more I think about it, the angrier I get. I'm ready to call the police and tell them what we know. What is happening here is horrific. I'm speaking both as a therapist and a person who has had a bit of a bout with an addiction to the bottle. I was a priest before I became a therapist. I was defrocked for reasons I won't go into, but a lot of my problems stemmed from my addiction. I made wrong choices, but at least I was the one making them. What Jeffrey is doing is addicting people who have no choice. We did not even know we were being given an addictive drug.

"I wonder how many other people have become addicted to Freedom. Their lives may be in shambles and they may not associate the Blue Coyote Motel with Freedom or even know they've become addicted. This is beyond anything I've ever seen, heard, or read about. When people discovered the atrocities that happened in World War II, like the gassing of innocent people, there was a global outrage such as the world has never known. I'm sure if people knew what was taking place here, they, too, would be outraged and if this maniac has his way and the means to do it, he intends to addict the world's population. Can you even begin to imagine the consequences of something like this? It's beyond the scope of my imagination to consider the logistics of how he plans to do this, but if even one more person is addicted, that's one too many.

"I've made my mind up that I won't buy the drug. I've had to break an addiction before, and yes, this motel was one of the reasons I was able to do it. But I refuse to become addicted again to any substance. If any of you want to talk to me about this situation, I would be happy to speak privately with you. As much as I want to call the authorities and have this madman put away for the good of society, I will wait until each of you decides what you intend to do."

Sam was the next to speak. "I am a man of medicine and a Native American tribal medicine man trainee as well. There is no way that I will be a part of any of this for a number of reasons. If I look like I'm shaking, I am. I've had anger issues in the past, but I have never felt the depth of rage I feel right now. I know what drugs and alcohol can do to people. The Native American populations have been decimated because of addiction. Once-proud people grovel on their way to the liquor store or drug dealer to get their fix. I won't do it or be a party to it," he said. His voice became louder and he was visibly shaking with anger.

"This madman must be stopped and we're the only ones who can do it. We have to agree as a group not to buy the drugs. When we leave, we'll contact the authorities and close him down. In his demented state, he'll probably go to a mental hospital for the rest of his life. The only way we can help ourselves and others is to see that Jeffrey is put away. None of you has the right to selfishly want to keep feeling good when who knows how many other innocent people will become addicted if he's not stopped now." Sam stopped talking and caught his breath.

Sean spoke again, "Sam, I agree with everything you've said, but as a therapist assessing Jeffrey, I don't think he's going to be capable of producing this drug for very long. And we don't have the right to judge the others who are here and may want to take the drug." He turned to them. "Each of you had your own reason for needing it in the first place. If any or all of you decide that you want to continue to take the drug, it may cause me to make a decision that will be in the best interests of the group, rather than what I would personally like to do."

He looked at the others in the room. "Jill, what are your thoughts?"

Jill started to sob. Tears ran down her face as she answered Sean. "I can't go back to the way I felt after Rick died. I didn't want to live anymore and I almost committed suicide. I just can't do it. I have a second chance at happiness with a man I love and I'm not willing to give that up. I may hate myself for doing what I'm going to do, but I need the drug. If that makes me weak, so be it." Her voice caught as she said, "I'm not willing to go without the drug."

"For God's sake, Jill, how can you be so selfish? What about all the others who will become addicted? Do you think you have the right to sacrifice other people so you can be happy?" Sam asked.

Jill was becoming hysterical. "I won't go back to the way I was before. I won't."

Sean walked over to her and placed his hand on her shoulder. His touch was comforting and she began to calm down. As a priest and therapist, Sean was very familiar with the frailties of the human soul. He knew Jill seriously wished she could do without the drug, but like most people, she would do anything to avoid the mental anguish she had suffered after her husband died. Sean also knew that whoever gave up the drug was going to be hurting.

Jorge was the next to speak. "Luisa and I talked most of the night. We both wish we were strong enough not to take the drug, but we're going to continue with it. We may be making excuses, but Luisa feels that our baby became very sick because she was withdrawing from the drug, was tense, and passed it on to the baby. We tried for so many years to have children and now that we have a child, Luisa is committed to doing whatever she has to do in order to insure that our baby is healthy and happy and that he has a calm, peaceful mother.

"As for me, I cannot go into the Amazon going through withdrawals. I don't talk much about it, but it is a very dangerous place. I only told Luisa last night just how dangerous it is. If I am not fully focused on my safety, there is a good chance I will be killed. If I were to go through a withdrawal phase, that would only increase my chances of having a fatal incident. I must be aware of everything I see or hear and I have to make extensive use of my sixth sense, knowing when something is wrong or off or when I may be in danger. To be killed in the jungle because I'm going through a drug withdrawal would not be fair to my family or to my employees who depend on me for their very existence. I'm sorry, but like Jill, Luisa and I will be buying the drug.

"Sam, I see how angry you are and I understand. I'm sorry. And Sean, is this madman committing outrageous acts on unsuspecting people? Yes, I agree with you; he is. Again, I'm sorry if we've disappointed you, but Luisa and I have made our decision."

Sean turned to Doug. "And you, Doug. What is your decision?"

"I've decided to take the drug. My life has turned completely around since I started taking it and if I stop, I stand to lose everything: my job, the woman I love, and most of all, my self-respect. Sean, yesterday I told you I decided to come back to the Blue Coyote after some sales calls in Las Vegas. That part was true. What I didn't tell you was that I lost over $1,000 gambling in a casino sports bar, drank myself into oblivion trying to feel better, and capped it off by spending some expensive and unmemorable time with a prostitute.

"I hate myself for what I've done and I am determined not to do it again. If that involves me taking the drug so I never return to being the man who did those things, I will. I'm sorry for others who may become addicted, but who knows, maybe they'll be able to turn their lives around like I have. And what if there were no more wars? What if there was peace in the world? Would that be such a bad thing?"

Sam looked at him, aghast. "You can't mean what you're saying, Doug. This is wrong on every level and much larger than you are. I'm pleading with you. Don't do this, I beg of you."

"I'm sorry," Doug said. "I hope that you can forgive me and Jill, as well as Luisa and Jorge. Maybe we're just not as strong as you and Sean. Speaking for them as well as for myself, I ask that you not go to the authorities. The police will want to interview us and even though we are innocent, our names will no doubt be disclosed in the press. People will think that we are common criminals and drug users like you see hanging out on a street corner in the worst part of town. That's not fair, given the fact that initially we didn't even know we were being given the drug."

Although Sam was obviously furious, he knew there was no point in arguing further with them. If he went to the authorities, these people's lives would be ruined. If he didn't go, there was a chance that more lives would be ruined. There was nothing more he could do. It was time to leave. It was apparent to him that he couldn't convince the others they were making a horrible decision. As he stormed out of Sean's room, he asked Sean for his business card and told him he would stay in touch, so the two of them might be able to help one another when they started withdrawing from the drug.

No one was happy as they filed out of Sean's room. Each one of them had his or her reason for their decision. Sean also knew that no one could make the decision for someone else. He knew how painful life could be and if they chose to avoid that pain by taking the drug, who was he to judge? He knew Jeffrey was on the edge of complete insanity and that sooner, rather than later, he probably wouldn't be able to even make the drug. He wasn't as worried about Jeffrey's manic desire to save the world from war and chaos as he was about the people who may have unwittingly become addicted to Freedom after staying at the Blue Coyote. Nothing more could be done here. It was time to go home. With hardly a word to one another, the five of them walked down the stairs and knocked on the lab door.

Jeffrey was already in the lab and opened the door for them, saying, "Good morning. Some of you may be in a hurry to check out of the motel, so let's get started." He was so certain that each of them would want a supply of the pills that he began directing them as to where they should put their payments. Jeffrey had even prepared envelopes with the motel's mailing address on it in case they had to send their payment to him by mail. He didn't seem to notice that Sam was not part of the group.

"Wait a minute," Sean said. "I've decided not to take the drug. I'm going to gut this out. I've seen too many people with addictions to subject myself to this. I've had enough problems in the past." He said good-bye to everyone, wished them well, and made his way up the stairs.

The others quickly took the white vials, putting their payments in the small dish Jeffrey had set out for that purpose. Doug asked Jeffrey if he could send him a check when he returned home. Jeffrey knew Doug needed the drug and agreed to let him take the pills, knowing that the check would soon arrive in the mail.

The guests all returned to their rooms. Although Sean had already departed, before he left he had placed one of his business cards under the door of their rooms. On each card was written, "If you feel that you need to call me, don't hesitate. Months or years from now you may want to talk to me and I'll be happy to hear from you. Good luck!"

Sean drove to Phoenix, buoyed by the fact that Sam had turned down the drug too. He knew as time went by he would probably hear from each one of them. The drugs might mask whatever else was going on in their personal lives, but eventually they, too, would fail and each person would have to face his worst fears. Sean vowed to be there when they called.

CHAPTER 34

Sean returned to Denver feeling good. He knew that in a few months the feeling would wear off, but for now, he had to admit, it felt good. He couldn't wait to get home and tell Jeanne everything that had happened over the weekend. She was adamantly opposed to drugs and he knew she would strongly support his decision not to take the drug.

He was glad to get back to the clinic and his life. Soon, the events of the Memorial Day weekend became a distant memory. Sean and Jeanne bought a cabin in the mountains near Cripple Creek and Friday afternoons found them on the road, ready for a weekend of birding. The highway was always busy and it seemed as if everyone in Denver drove to the mountains on Friday and returned on Sunday evening. Jeanne and Sean shared the driving and each of them looked forward to their weekends in the mountains.

The birding was fabulous. He loved his new life. Sean and Jeanne were equally comfortable in the clinic and in the mountains. The clinic received a large grant from the federal government, allowing it to expand. It was gaining a reputation as the best clinic of its kind in the Western states. Many a day found Sean giving tours to visiting psychotherapists, politicians, and anyone else who had an interest in what the clinic was doing. He was a much sought after speaker, charismatic and knowledgeable. He soon found himself traveling all over the United States, representing the clinic and sharing its success with others.

Occasionally, he wondered about the guests at the Blue Coyote Motel and how they were. He thought they were all doing well since they were still feeling good, as he was. He expected to hear from Sam and knew it would be good for them to check on each other as the drug began its gradual withdrawal from their systems.

One Thursday night several months after the Memorial Day weekend at the Blue Coyote Motel, Sean went into his office and saw the message light on his phone blinking. He played the message.

"Sean, it's Sam Begay. You may remember me from the Memorial Day weekend a few months ago at the Blue Coyote Motel. When you have time, please call me at this number. It's my cell phone and I have it with me all the time. I don't know about you, but the good feelings are starting to leave. I'd like to talk to you."

Sean knew exactly what Sam was feeling because he was going through a similar loss. He was fortunate to have Jeanne to talk to, his own live-in therapist.

He dialed the number. Sam answered on the first ring. "Hello, this is Sam Begay."

"Sam, it's Sean. I'm glad you called and I think I know why. If you're anything like me, you're probably coming down from the drug Jeffrey gave us. Am I right?"

"Sean, thanks for returning my call so quickly. Yes, I am coming down and it's not pleasant. I can feel the old anger returning and I find myself short-tempered with everyone. I still refuse to buy the pills and take them, but I'm not enjoying this."

"Sam, I've spent some time thinking what we could do to help each other. I know alcohol has often been abused by tribal members. As a doctor, you're probably familiar with AA and how it brings together people who share the same problems."

"Yes. It was started by a doctor and a friend of his who had no success in trying to quit their addiction to alcohol. What worked for them was being able to help each other stay away from alcohol."

"I think we should do the same," said Sean. "I have Skype and if you don't have it, you can easily get it. If you're not familiar with it, it's a camera that works through a computer so you can see the person you're talking to. We could agree on a time, say once a week, when we would meet and talk using Skype. We could discuss what's bothering us. It's not the magic pill we could have gotten from Jeffrey at the Blue Coyote, but if it worked for Dr. Bill and Bob, the founders of AA, and a lot of others, there's a good chance it will work for us. Want to try it?"

"Yes," Sam replied. "I like the idea. So when do we start? I can adjust my schedule to fit yours. It would be a lot easier for me to have the pill and the happy feeling the drug brought, but it's time for me to deal with the devils that haunt me once and for all."

They agreed on Wednesday evenings at 9:00 p.m. because both of them would have finished with their patients and they wouldn't feel rushed. Sean went downstairs to tell Jeanne what had happened.

When he told her about his conversation she said, "Sean, I think that's a wonderful solution. I am more than happy to listen to you, but it's far more effective to talk with someone who is in the same situation. That's one reason why AA has been so successful. It's hard for me to completely understand what you're going through because I haven't been there. From what you've told me of Sam, he seems like a good man and I think it's great you're both doing this. I'll make sure to keep Wednesdays clear."

She walked up to him, putting her arms around him. "I love you so much. This will work. I know it."

CHAPTER 35

The last five months had gone by quickly for Luisa. Carlos was nine months old, putting anything and everything in his mouth. He was an adorable, inquisitive, and very happy child. Carlos' colic had cleared up soon after Luisa returned from the Memorial Day weekend. She was far more relaxed and Carlos' improved health reflected the changes in her.

Jorge had adjusted to his trips to and from Brazil. While he didn't like being away from Luisa and Carlos, his time in Brazil had been productive. Under Jorge's watchful eye, Ortega & Ortega had been able to gain the respect of the indigenous people as well as the environmentalists. Although they were removing a valuable natural resource from the land, they were doing it in a manner that was respectful of the environment, something no other gold mine owner in Brazil had ever done. They still had problems with lawlessness, but that was to be expected anytime there were huge amounts of money at stake.

The memory of the Memorial Day weekend at the Blue Coyote was simply that, a memory. It only became real when Luisa opened the drawer where she kept her cosmetics and saw the two white pill bottles at the rear of the drawer. She and Jorge had spoken often about when they would start taking the pills and both knew the time was coming. They could feel that the "pick-me-up" they had received over that weekend was wearing off. She was beginning to feel nervous and anxious once again. For his part, Jorge was beginning to dread the Brazilian trips. They decided to take a pill on a Saturday in late October. It seemed to work just as Jeffrey had said it would and within hours they both felt much better. The anxiety and restless anger they both had been experiencing was soon gone. Life looked good again.

Three months went by and on a sunny January day, Luisa kissed Jorge good-bye as his driver arrived to take him to the Los Angeles airport. When Jorge left the house, he said, "I'll be back from the Amazon in two weeks. We need to plan some trips to Catalina Island with the boat. It makes no sense to own it and belong to the yacht club if we don't use and enjoy both of them. Carlos is old enough and I'm ready to start spending a lot of time at the island. When I get back, let's decide which weekends this coming spring will work for us." Luisa was just as ready. She needed something to look forward to now that the holidays were over.

"That sounds wonderful." Luisa said. "I'll look at our calendar while you're gone and come up with some tentative dates. Be safe. I love you." She waved good-bye as the big silver Mercedes pulled away from the house. Even though Jorge had started to drive after their move to California, he still relied on a driver to take him to the airport and pick him up.

Luisa went upstairs and as she walked by her bathroom to check on Carlos, she noticed that she hadn't fully closed her cosmetic drawer earlier that morning. When she shut it, she saw Jorge's little white vial of pills in the back of the drawer and realized that he had forgotten to take his pill with him and he was due to take his monthly pill tonight. They had both been taking the pills for a couple of months and Jeffrey had been right; the little pill continued to work its magic in just a few hours. She hoped Jorge would be all right without it for two weeks. She wondered if she should call him to come back and pick it up, but she became distracted when Carlos tried to climb out of his crib and she forgot about it. Several hours later it crossed her mind when she opened the drawer to get her makeup removal cream and once again saw Jorge's white vial. *Well, she thought, Jorge's already in the air and there's nothing I can do about it now. I'll remind him the next time he goes to Brazil to be sure and take some pills with him and keep them at our home in Rio.*

Jorge slept fitfully on the plane and awoke shortly before the big jet landed in Rio. His Brazilian driver was waiting for him. Jorge would spend two nights in Rio, meeting with his father and taking care of routine business matters, and then fly by company plane to where the company boat was kept, which would take him to their gold mine operation deep in the heart of the Amazon.

When he landed in Rio, he went directly to the offices of Ortega & Ortega. Soon he was immersed in the business decisions that being a co-owner of the largest gold mine in Brazil brought. It was late when his driver took him to his home. He had felt "off" for a few days and eagerly looked forward to the relief the little pill he had brought with him would bring. He poured himself a glass of water and reached into the side pocket of his attaché bag for the pill bottle. He couldn't find it. He took everything out of the bag, turned it upside down, and shook it, but it wasn't there. Now that he thought about it, he couldn't remember actually packing it. *Well, it's only for two weeks,* he thought. *I'll take a pill as soon as I get back to California.*

After a sleepless night, he went to the office early the next morning and began tackling the paperwork which had piled up since his last trip. He knew he had a number of meetings scheduled and he was anxious to get this task behind him. When his secretary arrived at the office, he called her into his office.

"Consuela, I see that you've made a mistake on my appointment schedule." He began yelling at her. "There is no room for anyone at this company who makes such stupid mistakes."

The outer office became very quiet as Consuela

began to softly cry. Jorge couldn't believe he had yelled at an employee and one of his most loyal employees at that. It was completely out of character for him to act in that manner.

"I'm sorry, Consuela. I'm feeling very jet lagged. Please forgive me." He knew it wasn't jet lag. What he really needed was Freedom and he couldn't get it. Even if he had Luisa send it to him, it would be too late. He would be deep in the Amazon jungle by the time it arrived. He would just have to hold on for twelve more days.

Later that day, his father called him into his office. Tomas was an avid collector of South American art and the displays in his office were often featured in various magazines and journals. His collection was one of the finest in the country. Jorge sat down in the chair across from his father, separated by the massive Brazilian mahogany desk his father had recently purchased. Jorge looked around the room. Tribal masks graced the walls along with brightly colored native art. Wooden carvings, totems, and textiles of all sorts filled other spaces. Jorge had always been fascinated by the nursing serape, which supposedly had belonged to the wife of a tribal chief. It was embroidered in various horizontal geometric patterns on a deep orange fabric. Embossed on each side of the central vertical opening for breastfeeding were brightly colored flowers. It was beautiful to look at and even if the story wasn't true, it always made for good conversation.

His father began, "Jorge, things have changed in the two weeks since you were last here. There have been a number of murders in the jungle. A tribal malcontent has been urging a group of young native men to attack the various gold mines in the area at night. When the guards step away from the others, generally to relieve themselves, they are attacked and killed. Their necks are slashed from ear to ear with the machetes these vicious killers carry. We haven't had a problem so far, but the Moreno family has had several of their guards murdered. The other owners have stopped going to the mines, letting their on-site managers run things. I'm concerned for your safety. Perhaps it would be wiser if you didn't go to the mines on this trip. Why don't you let Jose, our manager, go on your behalf?"

Jorge thought for a moment and responded, "Well, I'm here. I have the best guards money can buy and I know they'll protect me. What kind of message would we send to these rebels and to our employees if I became afraid to go to the mines? One of the reasons we've been so successful is because we personally go to the mines and know exactly what's going on at each one. No matter how much we trust Jose or any of the others, it won't be the same. When these malcontents see that the owner of the mines doesn't fear them, it will send a very powerful message. Don't worry. I will be careful."

His mind flashed back to the Memorial Day weekend at Blue Coyote and he remembered when he had told the other guests that he was going to continue to take Freedom; he couldn't go through a drug withdrawal in the Amazon. It would be too dangerous and not fair to Luisa, Carlos, and his employees. The words were coming back to haunt him as he feared that was exactly what was going to happen. He tossed and turned all night, getting up before dawn and packing for the plane ride and the trip on the river. He was exhausted. Not a good way to go into the Amazon when you had to be alert to everything because of the ever-present dangers. And now there was this new danger, a group of dangerous natives, bent on wreaking death and destruction on the mines and their owners.

The plane ride and the river trip were uneventful. Jorge still marveled at the unending canopy of vibrant green trees beneath him as the small company plane flew over the jungle. They landed at a small airstrip near the city of Belem. Within minutes, Jorge's gear was transferred from the plane onto the waiting boat. Jorge made sure the pistol he wore at his hip was loaded and checked to make sure the large knife he concealed in his boot was also there. He was flanked by seven guards, all heavily armed. He felt safe.

Jose accompanied Jorge and as soon as they arrived at the mine, Jose gave him a quick tour of what had happened in the two weeks since he had last been at the mine. It was amazing that the land could continue to yield so much of the treasured gold. Because of a worldwide economic recession, investors wanted more and more gold to act as a hedge against declining prices on the worlds' stock markets. The demand was outstripping supply and driving up the price.

During the tour, Jorge carefully reviewed the

procedure the company used to ship the gold. The gold always left the mine locations in heavily armed boats. They were small and fast and could outrun any other boat intent on piracy. They carried four men, two at the helm, one aft and one in the front. A stack of gold ingots that had been smelted at the mine was positioned in the center of the boat. All of the men had submachine guns slung over their chests with a holstered sidearm on each hip. Although each man knew that piracy was always a possibility, there was very little chance that the boats or the men would become captives.

Night came quickly in the jungle. Fires were lit and the guards assumed their positions around the perimeter of the mine. Several men were sitting and standing around Jorge, making sure that no harm would come to the "chefe," as they referred to him. He slept in a hammock tied between two trees. One didn't sleep on the ground in the jungle. Not only did things go bump in the night, they slithered as well. He was exhausted, but sleep eluded him. In the past, he had found the jungle sounds soothing, but tonight they were frightening. He longed for Luisa and Carlos and his warm bed in California. He also longed for the comfortable feeling provided by his Freedom pill.

Sometime just before dawn, when the jungle was at its darkest, he felt nature's call. He thought if he relieved himself, he could probably get some sleep. He debated with himself whether to get up or wait for dawn. The pressure on his bladder finally won.

He swung his feet over the side of the hammock

and, exhausted, almost fell to the ground. He steadied himself and took a few steps away from the fire, but his judgment was off. Freedom was no longer in his body and he neglected to have one of his guards accompany him, a mistake he had never made in the past.

In the moonlit night he thought he saw a glint of flashing steel behind him. He turned quickly, but the cold blade of the heavy machete was quicker, slitting his throat from ear to ear. His last thoughts were of Luisa and Carlos. *Dear God, watch over them,* he prayed as his blood spurted from his throat, shooting in every direction. He pitched forward and before he hit the ground, the murderers beheaded him, taking their prize and leaving the body for his guards to find. It was all done within a matter of seconds.

One of the guards thought he heard a strange sound. He turned, realizing that Jorge was not in his hammock. He immediately sounded the alert and within minutes they found Jorge's body, still warm, lying in a massive pool of blood. The head was missing. Only his body was left at the bloody scene.

They quickly got Jose who wanted to know why Jorge had gone off without one of his guards. He took all of his pain and anguish out on the guards, screaming at them and blaming each one of them for letting this tragedy occur. Finally, he realized that it was not the fault of the guards. For some reason, Jorge had not taken a guard with him when he went left his hammock to relieve himself. Jose didn't know about Freedom and how it had resulted in Jorge's lack of judgment. He instructed the guards to wrap Jorge's body in blankets and told them they were to go with him to escort the body back to Rio. No one wanted to be the one to tell Tomas. That task fell to Jose, the man now in charge.

Jose and several of the guards made their way to the offices of Ortega & Ortega in Rio. They had left Jorge's headless body, guarded, in a commercial cooler at the airport. In the way of the jungle, they knew that Jorge's head would soon be brandished on a spear for all to see. Those who had taken the head would be considered heroes by the malcontents and some of the indigenous tribal people.

When they entered the large office building, Jose and the other men went directly to the office of Tomas Ortega. The secretary recognized Jose and realized from the somber faces that something very bad had happened. She called Senhor Ortega on the intercom; then opened the door to his office. Jose and the men entered and within moments she heard a primal scream. Jose threw the door open. "Water!" he yelled to Senhor Ortega's secretary. "Quickly, bring some water." She poured a glass of water from the carafe on the reception table and ran into the office where Tomas was slumped in his chair, his face chalky white. He tried to hold the glass in his hands, but they were trembling so badly he nearly dropped it. Jose held the glass to the old man's lips and told him to drink the water.

Grief-stricken, the old man wanted to know how it had happened. He listened intently as Jose told him everything he knew. Tomas could not understand why Jorge had not taken a guard with him. Jose had no answer; he only knew what the guards told him, that Jorge had not asked anyone to accompany him. Within minutes, they left the Ortega & Ortega office building and drove Senhor Ortega to his home. Tomas seemed to have aged twenty years in the last hour.

"Who have you told about this tragedy?" Tomas asked Jose.

"No one. We came here immediately. I did not want to be the one to tell Luisa. It's not my place to do so and I knew you would want to be the one to tell her. I am concerned that your employees probably know what happened. Luisa should be told as soon as possible before she is called by the press or hears of it on the news.

"We must fly to California immediately. I need to tell her in person. You will come with me. There are questions she might ask that I can't answer," Tomas said. "I will call her parents when we land in California so they can be with her. Make all the arrangements necessary to have his body cremated immediately." Tomas did not want to see his son's body and he certainly didn't want Luisa to see Jorge's brutalized remains.

He went on, "Luisa will want a funeral service for Jorge to take place here in Rio. She may also want to have a small service in California. The families are so well known here that plans must be made. A funeral Mass for him will be attended by many. He can be cremated, but his ashes can't be scattered. See that the church has a place ready for his entombment, a cremation vault."

Jose silently vowed to never let Luisa know that her husband's head was probably on a spear somewhere in a remote jungle village in the Amazon. He only hoped the old man wouldn't hear about it, but from Tomas' discussion of cremating Jorge, he knew that the old man probably knew as well. Jose took care of the details for the service as they made their way to the airport to catch the long non-stop flight to Los Angeles.

The flight to California was a nightmare. Senhor Ortega wept on and off during the entire flight. Jose was glad they were in first class. At least there were fewer people to witness his grief. The thoughtful flight attendant kept a supply of Kleenex available. By prearrangement, Jorge's California driver met them at the airport. Jose told him what had happened and he, too, wept. Jorge had been much loved by the people who worked for him.

Tomas had been to California several times since his son had moved there, but the heavy traffic on the 405 Freeway in the airport area made his sad journey even worse. He wanted to tell Luisa and get it over with and being stuck in traffic just added to his grief. It was one o'clock in the afternoon, yet every traffic lane was filled with cars. It was like a giant parking lot snaking lazily into the distance.

He called Luisa's parents from his cell phone once he and Jose had an idea of what time they would arrive at Luisa's home. There was no way to break news of this type gently. Diego answered the phone. Tomas took a deep breath and began, "Diego, this is Tomas Ortega. I have some very sad news. My son was murdered yesterday at one of the company mines in the Amazon. I have flown from Rio with my manager, Jose, to tell Luisa, but I think it would be good if you and Juanita were with Luisa when she is told. We are just now leaving the Los Angeles airport for her home."

The news of Jorge's death devastated Diego and Juanita. Once they had a chance to digest the terrible news related to them by Tomas, their thoughts turned to Luisa and Carlos. They agreed with Tomas, that it would be best if they were with Luisa when she was told. Arrangements were made for Jose and Tomas to pick up Diego and Juanita and then go directly to Luisa's home. "Do you think Luisa will be home?" Tomas asked Diego.

"Yes, it is Carlos' naptime and she never goes anywhere during that time. We will see you shortly."

Tomas and Jose picked up Diego and Juanita and drove to Luisa's nearby home. They were all quiet. What was there left to say? With heavy hearts, they got out of the car. Tomas told the driver to wait, as he and Jose needed to return to Rio. Jose had made reservations for them on a flight that left at eight p.m., but with the traffic, an international flight, and security lines, one had to plan on being at the airport several hours before the departure time for an international flight.

Luisa's maid opened the door in response to the doorbell. If she seemed surprised to see all of them, she didn't show it. "Mrs. Ortega, you have some guests. If you need me, I will be in the kitchen," Ana said.

Luisa came down the stairs, clearly surprised to see the four of them standing there, particularly Tomas and Jose. She looked at their faces and knew something had happened to Jorge. "What is it? What's happened? It's Jorge, isn't it? Where is he?" Her parents quickly crossed the tile floor and held her. She pushed them aside. "What's going on? Tell me." Her voice began to shake with emotion.

"Jorge was murdered yesterday in the Amazon by members of a lawless band of angry men led by a man who is intent on closing down the mines. It was a quick death. He didn't suffer," Tomas said, tears once again running down his cheeks.

Luisa's knees buckled. Diego caught her and led her to a nearby couch. She began to cry. "Dear God, what do I tell Carlos? He loved his father so much. We had a calendar and we would mark off each day until he came back. As young as he is, I think he understood. How do I go on without him?"

There was no way to respond to her questions. Tomas walked over to her. "I am so, so sorry. I asked him not to go. I told him the jungle had changed in the short time since he had last been there. He felt he would be safe and insisted on going. I will regret with every breath I take for the rest of my life that I did not forbid him to go."

Diego called Father Connery at the church. "Father, this is Diego Chaves. There has been a tragedy in our family. Could you come to Luisa's home? You've been here before. Please hurry." Father Connery said he was on his way. The Ortega family had been very generous to the church and Father Connery was ready to help in whatever way he could. Next, Diego called Selena and told her what had happened. She told him she would leave work immediately and be there as soon as possible.

As the tragic death of Jorge became a reality, they started the difficult task of making plans for the memorial services, both in Rio and the one Luisa wanted for Jorge in California. Tomas told Luisa that he had authorized the cremation of Jorge's body and Luisa agreed that this was the right decision to have been made under the circumstances. He told her that they would have a funeral Mass in Rio as well as at the local church and that Jorge's cremated remains would be entombed in Rio in an underground crypt in keeping with the tradition of cremation in the Catholic Church.

Tomas' secretary kept calling, telling him that the newspapers and others were asking for a statement from the company regarding the murder. Evidently one of the guards who had come from the mine had leaked the story to a newspaper in return for money. There were people to be called and things to be dealt with when a life was shortened by murder.

The next few days were a blur for Luisa. Although Carlos had been told, he was too young to realize what it meant. A funeral Mass was held at the local Catholic Church in Huntington Beach, attended by the few people Jorge and Luisa had come to know since moving to California.

Luisa and Carlos flew to Rio, accompanied by Diego and Juanita. Both families had been members of the oldest Catholic Church in Rio for decades. The large funeral Mass was attended by all of Rio's society, politicians, business community, Jorge's beloved employees, and the press. It was one of the largest funeral services to ever take place in the Church. Every pew was filled and cameras filmed the service, feeding it to an overflow crowd gathered in an adjoining building.

Although the death was tragic, it was a story made for the newspapers and the Rio newspapers made the most of it. A wealthy gold mine owner from one of the founding families of Rio murdered by indigenous tribesmen in the Amazon, leaving a beautiful young wife and infant son was a story that even made its way into *People* magazine and the supermarket tabloids.

Unfortunately, the story also told how Jorge's head had been paraded on a spear deep in the Amazon. In true tabloid fashion, some unknown member of the "paparazzi" had managed to find his way to the remote village where Jorge's head was displayed and had taken a photograph of it. Grief stricken, Luisa stayed at home most of the time and avoided any painful interviews with the press. When she finally ventured out, the tabloids had already moved on to the next "big" story.

Even though she was burdened by a broken heart, there were decisions that could only be made by Luisa. Should she sell the Rio condominium? Close out the Rio accounts? Go into the family gold mining business? Stay in Rio? Go back to California? Sell the boat? Sell the Huntington Beach house? Move to a smaller home in California? Her mind spun with all the critical decisions that had to be made. While most experts say no big decisions should be made until a year after the death of a loved one, many of Luisa's decisions simply couldn't wait.

After being in Rio for a few weeks she decided to permanently move back there. Although her sister and parents still tied her to California, without Jorge, the big house on the water held little appeal for her. She decided to sell it. She called John and asked him if he knew someone who might be interested in the boat. She didn't care about making a profit on the house or the boat. Given her state of mind, she couldn't deal with such details.

When she told her parents that she had decided to move back to Rio, that her roots and Carlos' were there, not in California, her parents decided to move back to Rio with her. They enjoyed California, but they missed their friends and other family members. They, too, would miss Selena, but they couldn't stand to be so far away from Carlos during his childhood years. With Jorge gone, they knew Luisa and Carlos would need them more than ever.

After many long talks with Tomas, Luisa agreed to join the family business. She promised her parents she would not go to the mines, but she would help run the company from Rio. Jose was promoted to General Manager of all the Ortega mines. He was highly respected and coming from the indigenous people, he would have no problem supervising the employees, which was such a large part of a successful gold mining business. Luisa and Jose got along well. She knew Jorge had completely trusted him and she looked forward to working with him.

When Luz and Manny found out that Luisa was moving back to Rio, they asked if they could have their old jobs back. Luisa was thrilled to have them in her employ once again. Luz told her to forget about looking for a nanny, that she could be a nanny and a maid. She clearly adored little Carlos.

With all that had happened in the last few weeks, Luisa had completely forgotten about Freedom. She had noticed that she was feeling tense, angry, and subject to sudden verbal outbursts, but she rationalized it all as being caused by Jorge's death. Now she realized she was two weeks late in taking her next Freedom pill and that the pills weren't in Rio; they were in California. *Well*, she thought, *I can take it when I return to California next week.*

Luisa had no desire to go back to California, to where she and Jorge had been so happy. She knew the memories would overwhelm her, but she also knew there were business matters to attend to there and she was the only one who could take care of them. She needed to put the house and boat up for sale and decide what to do with their household goods. It would be a very busy time. Fortunately, her parents had decided to travel back to California with

Luisa and Carlos as they, too, needed to take care of business matters before returning permanently to Rio.

The thought of Jorge and his forgotten pill crossed her mind. Once again she wondered if it had played a part in his death. When Tomas had told her that Jorge had not taken a guard with him when he went to relieve himself, she was pretty sure that his lack of judgment was from drug withdrawal. She would never know, but she began to develop a hatred for the drug on which she had become so dependent.

The night before she was to fly back to California, Luisa suddenly woke up shaking, not an uncommon occurrence for her since Jorge's death, but this time it was different. She had been dreaming and Jorge had spoken to her in the dream. He told her he had caused his own death because of faulty judgment brought on by his failure to take his regular dose of Freedom. So strongly could she sense his presence, it was as if he was in the room with her.

He pleaded with her to quit taking the drug. He told her he knew she might have some rough times caused by withdrawal symptoms, but that eventually she wouldn't feel she needed the pill. He begged her to stop for Carlos' sake. Carlos needed her to be drug-free. Jorge reminded her that anytime Jeffrey wanted to withhold the pills for whatever reason, he could. He reminded her of how crazy and unpredictable Jeffrey had seemed when they saw him during the Memorial Day weekend. What if

Jeffrey really went off the deep end and she could no longer get the pills? He told her to get rid of her reliance on Freedom and that the longer she waited, the harder it would be. He told her to call the psychologist, Sean, so he could help her. Although the dream was both startling and vivid, gradually it subsided.

She decided she would call Sean in the morning. With her decision made, she fell back into a deep and dreamless sleep, waking rested for the first time in weeks. After taking into account the time difference between Rio and Denver, she called Sean.

"This is Sean Moriarty, may I help you?" the voice on the other end of the phone said.

"Yes, you may remember me. My name is Luisa Ortega. We met at the Blue Coyote Motel. My life has changed dramatically since I last saw you. My husband, Jorge, was murdered in the Amazon and I've decided to take my son and move back to Rio. But that's not why I'm calling. I feel that Jorge's death was somehow related to his forgetting to take his Freedom pills to Rio with him on his last trip. I need to get off the pills. I'm two weeks past when I should have taken one and I feel foggy, kind of 'off.' I've even had bouts of sweating and the shakes.

"I kept your business card and you said to call if any of us ever wanted to talk. I remember that you chose not to take the pills. Maybe you can help me. I have decided I can't take them any longer. I have to be there for my infant son and the pills are interfering with my duty as a mother." It was a long explanation of her concerns, but Luisa felt much better after she had spoken.

Sean said, "Of course I remember you and I am so sorry to hear about Jorge. I liked him. I think I can be of help. You may remember Sam. He, too, decided not to take the pills. We knew we were going to go through some rough times and we have, but it's much better now. Sam and I decided to talk once a week via Skype. We formed a two-person group based on the successful model used by Alcoholics Anonymous. The basic premise is that you can't deal with problems of addiction by yourself, but you can help someone else and someone else can help you. The two of us are helping each other. You are welcome to join us. We talk at 9:00 p.m. every Wednesday night. If you're not familiar with Skype, have someone install it for you on your home computer and have them show you how to use it. With Skype we not only talk, but we can see each other as well. As I said, it's all done with your home computer. Skype also has the ability for group talks. I can set that up for the three of us. Sam and I are doing very well. I really think it would help you if you would join us on Wednesday nights."

Sean was surprised at how true his words were. He and Sam were both doing very well. The cravings for Freedom were becoming less and less frequent. Sean felt a lot of it was because he and Sam talked about their feelings and cravings. He was sure if Luisa joined them she would be helped too.

"Oh, Sean, thank you so much. You're offering me hope. When I made the decision last night, on one hand, I was sure it was the right one, but on the other hand, I was dreading what I might go through. If I have someone to talk to, it will be much easier," Luisa said, clearly grateful for Sean's help.

"And Luisa, don't forget. I'm a psychologist and Sam is a doctor so you're getting two professionals helping you for free."

They both laughed, knowing full well that Luisa could afford any professional she wanted. She told him she would have Skype installed and would call at 9:00 p.m. next Wednesday. She hung up feeling hopeful, as if a huge burden had been lifted from her shoulders. If she could get help from Sean and Sam, she felt she could make it through this time of almost insurmountable grief. She was eager for Wednesday to arrive.

CHAPTER 36

After leaving the Blue Coyote Motel on Memorial Day weekend, Jill drove to her home in the desert feeling great once again. She'd always loved the desert and even more so on late spring days like today. There was a little nagging voice in the back of her mind, a reminder that Rick still watched over her. She knew that he would have been unhappy with her decision to take Freedom, but she just didn't think she could go back to how she felt after his death. She was finally enjoying her life and had no desire to return to a mental state where she didn't care whether she lived or died and had seriously contemplated suicide.

When she got to her desert home, she called Aaron, who had become her best friend, her lover, her confidante, and her constant companion whenever they could arrange it. When he answered the phone, Jill said, "I'm so glad I went to that little motel in the desert. I really feel better and I think I look better too. I was probably overly tired, but I'm feeling fine now. You've never been to my home here in the desert. Why don't you fly into Ontario airport next Friday and I'll pick you up. It's only about an hour's drive from the airport to my home. The desert is so beautiful this time of year. Bring your clubs and I'll make a golf reservation for us."

"I've been so worried about you," Aaron said. "This is great news and a celebration is definitely in order. I'll meet you at the airport on Friday. My scheduler will make my flight reservation and I'll get back to you with my arrival time. I haven't played golf in a long time, although I've been meaning to take it up again. I never could seem to find the time for it, but I guess the time is now. We've never talked about this. Are you any good?"

"Well, I haven't played for a long time either, but at one time I could play without totally embarrassing myself. I'm not sure how I'll do now, but I'm game. I can't wait to see you!"

When Jill hung up, she realized just how true that was. She had missed him more than she had thought possible. She wasn't sure just how long she wanted to continue a long distance romance. The times she spent in between seeing him were getting terribly lonesome. Aaron had built a very lucrative and successful medical practice and she knew that if any future moves were to be made, they would have to be on her part.

As she unpacked, she noticed the little vial of Freedom pills in her suitcase and made a mental note to put them in her medicine chest when she returned to Newport Beach. She thought that Aaron, like Rick, would probably not be in favor of her decision to continue with the pills. It was something she'd hold off telling him, if she told him at all.

Jill picked Aaron up at the Ontario airport at 3:00 p.m. on Friday. They had to wait a long time for his golf clubs, but they finally slid down the chute marked "Oversize Luggage." Aaron wasn't the only one to ship golf clubs to the Ontario airport to be used in Palms Springs. The area had a worldwide reputation for having some of the finest golf courses in the country. A large number of golf bags joined Aaron's in the baggage claim area.

They had an easy drive to the greater Palm Springs area, arriving at Jill's home just before dusk. Aaron left his clubs in the car while they hurried into the house, poured a glass of wine, and took their drinks out to the patio. Her home faced the seventeenth hole of an exclusive golf club and was a perfect spot to watch the sun set. It was a beautiful evening and the desert was magical with breathtakingly beautiful pinks, purples, light blues, and dark blues. When it was finally dark, the sky was filled with stars.

"We don't have nights like this in San Francisco. There's too much fog and too many lights from the city. This is really something," Aaron said. "I don't remember seeing a sky like this in Newport Beach either."

"Newport is the same as San Francisco," Jill said. "Too many city lights; the desert has a beauty all of its own. I love to come here because I always feel like I'm on vacation."

Aaron said, "To change the subject. Do you remember Lenore? You met her at a hospital fundraiser when you were in San Francisco with me. Evidently, she's a good friend of your friend Marge, who, as I understand it, is the chairperson of the big Newport Hospital fundraising gala. I believe you handled the last silent auction for her. Anyway, Marge was going on and on about how successful it was because of you, so Lenore called me to see if you would be interested in moving to San Francisco. They're at a place where they need a full-time fundraising director at the hospital and they've decided to create this new position. I understand that it pays well and I think you would be great for it."

Aaron took a deep breath and went on, "I know it's early in our relationship, but I'd like you to move in with me and let's see where this goes. I've never been married and I'd like to take my time before either of us makes any permanent decisions. Take your time and think about it as long as you like, but please say yes."

Jill sat perfectly still, barely able to comprehend what she had just heard. A job in San Francisco and Aaron asking her to move in with him? She hadn't known what she wanted, but now that it was presented to her, this was exactly what she wanted.

"I don't even need to think about it," she said. "Absolutely! How soon does she want me to start? I'll need to take care of a few things before I can move to San Francisco, but I'll make it work. Oh, Aaron, I love you and I want to be with you. I've been so worried about the future of our relationship. I didn't know how we were going to make it work. This is a miracle."

Aaron reached out and took her face in his strong hands. "I promise I will do everything in my power to make you as happy as you're making me at this moment. Let's celebrate by going out to a fancy dinner, but first I'd like to celebrate privately in the other room."

He stood up, took her hand, closed the patio door behind him and gently pulled her into the bedroom. The celebratory dinner had been a great idea, but the private celebration was much better and lasted the whole night.

Aaron woke up to the smell of bacon sizzling on the stove griddle along with the smell of freshly made coffee. He walked into the kitchen to find Jill setting the breakfast table on the patio. She had squeezed fresh orange juice for their mimosas and was getting ready to mix the hollandaise sauce for their bacon eggs benedict. He helped her carry the plates out to the patio table where a big bouquet of flowers she had brought from inside the house sat in the middle of the table.

"I could really get used to this. Do you cook like this all the time?" Aaron asked. "I'm sick and tired of eating on the run and I'm no good as a cook. Think you can do some cooking like this when you get to San Francisco?"

"You're in luck. I love to cook. Guess I'm just a frustrated chef and cooking just for me is not a lot of fun. Get ready! This is the part of our relationship I think you're really going to like," Jill replied.

"Actually, there aren't any parts I'm not liking," Aaron said, grinning.

As she sat in the warm morning sunshine looking out at the perfectly maintained golf course, enjoying breakfast with Aaron, the image of the white pill vial containing her supply of Freedom pills flickered briefly through Jill's mind. She quickly shut it out, not wanting anything to destroy this moment. *I'll think about it later*, she thought. *I'm probably going to have to do something about this pill thing, but for now I'm just going to enjoy the ride.*

Jill had reserved a tee time for 9:00 a.m. The desert could become brutally hot in the afternoon and she wanted them to finish their round of golf before the heat made it unbearable. Given the fact that neither one of them had played any golf for a long time, they both played fairly well and promised each other they would continue to play regularly when Jill moved to San Francisco.

Aaron had belonged to an exclusive country club with a beautiful golf course for several years, but he'd never taken the time to play there. When he'd used the clubhouse for luncheon meetings, he'd often admired the course. It would be fun to take Jill there and play the course on a regular basis. There were a lot of things in San Francisco he wanted to share with her.

The parking lot in the Italian restaurant where Jill had made dinner reservations was jammed with Bentleys, Mercedes, and BMWs. When she saw the parking lot, she was doubly glad that she'd called for a reservation. She'd read in the local newspaper, the Desert Sun, that you couldn't get a dinner reservation for the weekend after Wednesday. They were always full. The hostess escorted them to a table for two. The place was packed and a quick glance at the food being served to the guests at the other tables reassured Jill that she'd made the right choice in selecting this restaurant.

Good wine, good food, good service, and a great ambiance. The restaurant scored a ten on all fronts. Satisfied and sleepy, they made their way back to Jill's gated community home.

They spent the following morning making plans for the future. Jill called Lenore at her home and talked to her about the job. Jill would be in charge of all fundraising for the hospital. She would meet with large donors and oversee the different fundraising groups that supported the hospital. It was a newly created position and Jill would be hiring her own staff. Jill accepted the position on the spot, knowing she would excel. She and Lenore agreed that Jill would start two weeks from Monday. Before they knew it, the day was almost gone and it was time to take Aaron to the airport.

Jill returned to her home in Newport Beach the following day feeling completely overwhelmed. How would she ever get everything done in just under two weeks' time? She remembered something she had read about breaking things down into parts when a person is confronted with a large project. The article suggested not thinking about the whole thing, just thinking about the individual parts. She made a list of the major things that needed to be done and broke each into separate parts.

The two biggest things on her list that had to be dealt with were her house and its contents. She had some valuable antiques that she and Rick had acquired over the years, some of which might fit into Aaron's condominium, but many of her other things would have to go into storage. Jill decided to rent the house rather than sell it, but she didn't feel comfortable renting it with all her furniture and valuable antiques still in it.

She called a property manager, making an appointment for the following day. Next she called a moving company, arranging for them to come on Thursday of the following week. Lastly, she called the storage company she had passed many times on the freeway, not too far from where she lived. She began to feel a little better. Those had been the major things.

Then she moved on to the lesser items on her list. She made a list of the clothes that she wanted to take with her to San Francisco. Other clothing would have to go into storage. She knew she'd be coming back from time to time, so if she needed something, she could easily get it later.

She wondered what to do with the books, CDs, and a houseful of plants she had accumulated. Jill's mind was whirling. By Monday evening she was exhausted from all the decisions she had made. She walked into the kitchen and poured herself a glass of Silver Oak Napa Valley Cabernet Sauvignon, one of her favorites. There were perks to having money and a good red wine was one of them.

As she walked back into the living room, she glanced at her collection of books. She loved the look of books as a decorator item in a house, but in her case, she'd read each and every one of them. She asked herself if she would ever read them again and had to admit, honestly, that she probably wouldn't. A donation to the Newport Beach Public Library seemed to be in order.

Next, she needed to deal with the houseplants. She made a note to call several of her friends to come over and take any plants that they might want along with their containers. Her large outdoor patio was filled with potted and hanging plants and every room in her house seemed to have one or more plants in it. As much as she had enjoyed them, she knew they would do fine in their new homes.

She had several valuable Oriental rugs and made a mental note to check with Aaron to see if any of them would work in his home. Back in the kitchen for a second glass of wine, she wondered what to do with all of the pantry items. The last time she had been in Aaron's home, she had made breakfast and noticed that salt and pepper were about as good as it got in his spice rack. She would have to hire a moving van to transport her clothes, some personal things, her spice collection, the Oriental rugs, and other odds and ends to San Francisco. She could donate the rest of the pantry items to "Someone Cares," the soup kitchen in Costa Mesa, which fed hundreds of homeless people every day. She knew they'd appreciate the donation.

Everywhere she looked something needed to be donated. *Well,* she thought, *I can call some charities and have them pick up the things I don't want. That will be a big help to them as well as solve some problems for me.*

The following days went by in a blur for Jill. A never-ending stream of friends rang the doorbell, wanting to personally say good-bye. There were endless decisions about what to take and what should stay. Each time a friend took one of her plants, she felt like crying. They were as personal to her as her books were. Jill had so many books that the library brought a van to her house to transport them. It was gut wrenching for Jill. She was a voracious reader who had first learned to read when she was three years old and she'd never stopped. She considered her books to be old, cherished friends.

The moving van arrived, packing up a lot of her life. The storage rental unit had a home service for people like Jill. They came to her home, packed up the items she indicated, and put them into a unit for her. For several days Jill felt like all she did was oversee packing for her storage unit. She was glad she'd decided not to sell the house. Several of her friends had commented that at least if things didn't work out, she had a safety net, her home. Jill was determined that things would work out, but only when she and Aaron were married would she consider selling her Newport Beach home.

In the short time since Aaron had asked her to move to San Francisco, everything had come together much easier than she had thought it would. Tomorrow she would be leaving her beloved home in Newport Beach for a new life in San Francisco. The house was empty and all that remained was a sleeping bag and two suitcases. The rest of her things would be arriving in San Francisco on Saturday.

She walked into her closet, taking out the last of her clothes, folding them and putting them in one of the suitcases. She opened her make-up drawer, removing items and putting them in a travel zipper bag. She had another one for her contact lenses and hair items. As she picked up the contact lens solution from the medicine cabinet, she saw the small white pill vial containing the Freedom pills. She stuck it in her bag and wondered when she would need to start taking them. It had only been a few weeks since she'd been to the Blue Coyote and she still felt fine. She'd find a place for the pills when she got to San Francisco.

The next few months of Jill's life passed by so rapidly she was surprised one day when she realized that she'd been in San Francisco for almost nine months. It had been perfect. She woke up each morning, eager to get to work. She really liked the staff that she had hired and it was as if the job had been designed with her in mind. She knew hospitals and doctors and she was perfectly comfortable with the donors. Jill easily spoke the language of the wealthy and they quickly embraced her as one of their own.

Aaron was everything she wanted in a future husband. They traveled whenever they could get away. Nearby Napa, with its beautiful rolling hills, world renowned wineries, and five-star restaurants, was high on their list of getaways. They loved staying at L'Auberge in the northern part of the Napa Valley with its wonderful view of the vineyards located in the valley below the hotel. Other places they visited included Sausalito with its bobbing sailboats, Half-Moon Bay, and the Russian River area.

Although Jill had visited San Francisco many times, she was enjoying becoming acquainted with the secrets of the city she and Aaron now called home. Under her guidance, he was quickly becoming an expert on food and San Francisco was a city that catered to those who liked to eat well.

Jill had started taking the Freedom pills a couple of months earlier when the familiar feelings of lethargy and depression began to reappear on a daily basis. She recognized the symptoms before she began having suicidal thoughts, took her little pill, and very soon felt good, really good.

One weekend morning when she was in the kitchen fixing breakfast, Aaron walked in with the little white vial in his hand. "Jill, when I was looking for a bottle of aspirin, I found these at the back of the medicine cabinet. Do they mean anything to you? There's no label on the bottle and I can't find anything identifiable on the pills themselves. I don't know where they came from. I'm going to dissolve them in water and then flush them down the toilet. Unmarked pills make me nervous."

Jill's mind raced. She couldn't let him put the pills down the drain. She was due to take one tomorrow and she knew that she couldn't get a new supply from Jeffrey for several days.

"Aaron, there's something I need to talk to you about. Please sit down as this is going to take some time."

She started at the beginning. He knew all about the first time she had stayed at the Blue Coyote Motel. Then she went on to tell him about the second trip, leaving nothing out. She told him she knew she was probably addicted to the Freedom pills, but that it was a pretty harmless addiction and she had the money to continue buying the pills. There hadn't been any side effects. When she finished talking, Aaron was silent for what seemed a very long time.

Finally he spoke, "Jill, I love you. You know that, but I can't condone what you're doing. This man sounds like he's ready to go off his rocker at any time and then what happens to your pills? At some point you're going to have to get off of them. I've got to be honest. I'm a doctor and I know what addictions can do to people, to relationships. This has been the best nine months of my life, but this is a deal-breaker for me.

"If you don't stop taking the pills, I'll have to end the relationship. I want to marry you; hell, I've even bought the ring. I was just waiting for the right moment to ask you, but this changes everything. I'm here for you and if you are going to go through a withdrawal phase, we'll face it together. I'm realistic enough to know that love isn't just about the good times, but if you choose the pills, I'll have to ask you to leave. Please, Jill, let me help you." Aaron was so distraught the last few sentences had come out in ragged breaths.

Jill tearfully replied, "Oh, Aaron. I'm so sorry to put you through this. I'm so scared. I never want to go back to the way I was before the Blue Coyote. You didn't know me then. I didn't care whether I lived or died." Tears poured down her face. Suddenly, she remembered the psychologist, Sean.

"Aaron, there was a psychologist at the motel. He and a medical doctor, Sam, chose not to take the pills. He gave the rest of us his business card and told us to call him if we ever wanted to talk. I trusted him. We all did. I'm going to call him. I think I kept his card in my wallet. Maybe he can help."

She stopped crying and began leafing through her wallet. She found the card and dialed Sean's number.

"This is Sean Moriarty, may I help you?"

"Sean, this is Jill Loren. I don't know if you remember me. I met you at the Blue Coyote Motel almost a year ago. We sat by the pool and had a long talk. When we left the motel on Sunday you had slipped your card under my door and wrote a note on it that I should call you if I ever needed to talk to anyone. I do."

"Of course I remember you, Jill. Tell me why you called," Sean said.

Jill began to cry again as the words tumbled out of her mouth in gasps.

"Jill, take a deep breath. I'm here for as long as you need me. Tell me everything."

Sean's voice was warm and comforting. Jill responded, telling him everything that had happened over the last few months. When she got to the morning's conversation with Aaron, once again she had trouble speaking. She stopped, took a deep breath, and finished by telling Sean how much she loved Aaron and how frightened she was that she couldn't stop taking the drug.

Sean replied, "You've probably heard of AA or Alcoholics Anonymous. It was started by a doctor and a stockbroker in the 1930s. Neither one could stop drinking. Nothing worked for either of them. They made a decision to help each other and finally, that worked. They found that if you helped keep someone else from drinking you helped yourself as well.

"Sam, the doctor you met at the motel, and I started our own version of helping each other several months after Memorial Day when the drug was beginning to leave our systems. It's worked. We both had some tough times at first, but we got through them and both of us are on the other side now. Finally, Freedom is out of out bodies and we are free from the addiction, but we still talk once a week. It's been a huge help to both of us.

"You may remember Luisa, the Brazilian woman. She's been part of our group for about four months. Her husband was murdered in the Amazon while he was there on business. She wanted to stop taking the drug because of her infant son. I would say she's doing quite well. She has some down days, but who doesn't? Are you familiar with Skype?" Sean asked. "It plays a big part in how I believe we can help you. We talk in a group call via Skype every Wednesday night at 9:00 p.m. I'd like to invite you to join us. Please, Jill, I can almost promise that you'll be helped."

"Thanks, Sean. You've given me hope that I can stop. If I can stop taking the drug, this wonderful life I'm sharing with Aaron is a real possibility. We already have Skype and I look forward to seeing as well as talking to you Wednesday at 9:00 p.m. And Sean, again, thank you for everything."

She turned to Aaron who had been listening to every word. He was smiling and held his arms out to her. "You can do this, Jill; you can do this," he said.

CHAPTER 37

The months following the Memorial Day weekend had not been kind to Jeffrey or Maria. Jeffrey continued his downhill slide into the depths of insanity. Maria realized that she could no longer reach him and thought he had probably gone mad. He continued with his experiments, but he no longer even came to their house, taking his meals in the basement lab and sleeping there. Maria had stocked the second refrigerator with things he could eat standing at one of the lab tables while he worked on his experiments, but Jeffrey often forgot to eat. He stopped shaving and his hair turned completely white. Piles of unopened mail and journals were stacked everywhere. When Maria looked into his eyes, she knew that the man she had known and loved had gone to a place far beyond her reach.

He stopped pumping Freedom into the motel rooms and there was only enough left to occasionally fill the office area. She didn't know how it worked and increasingly, he neglected to turn it on. Maria knew the day was rapidly approaching when it would run out and she was also out of her anti-aging hormone injection.

Early one afternoon, Maria went down the dark stairway to the lab, intent on trying to reason with Jeffrey by taking him his favorite meal. Maybe that would work and she could get him to make more of the anti-aging hormone for her. She was concerned that he may have slipped too far out of her reach and he could not or would not create the hormone injections for her any longer. She had to try one more time, vowing to herself to ignore the rats.

"Jeffrey, I've brought you some of your favorite foods. Why don't you take a break and eat them while they're hot?" She set down the large tray filled with plates of slow cooked ribs, mashed potatoes, bacon braised Brussels sprouts, freshly baked bread, and chocolate mousse. He barely acknowledged her, intent only on the food she placed in front of him.

Maria wondered if he even knew who she was. The thought occurred to her that if she could get a supply of the anti-aging hormone, it might be time to take the money in their checking account and just leave the country. Maybe she could go to a country where women weren't afraid of aging. She'd read that women in France aged gracefully. Older women there were just as desirable to men as younger ones. Maybe she should go there. Maria did all their bookkeeping and knew to the penny how much money they had in the bank and they had a lot. There certainly was enough for Maria to live very well in another country for the rest of her life.

Sooner or later she knew that she was going to have to get used to not being able to get Freedom or her anti-aging hormone. *Well,* she thought, *other people have lived through withdrawals, I guess I can too.*

But she thought she'd at least try to get Jeffrey to give her a supply one last time.

While he was eating, she looked around for her hormone injections. Jeffrey had always kept the hormone in a drawer in the large desk under the television screen. His face was nearly buried in his plate. He had begun eating like an animal, shoveling the food into his mouth, no longer even bothering with silverware, although he had taken a big knife he used in his experiments from a drawer to cut the ribs.

Closely watching him, she edged over to the desk. She put her arm behind her and quietly pulled the drawer open. Her hand searched the drawer from front to back, from side to side, but nothing was in there. Just as quietly, she closed it. Maria thought of ways she could approach Jeffrey to get the drugs she wanted, finally deciding to use the oldest method known to women. She knew he had once loved her deeply. She decided to try and tempt him with thoughts of having sex with her. In his present state, she didn't know if anything would work, but she was determined to try.

"I hope you like your meal," she said. "I want to please you, Jeffrey. It's been a long time since you came to the house. After you finish eating, why don't we go there together? We could go to the bedroom and spend a long, lovely afternoon together. I really have missed you," she said, looking for any signs that her words were registering with him. When he answered, she knew they had registered and that she would never again get him to provide Freedom or the anti-aging hormone to her.

"Maria, I know what you want and why you came down here. Do you think I'm stupid? You want your 'medicine.' Well, not any more. I know the only reason you married me and stayed with me is because of the hormone and then Freedom. You wanted the hormone so you would always be beautiful. You never loved me. I want you to be ugly. It shouldn't take too long for you to start aging. First, the lines in the face will come. Then your hair will begin to lose its shine and your body will change. After a few years, your chin, jowls, and breasts will sag. No, you won't be beautiful at all. You'll be the person you were always afraid of becoming, old and ugly."

Jeffrey laughed a maniacal laugh. Maria hadn't felt terror like this since she was gang raped so many years ago. She knew with certainty that her life as a beautiful young woman was over. She knew Jeffrey was right. She would start aging and eventually become ugly and old.

Maria pleaded with Jeffrey. "Please, if you ever loved me, please make the hormone for me. I promise I'll stay. I promise I'll never leave you, just make me the hormone. We can start again. I've been a good wife to you and I will continue to be a good wife. I'm not interested in anyone else. Please, please, won't you make me the hormone?"

He looked at her coldly. "Maria, I don't care what happens to you. You can rot in hell for all I care. This lab is my home. The rats are my friends. I don't care what happens to me. There is nothing you can give me or promise me that will change how I feel towards you. I hate you just like you've always hated me. I've seen how you look at me. Get out, get out of my lab and don't ever come back."

Maria felt panicky. She had to get the hormone. The hormone was far more important to her than Freedom. She remembered that Jeffrey kept a gun in one of the desk drawers. The crazier he had become, the more paranoid he had become. He was certain people were looking for him, trying to steal his discoveries. He thought the gun would stop someone from stealing his inventions. If she could get to it, she could threaten him into making the hormone for her. He turned his back to her and continued eating, dismissing her. Maria silently crept over to the desk, opening the bottom drawer with her foot. In one motion she knelt, grabbed the gun, and cradled it in her hand.

She began to speak in a voice completely unlike her own. She seemed to be possessed. "Jeffrey, look at me. I have your gun and I'll use it if I have to. I need the hormone. Make it, now," she said.

Jeffrey quickly stood up, grabbed the knife he had been using to cut his ribs, and charged her. She backed up, certain he intended to use the knife to scar her or worse.

"Maria, drop the gun or I will make so many cuts on your face, you won't need to worry about aging. You'll be so ugly no man will ever want you. Give me the gun, Maria. You don't know what you're doing. Just drop it!" He was screaming, the knife held over his head, intending to bring it down, slashing her face. Once again he shouted at her, "Give it to me, Maria! You don't know what you're doing."

He looked into the barrel of his own gun and at the stranger holding it. In the few minutes Maria had been in the lab, she had changed. What he saw before him was a strong woman holding a gun and not afraid to use it. This was definitely not the soft, compliant woman he had always known Maria to be. Even in his deranged state, he recognized that there was a stranger standing in front of him, holding his gun, and he wasn't sure what that stranger was capable of doing.

At that moment, somewhere in the depths of his demented mind, the need for self-protection kicked in. Even in his crazed state of mind, he knew that guns kill and he might be the one killed. He grabbed for the gun and at the same time, started to plunge the knife into Maria. He was certain that Maria wouldn't know how to release the safety on the gun before he grabbed it away from her.

Jeffrey had forgotten that he had previously released the safety on the gun. In a state of paranoia, he thought it was best to have the gun ready to fire in case someone came to get him. It was the last thought he ever had. The shot that rang out instantly killed him. Maria had pointed the gun at his chest at point blank range and the bullet hit him dead center in his heart. He fell to the floor, blood pouring out of him and pooling on the floor. It happened in the blink of an eye.

Maria looked at Jeffrey lying on the floor and realized he was dead. It was over. There would be no more Freedom and no more anti-aging hormone. The horror and enormity of what had just happened washed over her. Her first thought was to run, to get away from the Blue Coyote as fast as she could. Fortunately, there were no guests at the motel and as remote as the motel was, no one could have heard the shot. She knew she had to get away from the motel and get rid of the gun.

She was afraid if she stayed, she would be arrested, possibly tried for murder and sent to prison. She could claim self-defense, but she was the one who pulled the gun on Jeffrey and threatened him. A jury might not believe her version of what had happened. She decided to run.

Maria threw open the door to the lab, taking the stair steps two at a time. She ran through the walkway to their house, opening drawers and cupboards, throwing things into a small carry-on bag. Her brain was whirling. It was only 1:00 in the afternoon so she had time to get to their bank in Phoenix and withdraw their money before it closed. Then what? She knew she had to get away, the farther the better, perhaps Italy or France. Sky Harbor airport in Phoenix was an international airport. After she went to the bank, she'd go to the airport and get a ticket to somewhere far away. The last thing she threw in her carry-on luggage was her passport. It was ironic that she had gotten the passport when she and Jeffrey had gone to Tuscany on their honeymoon.

She got in the van and turned it towards Phoenix. There was a rest stop not too far from the Blue Coyote on the freeway that led to Phoenix. She pulled into the parking lot, grateful for the open spot in front of a trashcan. There was a grocery bag in the van from the last time she had made a food run to Blythe, filled with non-perishables. She'd been too tight on time then to take it into the motel kitchen, making a mental note to do it later. Right now she was very glad it was there. In the sack she found a box of plastic gloves, which she wore when she was preparing food for the motel. They would work. She slipped a pair on and began to towel off the gun, trying to get rid of any of her fingerprints. Then she wrapped the gun in fresh towels, placing it in the empty plastic glove box.

Maria opened her door to the van and walked to the women's restroom. To anyone watching, it would look like she had gone to the restroom and then decided to get rid of some trash, a perfectly normal occurrence. When she returned to the van, she opened the door and pulled out the plastic glove box holding the gun, casually throwing it into the half-full trashcan. Breathing a silent sigh of relief, she got back in the van and made her way onto the highway, certain that no one had seen her. Even if they had, nothing she had done would trigger someone's memory. She was simply a woman wearing a scarf and sunglasses, throwing away some trash.

As beautiful as she was, she was used to people staring at her. Until she was safely out of the country, being stared at was the last thing she wanted. When she was getting ready to leave the motel, she remembered that a Muslim guest had left a burkha behind. Maria had put it in the storage area of the office in case its owner ever wanted to reclaim it. She had taken it with her when she left the Blue Coyote, thinking it would be a perfect way to hide her hair, her face, and her body. When she got to her final destination, she would get rid of it somewhere. At a desolate freeway off ramp she pulled off and quickly changed into the burkha. She was back on the highway in less than three minutes. The burkha might draw attention for the next day, but nothing like the attention she normally received.

At the bank in Phoenix, she easily withdrew $10,000 in cash. When Maria first suspected that Jeffrey was going mad, she had opened a bank account in the Cayman Islands and from time to time, she sent money there. She transferred almost all of the substantial amounts in their checking and savings accounts to the Cayman Island bank account, knowing she could withdraw it as needed when she got settled. The tellers weren't familiar with her, as almost all of her banking had been done online. Having made arrangements for the funds she'd need immediately and those she would need in the future, the most important thing now was to get out of the country.

She parked the van in a Wal-Mart parking lot off the highway leading into Phoenix and retrieved the registration and insurance papers from the glove box, throwing them in a trash can as she walked to the front door of Wal-Mart, carry-on in hand. She couldn't risk drawing attention by taking off the license plates. Anyway, she knew the car would be traced to her eventually. She called a taxi from her cell phone and then threw the cell phone in the trash as well. Cell phones could be traced and she could probably buy a disposable one at the airport. The yellow taxi cab pulled up to the front of Wal-Mart. "Sky Harbor airport, please." she said as she got in. "International terminal."

A few minutes later, she entered the terminal and quickly found the departing flight screen. Her first choice was Italy, but she worried that someone might remember that she and Jeffrey had gone to Italy on their honeymoon and law enforcement might look for her there.

Maria vaguely remembered a conversation she and some of Jeffrey's friends had years ago about extradition. She remembered that the countries who didn't have agreements with the United States were all countries she never wanted to go to anyway, third world countries where her safety would be an issue. Well, now her safety would be an issue wherever she went, so she might as well go to France. As long as she was going to age, it would be better to be in a country known for being kind to aging women. She'd never been to the Provence area of France, but she'd heard it was as beautiful as Tuscany. She bought a ticket to Marseille. She would fly to Paris, transfer planes, then take a smaller plane to Marseille, get a hotel, and then find a place to rent. From there, who knew?

CHAPTER 38

Ralph Martin had a secret. He was hopelessly in love with Maria, the woman who owned the Blue Coyote Motel. She made the best coffee around and her banana bread could sustain him for hours. He was a big rig truck driver and whenever he found himself making the run between Los Angeles and Phoenix, the truck automatically turned into the Blue Coyote for some of Maria's coffee and freshly baked breads.

He knew she was married. Hell, he was too. But there was something about Maria, something that fascinated him. It wasn't just her beauty. There was something mysterious about her, things she knew but would never tell. Ralph thought about her a lot when he was on the road. He had never told anyone about her and never would. Ralph discovered both the Blue Coyote Motel and Maria when he pulled into the Blue Coyote one cold wintry day, desperate for a good cup of coffee. Phoenix and Blythe were too far away and when he saw the Blue Coyote sign, all he wanted was hot coffee.

What he found was a beautiful woman, great coffee, and even greater food. The times he spent at the Blue Coyote were the only perks of his numbingly boring desert travel route. He found it increasingly hard not to compare Maria to Linda, his pasty-faced, overweight wife. Maria had a figure that made everything she wore look like it had been bought at an expensive Italian boutique, even her jeans and tees. He couldn't help contrasting Maria's clothes with Linda's bib overalls, Maria's freshly ground coffee with Linda's instant coffee, and even Maria's homemade cooking with Linda's Betty Crocker and Hamburger Helper boxed meals. It was an uneven playing field. Linda was no match for Maria.

He often asked himself why he even bothered to stay married to Linda. It was not an easy answer, but children, a mortgage, and the church were involved. Both he and Linda were devout evangelicals. Their life pretty much revolved around their church. Ralph was a lay pastor and Linda taught three Bible study groups a week in their home. He supposed he was about as happy as a man was supposed to be, even with his secret fantasy about the beautiful lady at the Blue Coyote Motel.

It was around 4:00 p.m. when he swung his big rig into the empty Blue Coyote parking lot. *Good*, he thought, *that means Maria and I will have some time to talk.* He was looking forward to the coffee and wondered what wonderful things she had baked this morning.

As he opened the door of his rig, something began to bother him. *That's it*, he thought, *the neon Blue Coyote Motel sign located on the side of the highway wasn't lit.* Whenever he'd been here, it had always been lit, even in the middle of the day. He thought that was odd, but decided that maybe the bulbs were burned out. There was a strong late winter wind blowing and the front door of the office was wide open. He closed the door behind him, looking around.

It was the same office area he'd entered many times before, but then again, it wasn't the same. There was no coffee on the reception table, no fresh baked goods. He could see into the kitchen and it was piled high with unwashed pots and pans. He knew from experience that Maria was a meticulous person. *Something must be wrong*, he thought. He hoped she wasn't sick. He walked around the motel to the attached house where Maria had told him she and her husband lived. He knocked and when there was no response, tried the door, which opened easily.

Ralph gasped as he entered the house. Clothing was spread everywhere. Dresser drawers and bathroom cabinets had been trashed and left open. This was not like Maria. He remembered a conversation they'd had several months ago about guests who left drawers and cabinets open. She liked everything in its place and couldn't stand it when people left things strewn about and drawers open. *No, Maria would never have allowed this.*

He wondered where her husband, Jeffrey, was. Ralph remembered Maria mentioning that Jeffrey had a laboratory in the basement of the motel. He vaguely recalled her telling him that Jeffrey was an inventor or some kind of a scientist. Ralph hadn't paid much attention. The last thing he had wanted to do was think about Maria's husband. He wondered if Jeffrey was in the lab or maybe Maria was ill and Jeffrey had taken her to Phoenix. Earlier, he'd noticed a door marked "Basement" at the far end of the motel rooms. He walked back from the house to the basement door. He opened it, his eyes adjusting to the dim lighting over the stairs leading to the basement.

Ralph pulled the handle on the lab door, bracing himself for a possible confrontation with Jeffrey. Ralph was a big man who worked out with weights whenever he was at home and if Jeffrey had caused Maria any pain, he would be sorry. The pedestal Ralph had placed Maria on was pretty high and he was prepared to keep her on it.

As soon as he opened the laboratory door, Ralph smelled Jeffrey before he saw him. Ralph had served in the Marines in Iraq and he recognized the smell of death. He found himself detaching, doing exactly what he had learned to do in Iraq to keep the horror of the war at bay. He simply took notice of Jeffrey, the gunshot wound, the pooled dried blood, and the remnants of food. Nothing could be done for Jeffrey. He closed the door and went up the stairs, taking a deep breath of the clear desert air when he got outside. The air in the lab had been stifling.

He dialed 911 on his cell phone. The dispatcher answered on the first ring. "My name is Ralph Martin. I'm a trucker and I stopped at the Blue Coyote Motel out on Interstate 10 for a cup of coffee. There's no one here and it looks like there's been a murder."

"Stay where you are. Don't touch anything. There's a patrol car in the area and they'll be there shortly," the dispatcher said.

When he hung up, Ralph began to look for Maria. If someone had killed Jeffrey, maybe Maria had been hurt as well. Maybe someone had taken her. He looked in each of the motel rooms, the refreshment area, and behind and in front of the motel. He looked in the pool and in the bushes around the area. There was no sign of Maria. He knew she drove a van, which was also gone.

Twenty minutes later, a patrol car pulled into the parking lot, red lights on and siren going full blast. A few minutes later, two more patrol cars pulled into the lot. A deputy sheriff got out and walked over to Ralph, introduced himself, and shook Ralph's hand. "Mr. Martin, I'll need you to tell me what you've seen and what you know about this place. I've driven by it a hundred times, but I've never stopped here."

After telling the officer who he was, why he was there, and what he had seen, Ralph took the officer to the steps that led to the basement laboratory. He had seen enough and let the officer go down on his own. A few minutes later the officer walked back up the stairs, cell phone in hand. He turned to Ralph. "I just called the dispatcher. They're sending a detective out here along with someone from the coroner's office. I need you to stay and talk to the detective. It will take a while for him to get here, so please be patient."

Soon another car pulled into the parking lot. Detective Lawrence got out of the car, introduced himself to Ralph and asked him to show him where the body was located. Ralph told him he'd show him the room where the body was, but that he'd seen enough of death and that he'd remain outside the lab if the detective wanted to talk to him. The detective began examining Jeffrey's dead body, trying to get some idea of when and how the victim had died. Because of the gaping hole in his chest and lack of powder burns on his body, it seemed unlikely that Jeffrey had committed suicide. The size and position of the gunshot wound indicated that the fatal round had been fired at close range, probably around five feet. There was such a look of disbelief on Jeffrey's face that the detective could easily believe that he had known the murderer. He noticed that the decedent was wearing a wedding ring. In cases like this, the obvious starting place was the spouse and since the spouse was nowhere around the area, a massive search for her would begin immediately.

Detective Lawrence then asked the other deputies to enter the lab. Ralph could hear the detective talking to his men, telling them what he wanted done. In a few minutes he came out of the lab and asked Ralph to go upstairs with him. His men had started collecting evidence at the crime scene. The coroner arrived to take the body to the morgue. Deputy Lawrence showed him where the stairs were located that led to the lab and Jeffrey's body.

Then he turned to Ralph and said, "I'm going to need a statement from you since you're the one who discovered the body. I also want to know anything you can tell me about the motel, the owners, guests, if you know, and anything else that might be relevant."

For the next hour, Ralph told the deputy everything he knew. The only thing he omitted was his secret love for Maria. That wasn't relevant. He did tell the detective that he was worried about her and how out of character it was for her not to be present on the premises. He told the deputy that the van she drove was also gone.

When they were finally finished, Ralph drove his big rig as fast as he legally could to Phoenix. He'd lost valuable time on his run, even though he had a good excuse. In his business, time was money, and he had just squandered both.

CHAPTER 39

Two weeks after Jeffrey's death, as Sean got ready to go to the clinic, he unplugged his cell phone from the charger and noticed that he had missed a call that had come in a few minutes earlier. The number wasn't one he knew and he couldn't place the area code. He returned the call, figuring it was someone who wanted him to speak to their group about the clinic.

"This is Detective Lawrence," the voice on the other end said.

"Hello Detective, I'm Sean Moriarty. I believe you called me a few minutes ago. How can I help you?"

Detective Lawrence continued, "Mr. Moriarty, I'm investigating the murder of Jeffrey Brooks, the owner of the Blue Coyote Motel. The records we got from the motel computer indicate that you were a guest there on two occasions. I was wondering if you could tell me anything that might help with the investigation. Have you ever met the owner, Jeffrey Brooks? He lived on the property with his wife, Maria, who is missing. She closed out their bank accounts, abandoned her van, and flew first to Paris, then on to Marseille. Her trail ends there. Did you ever talk to her about her husband, their life, France, or anything else that might shed some light on this case?"

Sean quickly made a decision not to reveal anything he knew about the Blue Coyote Motel. As a psychologist, he was a keeper of secrets and there was nothing to be learned from the secrets he carried about the motel.

"Detective, I wish I could help you. I stayed there twice. It was a convenient place to stay when I was on the road between Los Angeles and Phoenix. I never met Jeffrey. My dealings were always with Maria, who seemed like a lovely young woman. I'm sorry for the loss of her husband. There must be some explanation for her leaving. I certainly never had the impression that she was anything other than a loving wife. Once I overheard her talking to someone about her husband. It seemed that she was concerned about his mental health, but that's just about the extent of my knowledge. Could he have committed suicide?" Sean asked.

"No. Our tests clearly indicate he was killed by a gunshot to the chest, but it was not self-inflicted. From the looks of him, he may have had a mental breakdown. Who knows? Maybe it was too much for her. Well, thanks. You have my number in case you think of anything else," Detective Lawrence said.

Sean texted the other guests who had been at the motel that Memorial Day weekend. He told them not to answer their phones and that he wanted all of them to join him in a conference call in two hours. He gave them the number to call and the code.

He didn't feel good about lying to the detective. He had met Jeffrey, but what use would it be to dredge up the Freedom gas, the Freedom pills, and the work that he was now doing with Sam, Luisa, and Jill? Enough pain had come to all of them. They didn't need to be involved and there was nothing that any of them could do for Jeffrey or Maria.

Sean justified his lie to the detective by telling himself that what he knew was privileged information. There was a legal right and requirement for him to keep confidential any communications between a psychologist and his patient. In reality, wasn't he doing therapy with all of them when they talked on Wednesday nights? He was well aware that a psychologist had the same confidential rights as a lawyer. Information about the patient could not be released unless the patient was intending to do harm to another. None of his "patients" were intent on harm. They were just trying to help themselves and doing a very good job of it.

Two hours later, with all of the Blue Coyote guests on the line in the conference call Sean had arranged, he told them about his conversation with Detective Lawrence. No one was surprised that Jeffrey had been murdered, but everyone was surprised that Maria was a person of interest. Everyone had liked her and there was concern for her safety and hope that time would reveal that someone other than Maria had committed the crime.

Their collective lives were going well and their addiction to Freedom was slowly fading. Sean had made it clear to them that they were the victims of an unintentional addiction. Theirs wasn't anything like other people who were addicted to cocaine, alcohol, or other controlled substances. None of them had willingly taken or sought the drug in the beginning. They had no idea that they were even inhaling a drug into their systems. Even though some of them had taken Freedom after their second visit to the Blue Coyote, what had changed in the last few hours was that they could never get Freedom again, so a relapse wasn't possible.

Sean told them to expect a phone call from Detective Lawrence and the position he had taken with the detective. He suggested they all do the same. There was nothing to be gained from telling the detective about Freedom. He told them he had lied about not meeting Jeffrey, but was loosely justifying it as part of the psychologist-patient confidentiality requirement. None of them wanted to get involved and they readily agreed to follow Sean's suggestions.

They said their good-byes and hung up, knowing they would "see" Sean on Wednesday at 9:00 p.m. Five minutes later, Sean's phone rang.

"It's Doug. I need to talk to you. I guess I'm the only one still taking the Freedom pills, but from what you said a few minutes ago, I won't be able to take them any longer. I took the last pill I had several weeks ago and was just getting ready to write a check to Jeffrey for another three months' supply. I couldn't afford a larger supply. Now I'm going to have to adjust my lifestyle and learn to get along without Freedom. Would it be possible for me to join your group?"

Sean replied, "Of course. We talk via Skype Wednesdays at 9:00 p.m. If you don't have it, get it installed. Our weekly sessions have been very successful. You're probably going to have a few uncomfortable weeks, but soon the whole thing will seem like a bad dream from the past. I remember you told me how wonderful your life has become. At the time, you didn't know it was because of the drug, but trust me, you can still maintain the good life you've made for yourself and you can do it without the drug.

"The others have all made it and so can you. Your body is going to go through a period of withdrawal. The Freedom drug is just that, a drug, and your body will experience withdrawal from an addictive substance. For a time, your body's going to crave the substance, but it will adjust to not having it and you'll get on with the business of life. I know it will work and welcome to our group. When you get to know all the people in the group better, you'll come to really like them. They're human. We all are."

Sean found Jeanne looking out the window at the snow beginning to pile up in the driveway. It had been a cold late winter in Denver. It felt good to be inside with a warm fire and the woman he had come to adore standing next to him. His past life, the alcohol problems, the young boys, the church, they all seemed like a distant memory. He had been one of the lucky ones. He silently vowed to help each member of his Wednesday group achieve the peace and love of life he felt.

CHAPTER 40

Detective Lawrence called Ralph on his cell phone two weeks later. "I told you I'd let you know if we found anything out about Maria. It looks like she left the country. She cleaned out their bank accounts, abandoned her van at a Wal-Mart on the outskirts of Phoenix, took a flight to Paris and then on to Marseille. Obviously, we don't have jurisdiction there and even if we did, we'd have to find her first.

"We haven't found the gun yet, but her fingerprints are all over the lab and everywhere else. So far we haven't found any signs that anyone else was ever in the lab. The bits of food we found on the plate in the lab match the food prepared in the kitchen behind the office. Looks like Maria took him a meal and then we just don't know. I'd feel a lot better if she hadn't skipped.

"There's something else. Evidently the decedent, Jeffrey Brooks, was a brilliant scientist. He was even touted as being a future Nobel Prize winner for his work on an anti-aging hormone. The company where he used to work, an outfit called Moore Scientific Laboratories, says he quit because of medical reasons. The unofficial word on the street was that he was giving the anti-aging hormone he had discovered to Maria, his beautiful wife. Evidently he violated company policy when he gave her the hormone and they fired him. They gave him a large sum of money so he wouldn't sell the formula to some other drug company.

"There's talk that he had become mentally unhinged, although we don't have any direct evidence of that. Anyway, that would be very hard to determine unless someone had been around him lately. From what we've been able to find out, he never left the motel, so we haven't run across anyone who saw him. Maria dealt with the public, handled the banking, and bought everything that was needed for the motel.

We found a computer in the reception area with information for the motel guests on it and we've already started contacting each of them to see if anyone has any information about Maria or her deceased husband, Jeffrey. So far it's been a dead end. The coroner did an autopsy on his body to see if he'd taken any drugs, but it'll take a couple more days to get those results. If you think of anything else, let me know and again, thanks for your help."

"I appreciate the call, Detective. I hope she's alright. She was a nice lady. If anything comes to mind, I'll call you."

All Ralph could think about was that Maria was gone. Nothing that he knew of Maria fit the picture of a woman capable of killing her husband, taking the money, and leaving the country. He prayed that there was a rational reason for all of this. She had been his dream woman, his private fantasy. She was the only thing that had kept him going during his long drives and his loveless marriage. Maria gone? He felt like he was the one who was dead. Secretly loving someone was lonely, and knowing he would never see Maria again made it even lonelier.

CHAPTER 41

Because of time zone changes, Maria landed at Orly airport in Paris the day after leaving Phoenix. She had slept most of the way, keeping her carry-on bag close at hand. The bhurka had served its purpose and she was anxious to get rid of it. She needed to keep it on for one more plane ride and security check. If the US authorities showed her picture to the French airport security, the burkha would effectively hide her face.

The one thing she couldn't do anything about was her passport. Maria knew that counterfeit passports were readily available in the States, but it had been more important for her to leave the United States than to stay there and get a fake one. There would be a trail to Marseilles and there was nothing she could do about that. Maria had plenty of cash and she knew that if you paid cash, you generally weren't asked for identification. When she got to wherever she was going, she would begin to form a new identity. She would color her hair immediately and look into getting some plastic surgery. Contact lenses could change the color of her eyes. She hated the thought, but it probably would be a good idea for her to gain about twenty pounds. She mulled over possible new names as she thought about her new identity.

When her plane landed in Marseille, Maria went into the airport women's restroom, entered one of the stalls, and pulled the burkha over her head. No one was in the restroom so she put it in the covered wastebasket and slung her carry-on bag over her shoulder. Dressed in jeans, jacket, and sweater, other than being uncommonly beautiful, she looked like any other American tourist. Once again, she wrapped a scarf around her head and put on her big Jackie O. sunglasses.

She told the taxi driver to take her to the Sofitel Hotel, which she remembered from a recent magazine article she had read about Marseille. She paid cash for three nights and declined to show identification or give them a credit card. Maria's instincts had been right. If you had enough cash, no one asked any questions, however, she did need to cut up her credit cards. That was something she hadn't had time to do when she left the Blue Coyote. Even though she'd slept on the plane, she still felt jet-lagged. She rode the elevator up to her room, pulled down the bedcovers, and quickly fell asleep.

When she woke up she felt refreshed and ready to begin her new life. She started a list of what needed to be done. The list was long, but one of the first things she had to do was find a permanent place to stay.

Maria had grown up in a bilingual household and Spanish was the language her family spoke at home. She had taken French classes in high school for four years, more than completing her foreign language requirement. She soon discovered that she had an ear for languages and they came easily to her. Even though it had been several years since she had spoken French, when she looked in the telephone book there were very few words she didn't know or couldn't guess at their meaning. There was a lot of similarity between Spanish and French. Maybe that's why it had been so easy for her in high school.

Maria got dressed, went to the concierge and asked him where she could find a real estate office. The language encounter with the concierge confirmed that she would be able to easily communicate in French.

She walked up and down the streets near the hotel, orienting herself. After a couple of wrong turns she located the real estate office that the concierge had recommended. Rather than enter the office, she decided to return to it on the following day, as she needed to take care of some other things before she was ready to talk to anyone.

She found a drugstore and bought a hair coloring kit and some scissors. At the women's clothing store next door, she purchased a couple of tunics and some very plain slacks. Everything in her railed against the dowdy look she was beginning to achieve, but it was critical that no one remember her. She needed to blend into a crowd.

Before she went to the real estate office the next day,

she needed to come up with a name. Maria decided she would go to the French Office of Immigration and Integration and tell them that all of her personal identification had been stolen from her while she was on the plane, that it must have happened when she went to the bathroom during the flight. She wore a money pouch beneath her clothing, but her passport, driver's license, credit cards, and social security number had all been stolen from her carry-on luggage. That was the story she planned to tell. She just hoped they'd believe it.

Walking back to her hotel, Maria stopped to eat at a brasserie located at the corner of Palais du Pharo and Boulevard Charles Livonbistro. She pulled the door open and was greeted by aromas of garlic and rosemary. Bouquets of lavender were everywhere. While she waited for her meal, she took out a pen and paper and continued with the preparations needed to reinvent herself.

Arriving back at her room in the Sofitel Hotel, she cut her hair; her beautiful long black hair laying in clumps on the bathroom floor. She couldn't help but cry as she prepared the light brown hair dye. Next she got out her make-up bag and tossed it in the wastebasket. She needed to look plain, so there would be no need for makeup. Looking in the mirror, she hardly recognized herself. Maria was gone. Finally, she needed to get rid of her credit cards. She cut them up into fine pieces and flushed them down the toilet.

The next morning she dressed in her new clothes. There was nothing to equate the beautiful young Hispanic woman with the mousy woman she had become. She took a cab to the French Office of Immigration and Integration where things went smoothly. They believed her story and gave her a one-year residence card, which the French called a "carte de sejour." She had become Elena Johnson.

At the real estate office, a middle-aged Frenchwoman named Simone asked if she could help Elena. She introduced herself and told Simone that she was interested in renting a cottage in Provence. Did she have anything available?

The agent told her that she had received a call earlier that morning from a gentleman who was an artist and had decided to move to northern France. He was anxious to rent his cottage. She hadn't seen it yet and was planning to take a look at it that afternoon.

"Would you like to accompany me?" Simone asked. "If you've not been to Provence before, I think you'll enjoy seeing the countryside and then, who knows, maybe you'll even like the cottage."

They agreed that Elena would return after lunch and the agent would drive them to see the cottage. The ride through the countryside was breathtakingly beautiful. Acres of vineyards, olive trees, and lavender fought one another for Elena's attention. Old stone homes and wineries were everywhere. She fell in love with the beautiful Provence countryside and knew she had made the right decision when she decided to make France her new home.

After an hour and a half, Simone pulled off the highway, entering a two-lane dirt road. Ahead of her, Elena could see a small village, which they drove around, continuing up a small hill. Near the top was a charming stone cottage with bright blue window shutters, surrounded by a stone wall with brightly colored flowers covering it.

Their knock on the door was quickly answered by a man who appeared to be in his 40's. He was of average height, but what caught Elena's attention was his bright red hair, which was pulled back in a long ponytail. His name was Michel. A tall woman wearing a Chanel scarf came in from the herb garden outside the kitchen and warmly greeted them, asking them to call her Suzette. There were packing boxes everywhere. It looked like they would be moving in a day or two.

Michel told Simone and Elena to take their time looking around. He apologized for not being able to show them the cottage and grounds, but said that they had to get the boxes packed as the movers were coming the following morning.

The cottage was perfect. It had a large room with a huge fireplace, a kitchen that had recently been renovated, two bedrooms, and a large bathroom with a claw foot tub. The location of the house was very private, but still within walking distance of the village

Michel and Simone discussed the rent. Elena told them she wanted to rent it and asked Michel when he and Suzette were going to move out. They told her that they would be leaving the following afternoon, after the movers had finished, and Elena could move in then.

While Michel and Simone filled in the blanks on a simple lease form that Simone provided, Elena strolled down to the village which consisted of a small market, church, petrol station, post office, bakery, bistro and about seventy-five or so homes. Beautifully colored flowers and vines trailed up the stone wall leading down to the village. Bikes filled the cobblestone streets, which were too small for modern cars. In the center of town was a stone base with a plaque attached to it honoring the men who had died in World War II. It was like taking a step back in time and it was a step Elena was more than happy to take.

She returned to the cottage after her brief walking tour of the village. As she stood in front of the cottage and once again looked down at the picturesque village, she took a deep breath and began her new life.

EPILOGUE

"This is Sean Moriarty, may I help you?"

"Hi, Mr. Moriarty. This is Detective Lawrence. You may remember that I called you a few months ago about a murder at the Blue Coyote Motel. I wanted to bring you up to date.

"The final autopsy results on Jeffrey Brooks came back. It looks like he concocted some drug that was similar to one he'd been taking for a manic-depressive mental condition. We located his psychiatrist, who told us Jeffrey hadn't kept his annual check-up appointment. Our lab tests discovered a drug in his system that doesn't match any drug presently on the market. We had it analyzed and it looks like Jeffrey miscalculated one of the ingredients he put in the drug. He was badly overdosing himself. The drug, in the huge amounts he took, would have caused anyone to slide into a state of mental insanity. We believe that's what happened to him. Apparently, he was a brilliant scientist, but it's ironic he was responsible for creating the drug that caused him to become mentally insane.

"We've never found Maria and we're getting ready to put the file in what we call cold cases. We think that Jeffrey probably went completely mad and she killed him in self-defense during some sort of confrontation, and then fled the country because she was afraid of being prosecuted. We found a knife at the scene of the murder which might have been part of the confrontation. Jeffrey's prints were all over it. It's sad because an attorney probably could have made a good case for self-defense for Maria. Guess we'll never know exactly what happened. She's completely vanished and her trail goes cold in Marseille. Have you thought of anything else?"

Sean was relieved to hear that Maria was free and not surprised that Jeffrey was responsible in some way for his own death. He mused that it was karma at its best.

"Wish I could help you, Detective, but I've told you everything I know. I'm just sorry for both of them. What a tragedy," Sean said.

"Well," Detective Lawrence said," I'm sure you'll never hear anything from Maria, but if you do, you know where to call, and again, thanks for your help."

Sean made a mental note to tell his Wednesday night session what the detective had told him. The last bad chapter of a bad book was thankfully at an end. Before he even thought about it, he realized he was saying a silent prayer.

"Our Father…"

ACKNOWLEDGMENTS

To thank all those who encouraged me to write this book and to all who read to this page. I am indebted to those who vetted the book, Susan, Jacquie, Mike, Noelle, and Tom, and to those who encouraged me to take my time with it. To my editor, Amy, and my graphic artist, Regina; to Barry, for giving me guidance on how to get from A to Z; to my family for their support and to my dog, Rebel, who was extremely gracious when I would feed him late because I'd been wrapped up in the book. But most of all, I thank Tom, my husband. Once he read it, he insisted that the book see the light of day and encouraged me every step of the way, spending hours editing, fine-tuning and pointing out things I'd missed.

To each and every one of you for reading it, thanks!

ABOUT DIANNE

Dianne divides her time between her homes in Huntington Beach and Sacramento, California, where her husband is a State Senator. She is currently at work on *Tea Party Teddy*, a tell-all novel about California politics due to be released in 2013, as well as a sequel to *Blue Coyote Motel*. She can be reached at www.dianneharman.com